crooked river

crooked river

VALERIE GEARY

WILLIAM MORROW
An Imprint of HarperCollins*Publishers*

HarperCollins books may be purchased for educational, business, or sales promotional use. For information please e-mail the Special Markets Department at SPsales@harpercollins.com.

FIRST EDITION

The bee image © by effrossyni/Shutterstock, Inc.

Library of Congress Cataloging-in-Publication Data has been applied for.

ISBN 978-0-06-232659-1

14 15 16 17 18   ov/rrd   10 9 8 7 6 5 4 3 2 1

In loving memory of my mother.
Also for Kristy, my best sister.

crooked river

sam

We found the woman floating facedown in an eddy where Crooked River made a slow bend north, just a stone skip away from the best swimming hole this side of anywhere. Her emerald-green blouse was torn half open and her dark, pleated skirt was bunched around her waist, revealing skin puckered and gray, legs bloated and bruised. Her hair writhed like black snakes in the current. I poked her back with a stick. Not mean, but gentle, the way you might poke someone who's asleep. She skimmed the surface, bumped against a half-submerged rock, and returned to where Ollie and I stood at the water's edge. She bobbed there in the shallows in a tangle of brown leaves, her arms outstretched, fingers reaching, and it seemed like she was settling in to wait for someone else to come find her. Like maybe we weren't good enough, Ollie and me, just two girls with skinny arms and skinny legs who didn't know the first thing about death. We did, though. We knew more than we wanted to anyway.

I dabbled the stick in the water near the woman's foot. "What do you think happened to her?"

Beside me, Ollie tugged her braid, a pale rope knotted all the way down her back. When she let her hair down, the ends curled near midthigh, almost reaching her knees, but since we'd buried our mother Ollie kept it all tied back and tucked away. And not just her hair, her voice, too—she hadn't said a single word in nearly four weeks.

"We should go back to the meadow," I said. "Get Bear."

Ollie, still clutching her braid, leaned into my leg.

"Well, cover your eyes at least."

But she didn't.

I was fifteen that summer, and Ollie was ten, and maybe we should have been more surprised or grossed out or whatever else normal kids might feel finding a dead body, but we were both still dazed from the funeral and everything that came before. Everything that came after.

I crouched close to the water, wanting to touch her, the dead woman, wondering if she would feel the way our mother had: cold, like rubber, a deflated balloon. All her life, breath, heat, gone. And in that moment before I reached and grabbed her shoulder, rolled her just enough to see her face, I felt a twisting dread that she would be no stranger at all, but someone we would recognize, another someone we loved taken too soon.

Her eyes were open, hazel and bloodshot. Her mouth, a dark gaping hole. One of her front teeth was missing. There was a deep gash above her left eye and something, a fish or a crawdad maybe, had pulled at the skin around it, eaten the flesh underneath all the way down to the bone. Mud streaked her shirt, weeds tangled in her hair, and welts covered her face, her arms, her chest and collarbone. The darkest marks, almost black against her faded skin, were around her neck. Here were impressions of fingers wrapping the circumference, thumbs pressing against her windpipe.

I stared at her face and then, when no name came to mind, I turned to Ollie. "She look familiar to you?"

Ollie pushed her glasses up high on her nose and shook her head.

"Me neither."

Still, she was somebody's somebody and we couldn't just leave her.

"We should do something. Shouldn't we? Tell someone?" And then again, because I couldn't remember if I said it out loud the first time, "We should do something."

I readjusted my grip on the woman's shoulder and tried to pull her closer to shore, but she was slippery and much heavier than I expected, and she dragged along the river bottom like something was snagged around her ankle. I dug my toes into the mud and pulled hard, but I wasn't strong enough. The dead woman slipped from my grasp and dropped facedown into the water again, creating a wave big enough to push her out of the eddy and into the middle of the river where the current raged. She spun halfway around until her head was pointing downstream, then she was sucked away.

I splashed in after her but stopped when the water reached my knees. Heavy spring rains and melting snowpack had turned Crooked River into a thundering flood. Boulders protected our swimming hole from the violent current, but past that, where I stood now, the river gathered itself up again and rushed north, curving around Terrebonne and connecting with the Deschutes River miles from here. White water slammed against my calves. My toes burned from cold. I kept waiting for the dead woman to snag on something, a log or a boulder, or get flushed into another eddy, but she flew straight and fast down the middle where the water was thick and churning. After a few seconds, she looked more like a stick than a person. A few seconds more and she disappeared completely.

Maybe she hadn't been real, only a trick of shadow and light. But my heart was thumping so fast it hurt and the hair on my arms stood on end, and I could still feel her cold flesh under my fingers, still see her face, her hollow eyes staring up at me. She was as real as real gets, and we had lost her.

A splash in the river sounded behind me, and then Ollie slipped her hand into mine. She was sucking hard on her bottom lip. The water surged around her waist. The greedy current clawed at her, trying to drag her under and away from me. I tightened my grip on her hand. Ollie blinked up at me and then looked behind us toward the woods and the path that would take us back to the meadow. She pulled my arm.

"Where do you think she'll end up?" I asked, turning my gaze again to the rapids.

Ollie pulled harder, tugging me toward the riverbank.

We waded ashore. Water dripped from our bare legs and shorts and turned the dirt around our feet to mud. We'd left our shoes on a log. I picked up both pairs by their laces and then put my arm around Ollie's shoulders and steered her toward the path.

"Bear will know what to do," I said.

We walked in silence, single file through the trees. Normally, the branches around and above us would be a bright symphony of bird-song and rustling leaves, but not today. The birds were hiding. The trees were still. Too quiet, and the shadows were cold. I urged Ollie to walk faster.

Bear's meadow was ten minutes from the river along a narrow path that wove through white alders and sugar pines. It used to be part of an alfalfa field. Then it was a horse pasture. When the horses died, Zeb tore the fence down and let the grass grow tall and the flowers bloom. Eight years ago Bear moved in, but he hadn't changed much. He put up a teepee and planted a vegetable garden, dug a fire pit and an outhouse, and brought in a picnic table, and of course there were the hives. But there was no electricity, only the sun. No plumbing, only the river and a barrel to catch the rain. No roof over our heads to blot out the stars, no television to drown out the bird and cricket songs, no asphalt to burn the soles of our feet. Most kids would probably hate a place like this, but to me it was home.

I'd been spending my Augusts in the meadow with Bear since I was seven. On the first Friday of the month, Mom would drive us from our house in Eugene to the Johnson farm just outside Terrebonne, where Bear would be waiting on Zeb and Franny's front porch. We ate breakfast together crowded around the Johnsons' kitchen table, and after, Bear and Mom would go and sit on the front porch swing. They'd rock and hold hands and talk in low voices. Ollie always tried to listen at the screen door, and I always pulled her away—what Mom and Bear whispered about out there was none of our business. When it was time for Mom and Ollie to drive back to Eugene, Bear and I walked them to the car. Mom pulled me close and kissed the top of my head and told me to be good and obey my father. Then she kissed Bear and told him she loved him for always. After they were gone, Bear and I walked a quarter mile from the farmhouse to the meadow along a dirt road pocked with holes. I picked flowers and told him about school and swim team; he carried my duffel and sleeping bags and told me what was new with his bees.

The first few summers I stayed with Bear, Ollie was too young to come along, and after that, when she was finally old enough, she decided to go to summer camp with her friends instead. This was the first year Ollie was staying with us in the meadow rather than going to camp. Our first year, too, without Mom.

The Johnsons technically owned the meadow and Bear paid them rent, but what had started out as a simple landlord/tenant relationship had, over the years, grown into something more like family. In the coldest parts of winter, Zeb and Franny let Bear stay in their guest room. If he needed to drive somewhere, they let him borrow their truck. They had him over for dinner a couple of times a week. In exchange, he'd do things for them around the farm—fix fences, mow grass, replace shingles. Bear's parents died before I was born, but from what I'd learned eavesdropping, they weren't the nicest people. And Mom's parents lived on the East Coast, visiting once a year at Thanksgiving and sending twenty-dollar checks on our birthdays. Zeb and Franny were more like grandparents to me and Ollie than our actual grandparents, and since they lived so close to the meadow, Mom never worried about me staying with Bear. She knew Zeb and Franny were watching out for me, too. I think that's the real reason Grandma agreed to let us stay here after Mom died. If not for Zeb and Franny, we'd be in Boston right now.

But this was only a trial period. We had six months to prove the meadow was safe and Bear was a good father. Six months to convince her we could thrive here. Three days in, we weren't off to a very good start.

When we reached the meadow, we found Bear in the apiary hunched over his newest Langstroth hive, billowing smoke into a narrow opening in the front panel. So intent was his focus on the bees, he didn't notice us stop in the shade to watch.

He wore long sleeves and pants, but no gloves, no veil, no hat. "Bees recognize those who cherish them," he told me once. "They can tell who respects their hard work and generosity and who just wants to take advantage. If you come to the hive humble and gracious, you won't get stung." He set his tin can smoker on the ground and lifted the cover. Bees flew lazy around his face and head, tangling in his grizzly-red hair and thick beard, but he didn't swat at them or try to pick them out. He was calm and his lips were moving, and even though we were too far away to hear, I knew he was asking after their queen and how the flowers were blooming this summer and if they would be so kind as to share their honey—the same questions he always asked this close to harvest.

With this newest addition, the hive count was up to eight. Bear had started out with two and every spring since had added one new hive. Most of the year the bees stayed here, at the west end of the meadow, well away from the picnic table where we ate our meals and bottled our honey, and even farther from the teepee where we slept. In early spring, though, Zeb brought his truck around and he and Bear loaded up the hives and divided them among the alfalfa fields and apple orchards for a few weeks. I was never around when this happened. By the time I showed up, the bees had been returned to their usual spot and were buzzing happily among familiar wildflowers.

When I learned they moved the bees from one place to another, I remember asking Bear, "Don't they get confused and try to fly back home?"

"Their hive is their home," he'd said. "Wherever the queen is, that's where they return."

"But what if the queen's not there?"

"The colony falls apart."

Since he'd started keeping bees Bear hadn't lost a single hive.

Ollie had grown tired of waiting and tried now to pull me toward the teepee.

"Wait," I said, tightening my grip to keep her from going anywhere. "He's opening the box. Maybe he'll let us have some of the comb."

Ollie had eaten Bear's honey before, but only what I brought home in jars. Not like this, not warm and fresh from the hive when it tasted like all the best parts of summer melting sweet on your tongue.

Bear pried the movable frames from the top section with his hive tool, a flat piece of metal that resembled a small crowbar. The bees filled cracks in the hive with a sticky resin stronger than glue, and the hive tool was the best way to unstick things. He worked at the frames, jamming one end of the tool into the hive and jerking it back and forth until a frame finally popped loose. Ollie flinched.

"Don't worry, the smoke keeps them calm," I said, and then, "That top box is where they store all their extra honey. And the bottom one is where they lay eggs and raise their brood. They store honey there, too, but we don't harvest it. You can't be selfish with bees or they'll stop working just to spite you."

She looked up at me, her mouth open a little like she was surprised, then she looked back at Bear. He tucked the hive tool in his back pocket, then brought the frame close to his face and blew gently on the bees until they started to crawl toward the edges. He lifted the frame to the sun, checking to see how many cells had been capped and how close we were to harvest.

I tugged on Ollie's hand, wanting to take her close enough to show her how when you tipped your head back to catch the light, a kaleidoscope of amber and gold glinted through the opaque comb, but she dug in her heels and wouldn't move.

She was shivering and staring up at me with puppy-dog eyes. Our clothes were still damp from the river, and though only the bottoms of my shorts were wet, Ollie was soaked all the way up to her chest. She leaned her weight toward the teepee and pulled on me.

"Go on, then," I said. "Go change. You don't need me to come along."

But she wouldn't let go of my hand.

"Fine," I said and went with her.

The teepee was larger on the inside than it looked from the outside. Bear's things were arranged neatly around the perimeter. The cot where he slept; the chest where he stored his clothes; the two-drawer filing cabinet filled with honey jars and beeswax candles; a folding chair and table; a single-burner propane stove; cast-iron pots and other dishes; a plastic tub for washing. Books were stacked in the spaces between. Feathers and dried flowers dangled from the ceiling alongside bleached-white deer antlers and charcoal sketches of bees and hives and trees and flowers, anything of interest that he found in the meadow. Several rugs covered the ground, and in the very center, Ollie and I had spread our sleeping bags. It was a little crowded, but it was also warm and dry and safe, and at night you could see stars through a small opening at the top, so I didn't mind if our elbows brushed every once in a while.

I waited by the door while Ollie changed out of her wet clothes into a pair of jeans and a blue-and-white-striped T-shirt that used to be mine. It was hot inside the teepee, sweltering and hard to breathe.

I reached for the flap. "You ready?"

Ollie adjusted her glasses and then glanced across the teepee toward the card table Bear used as a desk.

"Come on," I said impatiently.

She frowned and walked over to the chair. Bear's worn-leather satchel hung across the back. It had a long shoulder strap and a deep pouch and a flap that buttoned closed. Perfect for gathering blackberries and dandelion greens, mushrooms and wild herbs. Bear carried this bag almost everywhere and had taken it yesterday, too, when he borrowed Zeb's truck to drive into Bend for supplies.

Ollie lifted the flap and pushed her hand down inside the satchel.

"What are you doing?" I asked.

She looked over her shoulder at me and then pulled out a jean jacket. She held it in the air between us, unfolding it and spreading the arms. It looked too small to fit Bear.

I hopped over our sleeping bags and grabbed the jacket from Ollie, turning it over in my hands. Dirt streaked the back, and the collar was torn a little on one side. The cut was tight in the shoulders and narrow at the waist, and the buttons were fake pearl bordered by decorative brass. A dark stain covered the left shoulder, maybe oil or ink or mud or something else I didn't want to say out loud. Still holding the jacket at arm's length, I looked at Ollie.

"This yours?" I asked, even though I already knew the answer.

She shook her head and pointed to Bear's satchel.

"He probably found it in the woods," I said. "It could belong to anybody."

Hikers often wandered into the area surrounding our meadow, and even more so in late summer when they veered off the main trail, seeking relief in the cool shade, chasing the sound of water tumbling over stones. This jacket could have slipped off any number of shoulders. A high school prom queen trying to keep up with her jock boyfriend; a twentysomething bird-watcher chasing the throaty call of a western tanager; a young mother bouncing one child on her hip and yelling at a second to watch out for rattlesnakes. There were any number of other possibilities.

Ollie folded her arms across her chest and raised her eyebrows.

"What?" I asked, lowering the jacket so it hung at my side. "You don't think . . . ?"

Ollie lifted her shoulders and let them drop again.

"Come on, Oll. Say something."

She sucked on her bottom lip. She'd done this kind of thing before, four years ago after Aunt Charlotte died. Ollie didn't talk to anyone for two weeks. Not a single word. And then, when she finally did start talking again and I asked her why she'd stopped in the first place, she'd said, "Aunt Charlotte's ghost stole my words."

"You know ghosts aren't real, right?" I'd told her.

She'd cocked her head to one side and said, "Tell that to Aunt Charlotte."

I thought seeing a shrink and growing up a little would be enough to keep this from happening again, but it wasn't. She'd stopped talking after Mom's funeral and though I was trying to be patient, the way Mom had been the first time, her silence was finally starting to wear me thin.

"Ollie," I said. "If you know something . . . if you know where this jacket came from, then you have tell me. Talk to me. I won't get mad. I promise."

She grabbed a pencil, reached for one of Bear's sketchbooks lying open on the table, turned to a blank page, and started to draw something.

I took the sketchbook from her and tossed it onto Bear's cot. "You're too old to act like this now. This silent treatment stuff? This drawing pictures instead of talking? It's for babies. If you have something to say, use your words."

She glared at me. I waited another few seconds, but she stayed silent. I shrugged and said, "Fine," and then folded the jacket over my arm and left the tent. Ollie followed, sticking close to me.

In the apiary, Bear was working on an older and more established hive. Despite the smoke, the bees were darting quick circles around his head, filling the air with loud and angry buzzing. They were agitated, crawling on his hands and neck and around his nose and mouth, and I was sure by now he'd been stung a few times. Still, he never once flicked or swatted them away; he didn't seem bothered by them at all.

"They're only defending their brood and stores," he told me the first time I saw a hive upset like this. "You can't get angry with them for that." Later, when it was time to actually harvest and not just peek, Bear would use escape boards, forcing the bees into the lower boxes so he could remove the top ones and extract the honey. For now, he let them do as they pleased.

He secured the top cover and patted it gently, whispering something only the bees heard. This was the last hive. He gathered his smoker and hive tool and walked toward the lean-to at the edge of the apiary where he kept his tools and supplies and where Ollie and I stood waiting.

Here was where I should have told Bear everything. It would have been easy enough: We found a woman floating in Crooked River, we found a woman dead. Then she got caught up in the current and drifted away. We found a dead woman and now she's gone and maybe we should tell someone so she can be found again and we think this jacket might be hers, too. He was the adult—this should have been his burden. Here was where I should have told. But I kept my mouth shut. Because he was close enough now for me to see two scratches on his right cheek, stretching parallel from the outside corner of his eye to the top of his beard. Two scratches, bright red and raw. Two scratches that hadn't been there yesterday.

He stopped in front of us and narrowed his eyes when he saw the jean jacket draped over my arm. Before I even had a chance to ask, he said, "I found that in the woods."

He tapped the hive tool against his leg. "I thought it belonged to one of you."

Ollie leaned into me. I shook my head and shoved the jacket toward him. "It doesn't."

He didn't take it. Instead, he asked, "Do either of you want it? I think Franny might be able to get that stain out."

This was the first summer I was tall enough to look Bear in the eyes without having to tilt my head up, but when I did so now, he dropped his gaze to the ground.

"We don't want it," I said.

He shrugged and took the jacket, draping it over his shoulder. "I'll leave it with Franny, then," he said. "She can drop it at the church donation box next Sunday."

"Sure," I said. "Whatever."

A bee flew right up close to us, darting back and forth, making a nuisance of itself. Ollie shrank away from it and swatted the air.

"They smell fear, you know," Bear said. "You can get stung real quick that way if you're not careful."

Ollie sucked in her breath and puffed her cheeks out huge.

The bee flew off, leaving the three of us standing there in a broken circle. Ollie and I watched Bear, Bear watched us, no one saying a word. Then he walked past us, swinging the hive tool at his side, and for the first time I noticed how thick the metal was, how blunt the edges, how weightless he made it seem. It wasn't very big, barely a foot long, but the potential was there. Lift it above your head, tilt it at an angle so the edges hit first, swing it fast enough and hard enough, crack a woman's skull, bludgeon her to death.

ollie

This night is made of ghosts. One stands behind me, at the edge of firelight and just out of reach. One sits beside my sister. Both wait for someone to look up and see.

I see.

I see things no one else does.

I see them there and wish I didn't. I want to tell and can't.

I try because my sister needs to know what I know about the jacket and this man we call Bear, who sits beside me, who is our father. I try, but my sister says I'm being a baby and she'll only listen if I use my words. But my words are gone and I'm afraid they're never coming back.

Bear throws another piece of wood onto the fire. Bright sparks leap, but they lack the spirit to become stars and fade before reaching the black-ink sky.

He stares across the hot red coals and smoke at my sister, who sits apart from us. "You're awfully quiet tonight."

She shrugs.

"You and Ollie both." He looks at me and winks.

But he doesn't say I'm crazy.

The day we got here, Grandma pulled me close and pressed her dry lips to my forehead and said to Bear, "I'm worried about her. Maybe she should see a doctor. There's still time for Al and me to cancel our trip. Stay here with the girls instead."

Bear told her I'd be fine, he'd look out for me. "Give the kid a break, Judy," he said. "She's been through a lot the past few weeks. We all have. She'll start talking again when she's good and ready." All I needed was a little more time.

The marshmallow on the end of my stick catches fire. I let it burn a few seconds before blowing it out. I like them this way, the bitterness of burnt. How the shell is crisp and smoky. How the center is gooey and sweet. Opposites and the same. I lick sugar from my fingers and take another marshmallow from the bag, hold it out to Bear. He doesn't usually eat this kind of thing, he says. He eats only what he can grow. But he bought them special for me and Sam because he doesn't want us to be sad anymore.

I wait one second, two seconds, three seconds . . . five and then ten. Finally his hand crosses the distance and his fingers brush mine.

The one at the edge of firelight smiles and tells me not to be afraid.

The one shimmering beside my sister turns her hollow gaze on me and I think, *Leave her alone.* She curls her lips, hissing, and gnashes her broken teeth.

sam

The next day I skipped breakfast and hiked into the woods alone. I followed the well-worn path toward Crooked River for a while, then veered right, following no path, making my own, weaving through bitterbrush and elderberries and sugar pines and red rock boulders twice as big as me. I didn't have to think about where I was going; my feet knew the way. I walked about ten minutes due east, far enough from the meadow that I couldn't hear Bear plucking at his banjo anymore, but close enough that if they needed me, or if I needed them, all we had to do was holler.

The poplars were waiting in their usual spot, old friends unchanged from last August, or the August before that even. Zeb planted the tallest ones years ago as a windbreak, but never much bothered with them afterward. Now they stretched roots and branches, intruding on a nearby field that had been overrun with dandelions and ryegrass. Three of the largest trees formed a lopsided triangle and, even though you couldn't see it from the ground, up in the leaves was a platform made of plywood and old fence boards. Bear helped me build it five years ago. He said every kid needed a place to go and be alone, a place all my own where I could just sit quiet and watch the birds, the clouds, the world go by. We were a lot alike in that sense. Bear and I both thought trees made better friends than people did. Mom was always worrying I was too much alone, that I didn't try hard enough to make friends with the kids at school. I had friends. Heather, who was on the swim team and sometimes sat with me at lunch, and Laura, my best friend since first grade. They were both at Mom's funeral with their parents, and it was awful and embarrassing and I hadn't talked to either one of them since. I was glad to be starting over at a new school in September where no one knew anything about me and no one had seen me cry.

I grabbed the rope ladder hanging from the bottom of the platform and climbed up. This high off the ground I could see for miles in every direction. Crooked River to the northwest. Zeb and Franny's house a quarter mile to the east. The dirt road connecting our meadow to their gravel driveway and the paved highway beyond. If I'd brought Bear's binoculars, I would have been able to see a small chunk of Smith Rock scraping the sky four miles west and the steeple of the First Baptist Church of Terrebonne glittering white three miles north. Year after year my view from the poplars stayed the same. The fields ever rolling green, the river curving around the usual bends, the water flowing on and on, the sky and earth reaching to infinity. Up this high the small changes, the slow erosions and fallen trees and gone-away people, were impossible to see. I sat with my back against one of the poplar trunks. A light breeze swayed the branches around me. I was embarrassed to admit it, but a small part of me had been hoping that this summer would feel just like every other summer. Ollie and I would pick wildflowers and float in the river until our fingers and toes went numb and watch clouds trip lazy across a perfect blue sky and not think a minute about how Mom wasn't back home waiting for us. I thought for a few days, maybe, we could forget.

Last night I dreamed about the dead woman we found in Crooked River. She was still alive and reaching for me, begging me to save her, but my feet were stuck good and fast in the shore mud; and hard as I tried, I couldn't break free. The river was pulling her away from me, and I screamed at her to swim, to move her arms and kick her legs and swim, goddamn it, *swim*! But the current was too strong, too fast, and she was swept away again.

I woke up in a panic. My mouth was dry, my tongue like cotton. The air inside the teepee was swollen and heavy, warming quickly now that the sun was up. I shoved the sleeping bag off my legs and stumbled outside where Bear was bent over the fire pit, stirring a pot of boiling water. I slumped down in a camping chair a few feet away from him.

He said, "How'd you sleep?"

"Fine," I lied. "What's for breakfast?"

"Oatmeal with honey and fresh peaches." Same as yesterday. "You want hot chocolate?"

And it all felt so usual. As if I'd imagined the dead woman and everything else; I'd dreamed it all and didn't have anything to worry about. Nothing had changed, and we were all going to be fine, just fine. Then Bear straightened and turned his face toward me. The scratches were still there below his right eye, red and starting to bruise around the edges. Maybe he had a good explanation for them. Maybe not.

Before I could ask him about it, Ollie came out of the tent. She was wearing the same shirt from yesterday and smelled like last night's campfire. Her braid was starting to unravel. I drew her close to me and started to fix it tight and smooth again. As I worked, she crouched, picked up a small stick, and drew something in the dirt at our feet. Two stick figures—one with curly hair, one with long braids—stood beside a river. I finished her braid and bent for a closer look. She'd drawn a body floating in the water and something like fireworks exploding above. She tapped the crude sketch once with the stick and then turned and pointed the stick at me.

"Go wash your hands," I said. "Breakfast is ready."

She tapped the dirt again, insisting. I scuffed out the drawing with the toe of my boot and said, "Stop it."

She scowled at me, then spun on her heels and stomped to the rain barrel to wash her hands.

Bear had been watching us and asked, "What's that about?"

I shook my head. He scooped oatmeal into a bowl and held it out to me.

"I'm not hungry," I said, rising and walking past him into the woods.

He called after me, but I pretended not to hear.

Maybe Grandma was right. Maybe Bear wasn't cut out to be the kind of father we needed. Monday night, the night before we found the dead woman, he left me and Ollie alone in the meadow. Normally, this wouldn't have been any big deal. Ollie and I were latchkey kids. We were used to coming home from school while Mom was still at work, letting ourselves in, fixing our own snacks, starting our homework, even making dinner sometimes. But Mom never left us alone for more than a couple hours, and if we called her office phone, she almost always answered on the first ring.

Bear was gone all night and there'd been no way to reach him. He said an order of jars and lids had come in at a supply store in Bend and he was going to borrow Zeb's truck to pick them up. He asked if we wanted anything special and promised to be back before dark. Ollie and I fell asleep waiting for him. One minute we were watching the stars spark to life through the small opening at the top of the teepee where the poles came together, the next we were waking, blinking back bright morning, and Bear was outside cooking oatmeal over a small fire.

He was wearing the same clothes as the day before and his cot looked like it hadn't been slept in, but I didn't get a chance to ask him where he'd been because by the time I wriggled out of my sleeping bag, dressed, and put on my shoes, he was already busy in the apiary. And then Ollie and I had gone down to the river for a swim and that's when we found the dead woman and I forgot all about Bear being gone until we were standing near the lean-to, and I glanced in at the shelves where he kept extra jars and noticed the number of jars was the same as when we got here on Saturday. He hadn't brought back any new ones like he said he was going to.

I tilted my head back and scanned a patch of open sky where the poplar branches didn't quite come together. Sometimes I saw bald eagles up there, but mostly vultures. Today, there was only empty blue. I sighed and stretched my arms, bounced my legs.

When Mom was alive, Grandma was always pleading with her to get a divorce, to leave that good-for-nothing sad sack of lazy bones and move on with her life, but she never did. She would always just smile sadly out the window and say, "Families come in all shapes and kinds, Mama. Love, too."

After the funeral, which Bear skipped out on, Grandma was all set to file and fight for custody of me and Ollie, but Grandpa had laid his hand on her arm and said in a low, gruff voice he only brought out once in a while, "Give him a chance, Judy. Poor man deserves at least that."

Bear was supposed to be using this time to find a job and a place for us to live with a roof and four walls. So far I hadn't seen him doing any of that. But Mom had trusted Bear. And I did, too. If I wanted to know where he'd been on Monday night, if I wanted to know about the scratches, all I had to do was ask, and whatever answer he gave, I'd believe it. I'd believe him.

I shifted my gaze toward Zeb and Franny's house. A car was coming down the driveway, a blur, really, dust billowing from the back tires. As it got closer, I recognized its boxy shape and bubble lights, the lettering on the side. Early on, the sheriff used to send deputies out to harass Bear about permits and squatting and proper disposal of waste, looking for any excuse to kick him out of town. After a while, they must have decided he wasn't worth the effort because they stopped coming. This was the first time in almost four summers I'd seen a patrol car headed our direction, and there was only one good reason I could think of for them to drive all the way out here now.

I jumped to my feet and scrambled down the rope ladder from my roost. Past the barn, the patrol car could go a quarter mile along the dirt road Bear and I walked every summer before it dead-ended against a hemlock stump. After that, the deputies had to walk another fifty or so yards to reach the meadow. I could get there first if I ran.

I broke through the tree line just as the patrol car reached the end of the road. Doors slammed shut. They left the engine running. Heavy boots crashed through the underbrush. Bear looked up from where he sat by the fire pit with his banjo, his hands frozen over the strings.

"Sheriff's here," I said, running past him to the teepee.

I ducked inside and not really thinking, just doing, I grabbed the jean jacket from the back of the chair where Bear had left it the night before. I stuffed it in his leather satchel and then stuffed the satchel inside my sleeping bag, pushing it all the way down to the bottom.

Ollie was sprawled out on top of her sleeping bag reading the same book she'd been reading since the beginning of summer: *Alice's Adventures in Wonderland,* a green, pocket-sized hardcover with an embossed white rabbit on the front. She and Mom had been reading it together, one chapter every night before bed. They only got halfway through. Ollie lifted her eyes from the page and stared at me. Outside, voices rushed together, murmurs at first, too soft and far away for me to make out individual words.

Then Bear raised his voice. "How many times do I have to tell you people to leave me alone? You're trespassing, you know. Not that you give a good goddamn."

Ollie frowned at the door flap, then at the lump in my sleeping bag, then at me.

"It's nothing," I said. "Pretend you never saw this."

Her frown deepened.

"I'll buy you two new books."

She touched the tip of her finger to her glasses.

"Fine," I said. "Four."

She tugged her braid. We had a deal.

"Girls? Sam?" A familiar voice called through the canvas. "Are you in there?"

The first time Deputy Santos came to the meadow, I was eleven and she was responding to a call from a concerned citizen who said there was a young girl living unnaturally in a teepee with a wild man out on the Johnson farm. She spoke awhile with Zeb and Franny, then with me and Bear, then she bought a jar of honey and went on her way. Every August after that, she made a point of meeting me for a sundae at Patti's Diner. We talked about ourselves, about life and school and work, and we talked about other people, too, the kind of talk you can only do in a small town. I liked her. But she wasn't family.

"Can you come out here? We'd like to speak with you."

Bear said, "Leave them be."

Ollie closed her book and sat up. She fumbled to tie her shoelaces. The look on her face was panic.

"Just let me do the talking." I took her hand, and we went outside together.

A few steps from the teepee, Deputy Santos stood with her hands on her hips, waiting. Her dark hair was pulled back and tucked under a brimmed hat. She smiled at me and Ollie, but there was sadness in the smile, a knowing. Someone had told her about Mom. Franny, probably, and I wondered who else in Terrebonne knew, and how many people I'd have to spend the next few weeks avoiding.

"You must be Olivia." Deputy Santos stuck out her hand. "Sam's told me so much about you. It's good to finally meet you in person."

Ollie stared at Deputy Santos's fingernails. They were painted lime green and starting to chip around the edges. After a few seconds where no one did or said much of anything, Deputy Santos cleared her throat and placed her hand back on her hip.

"What's going on?" I asked.

Beside the fire pit, Bear stood with his hands shoved in his pockets. His banjo leaned against a stump we used as a stool, and on the other side of that was a man I'd never seen before. He wore a navy blue suit with shiny, fancy black shoes, not the brown uniform and boots I was used to seeing on deputies. But he had a badge and handgun clipped to his belt, so he must have been an officer of some kind. He was bald and thick across the shoulders and kept tugging at his sunset-orange tie like it was choking him.

"That's Detective Talbert." Deputy Santos nodded at the man. "And we're hoping you all can help us out by answering a few questions."

"You don't have to talk to them," Bear said to me, and then to Detective Talbert, "You don't have my permission. They're minors. You have to have my permission."

"It's all right, Mr. McAlister," Detective Talbert said. "No one's in trouble here."

Deputy Santos took a small notebook from her pocket. "We just want to find out if you've noticed any suspicious activity in the past few days. Any strangers bothering you? Odd noises in the middle of the night? Anything out of the ordinary? Anything you can think of?"

"No," Bear said.

Deputy Santos watched his face carefully, like she was looking for signs he was lying. Detective Talbert tugged his tie. Tugged and tugged. A muscle in his jaw twitched. The officers were wary of Bear, and I didn't blame them. His hair tangled with leaves, the dirt on his hands, his shabby clothes and frayed moccasins, the way he jerked a hand out of his pocket to pull at his beard. Those scratches under his eye.

"Even something small," Deputy Santos said. "Something you might not have thought was important at the time could be helpful."

"Helpful for what?" Bear stared hard at Deputy Santos, and then at Detective Talbert. "Why are you here? Has something happened?"

Detective Talbert cleared his throat and smoothed his tie flat against his chest, his hand lingering at the end.

Deputy Santos said, "A woman's body washed up in Smith Rock Park sometime last night. Early this morning, maybe."

Something pinched inside my chest. Ollie rocked away from me and then back, bumping lightly against my leg.

"Tony Grant was out for a sunrise climb and saw her in the water, tangled up in some tree limbs," Deputy Santos continued. "We thought she might have come from somewhere upriver, so we're asking everyone who lives nearby if they saw anything. Just trying to get some answers for this girl's family."

Bear kept staring at Detective Talbert. He didn't blink or flinch or give any kind of sign that he knew what they were talking about.

Finally, he said, "We don't know anything about it."

He picked up his banjo, sat down on the stump, and started to play.

Deputy Santos and Detective Talbert exchanged a glance I didn't understand. Then Deputy Santos turned her attention to me and Ollie. "What about you girls?"

"You don't have to answer her," Bear said over the sound of his plucking. "Like I said already, we don't know anything about it. We didn't see anything, hear anything. Go on and leave us alone."

I said, "It's all right."

"You don't have to say a goddamn word." Bear bent his head down over his banjo and let his fingers fly.

Ollie squeezed my hand, and I squeezed hers right back.

Deputy Santos asked, "So yesterday? Anything strange happen? Or the day before?"

How much time do you have? I wanted to ask. And where should

I start? With Mom's funeral? Or a week earlier, on the Fourth of July, the day she died? Or should I skip all that stuff and get straight to the part where Ollie and I just wanted to go swimming and pretend our lives were ordinary again, but when we got down to the river we found another dead woman instead? Everything about this summer was ending up strange, one thing no more than another.

I glanced at Bear. He still had his head down, his fingers moving quick over the fret board. I swallowed all the words that had started to bubble up. If he wasn't talking, then neither was I.

I looked Deputy Santos straight in the eyes and shrugged. "We haven't seen anything."

It would have been hard enough to explain why we hadn't told somebody right away, why we let the dead woman drift downriver without going for help. And harder still to try and convince them that Bear had nothing to do with it. I knew what they said about him behind his back. How he couldn't be trusted, a man living out here all on his own, abandoning his wife and kids the way he had, a selfish man, a bad man. I knew what they said and considering everything else—how he'd left me and Ollie alone all night, returning with scratches on his face and a bloodstained jacket, how he was acting now, all guarded and hot-tempered—I knew they'd find him guilty before they even held a trial. Before I ever had a chance to hear his side of the story. I needed to hear his side.

"What about you, Olivia?" Deputy Santos asked. "Did you see anything?"

Ollie glanced up at me and then shook her head.

Deputy Santos closed her notebook and tucked it inside her pocket again. She handed me a business card. "If you think of something, anything, call me. Okay? If I don't answer, leave a message."

I held the card flat against my stomach and nodded.

She hesitated another second, watching me, then she sighed and motioned to Detective Talbert that they were done here, it was time to go.

The detective ran his hand over his scalp and said, "Appreciate your time."

Bear didn't look up from his banjo, didn't even stop playing.

Deputy Santos and Detective Talbert disappeared into the trees, and then it was just the three of us again. Me and Ollie and Bear. And all the lies we'd told.

Later that afternoon in the garden, I kneeled in the dirt and yanked weeds from a long row of tomato plants. Bear was crouched a few rows over beside a squash plant, pushing aside leaves, looking for fruit. I reached the end of a tomato row and started on another. When the tomatoes were finished, I worked my way over to the green beans. I wasn't meticulous the way I was with Mom's flower beds. Bear didn't care if his garden looked nice, only that it was productive, so I pulled just the biggest weeds, the ones that were starting to overtake the vegetables, threatening to steal precious sun and water. I worked quickly, carelessly, leaving behind clumps and patches of smaller weeds. My shirt stuck to my back and sweat dripped down my forehead. My shoulders ached and my knees, too. My hands were covered in dirt. I kept picturing the woman's shattered face and reaching arms and wondered what difference it would make to tell the truth now. Nothing was going to bring her back to life.

I grabbed a large dandelion at its base and pulled, but it didn't budge. I scraped away the top soil around the roots and pulled again, harder. The dandelion snapped in half somewhere beneath the surface, leaving me holding the greens. I tossed them into my weed bucket and looked over at Bear.

"You think that woman they found is from around here?" I asked.

He picked a squash from the vine and turned it over in his hands. It was close to a foot in length, slender at the top, bulbous at the bottom, a delicious butter yellow.

"Don't know," he said.

"You think Franny'd know?"

He put the squash in an empty bucket and reached for another behind the leaves. He didn't say anything for a while and then, "Does it make a difference if she's from around here or someplace else?"

I sat back on my heels. "How did you get those scratches?"

Bear touched his cheek and looked off into the trees. "Blackberries caught me when I was out walking."

"And that jacket? You found it just lying on the ground? Or what? Hanging from a branch or something?"

"It was tangled in some bushes by the river." Bear carried his bucket half full of squash to a row of tomatoes. "I told you already, I thought it was yours. That's why I brought it home."

I shook my head, then reached and pulled a tall thistle from between two bean plants.

"You don't believe me," he said.

"You weren't back before dark," I said.

"What?"

"Monday night. You said you'd be back before it got dark."

Bear was shuffling between the vines, gently squeezing the reddest tomatoes and picking the ones that were ripe. He glanced at me and then looked away.

"Where were you?" I pressed.

He sighed and dug his knuckles into his low back. "Communing with the stars."

"You were gone for a long time."

He bent over the tomato plants again.

"Ollie and I were worried sick."

"I can take care of myself."

I glared at him. "It's not just you out here anymore, you know. It's not just you who needs taking care of."

"You sound like your mother."

I snapped a green bean from the bush I was weeding under, broke it in half, and stuck both pieces in my mouth. I liked them best like this, straight from the garden, crisp and sun warmed. I chewed and chewed until I no longer felt so much like screaming.

I swallowed the green bean and asked him straight, "Did you have something to do with that woman?"

He dropped a tomato in the dirt, then picked it up and shined it against his shirt. "What the hell gave you that idea?"

"You didn't tell that detective about the jacket." I picked at the dirt under my fingernails.

Bear placed the tomato in the bucket with the others, slowly like he was thinking over something, and then he straightened up tall again and caught my gaze, held it steady. "Neither did you."

We stared at each other for a few seconds. I looked away first.

"Something you need to tell me, Sam?"

A chunk of hair had fallen in front of my eyes. I tucked it behind my ear, but it came loose again. My auburn curls used to be long, hanging just past my shoulders like Mom's, but they were chopped short now and I still hadn't gotten used to them tumbling and springing all over the place. I'd done it myself a few hours before Mom's funeral. Took a pair of scissors into the bathroom, locked the door, and hacked away at my curls until they lay in a penny-colored heap at my feet. When I finally came out again, Grandma had asked, "Do you feel better?" And I had said yes, even though it wasn't true.

"Sammy?" Bear said again, softer, taking a small step toward where I sat in the dirt.

I looked up at him. His eyes were the same color as Ollie's—amber with gold and green flecks—but I hadn't noticed until now how sad they looked, how many new wrinkles had formed around the edges.

He said, "I didn't hurt that woman, if that's what you're thinking. I would never do something like that. I would never put our family in trouble that way, not after everything . . . Sam, I would never—"

"Me and Ollie saw her," I blurted out.

He pulled back a little, surprised. "What?"

"In the river." I was rushing, trying to say everything before I lost my nerve. "Yesterday morning. We went to the swimming hole and she was, she was . . . there floating. And dead. She was dead."

"Oh my God."

"We tried to pull her onshore, but she was too heavy. We tried, but . . ." My voice cracked. I hadn't cried since Mom's funeral, but all of a sudden pressure was building behind my eyes and my throat was stinging. If I started crying, I wouldn't be able to stop. I sucked in a deep breath and wiped the back of my hand across my nose. I sniffed and said quietly, "The current got her."

Bear set down the bucket and came closer. He crouched beside me in the dirt but didn't seem to know what to do with his hands. He reached for me, then pulled away again, patted my shoulder, pulled away. He worked his thumb over his knuckles and said, "So the jacket's hers?"

I nodded. "I think so."

"Then we need to give it to Detective Talbert."

I stared at my dirt-covered palms. "Can't we just put it back where you found it?"

Bear laughed a little, but I didn't see what was funny.

"No," he said. "We can't. We need to tell them."

"What if they think you did it?" I mumbled.

He shifted his gaze toward a patch of grass just outside the garden where Ollie sat, making a daisy chain. He took a handkerchief from his pocket and wiped his brow. "We'll be all right, Sam. If we tell them the truth, we'll be all right."

He rose to his feet and squinted up at the sun. "Think we might reach a hundred today?"

I didn't answer. I stared as he walked away from me, as he lifted the bucket of squash and tomatoes and carried it out of the garden. When he was out of sight, I reached beneath the beans and yanked out another weed. Adults were supposed to fix things, not make them worse.

ollie

Four weeks, one day, fourteen hours, forty minutes, thirty-two seconds, thirty-three, thirty-four, thirty-five . . . This is how long my mother has been dead and how long I've been living without her. Add fifteen more seconds. Another minute and another until I lose count and have to start again at the beginning.

July 4, 1988.

Time of death: 10:26 P.M.

Four weeks, one day, fourteen hours, forty-nine minutes.

And counting.

Bear pours water around the base of a tomato plant. My sister pulls weeds. A daddy longlegs crawls over my shoe. A white butterfly dances above orange marigolds. I lift a leaf, look under, and find a ladybug. If I squint and imagine, the cornstalks grow a little taller.

A shadow moves between the rows.

She's trying to hide, but I see her anyway. And I know who she is. She followed my sister up from the river, full of poison and rage. She wants our help. She wants revenge. I turn my head away from her and distract myself with daisies.

Bear takes his empty bucket to the rain barrel to fill it up again.

My sister sits back on her heels, wipes her hands on her pants, and squints at me. "It'd go a lot faster if you helped."

But the shade is cool. And my stomach is full. And every time her fingers work the dirt, I see my own hands scooping damp earth, holding it over an open hole, letting it stream through my fingers, down and down, hitting the coffin lid. Grandma said it was the proper way to say good-bye, and that even though I wasn't ready and didn't want to I had to be a brave girl and do it anyway. She said we weren't leaving until I did. And I wanted to leave because there were so many Shimmering and I was having trouble catching my breath.

I looked for my sister, but she was already done, already walking back through the cemetery to the parking lot.

I scooped up dirt and let it spill down and down and thought, *I'm sorry, please, I take it back, I take it all back*. Like blowing out birthday candles or breaking the wishbone and getting the bigger half, it's magical thinking and changes nothing.

In Grandpa's car I stared at my mud-streaked palms, trying to ignore the Shimmering who followed me from my mother's open grave to the parking lot to here in the middle backseat. My sister stared out the window all the way home. The one between us cried and cried and made my stomach hurt.

Four weeks, one day, fourteen hours, fifty-three minutes and she's still here, sitting in a branch above my head and swinging with the wind. She wants me to look up, but I won't.

She says my name, and I ignore her.

She says, *God made dirt and dirt won't hurt.*

And I think she's being childish.

She says, *Listen to your mother.*

I think, *My mother is dead.*

She sighs and the sound is rattling leaves and crackling bark. She sighs and my heart wants to crash out of my chest. I jump to my feet and walk away fast.

"Where are you going?" my sister calls after me. "Ollie?"

I pass Bear on my way to the teepee. He stops and sets the bucket on the ground. Water sloshes over the edge.

"You okay, kiddo?"

I walk faster though I know it won't help. She is right behind me and getting closer. She will wrap her arms tight around me and squeeze out all my breath. I cannot shake her.

I am living, and she is stuck in between. Where I go, she goes. She is my punishment. For the terrible thing. The worst thing I've done in my entire life. She is my reminder every minute, every day of what I did and am trying so hard to forget.

sam

See if this fits." I positioned my bike helmet on Ollie's head. It was a little too big for her, but her helmet was packed away in a box somewhere and she wouldn't ride without one. I cinched the straps tight under her chin and rapped my knuckles lightly on the plastic. "Snug as a bug."

She grabbed the handlebars of my blue-and-white Schwinn and swung herself onto the seat. Her toes barely reached the pedals.

"Get off," I said.

She jumped to the ground again, and I adjusted the seat lower. This time when she climbed on, her feet reached just fine. She pushed off and away from me, pedaling slow at first, finding her balance, then picking up speed, bumping across the uneven grass toward the path that led out of the meadow.

"Ollie! Wait up!" I hoisted my leg over a taller, heavier, black-and-red Schwinn and pedaled hard after her.

We followed the narrow path, dodging sharp rocks and twigs, our nubby tires chewing through dirt and shredding weeds. Sunlight broke through the canopy, splashing gold on our arms in patches and streaks.

Bear bought both bikes four summers ago. He told me he used our honey money, but Mom must have helped out some, too, because I knew for a fact we didn't sell enough jars to afford two brand-new Schwinns. He also told me he'd bought them so he and I could ride into town together, but I'd only ever seen him ride once and he was so wobbly and slow, the whole time I was afraid he was going to fall and break his arm. I think he really bought two bikes hoping one day Ollie would come and stay with us in the meadow. I think he'd always meant for it to be me and her, sisters tearing up roads and chasing the wind.

Approaching a slight dip in the path, I pedaled faster, and for a split second, my tires lifted off the ground. My stomach dropped, then pulled up again, and I was flying. I gave our battle cry, a combination howl and whoop—a sound I was too old to make but made anyway, just this once for Ollie—and waited for her echo, but she pedaled on silently without even a glance back over her shoulder. The front tire of my bike slammed down hard on a patch of loose dirt and started to skid. I leaned to keep from toppling, and the leather satchel I was carrying over my shoulder shifted. The strap cinched around my chest. I pulled it loose again and hurried to catch up with Ollie. When we passed the hemlock stump and the path widened into a road, I stood on my pedals and steered around her, taking the lead.

I wanted her to shout at me, to get upset and say "I'm not staring at your big butt the whole way there. No way, José!" and pedal faster so we were racing neck and neck, but she didn't. She kept her steady pace and pedaled on silently. I sat back down on my seat, focused on the road ahead. The long grass growing in between the tire ruts hissed and snapped, tangling in our spokes.

We went around a final, sharp bend, and then it was a straight shot past the barn, past Zeb and Franny's house to the end of their driveway and Lambert Road. From there it was another three and a half flat miles past grass fields and sheep pastures to Smith Rock Way, the two-lane road cutting through downtown Terrebonne.

There were more vacant houses and overgrown yards than I remembered from the years before. More FOR SALE and NOW LEASING signs in empty storefront windows. Fewer cars driving through. Fewer people coming in and out of the shops and restaurants along the main strip. Terrebonne had always been a small town that moved at its own slow and quiet pace, but recently it seemed to be moving even slower, getting even quieter, the whole town shrinking smaller and smaller until one day it might just disappear.

I steered my bike onto the sidewalk and stopped in front of a single-story brick building with a large picture window overlooking the street. Stenciled on the glass in white cursive letters was the name *Delilah's Attic*. A toy monkey with brass cymbals attached to his paws grinned at us from inside. Propped beside him was a small cardboard sign that read DREAMERS WELCOME. I didn't come here often. Part antique business, part curiosity shop, the store was filled with too many breakable things, and the woman who ran the place didn't seem very fond of kids, even though she had a son a few years older than me. But it was the only place in Terrebonne with books for sale, and I'd promised Ollie books.

We leaned our bikes against the front of the building and went inside.

A bell rang, and a woman called to us from the back room, "I'll be right out!"

There was a shuffling, like someone was moving boxes, then the woman said, "Mama Rose's granddaughter wants to bring me the leftovers from that estate sale they had last weekend. Bless her heart." Something metallic and heavy scraped across the floor. "I'm making a bit of room before she gets here."

"It's okay," I said, raising my voice to be heard above all the noise. "We're just browsing."

The sounds in the back room stopped completely for a few seconds and then started up again, her voice drifting out to us again above the scraping, "Let me know if you need help finding something."

I nudged Ollie toward the other side of the store. "The books are over here."

Past steamer trunks and aluminum milk jugs. Past Victorian-era dresses and dusty faux fur coats. Past top hats, and billiard balls, and snow globes, and empty cigar boxes. Tea sets, washboards, old radios, and Japanese screens. Pastoral paintings, jewel-toned vases, and art deco lamps. Boxes and boxes of costume jewelry. And finally, here in the back, four large shelves stuffed with books. Romance novels, mysteries, horror, classics, cookbooks, and how-tos. Hardcover, paperback, a treasure trove of words. The shelves reached to the ceiling and there wasn't a single, empty space.

Ollie looked at me and then at the books.

"You think you can find four you haven't read yet?"

She pushed her glasses up higher on her nose and moved along the first shelf, her head tipped to one side, her hand brushing over the spines. When she reached the end, she stopped and focused her attention on a purple, wingback chair wedged in the corner and a large gray tabby sleeping on top. The cat opened his eyes and blinked at us. He twitched his tail back and forth, and then, when we didn't come closer or try to pet him, he closed his eyes again, buried his face in his curled paws, and started to purr.

Ollie returned her attention to the books. I glanced over my shoulder. The store owner was still in the back, moving things around. Other than her, Ollie and I were the only people here.

Ollie pulled two books from a shelf and added them to a stack she'd started near the purple chair. I wrapped both hands around the satchel strap.

"Listen, Oll," I said, glancing again at the deserted front counter. "I have to . . . I need to go take care of something really important."

Ollie stopped searching the shelves. She held a book against her chest and chewed the corner of her lip.

I said, "Just for a few minutes. You'll be fine here."

Ollie glanced at the dozen or so books she'd collected already, then looked over my shoulder toward the front counter and a curtain that must have led into the back room. After a few seconds, she tugged her braid.

"Five minutes," I said. "That's it. And then I'll be right back. I promise."

Ollie turned away from me and added another book to her growing pile beside the chair.

"Don't leave the store," I said.

She stood on tiptoe, reaching for a book on the very top shelf. I left her there and hurried outside.

Before breakfast this morning, while Ollie was still asleep, Bear and I walked to the river together. The rising sun warmed the sky orange and painted the trees yellow. Neither of us spoke until we reached the swimming hole.

"She was right here," I said, pointing to the eddy.

Bear scratched his beard and stared at the churning, dark water. He looked upriver, then let his gaze drift down and down, following the current to the rapids where the dead woman had disappeared. He sighed, and the sound was weighted with all the sadness in the world.

I said, "What if I tell them I found the jacket?"

"Sam . . ."

"No, listen. It'll work." I hadn't thought it through, but as I kept talking, I convinced myself it was a good plan, the best plan—the only one that would keep Bear out of trouble and our family from being broken apart again. "I'll take the jacket to Deputy Santos by myself and tell her I found it at the exact place you found it, but I didn't want you to know about it because I was afraid you'd get mad at me for wandering so far away from the meadow and then . . . and then I'll tell her how me and Ollie found the body, too, but we didn't tell anyone because we thought we'd get in trouble for not being able to pull her out of the water and . . . and . . ." I looked up at him. His head was lowered. "Please. Let me do this."

He turned and looked at me with bright, damp eyes. His lips twitched, like he was about to speak.

I said, "We can't lose you too," and slipped my hand into his.

He stared out at the river again, squeezed my hand once, and let go.

After lunch, we stood facing each other in front of the teepee. He clutched the leather satchel in his arms and told me exactly where he'd found the jacket. Along a service road that was a mile and a half south of Zeb and Franny's house. About fifty yards in from Lambert Road, tangled up in a hawthorn bush.

I held my hands out, but instead of giving me the bag, he said, "If your mother knew about this, she'd kill me." He flinched hearing the words out loud.

"No, she wouldn't," I said. "She'd want me to do this."

He shook his head but handed me the satchel anyway.

In the alley behind the Attic, outside the Staff Only entrance of Patti's Diner, I found a Dumpster overflowing with black garbage bags, rotten vegetables, and soggy cardboard boxes. If I shoved the jacket down far enough, no one would notice it as anything but trash. Then, in a day or two, a garbage truck would come and haul everything away and the jacket would be gone. Forever. No one else would know it had even existed, and no one—not me, not Ollie, not Bear—would get in trouble. The meadow would go on being as safe as it had always been, and Ollie and I wouldn't have to move to Boston with our grandparents where we'd end up trapped and suffocated by all that glass and brick and concrete. We could stay in Terrebonne. We could try and be happy again.

I unbuttoned the satchel and took out the jacket. The back door of Patti's popped open. I tried to duck out of sight, but I wasn't fast enough.

Someone called out, "Hey! Hey, you!" And then, "Sam!"

The door thumped closed.

I froze and turned slowly, clutching the jacket tight against my chest.

I recognized him right away. Travis Roth. His mom owned Delilah's Attic and I'd seen him running the register a few times. I'd also seen him at Patti's, where he worked as a busboy. He was taller than me, older too, but not by much. His dark hair was cut short and spiked up a little with gel. He was dressed in a black T-shirt and black slacks, a stained apron tied around his waist, black army boots laced up tight. He walked toward me, smiling. Dimples creased his cheeks.

"Almost didn't recognize you." He reached and twitched a strand of my hair. "I like it."

I blushed and took a step back, tucking the chin-length tresses behind my ears. We hadn't said more than a few words to each other in all the summers I'd been visiting Bear. Until today I didn't even think he knew my name.

His gaze shifted to the jacket I was still clutching in one hand, and he asked, "What are you doing back here anyway?"

"Nothing." I stuffed the jacket into the satchel and buttoned the flap closed. "Just . . . you know . . . enjoying the view . . ." I tossed my hand in the air and then let it fall limp at my side. I wanted to crawl away, hide in the tall grass on the other side of the fence, be anywhere but here making an idiot of myself.

Travis pulled a pack of Marlboros from his apron pocket and offered me one.

I shook my head. "Those things will kill you."

He shrugged and cupped his hands around the cigarette, lighting one end with a shiny gold lighter. He inhaled deeply, held his breath a second, then tipped his head back and exhaled a stream of smoke straight up like a chimney.

We were both quiet a moment, watching the smoke curl and disappear, then Travis said, "So did you hear about that woman they found at Smith Rock? It's all anyone's talking about."

"Yeah." I wrapped one arm around the satchel. "Yeah, I heard something about it."

"Big deal, right? Haven't seen people this excited since Johnny Sommers won that hot dog eating contest at the State Fair three years ago." He took another long drag and then tipped his head toward Patti's back door. "There's people taking bets in there."

"On what?"

"You know. How she was killed. Who did it. That sort of thing."

I felt sick to my stomach. "Who did it . . . ?"

"Yeah, like her boyfriend or a jealous ex-wife. A trucker. Or some long-gone drifter. Or even someone living right here in Terrebonne. Pastor Mike, maybe." He grinned. It was supposed to be funny, the part about Pastor Mike, but if his name was being thrown around, even in jest, then chances were Bear's name had come up, too. And I bet no one laughed when it did.

"I've got twenty on a drifter," he said.

I stared at my shoes.

A long time must have passed with me staring at the ground like that, trying to think of something to say, because the next thing I knew, Travis was touching my shoulder, saying, "Hey. Are you okay?"

"What?" I lifted my gaze.

The back door swung open again. Travis let go of me and took a step back.

A redheaded kid I'd sometimes seen hanging around Travis poked his head through the doorway and said, "Hey, dumbshit! Let's go! Something's happening at the Meadowlark. They've got it all roped off. A bunch of black cars and men walking around in suits—" He noticed me standing there and his expression changed, like he'd been caught doing something he shouldn't. "Oh. Hey." And then talking to Travis again, "Looks like you're busy out here, man. Sorry to interrupt."

"Not busy. Just having a smoke." He took one last pull on the cigarette and then tossed the butt away.

It landed in a clump of tall grass at the edge of an abandoned field, and I watched it, waiting for the whole thing to go up in flames, but there was only a thin ribbon of gray and then nothing.

The kid jerked his thumb over his shoulder toward the front of the building. "So you coming or what?"

"Yeah. We're right behind you." Travis untied his apron and draped it over his arm. He turned to me, arched his dark eyebrows, gave me a sly grin, and said, "You got anything else going on right now?"

I didn't think about Ollie or how I told her I'd only be a few minutes. I didn't think about the jacket or Bear waiting for us back at the meadow. Right then, the only thing I was thinking about was that if this had anything to do with the dead woman, I needed to be there. I needed to know what was happening.

The deputy inside the taped perimeter waved us away from the yellow line. "Stay back, folks! Give us some space."

Travis and I stood on the sidewalk, part of a gathering, gaping crowd that was starting to spill into the street. If I had bothered to look around, I might have recognized some of the people knocking up against me, trying to push forward even as we were being pushed back. But all my attention was on Detective Talbert and room 119. Everyone and everything else were just part of the scenery, blurred shapes shifting in my peripheral vision, jumbled voices rising up, falling down.

"I bet she was a whore—"

"A drug dealer—"

"A crack addict—"

"Maybe she got what she deserved."

Detective Talbert knocked only once before taking the keys from the motel manager and opening the door. He disappeared inside the room for several long minutes, and when he came back out, he was holding his suit jacket over one arm and rubbing the top of his bald head. He stared across the parking lot to where an entire town waited, holding its collective breath.

Was this where she'd stayed in the days leading up to her death?

Was this where she'd dreamed her last dream? Taken her last shower? Watched her last news program? Eaten her last meal?

And her things—her clothes and shoes and makeup bag and whatever else she carried with her to places like this—were all her belongings still inside, barely unpacked, spilling from an open suitcase?

Did they know now who she was? Were they finally going to give us her name?

Detective Talbert nodded to a group of people all dressed in dark blue shirts and black trousers, huddled together under the awning a few steps from room 119.

Her room.

The group broke apart and set to work. Three of them, one with a camera around his neck, followed Detective Talbert back inside. The rest remained in the parking lot with a few of the sheriff's deputies, fanning in a wide arc to search potholes and sidewalk cracks, gutters and storm drains, and all possible places in between for blood, hair, shoeprints, cigarette butts, gum wrappers, anything and everything that might hold some importance, a revealing piece of evidence to help reconstruct her final hours.

Someone bumped into me, jostling the satchel, and I panicked, thinking how stupid I was to bring the jacket here to the one place where every person might be a suspect and every unclaimed item a clue. I tried to step back from the tape and bumped into a thick wall of people pressing forward for a better look. I twisted, searching for a break in the crowd, some narrow opening to squeeze through, but we were packed in too close, our elbows and shoulders touching, our legs and breath tangling. I was stuck.

"Sam? Are you okay?" Travis touched my arm.

I flinched away from him and bumped into a woman standing beside me.

"Sorry," I mumbled, gathering my arms close against my body.

"Hey," Travis said. "You don't look so great."

I nodded and said something about the heat, about not drinking enough water, about feeling dizzy. He pulled me along with him, forcing a path through the crowd, away from the yellow tape and chaos, the deputies and the dead woman's room.

We crossed the street and ducked into the shade of a maple tree growing in front of the First Baptist Church. I shrugged the satchel from my shoulders and let it slide to the ground.

"I'll get you some water," Travis said.

Before I could stop him, he was halfway to the church. The front doors were open, and he went inside.

I leaned against the maple tree and stared up into its twisting branches. The dark green leaves were still, even as the air vibrated with heat and light and shimmering, ocher dust.

Travis returned with a Dixie cup of cold water. I drank it in one gulp.

"You want more?" he asked.

I crushed the empty paper cup in my hand and shook my head. "Thanks."

"You gotta be careful in this heat," he said. "Gotta keep hydrated."

He kept glancing at the Meadowlark. My gaze wandered there, too, but the crowd was too thick. Nothing to see but the backs of heads. I rubbed my eyes, wiping away sweat and dirt and the image of the dead woman's battered face. Summer was supposed to be drowsy and carefree, measured by days and weeks of aimless roaming, doing whatever we wanted, lazy and young and unaware. Not this senseless violence and terrible death and so many questions unanswered, so many secrets and lies.

Travis was kneeling on the ground beside the satchel, tying his shoe. He straightened when he saw me looking down at him.

"Do you think they've told her family yet?" I asked.

"If she even has family." He picked at the tree trunk, pulling off small strips of bark and tossing them into the air, watching them fall.

His mouth was turned down and his brow crumpled, his shoulders slumped. He wouldn't look at me. This was the Travis I remembered, the boy from summers before who scowled at his feet if we passed on the sidewalk, who was always aloof and detached and so much cooler than me. Then he lifted his head and looked me straight in the eyes. He smiled, and I wondered if maybe I'd been wrong, if maybe he wasn't cool at all. Maybe he was just shy. Like me.

He said, "I guess everyone has some kind of family somewhere, though, don't they?"

"Shit," I said, picking up the satchel from the grass and slinging it over my shoulder. "I have to go."

I hurried away from Travis and the church.

How much time had passed since I'd left Ollie? Twenty minutes? Thirty? A whole hour? Long enough, I was certain, for her to worry and start thinking something bad had happened, that maybe I wasn't coming back at all.

"Sam, wait," Travis called after me. "Did I do something wrong? Did I say something?" He caught up with me quickly and grabbed my elbow, pulling me to a stop. "I didn't mean to upset you."

"No, it's not . . . ," I said, shaking my head. "It's just my little sister. I—"

"You have a sister?"

I nodded.

"Oh."

"I left her at your mom's store."

He let go of my elbow. "By herself?"

"She's reading books." As if that explained everything and made my leaving her okay.

"I'll walk back with you," he said, lighting up another cigarette.

ollie

When the pale girl and the man who does not know he's being followed come around the bookshelf, I hear tires screeching first, rubber burning pavement. Then glass shattering. They stop right in front of me. The shadows in this corner are dark enough that I can see the outline of her lowered head and her two yellow braids swinging loose, how she keeps her arms cinched around her waist and stands with her toes turned inward.

She's young.

My age.

Younger.

I sag the way she sags. The weight of so many awful things presses down on my chest, making it hard to breathe.

The man stares. He jerks and flinches and rolls his head. His long, gray hair, pulled back with a rubber band, snaps the air. His fingers twist together as he says her name, "Delilah?" But he's staring at me, not her.

I shake my head and back up to the purple chair where the one who follows me is coming apart. Gold bursts of light. Snapping like firecrackers. I press my hand to my chest because I, too, am coming apart. This is what happens; I feel what they feel.

I feel everything.

The man frowns, says, "I'm sorry. I didn't mean to scare you like that. It's just you remind me so much of my daughter. My Delilah."

The pale girl behind him lifts her head and blinks at me, like she's coming out of sleep. I plead with her, *Make him go away.* But she drops her gaze again, too weak to do anything except sigh.

The gray cat on the back of the purple chair hisses and swipes the air. He senses the Shimmering, knows they are here and unsettled.

The one who follows me wants me to open my mouth and scream, but I'm afraid that once I start, I won't be able to stop and I'll go on screaming forever.

"She had hair like yours." The man reaches for me.

The pale girl hugs herself tighter.

"Such long, beautiful hair." A step closer.

I shake my head harder and hold my hands out like shields.

The one who follows me splits and comes together again in the empty space between him and me. But his hand goes straight through her, and his fingers come out the other side brushed in gold and silver and white and red and other colors that don't have names. There is nowhere for me to go.

I bump into the purple chair. The gray cat screeches and leaps away, disappearing into some dark crack between the shelves, leaving me alone with them.

The man smiles and his fingers stroke my braid. "Spider silk. That's what we used to call it. Spun gold."

The woman from the back room calls, "Billy?" She's somewhere close, but out of sight.

"Back here, Maggie." The man replies, then drops his hand and smiles at me. "Remarkable."

"Billy? What are you doing?" She comes around the corner, sees us standing too close.

She hurries. She takes his elbow and turns him away, leads him

45

toward the front of the store. "I need your help moving some boxes."

She glances quickly over her shoulder and we connect, but only for a second before she looks away again.

The pale girl shuffles after them. But even after she's out of sight, I hear ripping metal and breaking glass, feel a heavy weight still pushing on my chest. Dizzy and too tired, I sit down in the purple chair, curl and tuck my legs.

The one following me crackles and sparks. I wish she would go away, too.

sam

Travis pushed open the Attic's front door, and the bell jangled. Barely a second passed before the curtain separating the back and front rooms was shoved aside. Mrs. Roth marched around the counter, moving quickly toward us. Her raven-dark hair was pulled into a severe bun, her thin, pale lips made even thinner by the way she was pressing them against her teeth. Her nostrils flared, and there was a second where I could have sworn her brown eyes turned infinite black, but maybe it was just a trick of light, a shadow cast by something hanging from the ceiling, because when she reached us, her eyes were a normal color again, her pupils a usual size. She grabbed Travis's elbow and pulled him behind the counter.

For someone so small—the top of her head barely reached Travis's chest and her frame was feather light—Mrs. Roth was surprisingly strong. Or maybe it just seemed that way because Travis wasn't putting up any kind of fight.

"Your shift at Patti's ended twenty minutes ago," she said. "Where have you been?"

I stood a few steps away from them, pretending interest in a stack of antique lunchboxes.

"We were over at the Meadowlark," Travis said. "The deputies were searching a room. That woman was staying there, I guess."

"What woman?" She inhaled sharply and then said, "I need you here today."

"I'm here." He shook off her hand.

Mrs. Roth arched up on tiptoe and sniffed the air around Travis's neck. She pulled back sharply, her lip curling. "Have you been smoking?"

Travis folded his arms over his chest. They stared at each other for a few seconds. Mrs. Roth started to speak, but a loud noise, like something heavy being dropped on the floor, stopped her.

Travis glanced at the curtain. "Dad's here?"

"Downstairs," Mrs. Roth said.

Travis started to move around her toward the back room.

She grabbed his arm, with less force this time, and said, "Leave him be."

"I need to talk to him."

"He's working." And then, "You know how he gets."

A moment passed where they just stared at each other, neither one saying a word. Somewhere in the mess behind me, a clock ticked off the seconds. Finally, Mrs. Roth let go of Travis's arm. He turned away from her and disappeared through the curtain.

She snapped her attention to me. "And you. What were you thinking leaving that child here alone?"

I twisted my head, looking toward the bookshelves. "Is she okay? Did something happen?"

"She's fine," Mrs. Roth said, sitting down on a stool behind the counter. "But this isn't a library, and I'm not a babysitter."

I ducked my head and mumbled something I hoped would pass as an apology and promised it would never happen again.

"See that it doesn't." Mrs. Roth gave me a hard and narrow stare and then started sorting through a stack of receipts, dismissing me with her silence.

I found Ollie curled in the purple chair, head leaning against one side, her legs tucked under her bottom and her arms wrapped around her stomach. She stared off into a dark corner, didn't even look up at me when I came closer. The gray tabby was gone.

I crouched in front of her. "Hey. You okay?"

She closed her eyes.

"Hey." I touched her arm. "I'm right here."

She uncurled her legs and threw her arms around me, burying her face in my shirt. I squeezed her as tight as I could.

"It's okay," I said. "I told you I was coming back, didn't I? You're okay. We're okay."

A few years ago, when Ollie was seven, Mom left her behind at the grocery store. We only got as far as the parking lot exit before I realized how unusually quiet it was inside the van.

I turned halfway around in my seat, saw the empty place where Ollie should have been sitting, and shouted, "Mom! You forgot Ollie!"

She cursed and slammed on the brakes so hard my seat belt locked, whipping my head forward and bruising my shoulder. She pulled a sharp U-turn, almost hitting another car, and drove too fast through the narrow aisles into a handicapped spot at the front of the store. She left the car running and we both raced inside the store.

"Manager!" Mom shouted at one of the checkout girls. "Where's your manager?"

The girl was startled and looked about ready to cry. A man with a goatee and an angry scowl marched up to us and said, "Mrs. McAlister?"

"My daughter! Where is she?" Mom was looking over the man's shoulder, but Ollie wasn't there.

He said, "Calm down, ma'am. Olivia's fine. She's in my office."

He seemed on the verge of a lecture, but Mom shoved past him and pushed through a door marked EMPLOYEES ONLY and into a small office with a metal desk and filing cabinets that took up more than half the room.

Ollie sat in a chair behind the desk. She was spinning and spinning, her head tipped back, her hair flying, a huge smile spread over her face.

"Ollie!" Mom knocked a stack of file folders off the corner of the desk trying to get to her.

Ollie stopped spinning and held out her arms. Mom lifted her up, held her so tight I was afraid she wouldn't be able to breathe.

"I'm so sorry, baby," Mom whispered into her ear. "I'm so, so sorry."

"It's all right, Mommy," Ollie said. "You always come back for me."

That night Mom made Ollie's favorite dinner. Spaghetti and hot dogs. When we were all sitting down, with our plates still empty, Mom leaned her elbows on the table and folded her hands together under her chin. She looked at me and then at Ollie and said, "I love you girls both so much. You know that, right?"

Of course, Mom, we said. *Of course we know.* We thought we knew. At the time, we were both still so young, and death was something we'd only ever encountered in stories. I don't think either of us understood what she meant. Not really. How terrified she'd been when she thought she'd lost Ollie. How she'd do anything, everything in her power, to keep us both safe. How one day we might lose her. One day she wouldn't come back for us and when that happened, she wanted us to remember love.

I understood. Now, I understood.

I held Ollie for another few seconds, until her breathing slowed and became less ragged. Then I pulled her away from me so I could see her face. "What happened?"

She looked over my shoulder. I turned to see, but there was no one there. I brushed my hand over her forehead the way Mom used to do. She was warm, but not feverish.

"I shouldn't have left you alone. I'm sorry. But you're okay. You're okay, right?" I rose to my feet but kept one hand clamped around hers. "Did you find anything good?"

The stack of books she'd been gathering before I left was gone, the floor cleared. I looked behind the chair, but there were no books there, either.

"Nothing?"

She shrugged and wiped the back of her hand across her cheek.

"Not even one?"

Ollie reached into her back pocket and pulled out a small, green hardcover. Her *Alice* book. She clutched it to her chest.

"Aren't you bored with that one yet?"

She shook her head.

I sighed and led her toward the front of the store. "You're still going to keep quiet though, right? About the . . . you know." I patted the outside of my satchel.

She squeezed my hand.

"I'll take that as a yes."

As we passed the front counter, Mrs. Roth cleared her throat. She eyed the *Alice* book Ollie was holding.

I put my arm around Ollie and said, "We brought it in with us. It's ours."

Mrs. Roth arched her thinly plucked eyebrows. A deep crease formed straight across the middle of her forehead. Before she could say anything, a loud crash came from the room behind her. The shelves and window glass rattled. The trinkets on the counter shook. Mrs. Roth jumped up so fast she kicked the stool over on its side. She glared at the curtain.

Voices, loud and sparring, forced their way closer to the front room.

51

"Would you just listen to me for one second?" I recognized Travis's voice, despite it being high pitched and frantic.

"Go! Get the hell out!"

"Dad, please. I'm only trying to help."

"If I wanted your help, I'd ask for it."

The edges of the curtain trembled.

Ollie tried to wiggle out from under my arm, but I held her tight.

The voices got louder, moved closer, almost right on top of us. Someone threw something hard against a wall. We heard a violent crashing and splintering, and then Travis shouted, "Fuck!"

Mrs. Roth turned her head, blinked at me and Ollie like she was just seeing us there for the first time. "I think you girls had better leave."

She didn't wait for us to go. She just turned her back on us and disappeared through the curtain.

"What is going on?" Her voice reminded me of Grandma's that time Ollie and I were visiting and tried to make milk shakes in her kitchen, but forgot the part about snapping the blender lid on tight.

Another something smashed and broke against the wall.

Travis shouted, "Shit!"

Mrs. Roth said, "Language." And then, "I will not have you two fighting in my store. This is neither the time nor the place."

The curtain twitched. Mrs. Roth's long fingers and violet-painted nails poked through, gripping the edge, readying to pull it open again. "Get a broom and clean up this mess," she said.

I rushed Ollie out the front door. We jumped on our bikes and rode hard and fast out of town.

Zeb and Bear sat side by side on the lowered tailgate of Zeb's truck, parked in front of the hemlock stump. They kicked their legs back and forth in the air like they were boys again and bored with summer. When Ollie and I came around the last bend, Bear hopped off the tailgate first. Zeb climbed down more slowly.

Two Decembers ago Zeb had broken his hip going down the driveway to get the mail. He wasn't watching where he was going, he'd said, too busy staring at the snowflakes coming down. He slid on a patch of ice and landed the exact wrong way. He'd recovered quickly for a man his age—seventy-nine and holding—and liked to say it was because he drank a glass of whole milk every damn day of his life as far back as he could remember. He used a cane for a few weeks after, but now he got around just fine on his own, only having trouble if he was climbing up or down from something, or if the weather was about to change. Even then, you'd hardly notice. A slow descent, carefully putting one foot down, testing the weight; a hand rubbing over the bad hip, massaging the aches away. Mom had once said that Zeb was going to outlive us all.

I got off my bike and leaned it against the side of the truck. Ollie dropped hers in the dirt and ran full speed toward Zeb. He crouched and held out his arms and when she ran into them, he folded her up and swung her around. For a few seconds he was as strong as Zeus, she was as light as a cloud, and there was no such thing as gravity. When he set her down again, she kept tight hold of his hand.

I was close enough now to see the equipment loaded in the back of the truck: a spray bottle of sugar water, a saw, a ladder, a bucket, an empty Langstroth box. My bee suit and helmet.

Zeb smiled at me and touched the brim of his straw hat, nodding once. He said, "There's a swarm trying to make a home in one of my apple trees. Your daddy said you might be able to do something about that?"

"Me?" I looked over at Bear.

He was leaning up against the truck bed, arms over the side, hands loosely clasped together in the air. He squinted off into the trees, worrying a long piece of grass between his teeth. Though I'd seen it done, I'd never captured my own swarm—that had always been Bear's job.

"You sure?" I asked. "You think I'm ready?"

Bear took the grass he was chewing on and tossed it aside. "You don't have to be ready. You just have to try." He climbed into the back of Zeb's truck and held his hand out for me. "I'll be right there, walking you through it."

I grabbed hold and swung myself up into the truck bed beside him.

"Ever seen a swarm scooped from a tree crook?" Zeb asked Ollie. Ollie shook her head.

"No?" Zeb's expression was the same as if she'd shaken her head no to his asking about whether or not she'd ever seen the ocean. "Well, then, I guess we'll have to go ahead and make a day of it."

He brought her around to the front of the truck and opened the passenger door. As she climbed in, Zeb said, "Did you know that the ancient Egyptians thought bees were messengers sent from the sun god Ra? The Greeks, though, now they believed bees were souls of the dead come back to keep the rest of us company."

"Don't tell her things like that," I said.

Zeb came around to the back of the truck again and lifted first my bike, then Ollie's, up to Bear, who found a place for them beside the beekeeping equipment.

"No harm in thinking there's some place to go after we're done with this life, is there, Sam?" Zeb shut the tailgate, walked around to the driver's side, and climbed in.

The back window of the cab was open. Ollie had her head forward, looking through the windshield, but I knew she was listening. I said, "It's bad enough already, her thinking she can see ghosts. She doesn't need any more excuses for not talking."

"But maybe she does see ghosts."

"There's no such thing." I sat down on the raised wheel hub, grabbing hold of the side for balance.

Zeb started the engine. He shouted, "Maybe there is. Maybe you've just never seen one is all."

I looked at Bear, wanting him to defend me, to say I was right and Ollie didn't need to hear any more made-up stories about spirits and souls and life going on after you're dead, but his head was tipped back and he was staring at a vulture circling high above us. If Mom was here, she'd agree with me. She'd tell Ollie the truth: Once you're dead, you're dead. There's just no coming back from that.

We bumped along the dirt road and then down another single track toward the apple orchard. Ollie stuck her arm out the open passenger window and moved her hand up and down, a rising and falling wave in the wind.

It only took a-few minutes to get there. Zeb parked the truck twenty feet from the tree where the swarm gathered and turned off the engine.

"Hear that?" he said to Ollie, holding his head out the window and cupping his hand around his ear. "Bunch of old souls singing about heaven."

"It's just bees, Ollie," I said. "Moving the air so fast with their wings we can hear their vibrations."

"Sounds like music to me," said Zeb.

I grabbed the sugar water and my bee suit and jumped out of the truck. Bear unloaded the rest of the equipment and joined me under the apple tree. Ollie stayed behind with Zeb.

Bees swarm whenever the colony grows too big for the hive and they get to feeling like they need more elbow room. The queen and thousands of workers fly off together to find some new place to call home, while the ones who stay behind in the original hive hatch a new queen and carry on about their honey-making business. Bear's colonies had swarmed only a few times, but he'd always caught them and set them up in newer, bigger hives before they'd gotten too far away. Sometimes, though, swarms showed up out of nowhere, maybe from another keeper's hives, maybe from a wild colony. Even though bees were their most gentle selves during a swarm, there was still something ominous and disturbing about the way they clumped together on a tree limb or under the eaves of a house. A shifting, dark mass sending out a low and constant drone, the sound of ten thousand wings beating an uncertain rhythm.

This swarm was balled together, hanging from a thin limb about fifteen feet off the ground. It could have been worse. Once Bear had to capture a swarm that was trying to make its new home in Zeb and Franny's chimney. I wasn't there, but Franny said it was quite precarious and Bear was crazy for trying.

Bear leaned the ladder against the trunk of the tree as close to underneath the swarm as he could get. "Ready?"

I zipped my suit, cinched my gloves, pulled the veil down over my face, and gave him a thumbs-up.

I was halfway up the ladder when he said, "Did everything go okay with Deputy Santos today?"

I missed the next rung and almost slipped off. I balanced, found my footing again, and kept climbing.

"Yeah," I called down to him. "She was a little mad at first, but she thinks the jacket could be helpful for setting up a timeline. Anyway, it's out of our hands now."

Bear nodded. "Good."

I was surprised at how easy and quick the lie came. Surprised, too, that Bear believed me.

He passed me the bucket and handsaw. "Watch it now. This part can get a little tricky."

ollie

My sister adjusts her helmet, her veil, her gloves.

Bear points at her empty bucket and says, "Set it right under that branch and hold it steady."

Papa Zeb offers me a sip of his Coke. "Think we're far enough away?"

The bees fly around the one from the river, outlining her shape in the air. She is trying so hard to make my sister notice. But my sister sees only what is right in front of her and says all the rest is fake, just light playing tricks, summer bending the sky. Impossibilities, imaginary friends, and all in my head.

Maybe she's right.

I wish she was.

As far back as I can remember I've seen them. In dim light, they seem almost solid. In bright light, barely visible. If I touch them, it's ice and fire, energy burning. They are glints and specks, here and then gone. Shimmering. Like heat rising off pavement.

When I was four, at the zoo with my sister and mother, I grabbed Mom's sleeve and said, "Who is that man over there?"

"What man, sweetheart?"

"The one beside the tiger cage. Under that tree. He's wearing a funny hat."

"I don't see anyone." She put her arm around me and squeezed. "Honey, there's no one."

When I was six, the night before Grandma and Grandpa came to stay with us for two weeks, Mom sat on the edge of my bed and told me Aunt Charlotte had an accident while climbing a mountain. She fell. She died. I would never see or talk to her again. She was gone.

And then she wasn't.

Then she was here at our house, coming through the front door behind Grandma and filling the rooms with cold and ice. But I was the only one who noticed, the only one freezing. I started to cry and Mom said, "Oh, honey, what's wrong?" and lifted me onto her hip. But I couldn't tell her. I couldn't tell anyone. Aunt Charlotte's voice smothered mine. Her words, trying, failing to escape, became trapped inside me. For days after, I kept my mouth shut tight.

Mom said, "Sweetheart, talk to me."

But I was too afraid to try, knowing that the voice I'd hear would not belong to me.

When Grandma left a room, so did Aunt Charlotte. When Grandma came into a room, Aunt Charlotte came in right behind her. Ice crystals formed on the inside of the windows. Snowdrifts piled in the corners. At night, I shivered beneath the covers.

When Mom tucked me in, she added another blanket, saying, "I hope it's not the flu."

During the day, my sister rolled her eyes and said, "Stop being a baby."

The first time I figured out they could speak, and that I could hear them, was at the funeral. Aunt Charlotte's voice, a fog-whisper across the back of my neck, *I'm not even in there, you know. They left me up on that godforsaken mountain. Said it was too dangerous to bring me down. That's just an empty box they're burying.*

Grandpa and Grandma and Aunt Charlotte left a few days later, and the house warmed up and the hand around my throat unclenched and my own voice returned. I asked Mom if the coffin was empty and why we'd had a funeral if there was no body.

Mom looked surprised. "Who told you that?"

"Aunt Charlotte."

"Your aunt Charlotte's gone, sweetheart."

"But she was at the cemetery with Grandma," I said.

Mom started to cry then and pulled me into the chair beside her and told me about heaven, how people went to live there after they died and Aunt Charlotte was smiling and singing with the angels. I let her say what she needed to say, even though I worried some of it might not be true.

I asked my sister once if she saw them too.

"What?"

"Shimmering. The shiny, light parts people leave behind when they die."

"You're talking crazy."

"Do you think they're ghosts?"

My sister rolled her eyes. "I don't believe in ghosts."

"What about angels?"

She shook her head. "Nope. Don't believe in them, either."

"Then what happens after you die?"

"Nothing."

"Something happens," I said.

"Nothing and nothing and nothing." She spun tight circles in the middle of the living room. "You get buried in the ground like Aunt Charlotte and then people come and cry over you for a while and then things go back to the way they were before. And that's what happens."

"But what about your soul?"

"If there is such a thing as a soul, it probably gets buried too."

"Of course there's such a thing as a soul," I said.

"What's a soul if you don't have a body?" My sister stuck out her tongue.

I stuck out my tongue too. I said, "What's a body if you don't have a soul?"

"I'm telling Mom," my sister said.

The doctor wore a plaid skirt and a red blouse and smiled too wide and called me Miss Olivia. One foot tapping, tapping, in constant motion.

"Tell me about these . . . Shimmering. How often do you see them?"

"Sometimes."

"Every day?"

"No."

"And how do they make you feel? Scared? Excited? Happy? Nervous?"

"Like someone's trying to open my chest and slip inside," I told her.

She wrote something on a yellow notepad, then smiled at Mom and said, "This kind of fantasy play is typical for kids her age, especially after losing someone they love in such a traumatic way. She's filling in the gaps. Try not to worry. She'll grow out of it. But just in case . . ." and handed her a slip of white paper.

In the car on the way back home, my sister pinched me and said, "You're a freak."

The one who follows me floats like a cloud above us. She flickers soft pink and rose red, sky blue and honey gold. She likes it when we're all together—my sister, my father, and me. She's pretending she's here with us too and that makes her happy. But she's not here. Not in the way that counts.

The one from the river coils tight and tighter around the leather satchel my sister left in the bed of the truck. She hisses at me, but I ignore her.

My sister uses the handsaw to cut the branch from the apple tree. Some of the bees fly close to her veiled face, but she keeps working, carefully, slowly, the way she's seen Bear work. She sets the cut branch and swarm gently into the bucket and covers it with a mesh lid.

"Good work," Bear says.

Papa Zeb shivers. "Makes my skin crawl."

My sister climbs down the ladder with her bucket of bees and brings it to the truck. The buzzing is so loud, I cover my ears.

sam

Friday breakfast at Zeb and Franny's was a standing tradition for Bear, and me when I was visiting, and now for Ollie, too. We were supposed to be at the house, sitting down at the table, by nine o'clock sharp, but when Ollie and I woke up that morning, Bear was gone. He'd left a note pinned to the inside of the teepee flap: *Be back soon*. I turned it over, looking for more of an explanation, but the other side was blank. Ollie and I waited until we couldn't wait any longer, then we walked the quarter mile to Zeb and Franny's without him.

They lived in a two-story farmhouse with a wraparound front porch and rooster-red shutters. Wind chimes and hummingbird feeders dangled from the eaves. They'd bought the house and eighty acres right after they were married. The plan, Franny told me once when I asked her why she and Zeb lived all alone in such a big house, was to fill the extra space with kids, and eventually grandkids, and, if God saw fit, great-grandkids, but their first daughter died of pneumonia when she was still a baby, and their second daughter died, too, when she was older, after falling off a horse. Though they didn't have any more of their own kids after that, they were foster parents for a long time, and Franny said all those kids had filled her heart with more than enough love to last until she died and then some. Besides, they had us now.

I opened the screen door. The hinges squealed.

Franny called from the kitchen, "Come in, come in! My babes from the meadow, come in!"

Ollie and I took off our shoes and crossed through the living room toward the back of the house. Framed photographs cluttered the walls, the shelves and end tables, even the top of the piano. Here were pictures capturing nearly a century of well-lived life. A sepia-toned portrait of Zeb in a suit and Franny in her wedding dress, holding hands, heads inclined toward each other. Black-and-white and color photographs of so many children I wondered how Franny and Zeb remembered all their names.

One photograph stood apart from all the others on an end table beside the couch. Taken three years ago, it was of Bear and Mom and Ollie and me bunched together on the front porch steps. Bear had his arm around Mom's waist, and Mom had one hand on my shoulder, one hand on Ollie's. Our smiles were silly and huge. Zeb stood by himself behind us, tall and straight and serious. It was Franny's idea to take the picture. She'd said she wanted all the people she loved most staring up at her from a single frame. I stopped in front of it and brushed my fingers across all our faces.

In the kitchen, Franny was busy plunging soft dough into a pan of hot oil, frying up her famous French crullers. The room smelled of warm cinnamon and powdered sugar.

She smiled when we came through the doorway. "My beautiful girls."

Ollie went over and hugged her.

"Papa Zeb could use a little help outside with the blueberries." She kissed the top of Ollie's head and pushed her toward the open sliding glass door.

A few seconds later, I heard Zeb outside talking and laughing, carrying on a one-sided conversation. I wondered how much Bear had told him about Ollie, if he knew it had been almost five weeks now since she last spoke.

Franny pulled a cruller from the hot oil and set it on a paper towel to drain. She said, "Papa's been out there for nearly an hour. Won't have any fruit for breakfast the way he's been picking. Slow as molasses on a January morning, that one is."

Though we both knew she didn't mind as much as she made it seem.

"I still can't get used to your new haircut," she said. "Reminds me of a 1920s starlet."

I touched my bare neck. "It's easier this way."

She nodded, gesturing to her own short hair, and then asked, "Your father back from his interview yet?"

"What interview?"

She frowned and wiped the back of her hand across her forehead, streaking her brow with flour. "He didn't tell you?"

I shook my head.

Franny dropped another raw piece of dough into the oil. It sizzled and popped. "Maybe he meant for it to be a surprise."

"What's he interviewing for?" I asked.

She hesitated, pinching her lips between her teeth and squinting up at the ceiling.

"Come on, Franny. Just tell me."

She let out her breath in a rush. "A janitorial position at the mill."

She lifted the golden brown cruller from the pan and continued, "That's what he told Papa yesterday afternoon anyway." She smiled at me, and I thought she looked a little sad. "Maybe he didn't want you girls to get your hopes up, and here I am flapping my gums. Forget I said anything."

I slumped against the counter and shoved my right hand into my pants pocket, wrapped my fist around the key I'd found last night in a small side pocket of Bear's leather satchel.

I was alone in the teepee, stuffing the satchel inside my duffel bag where no one would find it, promising myself that as soon as I had a chance, I'd get rid of the jacket like I'd originally planned. In my rush, the bag tipped on its side and a silver key fell out onto the ground. It had a narrow, rectangular head engraved with the word *Toyota*. I didn't know anyone who drove that make of car. I'd turned it over in my hand, feeling the weight of it, the coldness against my palm, then I put the key in the pocket of my jeans to ask Bear about later. But between last night and this morning an opportunity had never come up.

I took my hand out of my pocket, turned, and opened the cupboard above the sink. Right there in front, like someone wanted me to find it, was Mom's favorite mug, the one she always used when she was here. It was round, almost as big as a soup bowl, ruby red with tiny white polka dots and a small chip on the handle. It had fit perfectly in her cupped hands. I started to reach for a plain, blue mug that wasn't important to anybody, but then stopped and took hers down instead. It was heavier than I remembered and looked strange with my small, stubby fingers wrapped around it instead of her long, graceful ones. I poured myself hot water from the kettle on the stove, stirred in three heaping spoonfuls of hot cocoa, and sat down at the table. The key jabbed sharp into my thigh. Maybe I didn't know Bear as well as I thought I did.

I sank low in my chair and blew across the surface of my mother's mug, curling the steam in wisps around my face.

After breakfast, after we'd finished washing the dishes and were separating the extra blueberries into pint boxes, Zeb cleared his throat and said too loudly, "Well, Mother, I suppose now'd be a good time for me to take little sister out to see the new chicks."

Franny wiped her hands on a dish towel, then slowly untied her apron and hung it on its proper hook beside the stove, taking her time like she was trying to figure out the best way to answer. Finally, she said, "I suppose now's as good a time as any."

"I thought Ollie could help me work the honey stand this morning," I said and shrugged. "But I guess we can see the chicks first."

Zeb and Franny exchanged the kind of glance that said nothing and everything at once. Then Franny said, "Why don't I help you get things set up at the stand and then when Ollie's had her fill of those chirping yellow fluff balls, Zeb can bring her out to join us."

That's how I knew Franny wanted to talk to me about something important, something she didn't think Ollie was old enough to hear, because in the three years I'd been selling honey at the end of her driveway, Franny had never come out to help. "This old body just doesn't work the way it used to," she'd say, by way of explaining, and pat her swollen joints. "I'd barely get halfway and then you'd have to carry me and I know you're not strong enough for that." Then she'd laugh and shoo me away. But today was different. Today, Franny insisted.

I brought up two full boxes of pint-size honey jars from the basement and loaded them onto the wagon with three flats of blueberries, a metal cash box, and a plastic folding chair for Franny. She came out the front door wearing large rubber boots and a wide-brimmed straw hat and took her time coming down the porch steps.

"You sure you want to come, Franny? It'll be boiling out there so close to the asphalt." I offered my arm for support, but she waved me away.

"It's about time I see what you've been up to out there, don't you think?" She reached the last step and paused a moment to catch her breath before stepping down to the ground.

We started up the gravel driveway, slow and shuffling, and this time when I offered my arm, Franny took it.

The stand had been my idea. People bought lemonade and flowers from the side of the road, so I figured they might buy other things too. Better, tastier things like honey. Zeb had built the simple wooden stand and painted it bright yellow. Bear had helped him carry it to a patch of grass at the end of the driveway that was set far enough back from Lambert Road to be safe, but close enough to be seen. I'd come up with a name and a design for labels that Franny helped me stick onto pint jars. Then we tied red ribbons around the lids, and she said it was the most beautiful honey she'd ever seen. That first summer, we didn't sell very much. Maybe a half-dozen jars, mostly to people who were friends with Zeb and Franny. But the next year those same people came back for more, saying Bear's was the best honey they'd ever eaten and their allergies weren't coming on nearly as bad this year, and you know what, come to think of it, they hadn't come down with a single cold all winter. Not even the sniffles. Those people told their friends, and those friends told their other friends, and by the second weekend, we were sold out.

Bear started taking special orders and making deliveries to keep up with demand, and sometimes he even sold honey down at Potter's Grocery Store where they kept shelf space for his jars between the jam and peanut butter. But he always saved some jars just for me. He told me whatever I earned at the stand was mine to keep. It seemed like a lot of money when I was younger—fifty, sixty dollars for a few hours' work. I'd been saving all of it, plus the money I got on my birthday and for doing odd jobs around the house, for a car when I turned sixteen. Last week I'd counted, and I had almost a thousand dollars. Last week, too, I'd decided the car could wait. Whatever money I had saved up already and whatever I earned this summer was going to pay for the first month's rent on an apartment or a new winter coat for Ollie or a new suit for Bear for job interviews. I had to start being more responsible now, pitching in where I could.

When we reached the stand, Franny collapsed into the folding chair and fanned her hat in front of her face. She exhaled, long and loud, more groan than sigh, and fanned under her arms too, where large patches of damp were visible against her pale green cotton dress. I started to unload the wagon, and when Franny made to help, I shooed her away.

"Sit," I said. "Relax."

She settled her hat atop her head again, crossed her arms over her chest, and stretched out her legs.

I arranged the jars in pyramids at just the right angle where when the sun hit them directly, the honey sparkled. The county road was empty, no cars coming in either direction, but it was early yet. Soon enough someone would come rolling over one or the other of those hills.

Franny said, "Deputy Santos stopped by the other day."

I unstacked the jars and spread them in a straight line across the top of the counter to see if they looked better that way. They didn't. I restacked them, three pyramids all in a row.

"Shame about that poor girl they found," Franny continued. "I can't even begin to imagine . . ." She shook her head. "Anyway, Deputy Santos was asking a lot of questions about your father."

"Like what?"

"Like if we'd seen him the day before," Franny said. "What he said to us. How he acted."

"What did you tell her?"

"The truth, of course."

A dark blue minivan appeared on the horizon, coming at us from the south. Closer, closer, it slowed as it passed, but then went right on by, picking up speed again on the hill headed toward Terrebonne.

Franny shifted her weight in the folding chair. The brim of her hat shaded her face, and I couldn't see if she was smiling or frowning or wearing any kind of expression at all. She said, "Your father borrowed the truck that night, Sam."

"I know. He told me." I turned one of the jars so the label faced the road. "He went to Bend to pick up supplies."

Franny nodded. "That's what he told us too. But then after Deputy Santos and that detective came around, I got to thinking about it again and there's things about it that just don't sit right with me."

Some two hundred feet south of us on the opposite side of the highway and set back a little from the road was Blue Heron Pond. A man-made reservoir used by farmers to irrigate crops, the pond was rectangular in shape with sloped dirt retaining walls and a gravel driveway and a chain-link fence guarding the perimeter. Sunlight brushed the surface of the water, glinting radiant white. I stared at the reflection until my eyes hurt. When I looked back at Franny, she was a blur, a thin, paper-white ghost. Blink, and she was solid again, her hands worrying the tops of her knees, the brim of her hat dipping lower like she was trying to think of the gentlest way to say whatever it was she'd been holding on to all morning. I imagined her thinking, *Poor girl's been through enough already.* But I needed to know.

"What things?" I asked her.

She glanced at me like she was still deciding. The brim of her hat tipped up just enough for our eyes to meet, and then she looked away again and said, "When he brought the truck back, the gas gauge wasn't much lower than when he took it. That truck's a hog. It takes a quarter of a tank just to get to Bend. Another quarter to get back."

"Maybe he filled it before he gave it back to you."

Franny stared at the pond and nodded slowly. "Maybe."

One explanation was that Bear had found a gas station between here and there that was open late and he had somehow scraped together enough change to refill the tank. The other explanation, the one I thought Franny was worrying about, was that Bear hadn't gone to Bend that night, hadn't gone very far at all.

She took off her hat and wiped her sleeve across her brow. Her cheeks were flushed red, her eyes pinched against the sun. She put her hat back on. "Has he been acting funny to you lately? Doing things out of the ordinary?"

I shrugged. "He's Bear. Everything's out of the ordinary."

But he *had* been acting stranger than usual recently. Leaving me and Ollie alone for long stretches of time, lying about where he was going and what he was doing, skipping Friday breakfast. All of which could be explained away as a husband grieving his dead wife, a father struggling to handle his new responsibilities. And then I thought about the key I was carrying around in my pocket.

"You can tell me, Sam," Franny said. "You don't have to be scared."

I turned my back to her and faced the road. "Tell you what?"

"If there's something you're worried about with Bear. Maybe you saw something or heard something that needs telling." The chair she was sitting in creaked. "I know it's hard. He's your father—"

"There's nothing," I said, but my voice cracked and Franny heard it.

She said, "That girl had family, too, Sam. Someone who loved her the way you loved your mama."

A crow landed in the middle of the road, walked a few steps along the center dividing line, then flew off again.

"Don't you think they deserve to know what happened?"

I reached behind me, picked up a pint jar, and held it to the sun, turning it until the light seemed trapped inside the viscous amber. In Greek mythology, the gods ate honey to preserve their immortality. I wished it could work like that for regular people too. Then at least we could have a choice about dying.

I set the jar back down with the others, trying to decide how much to tell Franny—if anything—how much was something to be worried about and how much was just coincidence. Blue and red flashing lights flickered on the hill and a patrol car came into view, coming fast from Terrebonne. Ominously, without sirens.

Franny leaned forward in her chair. "What's all this, now?"

Another patrol car, this one with both its sirens and lights off, crested the hill and started down. A tow truck followed close behind. The lead car started to slow a few feet shy of Zeb and Franny's driveway and I thought, *This is it. This is where it all falls apart.* Another second, maybe two—snap your fingers and your entire future changes course. Blue flashed red flashed blue flashed red, burning my eyes, making me blink too fast.

The first patrol car passed the driveway, and all I saw were brake lights. The driver was stopping, pulling off to the side of the road, but not here in front of us, not here for me.

The car parked on the gravel shoulder beside Blue Heron Pond, and the driver's door opened. Detective Talbert stepped out. He hitched up his pants, checked to make sure the other cars were on their way, then turned and walked over to the reservoir's main gate. He stood a moment with his hands on his hips, staring at the padlock, then he took a radio from his belt and spoke into the mouthpiece. We were too far away to hear what he said.

"Must be having trouble with trespassers again," Franny said, lifting the brim of her hat to see better.

I curled my fingers around the overhanging edge of the honey stand.

The second patrol car parked on the shoulder behind the first. The tow truck pulled up beside them both and idled there in the northbound lane, waiting for whatever was coming next. The driver hung his elbow out the open window.

I recognized Deputy Santos as soon as she got out of the car. She spoke briefly to the tow truck driver and then joined Detective Talbert at the gate, which she pushed open without any trouble. Seemed that the chain had been cut, because I didn't see her turning a key and when the gate swung wide, both the chain and the padlock slid to the ground. They stood outside the fence awhile, staring down the short driveway that led to the reservoir, staring out across the water. Detective Talbert raised his arm and pointed to something I couldn't see. Deputy Santos turned her head toward the tow truck and motioned for the driver to start backing up. Then she caught sight of the roadside stand and of me and Franny, sitting, watching.

I wanted her to wave, to lift her hat off her head and sweep it in the air like she was in some grand parade, like this was just a routine call, nothing serious. Nothing to do with that woman. But she didn't. She nodded, just once, then turned her back on us and walked toward the water. I grabbed the wagon, rolled it up close to the stand, and started to repack the blueberries and honey.

"You giving up already?" Franny said. "We haven't been out here very long."

The glass jars clinked together.

I said, "Franny, have you ever been wrong about a person?"

"Now, I'm not sure what you mean."

I stopped stacking jars for a second. "Have you ever thought somebody was one way, but then something happens and you find out they're something else entirely? That they were just pretending so people wouldn't see their true self?"

Franny tipped her head up just enough so I could see her blue-gray, ancient eyes under the brim of her hat. She stared at me so long and sat so motionless, I thought maybe she still didn't understand what I was asking.

Then she sighed and shifted in her chair and said, "People can only hide who they really are for so long. After a while, all that pretending becomes exhausting and, soon enough, their true stripes and spots start to show through." She scratched the palm of her hand. "You thinking about someone in particular, Samantha?"

And the way she said my name reminded me of Mom and made it hurt to breathe and I had to look away. I shoved my hand in my pocket, wrapped my fist tight around the key.

On the other side of the highway, the tow truck had reached the reservoir. The back tires were half sunk in brown water, and the driver was standing between Detective Talbert and Deputy Santos at the edge where the gravel driveway disappeared into the pond. All three of them stared across the glassy surface, stared and didn't move, and I wondered what was taking so long. Finally, the tow truck driver walked away from the water, returned to his truck, and punched a switch near the back. The winch unraveled. A metallic grating and clattering echoed across the road.

"What in the world?" Franny said under her breath.

The driver waded waist-deep into the water and attached the winch to something beneath the surface. He splashed back to his truck and hit the switch again. There was a low grinding sound, the awful noise of metal scraping rocks, and then sunlight flashed off bright white paint as the tow truck pulled a small sedan from the pond.

"Franny?" I said, turning to face her and pulling the key from my pocket, holding it flat in the palm of my hand. "It might be nothing . . ." I glanced back at the white sedan.

She squinted, leaned in a little closer, and then her eyes widened, her hand fluttering to her chest. "Where did you get this?" she asked me.

I told her then about finding the dead woman and the scratches on Bear's face and how Monday night, the same night he borrowed the truck, Bear had left me and Ollie alone in the meadow for hours and hours after dark. How I'd found the key in his satchel. The one thing I left out was the jacket. I didn't want Franny to know how I'd convinced Bear to let me take it to the police by myself, how I'd lied and tried to get rid of it instead, how much worse I'd probably made things for him, for all of us, by not coming forward right away.

When I was finished, Franny started to get up from her chair. "You need to march right over there and tell all this to Detective Talbert," she said. "You need to give him that key you're holding on to so tight and let him sort this whole thing out."

I stared across the highway where the detective and Deputy Santos were walking around the car, peering in through the windows, taking notes.

"No," I said. "No way."

"Then I will." She reached for the key.

I curled my fingers around it and backed away from her, shaking my head, fighting a rising panic that I had made a mistake telling her. There would be no keeping it quiet now, no more pretending we weren't a part of this.

"He didn't do anything wrong." I stumbled over the words.

"I never said he did. But, Sam, we still have to tell Detective Talbert. If we know something about that poor girl's death . . . if we *think* we know something, even if it's nothing . . . we still have to tell them. It's the right thing to do." She reached for my hand. "We'll go together."

I ducked away from her and sprinted up the driveway back to the house. Franny called after me, but I didn't turn around and I didn't stop running until I got to the front porch. I leaned a moment against the railing to catch my breath before going inside to get Ollie. I was still holding the key, clenching it in my fist. I uncurled my fingers. The teeth had left dents in the palm of my hand, turned my skin bright red. I shoved the key back into my pocket and took the steps two at a time.

Zeb and Ollie were playing Slap Jack at the kitchen table. I interrupted them, saying, "Ollie, let's go."

She ignored me at first, turning a card over and placing it in the center of the table.

"Ollie!" I snapped, grabbing her by the arm, lifting her to her feet.

She huffed, threw her cards onto the table, and pushed her chair back hard, scraping the legs against the wooden floor. She wriggled from my grasp and shoved past me, dashing through the living room and outside. The screen door slammed shut. She pounded down the steps. Zeb started to say something, but I didn't stop to listen. I ran away from him, too.

The rock flew straight and fast from my fingers and hit the pine knot I'd been aiming at with a dead, solid *thunk*. I stooped, plucked another rock from the pile at my feet, and tossed it in the air. I caught it coming down, curled my fingers around the shape of it, and held the stone in my fist, feeling its weight. One hundred steps from the pine tree and my target knot. My best distance yet. Some fathers teach their kids how to play baseball. Mine taught me how to chuck rocks.

My first summer in the meadow, Bear handed me a stone so big I could barely get my fingers around it. He'd pointed at a fir tree some twenty feet away and said, "Show me what you can do." I remember pulling my arm back so far, feeling the muscles in my shoulder blade tightening until I thought they would snap, shouting as I let go, thinking that would make the rock go faster, farther. The stone had clattered into the dirt about five feet from where we stood and nowhere close to the tree. Bear had handed me another rock and said, "Keep practicing."

The trick was to aim a little higher than where you actually wanted to hit, on account of gravity, and to throw with your entire body. That's how Bear taught me anyway. I drew my arm back, then pitched it forward, releasing the stone at the high point of the arc, following through, watching the rock spin and spin and hit its mark. Most of the time I think I just got damn lucky.

Over an hour had passed since we'd left Zeb and Franny's house, and Bear still wasn't back from his interview. I kept glancing at the path, expecting Deputy Santos and Detective Talbert to come storming through those woods at any second, demanding the key, the jacket, my father. I was sure Franny had told them everything by now, but the sun ticked a little higher and a little higher after that until it was right on top of us and still no one came.

I picked up another rock and rubbed my thumb against its smooth side. "You want to give it a try, Oll?"

She was stretched out on her stomach in the grass under a tree with her *Alice* book, reading and ignoring me completely. I held the stone out to her. She lowered the book, looked at my outstretched hand, and shook her head.

"It's not as hard as it looks," I said.

Ollie didn't move.

"Come on. It's really fun." I waved the rock like I was tempting her with a piece of candy.

She lifted the book, hiding her face.

I shrugged and said, "Fine. Be that way," trying not to sound too disappointed.

This time when I threw it, the rock hit a few inches lower than the target, but it still hit the tree and that had to count for something.

In the distance, I heard an engine whining closer, too fast and high pitched to be a car. It sounded like a dirt bike. Ollie turned her head toward the sound. She closed her book and sat up. We watched the tree line and shadows, waiting.

The engine sounds stopped, and birdsong flooded the silence. A few seconds later, Travis came through the trees with a white pastry box under one arm. At the edge of the grass where thin scrub gave way to wildflowers and shade gave way to sun, he hesitated. He was dressed more casually today than when I saw him yesterday—a faded gray T-shirt tucked into the waistband of his dark jeans and a pair of red Chuck Taylors, the laces untied.

He smiled and came toward me. "Hey."

And I found myself wishing I had taken time this morning to put away the gardening tools and wipe dust off the tops and sides of the beehives and take the clothes off the line, hide these ordinary parts of our lives out here. I wanted him to see the beauty of our meadow, not the drab. Only the flowers and light, the bright shock of summer, the wide-open pasture and crisp, blue sky all around, the soul of this place.

We met at the picnic table. I brushed dirt off the bench and sat down. He sat down across from me, set the pastry box on the tabletop in front of us, and opened the lid. "Blackberry cobbler from Patti's. Still warm."

He pulled three forks from his back pocket and held one out to me.

I took it. "What's this for?"

"Yesterday," he said. "An apology, I guess. For how I acted at the store, yelling the way I did, making a scene. Upsetting people."

"It wasn't a big deal."

"Yeah, well. My mom thought it was." He spun a fork in his fingers. "But it was as good an excuse as any."

"Excuse for what?"

"To see you." He stared so hard, I had to look away.

Laura was always whispering about the cute boys in our class and writing their names in her notebook. She'd even kissed Derek Bosch last summer. But the most I'd ever done was hold hands with Gavin

Thompson on the bus to the science museum in fifth grade. I didn't pay much attention to boys, and they didn't pay much attention to me. But Travis was different, and I thought maybe I was starting to like him, which was pretty bad timing, considering everything else going on in my life right now.

I jabbed my fork into the cobbler and took a large bite. It tasted rich, sweet, like those long days of summer when you spend entire afternoons just dangling your bare feet in the river, and the whole world breathes fresh honey. I swallowed and nodded and said, "This is really good."

Travis ate a few bites. "Best cobbler west of the Mississippi."

"Is that true?"

"It should be."

I laughed a little and ate more and, after a few minutes, half the cobbler was gone.

Up to this point, Ollie had been watching us from the grass. Now, she got up and, with her book still in hand, walked slowly toward the table. She stopped a few steps away.

Travis offered her the last fork. "Get it while it's hot."

She stared at him, not blinking.

He shifted on the bench, waved the fork a little, and said, "I brought it for both of you."

Keeping her eyes fixed on Travis, Ollie came right up next to me and leaned hard against my shoulder. She plucked on my T-shirt sleeve.

"Don't be rude," I said to her.

Travis smiled and shrugged. "It's all right. More for us." He placed the extra fork on the picnic table and took another bite of cobbler.

Ollie looked back and forth between me and Travis. Her mouth twitched. She pushed her glasses up and yanked harder on my shirt.

"Stop being such a pest, Oll." I brushed her off. "Leave us alone."

She gave me a final piercing stare and then turned and ran, full sprint, to the teepee.

Travis shook his head. "I've never met a kid who doesn't like sweets."

"She just gets shy sometimes." I watched the tent flap, waiting for it to open again and Ollie to come back out. She didn't.

Travis stared off into the woods in the direction of Crooked River, then turned to me again and said, "You want to walk down to the water?"

"Sure," I said with a small shrug, like it was no big deal.

Travis closed the pastry box and stood up from the table.

I went to the teepee and poked my head inside to tell Ollie I wouldn't be gone long and if she needed something to come get me. She was standing over the card table, scribbling on a piece of paper. There were other papers wadded up and tossed aside, growing in a pile on the rug by her feet.

"What are you doing?" I asked.

She glanced over her shoulder at me but kept scribbling.

"I'm going down to the river with Travis," I said.

She wadded up the paper she was writing on and threw it at the teepee wall. It bounced off the canvas and rolled underneath Bear's cot. She tore a blank piece of paper from Bear's sketchbook and pressed the pen down hard.

I left her there alone and walked with Travis into the trees.

ollie

I follow them. My sister and her new friend who is hiding something. Travis, who is stitched together with secrets and dark threads. He says something I can't hear. My sister laughs and touches his arm. The one from the river coils around my sister's ankle and leg, wraps around her torso and squeezes. My sister feels nothing.

But I do.

My stomach twists. I can't catch my breath. I lean one hand against a tree trunk and wait for them to move farther away.

I keep my distance, being as quiet as I can. Light feet, ghost feet: what Mom used to say when I would sneak up on her.

They do not see me. They do not see anything but each other.

Travis slips his hand into his pocket. He walks this way for a while, one hand tucked out of sight, the other swinging loose at his side.

They have almost reached the place where the trees end and the grass skims my waist. The path here is narrow and half buried in weeds. They have to walk single file. My sister goes first, leading the way. The one from the river slides through the grass behind her and

Travis comes after. He slows his pace, stretching the gap between them. I am last and far behind, but close enough to see him pull his hand from his pocket and open his fingers. Something falls to the ground, but he doesn't stop to pick it up again.

He catches up to my sister, and they disappear over a small hill.

I stay in the trees.

What he dropped glints in a sun-yellow polka dot. The one who follows me floats over the top of it, too. She's a glowing orb, changing red to blue to green to bright white. I bend and pick up what he left behind. A lighter. Heavy, solid, made of gold. One side is smooth. I turn it over and rub my thumb across an etched rattlesnake, coiled and ready to strike.

I hear their voices up ahead, but their words are lost to me. I put the lighter in my pocket, where it will be safe, and go back to the meadow to wait.

I do not like this in-between boy, this almost man.

I tried to tell my sister before she left with him. I went to the teepee knowing she'd follow. I went to the teepee and grabbed a pen, pressed it to paper, tried to write her a warning.

It should be easy. The words played over and over in my head:

He's not who you think he is.

He's not your friend.

We can't trust him.

He'll hurt us.

Tell him to go away.

But trying to write is like trying to talk. The Shimmering want to climb inside me and write their way free. But if I let them in, I'm afraid they'll never leave.

My sister came into the teepee, and the one from the river was right behind her. She was upset. They both were.

The one from the river slid up beside me and put her hand on my hand and tried to move the pen across the paper. It felt like needles being jabbed beneath my fingernails, like someone twisting my bones. The worst Indian burn in the history of all Indian burns, and I jerked my hand away from her. The pen went sideways, streaking ink across the paper in jagged lines and bleeding scratches.

"What are you doing?" my sister said.

She has to know, and I am the only one here who can tell her.

I tried to write a *T,* but my hand was shaking so bad, it came out looking more like an *S.*

My sister stared at me the way she did after the funeral when she found me in Mom's closet, wrapped in Mom's gray peacoat and all her winter scarves, wearing her pink rain boots, reading *Alice* by flashlight. She stared at me like she didn't know who I was anymore.

I wadded up my useless scribbles and threw the paper as hard as I could.

My sister said, "I'm going down to the river with Travis," and left.

I have to find another way. I have to make her see, before it's too late.

sam

It had only been three days since Ollie and I found the dead woman floating in our swimming hole. Three days that stretched into forever.

I got to the riverbank before Travis and took off my shoes and socks. At a glance, everything looked the same. Same white alders huddled on the banks. Same rapids twisting, crashing, spilling down-river. Same paddle bugs skimming across the shallows.

And yet.

A dark stain spread over the surface of my swimming hole, swelling, growing darker, like a body rising from the deep, like black fingers reaching toward me. I blinked, and the stain moved away. Not a stain at all, only a cloud crossing in front of the sun, and the water sparkled again, swirling slowly as the current moved around the rocks, lapped against my toes, beckoned. I took a long step backward, putting distance between me and the river.

Travis crashed through the brush behind me. He took off his shoes, too, stood next to me in the sand, and stared out over the water.

"I bet she floated right by here," he said in a quiet voice.

He seemed to be waiting for me to say something, but I was caught up in thinking about the dead woman and how even though she was probably in some hospital basement, zipped up in a body bag, and not here, not anywhere near here, I still saw her floating. Just there, beneath the dark glass of my swimming hole. Sunlight reflected off her pale skin, and then she was coming closer, pushing to the surface. Her fingers broke through first, then her face, her eyes and mouth wide open, water streaming from her bruised purple lips and tangled black hair. She gasped my name and reached for me, then slid under again, sinking into the dark. Ripples cut through my swimming hole, out beyond the half-sunk boulders and into the main current where they were swept downstream. Echoes of her.

Travis nudged my shoulder. "Earth to Sam."

I squeezed my eyes shut, and when I opened them again, she was gone. It was all in my head. *She* was all in my head.

"Do they know who she was yet? Why she was in Terrebonne?" I asked, climbing onto a large, flat rock that extended a few feet over the water. I pulled my knees to my chest and curled my bare toes against the sun-warmed stone.

Travis climbed up next to me. "There was an article about it in the paper this morning. She was from Eugene, I guess. Her parents are driving in tomorrow to ID the body."

"It's so sad," I said.

Travis nodded and squinted at the trees crowding the opposite bank.

We sat close together, our shoulders brushing, and listened to the river hiss, birds chirp, a hawk scream.

Picking at a bit of moss growing on the rock, I glanced at Travis and asked, "Does your dad get angry with you a lot?"

His arm twitched against mine.

"I'm sorry," I said quickly, wishing I could take the question back. "I shouldn't have—you don't have to answer that."

"No. It's all right," Travis said. He stretched his legs out in front of him. His bare feet dangled above the water. "He's been spending a lot of time in his studio lately getting ready for a show in New York at the end of the month. Things can get a little . . . tense . . . this close to opening night."

Billy Roth was Terrebonne's most famous artist-in-residence, or used-to-be-famous, as Deputy Santos had once called him, since he hadn't sold a single new piece in over ten years. He was a sculptor who'd stopped sculpting. A has-been, all washed up, used up, dried up. If he was working again, preparing for a new show, that was a big deal. I didn't know much about his rise and fall—when he started, why he stopped—only that his pieces were strange and sold for a lot of money in certain circles. Though some people—Franny—called them abominations, it seemed to me that a new piece, or pieces, from Billy Roth could bring in much-needed income for his family. For the whole town of Terrebonne, even.

"That's great, Travis," I said, bumping him with my shoulder. "You must be so excited!"

He shrugged.

"Have you seen what he's working on?"

He shook his head. "He keeps the door locked. I don't know what the hell he's doing out there." He took a crumpled pack of Marlboros from his pocket and tapped it against his knee. "Mom's seen it, though."

"Yeah?"

"She seems to think it's worth something, I guess. She keeps saying it's 'unlike anything he's ever done before.' Experimental. Edgy. Even more so than his older pieces. She thinks it's going to be his grand re-entry into the art world. His 'resurrection.'" He took a cigarette from the pack, lifted it to his lips, then stopped and stared at it like he didn't know how it had gotten there in the first place. He stuffed the cigarette back in with the rest and rolled his eyes. "Sounds like a bunch of bullshit to me."

"Maybe you should wait until you see it and then decide," I said.

He grunted and changed the subject. "So what's the deal with your sister?"

"What do you mean?"

"She's kind of . . . weird. Right?"

I chewed on the inside of my cheek, trying to come up with a good answer.

Travis folded his knees to his chest, so we were sitting almost the exact same way. "I'm not trying to be mean or anything. She just seems . . . I don't know . . . quiet."

"It's been a rough summer," I said.

"Tell me about it."

We were quiet for a few minutes, each of us lost in our own private thoughts, and then Travis asked, "Where's your mom?"

I stiffened but said nothing.

"She doesn't stay in the meadow with you guys?" he pushed.

I folded my hands together and squeezed until my fingers started to hurt, not sure what to say, what not to say, not knowing how much he knew already and how much I was willing to tell. A yellow-and-black butterfly flitted past us and disappeared across the water.

He touched my arm. "Sam?"

My fingertips had turned white, but they didn't hurt so much anymore. Not compared to the lump growing in my throat and the headache starting to pulse at the base of my neck. I stared at part of a wooden fence visible through the trees on the other side of Crooked River, stared and tried not to cry.

I hugged my knees as tight to my chest as I could and said, "Our mom . . . ," but I couldn't think of a good way to finish.

Died seemed too blunt and cold, too much like being punched in the ribs by a stranger. *Passed away* was filled with too much sighing and melodramatic clasping of hands. *Kicked the bucket* turned the whole horrible thing into a child's game. Finally, I settled on, "She had a heart attack."

Travis turned so he was facing me and said, "Oh my God. I'm so sorry. Is she . . . She's okay, right?"

I wanted more than anything to say yes, yes, she was fine; she was spending the summer in Greece or Spain or Fiji. Someplace warm and beautiful and interesting. In a few weeks, she would come back for me and Ollie, come and take us home.

"Sam?" Travis squeezed my arm.

I looked at him, then looked away again so I didn't fall apart, and in that single second, in that swinging glance, without me ever having to say a word, he understood what had happened. He let go of my arm and buried his fingers in his hair.

He shook his head and said, "I'm sorry. I'm so sorry," even though none of it had anything to do with him.

I stared into the sun until my tears burned dry.

"It's okay," I said. "I'm fine. I'm getting used to it."

I wanted to change the subject. I wanted to slide off this rock and slink away. I wanted Travis to stop rubbing the heels of his hands into his eyes and apologizing. I wanted him to smile instead. He was cute when he smiled.

"Maybe you should have brought me two cobblers," I said.

Travis stared at me. He shook his head and said, "You don't have to do that."

"Do what?" I frowned.

"Pretend it's not important."

I shrugged. Pretending was easier.

Travis sighed and stared out across the water again. After a few seconds, he said, "I bet you didn't know I had a sister."

"You do?" I was embarrassed for not knowing this. Terrebonne's population was 916, on a good day, and even though I only lived here a couple weeks a year, between Franny and Deputy Santos I heard enough about everybody else's business that I should have known Travis had a sister.

He cleared his throat. "I *did*." He reached for his Marlboros but didn't pull out a cigarette. It seemed enough for him to just hold the pack. "She died a long time ago."

I leaned into Travis's shoulder to feel his warmth and the pressure of him there, to feel him push back. "How?"

"Car accident." He pinched the skin on his wrist. "They said she died instantly, that she didn't feel any pain. But I think they just said that so I'd stop crying."

"How old were you?" I was whispering now, unable to force the words louder.

"Seven," he said. "She had just turned nine. It was her birthday, and they were coming home from her party."

There was a stone in my throat making it hard to swallow, a fist in my chest making it painful to breathe.

Travis went on, "Dad was driving. Mom and I, we were supposed to be in the car too, but I woke up with a bad fever that morning so she stayed home with me. Some asshole crossed the center line. Pushed them straight into a tree."

"Oh my God." My words barely a whisper.

The river flowed into our silence, rushing and tumbling without end.

"It never really goes away, you know," Travis said, reaching over and pressing one finger to the base of my throat near my collarbones. "That sharp ache you feel right here. You get used to it, but it's always there."

"Like a bee sting that won't quit," I whispered.

He nodded and lifted his hand, but I could still feel the pressure of his finger, the heat burning there at the surface. I gulped air and swallowed and tried to think of something, anything else, but I kept seeing her. Mom, lying on her back on the blue-and-yellow quilt, eyes open, staring up at the stars. Fireworks boomed overhead, and she was staring and staring, but not seeing. And her skin was so gray. So completely and finally gray. Wiped of color, of life, of love. And then Ollie, kneeling beside her, grabbing her arm and shaking hard, saying, "Mom? Mom? Mom, wake up," over and over. I had pushed her back, screaming at her, "Don't touch her! Don't touch her!" because, even though I didn't believe in that kind of thing, somewhere before I'd heard it was bad luck to touch the dead.

"We were right there," I said. "Ollie and me. Sitting right there with her and we never knew anything was wrong until it was too late. Maybe it was because the fireworks were so loud or because there were so many people screaming. We were all screaming. The stars were so big. The night was on fire. It was all so beautiful. Until."

I squeezed my eyes shut, shook my head, opened them again, but the terrible images remained.

"I pushed Ollie away from her." My voice wavered. "I shoved her like Mom was contagious or something. I just kept thinking that if Ollie touched her, she'd die, too."

I didn't realize I'd been crying until Travis brushed his fingers over my cheek. I pulled away from him and wiped my own tears.

Laughing a little and squinting at the churning white water, I said, "It was her one chance to say good-bye, her last chance to say 'I love you,' and whatever else needed saying, and I couldn't even let her have that much."

"Sam . . ."

"The paramedics came and some old woman named Marge drove us to the hospital and we called Mom's best friend, Heather, and then Bear and Grandma and Grandpa, and then we waited in the chapel with a social worker who had hot pink fingernails and kept popping her gum and looked way too young to be there. When I asked when we could go see our mom, she kept saying, 'In a little while, honey-cakes. In a little while.' And then Heather was there, crying and shuffling us out of the hospital and back home where she told us to go to bed, that Bear would be there when we woke up and everything would be fine." I shrugged and tossed a mangled piece of moss into the water. "Bear was there in the morning. So were Grandma and Grandpa. But nothing was fine. Nothing has been fine since."

Travis didn't say anything for a few seconds, then, quietly, "Did you get to see her again? Did you have another chance to say good-bye?"

I shook my head. "Grandma said it was a bad idea."

"What about at the funeral?"

"Closed coffin. Anyone could have been in that thing. Or no one."

He rocked back a little, his shoulder sliding against mine. He said, "I didn't get to say good-bye either."

Neither of us said anything for a few seconds, then Travis's voice shifted to something dark and secret. He said, "You have to promise you won't say anything because it's not technically legal . . ."

I nodded and he continued, his voice still hushed, almost a whisper, "Mom and Dad buried her out in the woods behind our house one night while I was sleeping."

I shivered even though we were sitting in the sun.

He said, "The next morning when they told me, I got upset about not being there and they told me it was better this way, that it wasn't the kind of thing a kid my age needed to see. I used to go out there a lot when I was younger and sit under the dogwood tree they planted, but then I started thinking about how she was just right there, rotting beneath me, nothing between us but a few feet of dirt." He shivered a little too. "I haven't gone to see her for years. Because she's not there, anyway, right? Not the part of her that matters."

I turned my head and for the first time saw how close we were, our faces nearly touching. He smelled like the river, like water rushing and snow melting and sun and green algae and beneath that, other things, too. The hint of wildflowers and honey and stretched-out days. He smelled like summer.

He reached his hand to my face, cupped my chin. I kept my eyes wide open. There were flecks of storm-cloud gray in his. I thought he might kiss me and I thought about pulling away, asking him if he was sure this is what he wanted, if he was doing this because he liked me or because he felt sorry for me, but I didn't. I stayed quiet and let him draw me closer. His breath was warm and fast. His cheeks flushed apple red with life.

A branch cracked somewhere in the woods behind us, and we jumped apart before our lips had a chance to brush together. Travis dropped his hand and turned away from me. Whatever thin thread had been drawing us closer snapped, and then it was just me again, unmoored and drifting. And Travis, standing up now, hopping off the rock into the sand, increasing the distance. My chances for a first kiss, ruined, but maybe it was better this way, less complicated.

Another branch cracked, and I turned to look. Bear stepped out of the trees onto the path. He walked slowly toward us. I climbed off the rock, gathered my shoes under my arm, and went to meet him.

"Where's your sister?" His eyes scanned the riverbank.

"At camp. She didn't want to come." I stared at his brown suit jacket and trousers, his white-collared shirt all buttoned and tucked in, his navy-blue-and-gold tie, his shiny brown shoes. His hair was slicked back, his beard combed, his face washed. "Where have you been?"

Bear jerked his head at Travis, who had come up behind me. "What's he doing here?"

"Franny told me you had an interview at the mill?"

"She shouldn't have." Bear clawed at his tie, loosening it, pulling it off. Like a snake shedding his skin. "I don't like you leaving your sister alone like this."

"She's fine. She's in the teepee reading." I grabbed the tie from him.

It was one I remembered from before when he had a real job and lived in a real house and kept his hair cut short. I ran my thumb over gold dots that were actually crested gold lions, running in a diagonal pattern across the dark blue background.

"How did it go?" I asked.

He took the tie back and stuffed it into his pants pocket. "I'm going to need you to start taking on more responsibility for your sister, okay? Especially when I'm not here."

"I told you, she's fine. If she needed something, she would have come and got me, or screamed or something. We're not that far away. I would have heard her."

"She's just a kid, Sam."

"She's ten."

"Your mom would want you to look out for her."

I glared at him. The words I wanted to say—*How the hell do you know what Mom would want?*—stuck in my throat. I shoved my feet into my shoes and, without bothering to tie the laces, started walking back to the meadow.

Travis followed me.

Bear called after us, but by then we were too far down the path to hear what he said.

Travis nudged my elbow. "Hey, I'm sorry if I got you in trouble."

"You didn't."

"You going to be okay out here?" he asked.

"Why wouldn't I be?" I slapped at a leaf dangling above the path.

"Well." He cleared his throat. "Because of Bear and everything."

"What are you talking about?"

"Are you sure he's safe?"

I walked a little slower. "What do you mean? Of course he's safe." But my mind kept slipping back to the night he left me and Ollie alone, to the scratches on his cheek and the key I'd found. I asked, "Why would you think that he isn't?"

"Since that woman turned up dead, people have been talking," Travis said. "They've been saying Bear might have had something to do with it."

"What people?"

Travis shrugged. "I don't know. Just people in town and stuff."

"And you believe them?"

He hesitated, and when he finally spoke, his voice was soft, the way it can get when someone's about to deliver bad news. "He's always been a little . . . eccentric. He's out here by himself all the time. He doesn't really get along with anyone in town. People think he might be dangerous."

I tore a leaf from a bush crowding the path, crushed it in my fist, and then dropped it. "That's the dumbest thing I've ever heard."

"Is it?" Travis grabbed my hand.

I shook him off and walked faster. "People should mind their own damn business."

"They're worried, that's all. About their families and kids," Travis said, catching up to me, keeping pace. "And they're worried about you, too. You and your sister, living out here with him, not knowing what he's capable of."

"Well, they're wasting their energy. Bear isn't dangerous. He wouldn't hurt a fly." But even as I said the words, I was starting to doubt them.

We had reached the edge of the meadow. Travis grabbed my arm and pulled me to a stop just inside the tree line. He said, "Just be careful. That's all I'm saying."

He looked genuinely concerned, and I didn't know what else to say, except, "We'll be fine."

I don't think he was convinced, but he let go of my arm and didn't say anything else about it.

Ollie was outside again, sitting with her book in the shade. When Travis and I emerged from the trees, she dropped the book on the ground, jumped to her feet, and ran over to us. She planted herself directly in front of Travis and extended a closed fist, fingers facing up. Her lips were turning white they were pressed so tight together, and the expression on her face was much too serious for any kid, though I'd seen it on Ollie more than once this summer.

"What is it?" I asked her.

She didn't even look at me as she uncurled her fingers and opened her hand. Resting flat in her palm was a lighter. In the sunlight, it glinted gold.

I looked at it, then looked at Travis. "Isn't that yours?"

"No." He shook his head and dropped his gaze. "No, I don't think so."
Ollie pushed the lighter closer.

"It looks like yours," I said, and then, remembering earlier how
he'd taken a cigarette from the pack but hadn't smoked it, "Check
your pockets."

He patted his pockets and, finding nothing, leaned in for a better
look. He rubbed his hand back and forth across his neck, and then
finally said, "You know what? Yeah. I think that is mine."

He plucked it from Ollie's palm and turned it over a couple of
times, then slipped it into his pocket.

"Thanks," he said, and then to me, "I better go."

I nodded, then put my arm around Ollie's shoulders and pulled
her close to me. "Thanks for the cobbler and everything."

He smiled, but it was a weak, halfhearted attempt, making him
look sad and hollowed out. He seemed about to say something else,
something important, but Bear emerged from the trees right then and
whatever Travis might have been thinking about saying he kept to
himself.

Shoulders hunched and hands plunged deep into his pockets,
Travis crossed the meadow alone. He reached the path that led to the
road, and I stood waiting for him to turn around and wave, but he
kept walking with his head down. A few minutes later, his dirt bike
started up and shrieked away.

That night, Bear fried up fresh trout for us over an open flame. The
meat was pink and tender and seasoned with pepper and a spoonful
of honey. I think it was his way of saying sorry, of trying to make up
for leaving us alone all day. Ollie grubbed down her piece of fish like
she hadn't eaten in days. I picked at mine, taking smaller and smaller
bites until finally I just stopped eating altogether.

Bear nodded at my plate. "Not hungry?" His lips were covered in
grease and shining in the firelight.

I shrugged and poked at my uneaten fish.

Bear stared at me across the flickering coals and then said, "I stopped by the house this afternoon."

I couldn't look at him.

"Franny was pretty upset. She said you were, too." He waited for me to say something. When I didn't, he continued, "We're going over there first thing tomorrow morning to set things straight, okay? We're going to call Detective Talbert and get everything out in the open the way we should have from the beginning."

I set my plate on the ground.

"You'll feel better after it's done," he said, leaning forward to scrape his sucked-clean fish bones into the fire. "I promise."

He was wrong, but there was nothing I could say to change his mind. I got up from my chair and started walking toward the teepee.

Bear called after me, "And stay away from that boy, Sam. He's no good."

ollie

The moon leans into our teepee. Tonight, she is half full and bright enough for me to see the shape of my hand in the dark.

Bear sleeps. His body, curled tight under blankets. His snore, a low growl.

My sister is awake. She's turning and tossing, her sighs uneven and loud. She throws her hands above her head and brings them down again, and her sleeping bag swishes.

She doesn't want to tell. Like me, she's afraid that they will see only what they want to see, not what is actually there. They will stop looking for the truth.

Bear thinks everything will be just fine.

I stare across the teepee through the gray night and Shimmering at the man who makes tomatoes grow and bees hum, who calls the stars by name and tells time using sun and shadow, who once gave me a thunderstone for Christmas and told me how even though the black and gray rock outside was strong, the sparkly purple crystals inside were fragile and that's what made it so special.

His breath is even and deep. He does not stir beneath his blankets. A guilty man would not sleep so peacefully.

I pull my book from under the pillow and turn to a page near the middle, to a sentence I've already underlined.

The one from the river crouches near the door and stares through the flap to the world outside. She is listening to the bees, tucked into their hives for the night, murmuring secrets to one another. A breeze lifts a corner of the flap, bringing in scents of ripe blackberries and warm honey. She turns her head, nods at my book, and then returns her attention to the night meadow.

I sit all the way up and push the sleeping bag off my legs.

"You okay?" my sister whispers.

I reach for my flashlight.

The one who follows me rains silver diamonds from the hole in the ceiling, and the falling, falling reminds me of a snow globe, shaken and set right again. She is a fountain, a spray, a rush of invisible moon-flakes, uneasy because of what might happen tomorrow. She wants to slip into our dreams and show us the truth, what will happen if the wrong man is accused. But this is impossible because for my sister, my father, even me, dreams are where we go to be alone.

sam

The numbers on Deputy Santos's business card blurred, then separated, then ran together again. I smoothed my thumb over the slightly raised surface and wondered what it would be like to be blind. When I closed my eyes, the numbers were still there, white against black. When I opened my eyes, black against white. I turned the card over, but the back was blank. I flipped it to the front again and read the phone number backward, wondering who might answer if I called that number instead.

Bear pushed the cordless phone across Franny's kitchen table. "Call."

He was making me do it because I'd lied to him about taking the jacket to Deputy Santos and hadn't told him about the key. He'd confiscated both items last night and put them in one of the filing cabinet drawers for safekeeping. I was supposed to tell Deputy Santos everything I should have told her in the first place, and then Bear would tell his part and then she would come out here and we'd give her the jacket and the key, and everything would be fine. That's what

Bear kept telling me anyway. I held the phone in one hand, the business card in the other. My thumb moved over the buttons, but I didn't press down.

Last night, Ollie had sat up in her sleeping bag, turned the flashlight on, and passed me her *Alice* book. It was open to the page she wanted me to read and she shined the light straight on it so I could see. She'd underlined a single sentence: *"It is wrong from beginning to end," said the Caterpillar.*

I closed the book and gave it back to her. "I'm sleeping."

She turned to another page and pushed the book into my face again. This time the passage was: *Alice sighed wearily. "I think you might do something better with the time," she said, "than wasting it in asking riddles that have no answers."*

I rolled over so my back was to her. She clambered over the top of me and stretched out so we were lying parallel on the floor, our noses almost touching. She was frowning and had the book clasped to her chest. I rolled onto my back and faced the moon. Ollie sat up, cross-legged. She rustled through more pages, then held the book out to me a third time.

"Go away," I whispered.

She snorted air through her nose like a goat.

I propped myself up on my elbows. "Fine. Give me some light."

The final underlined passage she wanted to show me was this: *"If everybody minded their own business," the Duchess said, in a hoarse growl, "the world would go round a deal faster than it does."*

I flopped onto my back again and closed my eyes. Ollie didn't move. She was waiting for me to finish the game; she would wait there all night if she had to.

I sighed and said, "I get it. You don't want us to call the police tomorrow. Now, please go to sleep."

She climbed back into her own sleeping bag and turned off the flashlight. I'd gotten it right, though it didn't change anything.

In the morning, Bear nudged us both awake and told us to get dressed because we were going to Franny's. Ollie and I dragged our feet and complained about being hungry, but Bear hurried us toward the house, saying we could have breakfast after this whole thing was over and done. Franny was waiting for us in the kitchen with the phone. She took Ollie into the living room and left me alone with Bear. I'd been staring at the phone for the past ten minutes, hoping something would happen—a fire, an explosion, the end of the whole world—so I wouldn't have to make this call. We'd lost Bear once before and, even though he kept telling me we were doing the right thing and everything would work itself out, I didn't believe it and I was terrified if we lost him again, we'd never, ever get him back.

"Give it to me," Bear said, reaching for the phone.

I pulled it away from him. "I'll do it. Just give me a minute."

He sat back in his chair and crossed his arms over his chest.

Today's newspaper was lying on the table between us, folded so her photograph was facing up. Facing us. She must have been looking straight into the camera when the picture was taken because her dark eyes followed me, no matter how far I shifted to either side. Even though the photo was grainy and a little blurred, I could tell she'd been beautiful once and that when she was alive her eyes were the kind that sparkled. So different from the day I grabbed her shoulder and rolled her onto her back, then let her slip from my grasp. She wore a necklace, some kind of pendant attached to a simple chain. Her hair was short in this photo, cut close to her scalp like a boy's, and she was younger, too. Or maybe it was just that her skin was intact and there were no bruises, and she was smiling back at the world—so full of promise still, so full of hope.

Bear was staring at the picture now, too, frowning and rubbing his beard. Without looking away from her, he said, "Ten more seconds, Sam."

"And then what?" I sat up taller in my chair. "What will you do if I don't call? Ground me? Send me to my room?"

He pinched his lips together and laid his hands flat against the table. There was nothing he could do to me, and he knew it. Short of sending us to live with Grandma and Grandpa, which he didn't want either, there was nothing he could say and no threat bad enough to make me dial Deputy Santos's phone number.

"I thought we raised you better than this," he said, lifting halfway off his chair, reaching again for the phone.

Again, I pulled it away from him, this time hiding it behind my back.

"Give me the phone," he said.

"No."

He stood all the way to his feet, bent with his hands pressed flat against the table. Color rose high in his cheeks. For the first time in years, he shouted at me. "I said give me the phone!"

I shrank lower in my chair.

He held out one hand, fingers stretched long, demanding, "Now, goddamn it!"

I shouted back at him, "This is stupid! It's going to ruin everything! *You're* going to ruin everything!"

He rose to his full height. His nostrils flared, his eyes sparked. I glared at him, not backing down.

Franny appeared in the doorway between the living room and kitchen. She leaned against the frame like she needed the extra help and said only one word, "Frank."

It was his real name, a name I hadn't heard since I was a little girl and one that had never quite fit him anyway. He flinched hearing it and folded in on himself, dropping his head, sagging his shoulders, curling his hands close to his body. He backed away from the table and, without looking at me or Franny, walked out of the kitchen, through the living room, and out the front door. A few seconds later, the front porch swing began to squeak a slow rhythm.

Franny sighed and sat down in the chair Bear had left empty. She picked up the newspaper and unfolded it, shaking out the wrinkles and clearing her throat.

"Taylor Bellweather." She read from the front page. "Age twenty-five. Recently graduated from the University of Oregon with a degree in journalism. Valedictorian. President of her senior class. Just started working as a reporter for the *Register-Guard*."

I brought the phone around in front of me again, but I still couldn't get my fingers to push the numbers. A loud rustling in the living room made me flinch, even though I knew it was just Ollie scribbling nonsense, wadding up sheets of paper and throwing them away—telling me without having to actually talk that she wasn't happy about any of this.

"Taylor Bellweather," Franny said the name again, louder, and this time when she said it she looked at me. The wrinkles in her forehead and around her mouth and nose looked deeper than I had ever seen them.

I looked down at my thumbs suspended over the keypad, suspended but not pressing down.

Franny snapped the newspaper once and continued, her voice stumbling a little over the words. "Only daughter of Mitch and Teresa Bellweather. Cause of death. Blunt force trauma to the head. Deschutes County Sheriff's Department is investigating this as a homicide and asking people to call with any information pertaining to the case. Says here that they're trying to establish her whereabouts and activity on the night she died."

From the living room, more crumpling and the sound of paper tearing. The porch swing continued squeaking back and forth.

Franny folded the newspaper and slid it over to me. She tapped her finger on the edge of the dead woman's photograph. Taylor Bellweather. She had a name, a birthday, a history, a family. She was a person now, as real as me and Ollie. As real as anyone. But I still couldn't push the buttons down. Even with her staring at me and Franny waiting and Bear telling me everything would be okay, even then, I couldn't do it.

I turned the newspaper over and shoved it away. Franny reached and squeezed my hand. Her skin was like tissue paper, chalky and thin. "You can do this, Sam."

I stared at the phone, my eyes blurring with tears. I wiped them quickly with the back of my hand.

Franny said, "I'm right here with you," and I punched in the first number, then the second and third, my fingers shaking so badly I almost messed up, but then it was ringing. Twice, three times, four.

"She's not answering," I said.

"Leave a message."

I counted ten rings before the answering machine picked up, but before I had a chance to say anything, we heard cars coming up the driveway, tires crunching the gravel, engines muttering.

Franny eased up from the table and shuffled toward the living room window. "Now, who could that be?"

I disconnected the call without leaving a message. There was just too much I needed to say to fit into such a short amount of time. I left the phone on the table with the newspaper and went into the living room.

Franny and Ollie were standing at the picture window, both of them staring out across the front yard. I went and stood next to them, watched as one patrol car, then two more—all with lights flashing, but sirens off—drove past the house toward the dirt road behind the barn.

The front porch swing was empty, still rocking back and forth, as if Bear had only just left. I looked, but didn't see him anywhere. Not at first. Large hedges grew against a split-rail fence running alongside the driveway, casting shadows deep enough to hide in. It was only when the hedgerow ended and Bear stepped out into the sun that I saw him: walking slowly away from the house, away from us, following the patrol cars back to the meadow.

Franny pressed her hand to her mouth, then turned away from the window and hurried back into the kitchen, saying something about Zeb never being around when she needed him most, and why'd he have to choose today of all days to disappear into his damn fields. It was the first time I'd ever heard Franny cuss.

I watched the cars until they disappeared around a bend and the dust they'd kicked up had settled again, until Bear, too, had vanished, then finally I turned and looked at Ollie. Her jaw was tense, her eyes wide and storming, staring hard at me, her arms folded across her chest.

I shook my head. "I didn't call, Ollie."

Her nostrils flared.

"No one called." I reached for her, but she spun away and stomped to the coffee table where she'd been drawing or writing or coloring or something before the patrol cars arrived. She grabbed a pencil and pressed it to a fresh sheet of paper. Her hand jerked sharply to one side, streaking dark lead across the top of Franny's white oak.

"Be careful!" I said.

She gritted her teeth and returned the pencil to the top of the paper, and again her hand jerked. This time downward, tearing jagged through the middle.

"Ollie! Stop it!"

She threw the pencil across the room, then crumpled up the notebook paper and threw that, too. The paper ball landed near the front door and rolled up against a coatrack, heavy with so many sweaters and hats and jackets. I wasn't sure if her aim was intentional, if she meant for me to see the jackets and make the connection—how much worse this was going to be for Bear if they found Taylor Bellweather's jacket stuffed in his satchel inside his filing cabinet, how much worse it was going to be for all of us—I didn't know if that's what she meant to do, but that was what happened.

I turned and bolted out the front door. The screen slammed shut behind me.

"Sam!" My name like a gunshot.

I tripped on the bottom porch step and fell forward, skidding my palms and knees across packed gravel. The tiny cuts burned and started to bleed, but I was able to stand and put weight on both legs and move both wrists full circle. Nothing broken. Nothing to cry about. I brushed my hands down the front of my shirt, streaking dark red across white cotton.

The screen door creaked open behind me.

"Sam?" Franny called out to me again, but I didn't turn around.

And I didn't wait to hear what else she was going to say.

I took off running. My lungs felt stretched thin. The cuts on my knees, like they were ripping wider with each step. But still I ran. Around the barn to the dirt road, between the fields, following the fresh-pressed tire tracks and my father's barely visible footprints to the hemlock stump. I was still over fifty yards from breaking through the trees and reaching the teepee when I heard Bear shouting.

"You're trespassing! Get the hell away from there!"

I'd never heard him sound so panicked before, so frantic.

"Mr. McAlister, please, stand back. Let us do our job," and I recognized Deputy Santos's voice, trying to calm him, talk him through the process. "We're just going to have a look around—"

"I know what you're doing," Bear interrupted. "I know why you're here. Don't touch that! I haven't given you permission. You can't go in there!"

Tree branches slapped my face. I held up my arms, pushing aside brambles and leaves, and then the path opened and I broke into the sun.

I stopped short at the edge of the grass. The tent flap had been pulled back and secured with a small piece of rope, and I saw flashes of movement inside, brown uniforms crossing back and forth in front of the opening. Bear stood a few steps away from the teepee beside Deputy Santos. I was too late. We both were.

"We have a search warrant, Mr. McAlister." Deputy Santos shoved a stack of papers into his face. "Signed by the judge last night. Read it if you don't believe me."

Bear scowled at her but didn't take the papers.

She folded the bundle into thirds and stuffed it into her back pocket. She said, "If there's anything you think we should know, Mr. McAlister, now would be a good time to tell me."

He folded his arms over his chest and turned his head away from her, turned and watched the men inside the teepee.

Deputy Santos sighed and pushed her hand under her hat, wiping sweat from her brow. Then she, too, folded her arms across her chest. She said, "Fine. We can wait."

Inside the teepee, they were moving furniture, lifting blankets, opening drawers. Something fell, shattering, and Bear's jaw tightened.

"You might have a search warrant," he said. "But you sure as hell don't have permission to break my things."

Deputy Santos grimaced. "Why don't we sit down?" She gestured to the picnic table behind them. "This could take a while."

Bear shook his head. "I'm fine standing."

"Whatever you want," Deputy Santos said.

They stood silently together, watching the deputies inside the teepee, and there was a moment when I really believed that they wouldn't find it. I really believed we would be okay.

I took a couple steps farther into the meadow, and a small branch cracked underfoot.

Deputy Santos turned her head, said something under her breath I couldn't hear, then turned to Bear and said, "Stay put. Don't interfere." She left him and came toward me.

Bear saw me, too, but he didn't say anything or make any gestures or beckon me closer. He glanced at me, then looked away, returning his whole attention to the deputies who were tearing apart our lives. I wondered why he was just standing there doing nothing, why he didn't tell them about the jacket and the key, all the things he'd been planning on telling them barely fifteen minutes ago. His silence twisted a knot in my stomach, and I couldn't stop myself from thinking that he hadn't told me everything, that maybe he really did have something to hide.

Deputy Santos stopped in front of me, partially blocking my view of Bear. "You're bleeding," she said.

I looked down at my knees. Blood trickled thin and red from a deep gouge just below my right kneecap. The other knee was scraped up pretty bad, too, dark with gravel and dirt, more rash than cut. And there was blood on my shirt from where I'd wiped off my hands, and fresh blood still seeping from cuts in my palms and blood between my fingers that was starting to dry.

"I fell," I said.

"What are you doing here?"

I looked over her shoulder. Bear hadn't left his spot next to the teepee, but he was tugging on his beard now and scratching hard at his scalp.

"I live here."

"Where's your sister?"

"With Franny."

"Why don't you head on back to the house? Stay put until I come get you."

"What about our stuff?"

Deputy Santos let out a long, slow breath. She glanced over her shoulder. "I'll bring it by later."

"Are you going to arrest Bear?"

Deputy Santos rubbed her eyes. "I don't know, Sam," she said, and it sounded like she hadn't slept in a few days. "But if we do, I don't want you to be here. I don't want you to have that memory. Please. Just go on back to Zeb and Franny's now. I'll come over as soon as I can and try to answer all your questions."

Now that I was standing still and I'd caught my breath and my heart wasn't pounding so hard and there wasn't so much adrenaline rushing through me, I felt my knees hurting. Like someone was striking my bones with a hammer over and over. I bent and picked a piece of gravel from the deepest cut and tried to brush the dirt off, but that only made it hurt more. I left it alone and straightened up again.

"I want to stay," I said.

"No." Deputy Santos shook her head. "Absolutely not."

"I'm not a baby. I can handle it."

She rubbed her bottom lip, like she was thinking about letting me stay, but before she could answer, someone in the teepee shouted, "Found something!"

Deputy Santos jerked her head around and then took a step back toward Bear.

I grabbed her arm. "Wait."

"Go back to Franny's. Now." She shook me off and left me standing there alone.

Bear didn't look at Deputy Santos when she came up beside him. She touched his shoulder, and he flinched. She took her hand away again, moving it instead to her holster. She stuck close to his side, her stance strong and ready, but for what I had no idea.

Three men came single file out of the teepee. First was Detective Talbert. The other two after him were deputies I didn't recognize. They went straight to Bear and stood in a disorderly line, the detective slightly ahead of the others, facing Bear directly.

He held out a large plastic bag with the satchel sealed inside. "Does this belong to you, Mr. McAlister?"

Bear nodded.

I shifted on the balls of my feet.

Detective Talbert licked his lips. He moved slow, like there was all the time in the world. He handed the satchel to one of the deputies and held up a second plastic bag.

"We found this jacket inside that shoulder bag, Mr. McAlister."

The blue cloth seemed oversaturated in the sunlight. Too dark, too midnight sky.

"Does this belong to you too?"

Bear squinted at the jacket but didn't give them an answer.

The detective held out a third, smaller bag. "And this key?" He gave an exaggerated gesture of looking around the meadow. "Where do you park your cars, Mr. McAlister?"

One of the deputies snickered.

Bear glanced over his shoulder, and our eyes met.

"I'm sorry," I whispered, but not quietly enough. Everyone, now, turned and looked at me.

Detective Talbert frowned. "What the hell is she doing here?"

Deputy Santos came toward me again, her expression one of shock. "You knew about this?"

"We were going to tell you."

Her eyebrows shot up.

I looked down at my feet. "I called a few minutes ago."

She sighed and spoke over her shoulder: "I'll handle this."

"God Almighty," Detective Talbert swore under his breath, sweeping his hand over his scalp.

Deputy Santos put one hand on my arm and started to turn me away. "We're going to have to take him down to the station to ask him some questions."

"No, don't." I shrugged her off.

"We have to, Sam." She reached for me again, but I sidestepped away.

"Please, don't take him. Can't you just ask your questions here? He didn't do anything wrong. I can . . . we can explain. Just . . . it's not what it looks like. It's not what you think."

Detective Talbert had been watching us silently. Now he sighed and said, "This is ridiculous. Wentworth, get her out of here."

One of the deputies broke from the line and came toward me.

Deputy Santos waved her hand at him, saying, "I got this. I can handle it."

"Don't touch her," Bear said.

They were the first words he'd spoken since the men had come out of the teepee. No one moved. No one spoke. We all watched him, waiting.

"Don't you dare lay a hand on her." He made as if to come toward us, as if he was going to fight all of them if that's what it took.

"Enough," Detective Talbert said, his voice echoing into the trees.

Bear rolled his head, but he didn't come any closer. He cracked his knuckles but didn't start swinging. When he spoke, his voice was almost too quiet for me to hear: "I'll come with you, but leave my daughter alone."

Detective Talbert reached for his handcuffs.

Bear took a step back.

"Precautionary," the detective said.

"I'm coming of my own free will," Bear argued. "You don't need those."

Detective Talbert leaned closer to Bear. The handcuffs rattled.

"Where'd you get those scratches, Mr. McAlister?"

He reached to try and brush his fingers across the two scratches on Bear's cheek. Even after four days they were still visible, though they were scabs now, more than anything.

Bear flinched away from him. "Don't touch me."

Detective Talbert scowled and pulled back his hand, then nodded at the remaining deputy standing beside him. "Get him loaded up in the car nice and easy now. I'll radio in and let them know you're coming."

The deputy stepped forward, his hand reaching, moving to grab Bear's arm.

Bear jerked away and started to walk on his own in the direction of the patrol cars. "I said, don't touch me."

When he passed and then disappeared into the trees, I tried to go after him, but Deputy Santos stopped me. She gathered me close against her side and put her arm around my shoulders. "Come on," she said. "I'll drive you to the house so we can get you cleaned up."

ollie

The car taking my father away passes first. No lights. No rush. A steady pace, tires rolling over dirt and hard-packed gravel, not slowing, not stopping here. The driver stares straight ahead. In the backseat surrounded by thick bars and wire mesh, the man who is Bear who is innocent lifts his head and looks at me through the tinted glass. His eyes are hollow and dark. His mouth is partly open. He looks so very sad.

Nana Fran lays her hand on my shoulder and says, "Come inside."

I shrug her away and take one, two, three steps down, off the porch and onto the stone-lined path.

"Olivia."

My name, a warning, and yet not enough to pull me back.

A second car comes around the bend, passes the barn, slows and stops in front of me. The driver's door pops open and Deputy Santos unfolds, stretches, puts her hat on her head, and nods at me and Nana Fran.

"What is it?" Nana Fran says from the porch, her voice hurrying where she cannot, carrying her down the steps to my side. "What's happened? Is it about that woman? Oh, sweet Jesus, I need to sit down."

A shuffle, a creak of old bones and wicker patio furniture. I do not turn around. I do not go to help her. I stare through the windshield at my sister who stares after our father. The other car, barely visible in the dust, turns onto Lambert Road and vanishes over the hill.

Deputy Santos bends over the open car door and speaks into the cab. "Come on, Sam. This is as far as I'll take you."

"I want to go with him. He needs me."

"What about Ollie?" Deputy Santos asks. "She needs you, too."

This is true. But not in the usual way. I need her to believe. I need her to see. I need her to say the things I can't.

The shadows inside the car are thick enough for me to see the one from the river, sitting in the backseat directly behind my sister. Her hair is snakes. Her teeth are fangs. Her eyes, cold, black stones that she turns on me. She sways and hisses. She wants to borrow my voice. She wants me to say, *This isn't right. It wasn't him*. But I can't.

I won't.

If I do this for her, then I have to do this for all of them; and if I do this for all of them, my words—my own, the ones that belong to me and no one else, the ones that are only mine—will no longer matter. They will be pushed aside and shoved down deep and trampled over by all these others.

So I am silent.

The one who follows me can't sit still. She is all explosion and light, here and then over there, burning scared. I am scared, too.

Deputy Santos says, "There's nothing you can do for him right now."

Nana Fran says, "Come inside, all of you. I'll make us some chamomile tea."

My sister says, "He didn't do it. He didn't hurt that woman."

The one from the river strikes at the window and the thick bars dividing the backseat of the patrol car from the front.

"Sam." Deputy Santos rubs the back of her neck. "Sam, get out of the car. Now. I won't ask you again."

I move closer to the hood. My sister sees me through the windshield. Her face is red like she's been crying, and I wish I could tell her none of this is her fault and we will find a way to fix it.

My sister sighs and gets out of the car. The one from the river follows. Together they walk past me into the house. The one who follows me drops like a falling star, lands in the dirt at my feet. I step over her and follow my sister inside.

sam

.

Later that evening, Franny came into the guest room at the top of the stairs. She sat on the edge of one of the beds and said, "Deputy Santos and I talked with the social worker. They're going to let you girls stay with us until we can get in touch with your grandparents."

Ollie and I were on the bed opposite her, sitting apart from each other. I was at the foot, nearly spilling onto the floor. Ollie was up near the pillows, pressed close to the wall. She was wearing one of Franny's old T-shirts and had her legs curled up inside it, her chin resting on her knees, making herself as small as possible.

Before Mom died, Grandpa and Grandma had booked a two-week cruise across the Atlantic from Fort Lauderdale to Lisbon for their fortieth wedding anniversary. A week before their departure date, they were all set to call their travel agent and cancel, but their tickets were nonrefundable and so I told them to go. Bear could take care of us just fine, they didn't have to worry. According to the itinerary they left with me, their boat was floating somewhere now in the mid-Atlantic. Deputy Santos might be able to reach them, but they wouldn't be able to do anything except worry about us until Thursday when they were expected to reach port in Lisbon.

So much could happen in those five days. So much could change.

I picked at the sleeves of the old flannel shirt Franny had given me to wear when she'd thrown my blood-streaked clothes in the wash. I could hear the machine somewhere below us, chugging and thumping.

"Our paperwork's not up-to-date," she continued. "But given the circumstances and the good word Deputy Santos put in for us, Child Services is willing to make a temporary exception."

"What about our things?" I asked.

"From the teepee?"

I nodded.

Franny said, "Maribel said she'd bring everything over as soon as they finished processing the scene."

The scene. Bear's meadow. *Our* meadow. Our home.

I rubbed my eyes. Ollie clutched her knees even tighter to her chest.

"There are those boxes in the barn, too," Franny said. "We can open those up tomorrow, see if we can't find you both some clothes that fit a little better."

After Mom's funeral, we'd gone through the house in Eugene, deciding what to keep and what to give away or take to the dump. The things we kept, we packed in boxes and brought with us to Zeb and Franny's. Storing everything in the barn was supposed to be a temporary arrangement. We were supposed to be moving into a bigger place, an apartment or a house, with rooms and closets and plenty of space to stretch out. We were supposed to be figuring out how to be a family again, not worrying about a dead woman and how long my father might be in jail.

"I know it's not what you're used to." Franny smoothed her hand across the pink-and-yellow quilt. "But the sheets are clean. And the fridge is full. And here, at least, you'll be safe. That's the important thing."

Ollie sighed.

"How about we go to the store tomorrow after church?" Franny said. "Stock up on a few things. Toothbrushes, underwear, socks. Mint chocolate chip ice cream." She smiled, but it didn't stick. She leaned forward and the bed creaked. She grabbed our hands and squeezed. "We want you girls to be comfortable here. Our home is your home. Whatever you need, just ask."

In the hallway, floorboards groaned, and Zeb cleared his throat.

"Mother," he said. "Time to let these girls alone. Let them have their rest."

Franny rose to her feet, rubbing her back. She shuffled to the door and stood there a moment longer, leaning in the frame, watching me and Ollie. Then she said, "We're right down the hall if you need anything. Anything at all."

She left the room—Ollie's and my room now—and closed the door behind her.

I woke tangled in sheets.

I woke suffocating, choking on a panicked, half-formed nightmare in which I was being buried alive inside a grave with Taylor Bellweather, who was also somehow my mother. Bear held the shovel. Every time I opened my mouth to scream, I swallowed more dirt. More and more until I couldn't breathe and that's what woke me—this feeling of drowning.

Kicking off the covers, I sat up and stared straight ahead into a dark too thick to be night. No crickets, no frogs, no wind. No scent of morning dew and damp pine needles. I wasn't used to sleeping indoors in August, stifling between four walls and a shingled roof. I needed air. I needed to see the stars.

I turned my head toward the room's only window. The curtains were partway open, letting in a thin slit of silver moonlight. I wasn't the only one having trouble sleeping. Ollie stood with one hand pressed to the glass, staring out into the yard. Her unbraided hair fell loose around her shoulders. The hem of her nightshirt, like an old-fashioned gown, brushed against the floor. She was still and silent, a silk-spun dream against the black night. She pushed the window open. A breeze rushed in, smelling of parched earth and stirring the hair around Ollie's face into a shimmering halo, a flutter of pale ribbons.

I stood, and a floorboard creaked.

Ollie swung her head around and then, when she saw it was only me, turned again to the open window.

We stood side by side, not touching, not talking, just staring out over Zeb and Franny's fields toward the distant, ragged trees that surrounded our meadow. The wind hissed through the tall grass and bowed the tops of the firs. The chimes on the front porch clattered, their songs erratic and shrill. This wasn't the kind of wind that pushed in rain clouds or cool mornings. It was a dust bowl wind, swollen with heat and sighs. The kind of wind that dried you out and left you feeling thin. In the morning, we'd wake with parched throats and burning eyes.

"I know you're mad at me," I said. "I know you think this whole thing is my fault."

Ollie gathered all her hair in one hand and curled it around her fist.

"And maybe it is. Maybe if I had turned that jacket over to Deputy Santos at the beginning the way Bear wanted, then things would have worked out differently."

Ollie pushed her lips out like a duck, then sucked them back in again, pressing them together between her teeth.

"But maybe not."

Ollie looked at me. The moonlight turned her skin gray and her eyes ink black. She let her hair go, let it slide and tumble and cascade around her shoulders again. She seemed to be waiting for me to say something else.

"I want to believe he's innocent, too, Oll," I said. "But there's a chance he might not come home. We have to be ready for that, I think."

She turned away from the window, crossed a few steps to her bed, picked up her *Alice* book, which was lying on the pillow, and returned to me. She held the book out, already opened to a page near the beginning. She pointed at the bottom, at a sentence that read: *After a fall such as this, I shall think nothing of tumbling downstairs.*

I laughed. She closed the book against her chest and leaned into my side.

When we had been waiting at the hospital for someone to come get us, Ollie was still talking then and she'd asked if I was scared. I didn't answer. She tucked her small body close to mine, covered my hand with hers, and said, "It's okay to be scared, Sammy." And then, after a long pause, "We can be scared together. Okay?" I nodded and swallowed back the lump in my throat and stared up at the ceiling until the tears stopped wanting to spill out all over the place. And then I pulled my hand away, stood up, and said, "I'm getting Skittles from the vending machine. You want anything?"

She wrapped her arms around her bent legs and rested her chin on her knees. "Do you think they have those mini powdered doughnuts? Those are my favorite." They did and I bought them for her and she ate all but one, rolling the packaging up on itself and setting it on the chair beside her. She said, "I'm going to save it for Mom for when she gets better," and then she leaned in close, cupped her hand around her mouth, and whispered, "Hospital food's the worst."

I didn't tell her that Mom wasn't going to get better, that she was already dead. I didn't tell her because I was too scared, but I wish I had. Maybe it would have been easier if she hadn't held on to hope for so long.

Grandma found the doughnut a few days later in Ollie's jacket pocket and threw it away. Ollie cried pretty hard after that. There had been so much going on—between the funeral and packing and Bear fighting with Grandma about what to do with me and Ollie—that I probably didn't do as good of a job taking care of her as a big sister should. I couldn't think of anything to say that would make her feel better. There was no good explanation for why such a terrible thing had happened and no magic words to fix us.

This time, I wanted to be a better sister. I wanted to try. I said, "I don't know what's going to happen to us now, Oll. I wish I did. I wish I could tell you that everything's going to work out and we'll be just fine. But I can't."

Her hand found mine. I loved how warm she was, the inside of her palm like a stone sitting in the sun.

"I wish there was something I could do to change everything that's happened," I continued. "I wish I could bring Bear back. And Mom, too." My voice cracked.

Ollie squeezed my hand as tight as she could.

"It's just us now," I said. "We have to look out for each other."

She leaned her head against me. Her long hair tickled my arm, but I didn't mind.

We stood together in front of the window until the moon slipped behind the trees and the barn became a hulking beast in the dark, until the air inside felt more like the air outside and the frog and cricket choruses were louder than our own thoughts. When we returned to our beds, we left the window open and the curtains fluttering.

That night, I dreamed us with painted faces. We crept through the woods together, hunting rabbits and howling like wolves. Living wild. And when they came looking for us, we hid in the tall grass and up among the tangled branches, and Ollie pressed her finger to her lips and we could not be found. And, after a while, they went away. They went and left us to our savage selves.

The next morning when Franny came to wake us for church, I told her I was sick. She leaned over me, laid her hand on my forehead, and said, "You do feel a little warm."

I nodded and closed my eyes. "I can still go," I said. "I can try . . ."

She pulled the blankets up over my shoulders and tucked them tight. "You're going to stay right here in bed and rest is what you're going to do."

She brought me plain toast and peppermint tea and a stack of old *Better Homes and Gardens*. "We'll be home around noon." She kissed my forehead and left.

It was another fifteen minutes before I heard their voices drift out the front door and the truck start up and drive away. And another ten minutes of silence after that before I got up, got dressed, put on my shoes, and went out the back door.

Earlier, Deputy Santos had stopped by to drop off our duffel bags. Her car pulling into the driveway had woken me, and I'd crept to the landing at the top of the stairs, sat tucked in shadows where no one could see me. They tried to keep their voices low, but I still heard every word.

"We've arrested him for Taylor Bellweather's murder," Deputy Santos had said. "Officially."

"Oh." This was Franny, her voice fluttering like a baby bird. "Oh no. No, no."

Zeb asked, "What about bail?"

"His arraignment's scheduled for Tuesday morning. Until then, we're going to have to hold him."

"There must be some mistake."

"There's evidence. Witnesses. Too many things pointing us in his direction."

"An explanation then," Zeb said. "He must have had some kind of reason, something that makes sense."

"He's refusing to cooperate. He said even if he told us the truth, we wouldn't believe him, that we'd already made up our minds. Then he asked for a lawyer."

"But that doesn't mean . . ." said Franny. "He couldn't have possibly . . ."

"It just doesn't look good. Things aren't adding up right. There's just too much . . ."

I went back upstairs at this point and buried my head under my pillow. When I told Franny I was too sick to go to church, I wasn't lying. Not exactly. But how much of my stomachache was from thinking of all those people packed so tight together staring and whispering and casting judgment between hymns, and how much was guilt for my part in all this, I couldn't tell.

My father, murderer. And yet, I didn't believe it.

The grass in the meadow was trampled and dull. Boot prints marred the dirt. A wadded-up latex glove had been dropped and forgotten under our picnic table. Yellow tape hung limp from a tree branch beside the path leading to our swimming hole. In the apiary, the bees flew in and out of their boxes. Nothing had changed for them. Though the police had left the hives alone, the lean-to where we kept our tools was empty. They'd taken Bear's hive tool and smoker and everything else he needed to take care of his bees. They'd even taken my suit. Evidence. That's what they were looking for; maybe that's what they'd found.

The bees would be fine by themselves for a few days, and the established colonies could go on indefinitely, if we left them to it. They had enough honey stored to last into next spring when the flowers started blooming again. It was the newer colonies I worried about, especially the swarm we'd just brought home. Those bees hadn't had enough time to prepare and, to survive the winter, they'd need our help. Wasn't anything I could do right now, though, nothing I was willing to do without my gear anyway. I left the hives and went to the teepee.

As I stood on the threshold, looking in, everything was chaos.

Bear's cot was flipped onto its side, his blankets heaped on the floor. The small chest was open, the clothing inside tossed. The filing cabinet drawers were open, too, and I saw now what that crashing sound had been yesterday. A jar lay in pieces, shattered around a thick puddle of honey. Between then and now, a few bees had followed the scent and found their way inside the teepee. They gathered up the amber sweetness, then swayed drunkenly out the open flap and back to their hives.

I righted Bear's cot, then picked up the folding chair that had also been lying on its side and returned it to its place next to the small table. I gathered up papers that had been strewn every which way and started to sort through them. Some were Bear's sketches, the ones he'd hung from the ceiling. I stacked those in a pile together on one corner of the table. Others were receipts and order forms, paperwork for the honey business. I stuffed those into an empty pillowcase to take back with me to Zeb and Franny's.

I found a photograph shuffled in among a stack of beekeeping magazines. It was one I'd seen before, but so long ago, I'd forgotten all about it. A clean-shaven young man with cut-short auburn hair had his arm around the waist of a fairy-sprite woman with high cheekbones and dark freckles, brown hair that fell in curls around her shoulders the way mine used to. She leaned close to him, her head tilted up, her ash-blue eyes fixed on his face, and her mouth frozen in a funny, crooked smile that held all their hope, all their love. Their entire future trembling on her lips: happiness, children, growing old together, dying together. When Mom showed me this picture all those years ago, she'd told me she and Bear had been on their honeymoon in the Italian countryside when a man named Giovanni, who'd been riding past on his bicycle, offered to take their picture in front of an olive grove. She'd said Giovanni had wanted them to kiss for the shot, but Bear had been too shy. I stared at the photograph another second longer, trying to recognize my parents in the faces of these strangers, this woman and this man, so young and in love. This woman with her whole life before her. This man who had nothing to hide.

I tucked the photograph in my back pocket and gathered up the last of the scattered papers. My name written at the top of one sheet caught my attention.

> *Dear Sam,*
> *I'm sorry.*

The rest of the page was blank.
I shuffled through the stack. Here was another one:

> *Dear Sam,*
> *There's so much I want to tell you about what*
> *happened but*

The last word ended in a streak of ink, like someone had bumped his elbow, causing the pen to skid.

Another sheet just had my name and a date from three years ago scrawled in the top corner, but nothing else. There must have been twenty or thirty of these things, letters started but never finished. Words scratched out, whole sentences sliced through with thick black ink. The paper was thin, the sharpness starting to fade. These letters had been written years ago. I tried to put them in order, but most didn't have dates. Even if they did, I still wouldn't have been able to sort out what he was trying to say.

He'd written only a few words on each piece of paper, mostly *I'm sorry* or *I wish things could have been different, I wish I could have been better.* The earliest one was written in January the year I turned eight, when I was still too young to understand much of anything. I had refused to talk to Mom for three whole days that winter, giving her the silent treatment because I wanted to punish her. Because I thought it was her fault Bear didn't want to come home, her fault we couldn't go live with him in the meadow permanently. Her fault our family was broken.

This letter started out the same as all the others: *Dear Sam.*
And then:

*It snowed today. Enough for me to make a snow
family. And when I look at the four of them standing so
silently in white, I am reminded of you and your sister
and your beautiful mother. I am reminded of what we
might have been.*

But after that, nothing. A bunch of blank lines.

I couldn't decide whether to feel grateful for these letters—
knowing my father thought about me when I wasn't around, knowing he tried—or pissed off because they didn't make sense and they
weren't finished and, even if they had been, he'd probably never in-
tended to send them to me. I settled for indifference and piled the
letters on the table beside Bear's drawings.

When I left, I closed the teepee flap behind me and tied it shut.

I carried the pillowcase over my shoulder. Along with the honey
paperwork, I'd also thrown in Bear's drawing pencils and empty
sketchpads, thinking he might like to have them in jail, if that was
even allowed.

I walked through the trees toward Crooked River. The deputies
had come through here, too, flattening the grass and Queen Anne's
lace, leaving deep depressions in the soft ground, tearing apart the
woods, looking for clues—small, large, anything that would prove
Bear's guilt beyond a shadow of a doubt.

On the short drive back to Franny and Zeb's, I'd told Deputy
Santos about finding and then losing Taylor Bellweather's body, hours
before Tony Grant found her a second and final time. I told her, too,
about how Bear had left us in the meadow all night and about finding the jacket in his satchel the next morning, the key a couple days
later. When she asked me why I hadn't said something right away, that
first time they came to the meadow, I told her I'd been too scared. I
thought we were going to get in trouble. I told her Bear had promised
me he'd had nothing to do with the murder, and I told her it was my
fault we hadn't contacted the police sooner, not his.

"I thought I could protect him." It was the exact wrong thing to say considering the mess we were in, but it was too late for me to take any of it back now.

Deputy Santos had tightened her grip on the steering wheel. "It's not your job to protect your father. He's supposed to be the one protecting you."

There was a time before the meadow when all four of us lived together in a two-bedroom duplex in Eugene, six blocks from the university. Mom laughed a lot and sang country songs while she made dinner. Daddy wore suits to work and came home for lunch sometimes. Ollie was a baby, not even a year old, but she'd already said her first word: *Pa*. I was five going on six and believed the world was Saturday cartoons and playing catch and mint chocolate chip ice cream with fudge sauce on top. We were happy. Then Daddy left.

Maybe it would have been easier if I had known it was coming. If he had packed a suitcase or kissed us good-bye or given us some kind of reason. But it wasn't like that. One day, he just didn't come home. I waited for him by the window, the way I always did, but the driveway stayed empty. I waited the next day, too. And the day after that. Finally, Mom sat me down and held my hand and told me he wasn't coming home, not for a while anyway. She said it wasn't anything we'd done, that he just needed some time alone to find himself again. And it seemed strange to me, that he'd gotten lost in the first place. To lose your own self seemed an impossible thing.

I stopped waiting by the window, but in the dark, after Mom tucked me in and kissed me good night, I made up stories to keep myself from crying. Stories that centered on Daddy being stuck somewhere because of circumstances beyond his control, stuck but desperately trying to find his way home. Stories like he'd been kidnapped and thrown into the back of a van, driven into the woods and left to wander, or his car had broken down in the middle of a desert, or he'd been flying somewhere for work and his plane had crashed on a tropical island. I thought it was only a matter of time before a rescue team found him or he stumbled into a gas station, and then the phone would ring and I would answer and hear his voice on the other end telling me not to worry, he was coming home.

The story I came back to most often was that he'd been in some sort of accident and hit his head, lost consciousness for a while, maybe even had amnesia. He'd lost his driver's license and didn't have any other sort of identification on him, and so the doctors and nurses had no way of knowing who he was, or how to reach his family. One night, almost a year to the day he'd gone missing, I so thoroughly convinced myself that this was the only explanation for his absence, that I ran into the kitchen, where Mom was boiling water for tea, and started shouting, "Where's the phone book?!"

She almost dropped the kettle on her foot. "What is it? Calm down. Why do you need the phone book? Sam, talk to me."

"The hospitals." I was close to hyperventilating, my head too light, my heart pounding too fast. "We have to call the hospitals."

Mom squatted at eye level and grabbed my shoulders. "Slow down. I'm having trouble understanding you."

"Dad," I said. "He's hurt. He doesn't remember who we are. We have to find him and help him remember."

I tried to pull away from her, to go and find the phone book on my own, but she'd clutched me tight, pulled me close to her chest, and whispered against the top of my head, "Oh, honey. Your daddy's not hurt."

And that's when I realized she knew exactly where he was. That's when I understood he wasn't lost at all. But when I asked her to tell me why he'd left and where he'd gone, she said it wasn't anything I needed to worry about. I was too young. No matter how many different ways I asked, she always gave me the same response, "When your father's ready, he'll tell you." But I didn't see how that was possible. He wasn't here. He wasn't anywhere.

Two years passed and life went on. Then one night, a Wednesday, we were eating dinner—meat loaf, green beans, and applesauce—and I was trying to convince Mom to buy me a new winter coat. She was in the middle of saying "Your old one still fits" when the phone rang.

Mom answered, and I could tell by the way she crumpled into a kitchen chair—her head falling forward, her hair covering her face, her hand bracing the weight of it all—that it was him.

"Where are you?" she said. "I thought you were going to call this morning?" And then she was silent for a long time, just listening, nodding her head like he was in the room with us instead of somewhere far away. Finally, she said, "Okay. Mm hmm. Okay. I love you, too," and then held the receiver out to me. "It's your father."

I pressed the phone to my ear but didn't say anything for a few seconds. I just wanted to hear him breathing. After a while, he said, "Hello? Sam? Are you there?"

"Yes."

"Oh, hi."

"Hi."

"It's so good to hear your voice."

"Where have you been?"

There was a long pause, and I thought he'd hung up on me. Then he said, "I needed to be alone for a while."

"Why?"

"I just needed some space to think."

His answers were terrible, but hearing his voice again after so long, I didn't even care. I asked, "When are you coming home?"

He didn't say anything.

"Tomorrow?"

He sighed and then, "No, not tomorrow."

"Maybe the next day."

"No, probably not."

"When?"

"I don't know, Sam."

"Oh."

"I need you to be a big girl for me, okay? I need you to be brave and take care of your mother and baby sister. Can you do that?"

"Okay."

He cleared his throat, and in the background I heard a car drive by. Then Bear said, "How would you like to stay with me for a few weeks this summer? We can sleep under the stars. And I can teach you how to fish."

"Really?"

"Would you like that?"

"Yes."

And so my father had finally returned, but not in the way I'd imagined. The first time I saw him after he'd been gone for so long, I didn't recognize him. I was afraid to get out of the car. Here was this bearded man standing not much taller than my mother, though I remembered him being a giant. Here was this sallow-faced stranger, so much thinner than I remembered, and I was sure there'd been a mistake. Then he smiled at me, and it was as if he'd never even been gone.

But now.

And again.

I was here, and he was not. I was alone, and he was lost. Only this time, there were no stories to give me hope and no Mom to keep me safe or hold me when I cried.

At the river's edge, I bent, picked up a flat stone, and tried to skip it across the water, but the current was too rough, the rapids moving too fast, and the stone was sucked away before it ever had a chance.

A dark speck darted past me. I followed its movement, watched it bob low and come up again, then drop quickly down to the shallow water a few inches from where I stood. I crouched on the bank and leaned in for a closer look. It was a honeybee, maybe one of Bear's, but that's not something you can tell just from looking. Her job today was to carry water back to the hive. She drank deeply, and after a few seconds she took off, bobbing, dipping, pulling up again, trying to balance. Then she circled once and flew upstream, away from me and in the exact opposite direction of Bear's hives. I jumped up and ran after her.

When bees fly back to their hives, they fly in a mostly straight line. Bear taught me that. He also taught me that the best conditions for tracking them is an overcast day when you can see their black bodies against pale clouds. Today's sky was piercing blue, but as long as she stayed out of the trees, I thought I might have a chance to find my first wild colony.

Bear was always saying you can't call yourself a real beekeeper until you've tracked a wild bee to her wild hive. In the past four years, he'd found six, and he'd said it was because he was patient and attentive and had eyes like a hawk. I always wondered, though, if maybe the bees just moved slower for him, because whenever I'd tried to follow them, I'd take only a few steps before losing sight and giving up. "Beelining is ten percent skill and ninety percent luck," Bear liked to say. Bees are small and move fast, tracking them is like trying to follow a dust mote in the sun. The best thing to do is lock onto their movement, ignore where you're putting your feet, and just run as fast and as straight as you can.

It felt good to feel the earth pushing back against my feet, to suck great gulps of air into my lungs, to crash and stomp and blaze a path through the brush. The pillowcase thumped against my back and every few steps I stumbled over a loose rock or a piece of wood sticking up from the dirt, but I didn't fall, I didn't slow down. The bee flew. I ran.

She stuck close to Crooked River for about a half mile, and it was easy enough to follow her. The shoreline south of my swimming hole flattened out, the river itself widening, the current slowing. Grass swished around my ankles. A flock of small birds exploded from a clump of cattails.

I'd explored this part of the river before, and there was still a ways to go before Zeb's property ended and somebody else's began. I didn't think the bee would go much farther now, and I was starting to get excited, imagining what it would be like to find a wild hive. It would be in a tree hollow or a rotten log or maybe even inside a cave, tucked under the rock eaves. Once I got close enough I'd start to see more bees, maybe even hear them humming. And I wondered if they'd sound the same as Bear's bees—comfortable, soothing, cheerful—or if the wild buzz would be more frenzied, more hurried, rushing and angry. And Bear. I pictured the look on his face when I told him how I'd tracked a bee all the way from our part of the river to wherever. Elated, grinning, proud.

I thought, *I have to be getting close now,* and glanced at the tree line. And that's when I lost sight of the bee.

You have to pay attention. Time and time again, Bear had told me this. You have to keep your head up and your eyes wide open.

I stopped running and twisted my head around, scanning the air, the sky, the trees, every possible place, but she was gone. Vanished in the blink of an eye. I kicked at a rock. It skittered away from me and splashed into the river.

The sun inched higher. I had an hour, maybe, before Zeb and Franny and Ollie got back from church. I was close to the service road where Bear said he'd found the jean jacket. If I followed it to Lambert Road, I could get back to the farm faster and easier than backtracking through the trees and meadow. I continued upriver a few yards, following the curve of the shoreline, kicking stones and thrashing at weeds with a broken stick. Finally, I reached a break in the brush, a place where the trees thinned.

This service road—rutted, packed dirt, grass growing down the center—was similar to the one that ran between the meadow and Zeb and Franny's barn, but instead of ending miles from the river, this road ran straight up to the water's edge. Maybe there used to be a bridge here, or a shallow place to ford. I looked across to the other side, where the trees grew thick and right up close to the shore. Didn't seem to me like a good place to cross. The water was too high, the current too swift.

A few feet downriver was a small island, a heaped mess of boulders, grass, and spindly trees that would never grow much taller than my waist. Debris collected against one end, limbs and leaves tangling, and it was here that the sun kept catching on something, glinting gold and reflecting into my eyes.

I took off my shoes and socks and set them with the pillowcase on a nearby rock. I rolled my pant legs up to my knees and waded into the shallows. The current wrestled me, threatening to pull me off my feet and drag me under. I leaned forward, pushing against it and wading deeper. When I reached the island, my pants were soaked through. So was the hem of my shirt. The river rushed around my waist, pressing me up against the rocks. I grabbed onto a sturdy-looking branch jutting out from the tangle of debris and held on tight with one hand. With the other, I reached for what I could now see was a necklace caught on a twig.

My fingers clasped the charm first. I tugged gently, but the necklace didn't budge. I wiggled the chain back and forth and, at the same time, pulled. The necklace slipped off the twig, and I curled my fist around it.

I turned, pushed off the island, and splashed through the churning water back to shore. In the shallows, my feet slipped across the algae-covered stones covering the bottom of the riverbed. I steadied myself and clambered to dry land.

Water dripped from my pants and shirt, dampening the sand around my feet. I opened my hand and brought the necklace close to my face. The chain was gold and simple, and a round pendant dangled from it, a dark stone set in an intricately patterned base. I recognized the shape of it and the etchings around the stone, could see now that they were snakes, not vines like I'd thought when I saw this same necklace in the newspaper. This same pendant hanging around Taylor Bellweather's neck.

I snapped my head up and searched the woods behind me. I'd gotten that feeling, the kind where your skin crawls and a shiver runs up your spine and you think you're being watched. No one was here with me but the wind and the trees and a forest full of birds.

I stared at the necklace again. The clasp was broken and a bit of mud was caught in between the stone and the setting, but it was hers. Definitely hers. And because of that, I looked around and started to notice other things.

Tire tracks in the mud ran from the road down to the water and then out again. Clean and pressed deep, they hadn't had a chance to crust over yet or get worn down by wind and rain. They were only a few days old, if that. And here, up next to one of the tracks, so close I almost mistook it for a tire tread, a single, perfect boot print. Bigger than any shoe I'd ever worn, with a waffle iron pattern and a logo that wasn't familiar to me, but seemed distinct enough to mean something.

Here was evidence. New evidence. Evidence that would prove Bear's innocence. Beyond a shadow of a doubt. I put the necklace in my pocket where it would be safe. Then I dug around in the pillow-case for the sketchpad and a pencil. I sat down in the dirt beside the boot print, turned to a blank page, and started to draw.

ollie

The waitress asks, "Just the two of you?"

My sister, nodding, says yes, even though there are two of us and two Shimmering.

The waitress, whose sparkle-blue name tag reads Belinda, takes menus from a box near the cash register and leads us to a booth. I slide in on one side, my sister slides in on the other. The one from the river and the one who follows me break apart in the bright sunlight coming through the naked window. They float like dust around us, brushing arms, cheeks, lips. Never settling.

Belinda lays the menus down in front of us. "Special's meat loaf and mashed potatoes. Kids' menu's on the back." She leaves us alone to decide.

Patti's is crowded for a Monday, and people are watching us. Those two men at the bar. That woman and her husband sharing a stack of pancakes. Those three gray-haired ladies who all look the same. They whisper behind their hands the way they did at church, but their voices are not soft enough today and I hear things like "poor girls," "arrested," "always suspected," "monster."

My sister clears her throat too loudly and shifts her body. The vinyl bench squeaks. She says, "Do you know what you want?"

I point at the grilled cheese sandwich that comes with a bowl of tomato soup. Comfort food because it's what Mom would have made me on a day like today. She would have cupped my face in her hands, kissed the tip of my nose, and said, "It's okay to be sad sometimes."

A bright speck floats close to my face. I wave her away.

She is not my mother because my mother is dead. And yet she is my mother. I have seen her face in the dark. We are stuck between hello and good-bye, here and gone.

Belinda comes back to our table holding a notepad and pencil. "So what'll it be, girls?"

My sister gives our order, and Belinda goes away again. When she returns with two glasses of water, my sister starts to ask a question. "I was wondering . . ." But then she stops and shakes her head, glances out the window, and chews on her bottom lip. As Belinda is leaving, my sister says, "Can I get some coffee, please?"

Belinda brings a brown mug to the table and pours coffee from a half-full pot.

My sister slips her hand into her front shirt pocket, then clears her throat and speaks in a too-loud voice, the way she does when she's trying to convince people she's older than she really is. "So, that woman they found . . . what's the word on that? Any new developments?"

Belinda draws the coffeepot close to her chest and holds it there with both hands. She watches us with thin-slit eyes. A bead of water slides down the outside of my glass. I catch the drop on the tip of my finger before it reaches the table and touch it to my lips.

It's a good question, but not the right one.

The silence worries my sister.

One hand is still in her pocket, clutching something I can't see, but the other is picking at the corner of her napkin, tearing away tiny pieces. She stammers, "I mean . . . since you get a lot of people coming through here . . . in and out . . . talking . . . I just . . . I thought . . . I thought maybe you'd know . . ."

"Do you want cream, honey?" Belinda asks.

My sister shakes her head quickly and grabs a sugar packet from a small container at the edge of the table. "No, thanks. This is good."

And then we are alone again, and I want to tell her that she's doing the best she can and to keep trying. We can't give up. Not now. Not ever.

Not until we prove the truth.

She takes a sip of coffee, makes a face, and pushes her cup away. She stares out the window, and when the sunlight hits her, that's when I know something is different. Something has changed. It's her: clenching and unclenching her jaw, drumming her fingers against the tabletop. But it's also the one from the river: coiling and uncoiling, trembling the air between us. Both of them, all nerves and racing pulse.

My sister has found something. Something important.

Something that changes everything.

sam

We went to Patti's because that's where Deputy Santos usually came for lunch when she was out on patrol. Today, though, her favorite booth was occupied by someone I didn't know. I was about to march right back out the door and straight to her house then, but Ollie was holding her stomach and staring at the pies in the glass case so hard I thought her eyes would pop. Early this morning Detective Talbert had called and asked Zeb to bring the truck in as soon as he could. For processing. Ollie and I hitched a ride with him under false pretenses of going to the public library a few blocks away. The plan was to meet in front of the diner at three. We still had a few hours yet, so I didn't see the harm in getting a booth and ordering lunch first.

I touched my hand to the pocket of my flannel shirt, checking for the thousandth time that the necklace was still there, that I hadn't imagined everything.

Yesterday, the second I got back to Zeb and Franny's, I'd zipped the necklace into a plastic bag for safekeeping and tucked the bag inside my pocket. I didn't tell Ollie about it because I didn't want to get her hopes up. And I didn't tell Zeb and Franny because they already had enough to worry about. I did call Deputy Santos, though, as soon as I could, but she didn't answer. That's when I decided to take the necklace and sketches to her in person. All the rest of yesterday and this morning, too, when we were eating breakfast and getting ready and even when Ollie and I went out to feed the chickens, every minute, every second, I kept the necklace with me, safe and secure. Once I gave it to Deputy Santos and showed her the boot print, it could only be a matter of time before they let Bear go free.

I looked around the diner, surprised at how many people were here. Nearly all the tables and booths were full, and the room was loud with laughter and gossip and coffee being poured, utensils clinking on plates. I paid particular attention to the men, their hands and feet especially. Most of them wore sneakers or dress shoes, but a few had on boots, and from where I sat they all seemed to be about the right size.

One of the men glanced over his shoulder at the exact same second I was staring at his broad torso and thick neck, staring and thinking how Taylor Bellweather would have been like a matchstick in his hands. Our eyes locked. I blinked but didn't look away. I recognized him now, his receding hairline and hooked nose, the way his mouth was always turned up at the corners even though nothing was funny, his tiny dark eyes sinking too close together.

My second summer staying with Bear, Franny came to the meadow the Sunday after I got there and told me to change into something nice because she was taking me to church. She said it was about time I felt the fear of God in my life. I told her I didn't believe in God, but if I did, I wouldn't be afraid of him. She told me I was going to church even if she had to drag me there. And then she said I was right, it wasn't God I needed to fear. I was shorter then, by a lot, so much smaller and younger, and Pastor Mike Freshour seemed to me a terrible giant. Leaning over the pulpit to get closer to the congregation, he near bent double. He clutched the sides and, as his words reached a crescendo, he bore down, white knuckled, and I remember being afraid that he would snap the sturdy wooden platform into a thousand tiny splinters. I don't remember what he preached about, but I do remember running outside as fast as I could after the final Amen, desperate for air that didn't reek of hellfire.

He was still staring at me, and now he took a napkin from his table and dabbed at his mouth. His hands were bigger than I remembered, all knuckles and sinew. I'd only gone back to Franny's church a few times since that first time—whenever I was visiting Bear and Franny got it in her head that my soul again needed saving—but Pastor Mike was looking at me like we were old friends, like he was about to get up and come over here and say something.

I looked away from him quickly, focusing all my attention on Ollie instead. She was staring out the window. Her fingers tapped against the cover of her *Alice* book lying on the table between us. She must have felt me watching her, because her fingers stopped moving and she turned her head and our eyes met. I smiled at her, trying to be reassuring. *We'll be all right. I've figured out a way to fix this.*

The corners of her mouth twitched a little, and I thought I might get her to smile, but then her eyes shifted focus to something behind me, and her mouth drooped, her frown intensifying. I turned to look.

Travis, untying his grease-stained apron, approached our table. He didn't smile when he said, "Surprised to see you here today."

It felt strange being this close, seeing him now, going on with life as usual after leaving things so unfinished by the river. Even though it felt like an eternity had passed, it had only been three days since our almost kiss, since we ceased being acquaintances who barely said two words in passing and had become something else I didn't yet know how to define.

"I guess you've heard about Bear?" I asked.

He nodded. "Yeah, it's all anyone's talking about."

I pulled my coffee cup closer, wrapping both hands around it, wishing I'd said yes when Belinda asked if I wanted cream. Bear

always drank his coffee with just a single spoon of sugar stirred in—
that was still too bitter for me.

Travis cleared his throat. "You know it's in the papers, right?"

"It is?"

He held up a finger—*wait*—and left our booth, dodging between
tables to the front counter, where he plucked a newspaper from a wire
stand near the register. He returned and laid the folded paper down
in front of me. Bear's mug shot took up the top half of the front page.
He looked startled, half crazy, and his beard reminded me of a tangled nest of barbed wire. The headline in bold and all caps read WILD
MAN FRANK "BEAR" MCALISTER ARRESTED AS PRIME SUSPECT IN LOCAL
MURDER.

I turned the front page facedown on the table without reading the
article. Ollie grabbed for it. I tried to slide it away to keep her from
seeing, but she pulled the newspaper from my grasp and flipped it
over again.

I sagged against the vinyl bench. "They arrested the wrong person,
you know."

"This whole thing. It sucks," Travis said, twisting his apron in
his hands. "Really sucks. But they wouldn't have arrested him if they
didn't have proof."

"What proof?"

Travis shrugged. "I don't know, but they must have something."

Ollie started to kick her feet against the bottom of the bench. I
glared at her, but she just kept kicking. *Thump! Thump! Thump!*

I said, "Yeah, well, I've got something, too."

Travis stopped twisting his apron. Underneath the table, Ollie
kicked my shin.

I yelped and pulled my leg out of reach. "What was that for?"

She blinked at me, but stayed silent.

I shrugged at Travis, said, "Sisters," and then immediately wished
I could take it back. I started to apologize, but stopped, shaking my
head, motioning him closer to me instead.

"I found something by the river," I said. "Evidence that proves Bear's innocent."

"Sam . . ." Travis drew out my name too long. He thought I was making it up.

"No, really. I'll show you." I started to reach into my pocket for the sketches I'd made of the boot print and tire tracks, for the necklace safe in its plastic bag.

Ollie lifted a straw to her mouth and blew. A spitball flew fast from the end and struck Travis's forehead. Hard.

He took a step back, rubbing his brow. "What the hell?"

"Ollie!"

The straw came up again. Ollie puffed out her cheeks.

"Stop it!" I lunged across the table and grabbed her arm.

She pulled away from me and shot another spitball. Travis ducked, and it flew harmlessly past his shoulder.

I caught Ollie's arm and yanked the straw from her fingers. "Apologize."

She turned her face to the window.

I said it again: "Ollie. Tell Travis you're sorry."

She ignored me.

Travis touched my shoulder. "It's okay."

"She knows better."

Travis shrugged. "She's just a kid." He glanced behind him at the swinging kitchen door like he'd heard someone calling his name. "Listen, I gotta get back to work. You staying with Zeb and Franny?"

I nodded.

"Maybe I'll come by after my shift is over. You can show me what you found?"

"Yeah. Sure. If you want." I tried another sip of coffee. It was lukewarm now and tasted even more disgusting than my first sip.

When Travis was gone, I turned to scold Ollie, but she was smiling, just barely—a hint there at the corners of her mouth—and I decided to let the whole thing go.

Our waitress came with food a few minutes later. She set plates down in front of us and then stood beside our booth for a stretched-out moment, tapping her pencil against the palm of her hand. She was a heavyset woman and every time she took a breath, she wheezed a little. Her bottle-blond hair was pulled back in a ponytail, her dark roots starting to show.

I pulled my plate closer.

Belinda stopped tapping her pencil. She said, "You should be careful who you talk to about that woman."

Ollie's spoon clinked against the side of her bowl.

Belinda continued, "There are a lot of folks around here that don't like your daddy and this whole situation, his arrest . . . well, it has them even more riled up than before."

"He didn't—" But she wouldn't let me finish.

"Now. I like you girls. And I liked your mama. And even though I probably shouldn't, I'm going to tell you what I remember, but you keep it to yourselves, you hear? Don't go telling anyone I told you or I could get in some real trouble." She waited until Ollie and I both nodded, promising our silence, and then she said, "As far as I can remember, that poor girl came in here two nights in a row. Saturday and Sunday. Sat right over there. Same booth both times. Ordered meat loaf the first night and a club sandwich, hold the fries, the second. Drank a lot of coffee. Two pots' worth, easy. Each night. And she was writing on something, always had her hand going. When she wasn't writing, she was flipping through a stack of old newspaper articles."

"Did she talk to anybody?" I asked.

Belinda scratched behind her ear with her pencil. "Well, she asked me if I knew anything about your daddy."

"And?"

"And I told her I didn't know any more than what those articles in front of her said."

The *Bulletin* had run some features about Bear when he first set up camp in the meadow. They praised his return to the land and quest for a minimalist life. Some even compared him to Henry David Thoreau. After he set up his hives, there were a few more articles about his honey business and how to care for bees, but the last article I knew about had been published over four years ago, and I didn't see any good reason why Taylor Bellweather would have come all the way from Eugene to write about someone as uninteresting as Bear.

"Was there anyone else she talked to?" I asked. "Maybe someone she seemed uncomfortable around? Someone she didn't seem very happy to see?"

"I know what you're getting at, and no. There was no one like that." Belinda shifted all her weight onto one foot. "Though, now that I think about it, I did see her talking to Pastor Mike. That second night she was here. But it wasn't for very long and she was smiling at him the whole time, so stop looking like that because he didn't have anything to do with this."

I leaned closer to her. "Did you hear what they were talking about?"

Belinda scowled at me and dropped her pencil into the front pocket of her apron. "Wasn't any of my business then, and it's none of your business now."

"It is," I said, pushing the newspaper, Bear's mug shot facing up, across the table to her. "Now it is."

She sighed and her expression softened. "I know he's your daddy and all. And I know you love him. And maybe he didn't have anything to do with all this. Maybe he didn't do a damn thing wrong. But maybe he did, and all I'm saying is you've got to be careful. Sometimes when you think you're looking straight at something, you're really looking at it sideways." She rapped her knuckles twice on the table, then smiled at Ollie and said, "Eat up, sweetheart, before your soup gets cold."

As she moved away from us, I had a clear view of the table where Pastor Mike had been sitting. His chair was pushed back and empty. His plate of food, abandoned.

Outside it was so hot our shoes stuck to the pavement.

"Hurry up," I said to Ollie, but she didn't walk any faster.

The sun was bold and the asphalt mean. My T-shirt was damp, clinging to my skin.

"Ollie, let's go!"

She had stopped in front of the Attic and was staring through the front window at the toy monkey. I grabbed her hand and tried to pull her away. Ollie shook me off and crossed her arms over her chest, refusing to leave.

"Please, Ollie. It's important."

I'd called the number on Deputy Santos's business card before we left Patti's. No one answered. I didn't have her home phone number, but she didn't live that far from here, about a mile give or take, on the north end of town in a cul-de-sac near the fire station. It would take us maybe twenty minutes to walk there, and twenty to walk back. Plus, if Deputy Santos was home, I'd need at least a half hour to show her everything I'd found and ask her what she was going to do about it, forty-five minutes because she might need convincing. If we wanted to be back in time to meet Zeb, we had to hurry.

I tugged Ollie's arm. "We can come back later."

Ollie stepped closer to the window. She lifted her hand and, with one finger, traced the stenciled letters on the window: *D-E-L-I-L-A-H.* When she reached the *H,* she went back to the *D* and traced it again. She ignored the *'S* and the word *ATTIC* that came after.

On the road behind us, a car drove slowly past. The engine rattled the way Zeb's truck did, and I turned quickly, thinking maybe it was him—maybe the forensic guys had finished early—but it was a burgundy minivan and no one I recognized.

I grabbed Ollie's elbow, saying, "Let's go," and dragged her a few steps along the sidewalk.

She pulled back against me, digging in her heels, throwing her whole weight into going the opposite direction, back to Delilah's Attic.

She'd gotten stronger in the past few months, taller, too. I used to be able to pick her up under her arms and swing her around in a circle. I used to be able to lift her onto my shoulders and carry her around for hours. I used to be able to make her do whatever I wanted.

I released her. She stumbled backward but didn't fall.

"Fine," I said. "You want to go inside?"

She nodded.

"Go, then."

She took a step toward the door, then stopped and glanced back at me.

"I'm going to go talk to Deputy Santos."

She pushed her glasses up high on the bridge of her nose, and worked her lips between her teeth, and it seemed like she was getting ready to say something and I thought, *Finally. It's about goddamn time.* But then she just shrugged. And said nothing.

"You can wait for me here," I said. "Inside."

Her nostrils flared a little.

"Either that or you come with me."

She looked at the door, then back at me, and I wanted to ask her what was so pressing about this place, what couldn't wait another hour? What was more important than our family? But I knew she wouldn't answer.

"I'm going," I said and turned away.

I walked to the end of the block slower than I normally would, giving Ollie time to think about it, change her mind, and catch up with me. When I reached the edge of the sidewalk, I stopped and looked back over my shoulder.

Ollie was gone, the sidewalk deserted. Maybe it was better this way—letting her hide inside books and imaginary worlds. Mom was always saying kids should stay kids for as long as possible. They shouldn't be in charge of the hard things. I guess sometimes I just forgot how young ten really was and how much growing up Ollie still had to do.

I hurried across the street in the direction of Deputy Santos's house, promising myself I wouldn't stay long.

W here did you find this?" Deputy Santos turned the plastic bag over, then brought the necklace close to her face.

Her eyes narrowed on the pendant, and she moved her thumb over it, smoothing the plastic, trying to see the details better.

"In Crooked River about a mile from the meadow," and I told her about chasing the bee and how I was going to take the service road back to Zeb and Franny's, but the gold chain had been glinting in the sun, begging me to wade out and see.

"It's hers," I said. "She's wearing the same one in that picture the newspapers printed."

Deputy Santos frowned.

"Right?" I pressed her. "It's the same one. Isn't it?"

"I think so." She set the bagged necklace on the table among a cluttered mess of scribbled-on notepads, photographs, file folders, to-day's newspaper still rolled and wrapped in plastic, and empty mugs stained dark with old coffee.

When I first came into the kitchen and saw her table like this, I thought she was busy with one of the cold cases she was always working during her off-hours. She'd bring home stacks of dusty boxes and sort through everything again, because sometimes it wasn't new evidence that solved a case, rather someone with a fresh perspective coming along and taking another look, staring at it from a different angle. She told me once that working cold cases was the best thing she could think to do with her spare time, that it was important to never forget about the victims. That they deserved answers. "We owe it to them to keep trying," she'd said. And that's what I thought she was doing today, when she opened the door and invited me in. But then I saw Taylor Bellweather's name scribbled on some of the papers, and my father's name jotted down on others, and knowing this case had become her most important one encouraged me.

Deputy Santos skimmed her fingers over the plastic bag, lingering a few seconds on the pendant. "You should have left it there. You should have gone straight back to the Johnsons' and called me right away."

"I did call," I said. "You didn't answer."

"You should have left a message."

"By the time you got there, it would have been gone." I wasn't lying, just stretching the truth a little, because I needed her to focus. "The current was pulling at it too hard."

"Why didn't you call the tip line, then? Or 911, for Christ's sake?" She folded her arms, cradling her elbows. "Someone would have come out right away."

"I put it in a bag as soon as I could. And I kept it with me the whole time." I shrugged. "I didn't think it would be a big deal."

She rubbed her eyes and sighed.

"You can still use it, right? You can dust it for fingerprints or something, can't you?"

She didn't answer me.

"Look." I took the sketches from my back pocket, unfolded them, and laid them on the table side by side in front of her. "There were these, too."

She picked up the drawing of the boot print, studied it a second, then put it down and picked up the sketch I'd done of the tire tracks. "Where?"

"In the mud a foot or so back from the waterline."

She set the tire tracks back down, too, and looked at them both together.

"I didn't touch the boot print or the tracks," I said. "They're probably still there. Exactly how I found them."

She stared at my sketches. The ceiling fan in the living room clattered loudly, like a bolt was loose or the pull string was slapping against a blade.

"So?" I touched the corner of the boot print sketch. "This proves it, right? Bear's innocent. You can let him go now?"

"This doesn't prove much of anything," she said. "Other than a possible dump site." And then she bit her lower lip like she regretted using those words in front of me.

"But it does." I pushed the boot print across the table, closer to her. "Bear doesn't wear boots like these."

"You don't know everything about him, Sam. There are things he doesn't tell you." She tried to say it gently, but it still felt like a punch to the gut.

"No. You don't understand," I said. "He doesn't wear boots. Period. He says the laces make him feel trapped, like he's walking around in chains. He doesn't own a pair of boots. He hates boots. He refuses to wear them."

Deputy Santos picked up the boot print sketch again, turned it upside down and then sideways. She said, "They're the right size."

"He wears moccasins." My voice pitched shrill. "Or he goes barefoot. Never boots. Never."

"That you know of." Deputy Santos laid the sketch down.

"You searched the meadow, right? You went through all his things. Did you find boots like this?" I jabbed my finger at the drawing. "Did you find any boots at all?"

She pinched her lips together between her teeth, and the creases in her forehead deepened. She said, "The arraignment's tomorrow. You know that, right?"

I nodded. Zeb had already promised he'd take me.

"So it's too late for me to do anything about it today."

I nodded again, even though it didn't really make sense to me how they could keep a man locked up like that when he was now so obviously innocent.

"Okay," I said. "But you'll take another look? Come at it from a different angle?"

I could tell by the sudden tightening corners of her mouth that she recognized her own words.

"I can't make any promises," she said. "But I'll do what I can."

I almost hugged her. Instead, I took the sketch out of her hand

and brought it close to my face, trying to remember if I'd gotten all the details right. "I have some ideas, too," I rambled. "About other people you might want to look into. Run a background check on at least."

"Sam, listen to me." She pushed the paper away from my face. "Things still might not work out the way you want them to. I'm going to look into the boot prints and the tracks not because you're asking me to, but because it's my job. Because they're an important part of this investigation. But they might just lead us straight back to Bear. You know that, right?"

"They won't."

"There's a lot you don't know about this case. A lot of things we haven't told you . . . haven't told anyone. We didn't just arrest your father because we're out to get him. We arrested him because that's where the evidence is leading us."

I rattled the sketch. "But now it will lead you in a different direction."

Deputy Santos closed her eyes for a few seconds. "I hope so," she said, opening them again and holding my gaze. "I really do hope so."

And for the first time in a long time, I felt optimistic, and it was like a thousand tiny finches singing together in the brush, like a burst of sunlight reflecting diamonds across the surface of my swimming hole. A few more days, that was all, then Bear would come home and we'd start putting the pieces together again. Things would get better.

"But I need you to promise me something, Sam," Deputy Santos said. "I need you to promise that you won't do anything like this again, okay? Don't go looking for evidence or witnesses or anything else like that. Don't be a Nancy Drew."

I wanted to tell her I hadn't gone looking, that the evidence had found me, that if maybe they'd done their jobs right in the first place, she wouldn't even need to be giving me this lecture. I kept quiet and let her finish.

"And if you do find something, accidentally . . . if you think it might be important, or it might have something to do with this case, don't touch it. Don't pick it up and put it in your pocket. Don't move it. Don't draw it. Don't breathe on it. Just leave it alone and call 911 immediately. Do you understand me?"

I nodded.

"I want you to promise that you'll let me and Detective Talbert do our jobs. Let us do the investigating. I don't want you getting hurt. Can you promise me you'll do that?"

I said what she wanted to hear. "I promise."

ollie

Standing in a carved-out hollow down three concrete steps, I reach for a brass doorknob.

The one who follows me led me away from the front door, around the corner, and into the alley where boxes get dropped off and garbage gets picked up. She shimmers behind me and whispers, *Go on. I'm right here with you.*

I turn the handle. The door swings open from the inside, and it's six wooden steps down into a dark basement. I hesitate in the doorway where light and shadow mix.

Listen.

Somewhere in the distance a dog barks.

Music drifts out a nearby window.

Wind hisses through the trees, or is that just me sighing?

I listen to her say, *Don't be afraid. I'll go first.*

She moves ahead and glides to the bottom of the stairs. She is pale blue edges with a dark gray center, and her hair is static electricity. She waves her hand, arcing sparks near her head and urging me to follow.

I glance behind me. The alley is empty.

I face forward. She flickers like a television screen. There is something down there, something I need to see, something that will help me understand, and now is the best, the only, time. I grab the railing and step down and down and down. When I reach the fourth step, the door behind me slams shut. I stop and blink hard and fast against the darkness, but my eyes do not adjust. I am blind.

If there is too much light, the Shimmering are invisible. The same if they are swallowed in darkness. They do not have enough thickness to make their own shadows, nor enough energy to create their own light. But even though I can't see her now, I know she's still here. Her heat burns my cheeks and the backs of my hands as she leads me through the dark.

Toe touches first. Then heel comes down. Keeping one hand on the railing, the other pushing through the empty space in front of me. Toe, then heel. Until I reach the bottom and the floor beneath my shoes is flat.

She focuses her energy on my left hand, and it's like I'm touching hot metal. I start to pull my hand close to my body, but that only makes it worse, so I push my hand out to the side and touch the wall. The heat moves forward and I follow, feeling my way until my fingers find a light switch. I flip the switch up, and yellow light melts the darkness.

There is another staircase opposite the one I came down, another door that must lead into the store above me. A metal desk sits beneath the bare lightbulb. The top of the desk is cluttered with accordion folders and spilled-out heaps of paper. A cobweb stretches from the bulb, attaches to a globe that sits motionless on the desk corner.

Several feet of empty space surround the desk, and there is a clear path between the staircase I came down and the one on the other side. But the rest of the basement is cluttered with unwanted things, and there is barely room to slip sideways between the overflowing shelves and boxes.

In this corner: a headless mannequin. Over here: a box full of plastic dolls staring at the ceiling, arms and legs all in a tangle. On that shelf: jars filled with body parts and tiny, wrinkled animals floating in a dense, yellow liquid.

Here is a black parasol. Here is a stuffed and tattered squirrel. Here, an open, empty coffin.

These are ugly and broken things, and I wonder why they are here at all, why no one has thrown them away.

The one who follows me floats close to the desk and points at a stack of papers. Beneath the dim bulb she glints like broken glass.

I walk past a rack of old coats; past a leaning pink-and-brown baby carriage; past a box of orphaned quilts and a barrel of prosthetic limbs; past a hanging brass birdcage, the gate open, the bird long gone; past a metal washtub filled with colorful doorknobs; past wooden doors that lead nowhere.

On the desk are pages and pages of lined paper filled with numbers and equations and scrawled words that make no sense. Some of the papers have pictures sketched in the margins, nightmarish pencil marks and blotted ink stains, hands and eyes, noses and lips, bits and parts of broken-up animals and people. I push the papers to the edge of the desk and underneath are photographs, some black-and-white, some color.

Footsteps cross the floor above my head. I stare up at the beams and hold my breath until they pass.

The one who follows me looks over my shoulder. The photographs seem unimportant, more for cataloging purposes than any kind of sentimental reason. There are close-ups and wide shots of at least thirty different sculptures, horrifying twists of metal and carved wood, animals that have been stuffed and morphed, given extra limbs and horns made of recycled scraps and tree branches, given strange new life.

Overhead, a bell jangles. Heavy footsteps cross quickly from one side of the store to the other, and then I hear muffled, rushing voices. I do not understand their words, only that they are upset, angry, scared.

Faster. Hurry.

They are right above me now, and my too-loud heart will give me away.

There is something here I'm supposed to find, but I don't know what. The one who follows me moves back to the alley door. She crackles and sparks and wants me to leave, but she brought me here in the first place and I won't go until I find whatever it is I'm supposed to be looking for. I open the desk drawers one by one. More papers and files and a shuffle of broken pencils and uncapped pens.

The bottom right drawer squeals.

The voices above me stop. Slow footsteps moving closer.

I glance into the drawer and shrink away from what's inside. A gun. With an ivory handle and a shiny metal barrel and spinning bullets. It looks like something a cowboy would have. I push the drawer closed and hurry toward the staircase that will lead me back outside.

The door behind me, the one that leads into the store, opens and more light spills into the dim basement. I duck between a refrigerator-sized box filled with rusted cookie tins and a tall, aluminum milk jug and curl myself into the small space, curl as small as I can.

"Hello? Is someone down there?" I recognize Travis's voice.

And then Mrs. Roth, "It's nothing. Probably a rat."

"The light's on."

"I was down there earlier. I must have forgotten to turn it off."

I hear them breathing at the top of the stairs. The light from inside the store is brighter than the bulb above the desk, and their shadows stretch overhead.

The one who follows me makes herself candle-flame small. She darts between my hiding place and the back door, anxious for me to leave.

Travis says, "I don't know why you let him keep so much junk down here."

"He uses this stuff in his sculptures. You know that."

"Ten years ago maybe."

Mrs. Roth sighs.

A dark shape unfolds from a pile of rags near my feet. I bite my lip, but then relax because it's just the gray tabby from before. He rubs against my legs, tail flicking. I push him away, but he keeps coming back.

Travis says, "I want to see it."

"He's not finished. You know how he feels about sharing a piece too early."

"You've seen it."

"You'll see it too, when he's ready."

The cat sits plop-down in front of me and starts washing his whiskers.

Travis says, "What if it's not done in time?"

"It will be."

"But what if it's not? What if he's taken on too much too soon?"

Mrs. Roth says, "The best thing we can do right now is give him space. Let him work."

"But maybe I can help somehow. Screw pieces together or paint or something."

"No, he needs to do this alone."

The gray tabby stares at me and meows. I flick my hand, and he springs away, darting toward the stairs.

Travis says, "Damn cat."

Mrs. Roth says, "Language," and then, "I know it's hard, but try not to worry. He'll finish in time. I'm watching him. I'll make sure . . ."

The boards creak and pop. They're moving away from the staircase. Travis says something too quiet for me to hear. The basement door slams shut.

I count to thirty, then go.

sam

A long chain running from Bear's handcuffed wrists to his shackled ankles made it so that even if he tried, he wouldn't be able to stand up straight. He kept his eyes on the floor, hadn't looked up once since the bailiff brought him into the courtroom. They'd shaved off his beard and trimmed his hair and put him in a bright orange jumpsuit that didn't fit. The sleeve cuffs fell only a few inches past his elbows, and the pant legs rode so high I thought at first he'd rolled them up on purpose. There was a fresh bruise, swollen and red, on his right cheek just below his eye. I tried not to think about how he got it.

When they brought him through the side door into the court-room, I drew back at the sight of him. Zeb leaned in close and whispered, "Mr. Clemens said the beard made him look guilty." But I thought this was worse. His eyes were set too deep in his head, his mouth stretched too thin, his angles too sharp, cutting the air like so many knives. This man in front of me was capable of doing horrible, terrible, awful things. Things my father, a softer, kinder man, would never, ever do. Not that it even mattered. Beard or no beard, I had a feeling public opinion would stay the same.

"How does the defendant plead?" Judge Latham asked the question like a yawn.

At the table in front of us on the other side of the railing, Mr. Clemens, my father's attorney, shuffled through a stack of papers.

"Not guilty," he finally said, and I worried that he'd needed his notes to remind him.

If my grandparents were here, they would have hired someone better, someone without so many cases, someone who was paid to give a damn. But neither our social worker, nor Deputy Santos, nor anyone else who'd tried had been able to reach them yet. They'd keep trying, but it would be another two days before the ship reached port and then probably another whole day after that before my grandparents arrived in Terrebonne. Until then we'd just have to do the best we could with what we had, and that was Mr. Clemens, Deschutes County's public defender.

I was sitting close enough to see yellow sweat stains on Mr. Clemens's starched collar and a purple birthmark peeking out from his hairline. He smelled like fried chicken and raw onions. He checked his watch every few seconds, clearing his throat each time.

Across the aisle from Mr. Clemens, the prosecuting attorney, a thin man with grease-black hair and a cut-marble jaw, rose to address the judge. "The State requests that the defendant be held without bail."

"That seems a little extreme, Your Honor," Mr. Clemens responded, shuffling through his papers again, barely looking at the judge or Bear or anyone else, like he didn't think we were worth his time and energy. "Hardly necessary considering my client has no history of violent criminal behavior. And though his living conditions are a little unconventional, he's been residing in the same place for the past eight years. His wife recently passed away, Your Honor, and he has custody of his two young daughters, one of whom is here today."

He flicked his hand toward me. I straightened my shoulders and lifted my head a little higher, ignoring the rustling, cruel whispers of all the people around me, people who had come here today to gawk and gossip. Some I recognized, some I didn't. The redheaded kid who worked with Travis at Patti's; a few people who bought honey from Bear every year; the man who ran the farm supply store where we sometimes bought seeds and fertilizer; a checkout clerk from Potter's Grocery Store. Every bench full, standing room only. There were reporters in the back jotting notes, and two benches behind me to the left was Pastor Mike. I'd seen him come in, and he'd seen me, and I could still feel his eyes on me even now, though I didn't dare turn around. Any one of these people was just as likely a suspect as Bear. Any one of them could have been standing where he was standing now. I stared at his lowered face and didn't look away, didn't duck my head, didn't show any shame. I wanted them all to know that I believed he was innocent. I wanted them to see my faith.

"My client is not a flight risk," Mr. Clemens continued. "His passport's expired. Given his limited and sporadic income, the defense requests bail be set at ten thousand."

Judge Latham's caterpillar eyebrows shot up. He leaned forward on his elbows and returned his attention to the prosecution's table, nodding at that attorney to go ahead.

"Your Honor." The prosecutor adjusted his tie and took a single step out from behind the table, as if what he was about to say was going to take up too much space and he needed to get out of its way. "Considering the violent nature of the crime with which the defendant has been accused, as well as his prior arrest and the fact that he has no ties to this community, the State believes holding Mr. McAlister without bail is in everyone's best interest."

And when he said "everyone," he turned and looked at me.

A drop of sweat ran down my forehead. The ankle-length wool skirt Franny had forced me to wear—"You don't want that old judge thinking your daddy doesn't know how to raise his babies up right, now do you?"—itched something awful, but I kept my hands folded in my lap and sat very still. Beside me, Zeb shifted on the hard bench. He squeezed his straw hat between both hands, squashing it down so small I didn't think he'd ever get it to fit quite right again.

The prosecuting attorney said, "A young woman was killed, Your Honor. Brutally murdered. Bludgeoned again and again by an animal who has no regard for the sanctity of human life. And when he was finished with her, he threw her out like so much garbage, dropped her in a river to be picked apart by trout and crayfish."

A woman sobbed loudly, but just once. An ugly, harsh sound that echoed through the open rafters and bounced off the painted-shut windows. Someone began to murmur softly, hushing her to silence. I craned my neck, trying to see who was voicing my grief, all the things I kept swallowing down, swallowing and swallowing until my mouth was dry and my throat on fire. She was sitting in the first row behind the prosecutor's table. Collapsed forward, her head was buried so deep in her hands I couldn't see her face. A balding, heavyset man sat beside her with one arm placed firmly around her shoulders, as if he thought his arm would be enough to hold her together. He fixed his gaze pointedly on Bear. His etched-deep frown showed more disgust than anger, the lines in his face like uneven ruts. Perspiration beaded his temples.

The prosecuting attorney finished by saying, "This is not the kind of man you can trust to stick around for his trial, Your Honor."

How would you know? I wanted to shout. *How would any of you know what kind of man my father is?* And I wanted to tell them about how every Christmas Eve, even though he got carsick and hated the city, he rode the bus from Bend all the way home to us in Eugene to sing carols and make sugar cookies and fall asleep under the tree waiting for Santa. How he brought us things from the meadow as presents: dried wildflowers pressed flat between the pages of books, a thunderstone cracked open and polished, a beaver figurine he'd carved from a small oak branch, a brilliant sapphire feather from a Steller's jay, a jar of his sweetest honey. And I wanted to tell them about the summer we found the fawn with the broken leg, and how it was bleating and bleating, but its mother never came, and how Bear carried it three miles back to the meadow and splinted its leg and kept it fed by dipping a rag in milk and letting it suck, and how a few months after that when it was old enough and strong enough and healed, the fawn had walked into the woods and disappeared. I wanted to tell them that my father had called that day to tell my mother and me and Ollie how much he loved us. I wanted to tell them he cried.

The judge shuffled through a stack of papers on the bench in front of him and scratched his cheek. Finally, he cleared his throat and said, "I'm setting bail at five hundred thousand dollars."

His gavel came down.

Zeb flinched.

Bear closed his eyes.

I dug my fingernails into my arm and sat frozen, staring straight at him until the courtroom cleared.

Cameras flashed. Reporters shouted my name. Zeb wrapped his arm around me and guided me through the crush of strangers crowding the courthouse steps. He held his hat in front of my face.

"Leave the girl alone," he said. "Go on. Git! You goddamn vultures!"

"Samantha! Samantha!"

"What do you think about your father's arrest?"

"How do you feel about the bail the judge set?"

"Samantha!"

"Has he ever been violent with you or your sister?"

"Has he ever hit you?"

"That's enough." Zeb pushed their microphones away, but he couldn't push away their questions.

"Samantha, do you think he's guilty?"

"There's a rumor going around that you and your sister found the body first. What did she look like? Did you see her face?"

"Samantha! Samantha! How are you handling all of this?"

"Will you testify?"

"What about your sister?"

"Samantha!"

"What's it like knowing your father's a murderer?"

I was glad Ollie wasn't here. She'd wanted to come, had even climbed into the front seat of the truck next to me, but Franny had pulled her out again and said this wasn't any kind of circus she needed to be a part of and it'd be better if she stayed at the farm and helped make blueberry pies. I was starting to think maybe I should have stayed behind, too.

The reporters broke apart, moving away from us and squawking someone else's name.

"Sheriff Harper! Sheriff Harper!"

I could breathe again.

Zeb wanted to keep going, hurry me along as fast as he could back to the truck before the reporters had a chance to come after us again, but I ducked away from him and stopped at the bottom of the stairs, under the shade of a reaching dogwood.

A tall, broad-shouldered man with a thick head of graying hair stood at the top of the courthouse steps. He held up his hands, silencing the reporters. He had a politician's smile and a fat gold ring on his pinkie finger.

"Sam." Zeb reached for my elbow. "Let's go."

"No. Wait," I said.

Deputy Santos must have told Sheriff Harper about the boot print and the tire tracks by now. Certainly he would make some kind of appeal for more information, more tips, or a brief statement about how they were still looking at the evidence, pursuing leads, that they hadn't stopped searching, wouldn't stop searching until they knew exactly what had happened to Taylor Bellweather that night and why. I wanted to stay and hear exactly what he had to say.

Zeb let out a frustrated sigh, but let me be. He fixed his hat on his head and turned his attention to the sheriff.

"I want to first express my condolences to the Bellweather family, and thank them for their continued cooperation during this investigation. When something as terrible as this happens to a community, to a family, it's hard to find the right words, any words really." He choked up here. His jaw trembled, and he blinked hard. And I couldn't stop myself from thinking that he was putting on a mighty good show.

"The Deschutes County Sheriff's Department is committed to doing everything we can to ensure justice for Taylor Bellweather and her family. We're working day and night on this investigation. We've made it our top priority. To that end, we're still asking anyone who believes they might have information about this case to please come forward."

For a second, hope.

Then a reporter shouted, "Does that mean you're looking into other suspects?"

"Not at this time."

I took a step back, bumping into the dogwood trunk. Zeb's hand found my elbow, steadied me.

Sheriff Harper said, "We are confident we have arrested the man who committed this heinous act."

"Do you have enough evidence for a conviction?"

"I cannot comment on the details of our case at this time." And then he winked. Or maybe there was just a bit of dust caught in his eye.

Zeb squeezed my arm. "You sure you want to be hearing all of this?"

I nodded. To prove them wrong, I needed to hear everything.

I needed to know every detail.

M y fingers shook, but I managed to press all the right numbers, and after three rings, someone on the other end picked up and said, "*Register-Guard,* how can I direct your call?"

Calling the newspaper Taylor Bellweather had worked for seemed the best place to start, especially after the papers reported she was in Terrebonne on assignment. They didn't say who or what exactly she was here for—her editor was quoted saying, "No comment"—only that she was here for a story. But it felt like something important to me. Something worth following up on.

I drummed the side of the metal phone booth and stared at the keypad and the buttons I'd just pushed, trying to decide what to say, if I should even say anything at all or just hang up and walk away because maybe this would lead me nowhere except straight into trouble.

"Hello . . . ?" the woman on the other end said and then again, louder, "Hello?"

I'd found the number in the phone book easily enough and had borrowed enough change from Zeb's cup holder to pay for at least an hour, though I didn't think it would take that long. After the hearing, Zeb said he needed to stop by the hardware store for screws. I was going to wait for him in the parking lot, but then I saw the phone booth reflecting in the side mirror and even though it was just a coincidence, it felt like a little something more, too. Like maybe everything had worked out in a certain order just to bring me to this point, this phone call.

"Is anyone there? Hello?" The woman was impatient with my silence. "Okay, I'm going to hang up now."

There was only one way to do this: hold my breath and dive in.

I curled my body around the phone and brought the receiver close to my mouth. "Joe Mancetti, please."

"And who may I say is calling?" She was shouting now, because I had whispered and she must have thought we had a bad connection.

I brushed sweat from my eyes. I had to get this right. I had to sound like I did this kind of thing every day, like I was official. I cleared my throat.

"This is Deputy Maribel Santos," I said, pitching my voice like hers. "I'm calling about the Bellweather case."

On the other end, there was a hesitation, a catch in the secretary's breath, and then she said, quiet now, no longer shouting, "One moment, please."

A click, and then silence. No muffled voices in the background, no keyboards clacking or phones ringing, no cheesy elevator music. Just the sound of my own shallow breathing echoed back through the receiver.

I wiped my face against my shirtsleeve. The sun was straight above me and scorching. I should be sitting in the shade beside Crooked River, dangling my feet in the water. I should be teaching Ollie how to swim. I should be and should be and should be. Doing anything but this.

A man's voice interrupted the silence, "Deputy Santos?"

"Mr. Mancetti," I said. "Thanks for taking my call."

"Didn't think I'd hear from you folks again after I spoke with Detective Talbert last week."

My fingers curled around the phone cord. Of course someone had already spoken with him. Of course they had. He was probably the first person Detective Talbert called after Taylor Bellweather's parents. And he'd probably already said everything he knew, everything important anyway.

I let the silence stretch too long.

"Deputy? Did I lose you?"

"No, I . . . uh . . . I . . ." *Get it together, Sam.*

I cleared my throat again and let go of the phone cord I'd twisted too tightly around my fingers. It fell away, swinging in the empty space in front of me.

"I'm still here," I said.

"Well, good. We've been having a little trouble with the phones this past week, which reminds me . . ." There was a rustling, his hand covering the receiver, and then a muffled shout, "Amanda! Call the phone company and make an appointment for them to come check the lines. This is getting ridiculous." Then his voice was loud again, slamming into my ear. "So, Deputy. What can I do for you today?"

"Um . . . well, Detective Talbert and I were going over his notes again recently and we just had a few more questions for you. Follow-up, that kind of thing."

"Right, right. Anything I can do to help. Anything at all. Taylor was an important part of our family, even though she hadn't been with us for very long. Such promise, that girl." His voice got softer, like he'd pulled the phone away from his mouth. He blew his nose.

I said, "I'm sorry for your loss," and the words tasted like pennies.

"Thank you." The phone up close to his mouth again.

I pressed this morning's newspaper, folded to the front page, against the side of the booth. Taylor Bellweather stared back at me. Not blinking. Blind, deaf, mute. Dead.

"When you spoke to the detective the other day," I said, trying not to choke, trying not to stammer, "you said Taylor was in Terrebonne to interview . . ." I rustled the corners of the newspaper and mumbled, "Let's see, I wrote it down here somewhere."

For a second, I felt bad about making Deputy Santos seem incompetent. Because she wasn't. She was one of the best. But then I thought of Bear still sitting in jail for a murder he didn't commit and I didn't care so much after that.

"We sent her out there to do a piece on Central Oregon's most famous recluse," Joe Mancetti said, and it sounded like he might be smiling, like he thought there was something funny about the whole thing. A small-town celebrity. Like the irony of it had only just struck him.

"Right. Of course." I chewed on the inside of my cheek, trying to think of how to ask him for a name without making it obvious that I had no idea what he was talking about.

"Special assignment," Joe Mancetti said. "Her first time handling a front-page story." There was a moment stretched long by heat and silence, then he continued, "I guess she still got on the front page, huh? Just wish it could've been for something good. Really . . . anything but this."

I made a noncommittal sound and stared at Taylor Bellweather's picture. I'd looked at it so often in the past few days that even with my eyes closed, I could still describe exactly how she was in the photo. Pixie haircut, arched eyebrows, impish stare, turned-up nose, thin lips, sturdy chin, long neck, young, alive—beautiful because of it. And I didn't think it was fair. That I could remember so much of her, a stranger, and yet whenever I tried to imagine Mom, a person I loved so much, all I could come up with was a grayed-out smudge.

"Was that all you needed, Deputy?" Joe Mancetti's voice drew me back to the present, and what I was supposed to be doing, why I'd made this call in the first place.

I folded the newspaper and shoved it into my skirt pocket. "Did you talk to her the day she died?"

It seemed like an innocent-enough question to me, a typical thing to ask in a case like this, but the silence stretched too long and when Joe Mancetti finally answered, his tone was no longer casual and warm; instead, his words were clipped and professional and coated in ice. "Like I told Detective Talbert the other day, she called me around six thirty that night."

"And after that?" I asked.

"Nothing," he said. "I didn't hear from her again."

"Did you try calling her?" And even though I tried, I couldn't keep the edge from my words, the anger that she had been sent out here alone and no one had bothered to check up on her, and that maybe if someone had, she'd still be very much alive.

"Yes. Of course I did," Joe Mancetti said. "She had an interview scheduled for seven and she was supposed to call me after, but she didn't. So I called her motel room. Several times. I even called the manager, had him go and knock on the door. You know, I already went over all of this with the other detective."

This was when I should have hung up the phone. I could hear the suspicion in his voice, how he was withdrawing from me, starting to think maybe I wasn't who I said I was, and yet I kept going because

I needed answers. Not just for myself anymore, and not just for Bear, either. But for Taylor Bellweather. For her dad and mom and everyone else who loved her. They deserved to know who. They deserved to know why.

"What time was that again?" I asked, not trying so hard to sound like Deputy Santos now.

"What? When did I call? Why does it matter? She was already—"

"No," I interrupted. "When was her interview? What day? What time? Where was she meeting him?" And it all came out strung together in one long question.

Joe Mancetti took a deep breath and then, slowly, "Who is this?"

I didn't answer.

He said, "Tell me who this is. Now."

I reached to disconnect the call. My fingers hovered over the lever, but I didn't push down.

"I know you're not Deputy Santos. I know that. Hello? Are you a reporter? You know it's a felony to impersonate a police officer, right? You know that, don't you? Hello? Hello. I can hear you breathing."

"Who was she writing the story on, Mr. Mancetti? Was it Frank McAlister? Is that who she was going to interview?"

"Frank who?" And then, "Goddamn it! Son of a— Who the hell do you think you are, calling here and asking questions you have no business asking? I can find out who you are, you know that, right? And when I do, I'm taking your name straight to the police and they'll throw your ass in jail so fast—"

I slammed the phone down and took a step back. My hands, my chest, my whole body shook. He hadn't recognized my father's name. Which meant Taylor Bellweather hadn't come to Terrebonne to interview Bear. Which meant the person she had come to interview, the only other person I knew of who lived in Terrebonne and fit the description of Central Oregon's famous recluse, was Billy Roth.

The phone rang, and I hopped back, startled by its shrill, knowing jangle, by the way it kept ringing and ringing and ringing, as if

Joe Mancetti could see me standing here and would wait all day if he had to for me to pick up the goddamn phone. I lifted the phone from its cradle, then slammed it down again. The ringing stopped.

"Shit," I said. My heart was beating too fast. My hands were numb.

The phone rang again. This time I lifted the receiver just enough to end the call, but instead of returning it to the cradle, I let it dangle by its cord, disconnected. If Joe Mancetti tried to call a third time, all he'd get was a busy signal.

"Sam?" someone called out.

I turned. Travis was coming toward me from the direction of the Attic, a few blocks down from the hardware store. He had both hands stuffed into the pockets of his jeans. His red sneakers scuffed the sidewalk.

When he got closer, he whistled and said, "Looking fancy. Don't tell me you dressed up and came all this way just to see me?"

I blushed and plucked at my skirt, feeling stupid for wearing it, for letting Franny convince me it was a good idea. I gestured toward the hardware store and Zeb's truck out front. "We were on our way back from Bend, and Zeb stopped to pick up a few things."

"Right," Travis said. "The hearing. How'd it go?"

"You weren't there?"

He shook his head. "Mom went. And she hates closing the store in the middle of the day, so someone had to stay and run the register."

I remembered seeing Mrs. Roth standing alone at the back of the courtroom near the doors, remembered how I thought she was looking at me so I waved, but she hadn't waved back.

"You didn't miss anything," I said. "Trial hasn't even started yet, but they've already made up their minds."

He looked over my shoulder into the phone booth, nodded at the receiver still dangling in midair. "Am I interrupting?"

"No, I was just . . ." I hung up the phone, then walked quickly away from the booth, crossed the street to the hardware store.

Travis followed me. "Hey, you're not mad at me about yesterday, are you? At the diner? I really did have to get back to work. It wasn't just a lame excuse to bolt on you or anything."

"Okay."

"And I wanted to come over last night," he continued. "I tried. But Mom had me working on some mailers for Dad's show and by the time I was done, it was almost midnight."

When we reached Zeb's truck, I leaned against the tailgate and crossed my arms over my chest.

"So." Travis stood in front of me, blocking the sun. "You going to tell me what you found or what?"

"What I found?"

"Yeah," he said. "You were going to show me something yesterday. Said it would prove Bear's innocence."

"Oh, right, that." I shrugged. "It was nothing."

Travis tilted his head to one side. "You sure?"

So maybe my conversation with Joe Mancetti changed everything, and maybe it changed nothing at all. The truth was, I didn't know much more now than I did before the phone call. Taylor Bellweather had come to Terrebonne to interview Billy Roth. So what? Obviously the sheriff's department was aware of that when they arrested Bear, and it hadn't made any bit of difference to them. Over and over Deputy Santos had reminded me that they had to follow wherever the evidence led, and the evidence kept leading them back to Bear.

The evidence. I needed to see the case file.

I pushed away from the truck. "Is your bike at the store?"

Travis hesitated, then said, "Yeah. Why?"

"I need your help with something."

"Okay . . ."

"And I need you to promise me you'll keep your mouth shut about it."

"What is it?"

"Promise me first."

He rubbed the back of his neck. "Mom's expecting me back at the store in an hour. She wants me on the register again tonight."

167

"It's about Taylor Bellweather."

"Sam—"

"No, listen to me. I know you think I'm crazy . . ."

"I don't think you're crazy."

" . . . but Bear didn't kill her. I know he didn't."

"I think you should just leave it alone." He kicked at a small rock. It bounced under Zeb's truck and disappeared.

I said, "I can't."

"Why not?"

"He's my father, Travis."

"Not a very good one."

"What's that supposed to mean?"

Travis folded his arms and shrugged.

"You don't know Bear the way I do," I said. "No one does. If they did, they wouldn't have arrested him in the first place."

"Maybe you've got it backward. Maybe you don't know him as well as you think you do. You only see him, what, once a year?"

"Twice," I said. "He comes home for Christmas."

Travis shrugged again. "How much can you really know about a person you spend so little time with?"

"Are you going to help me or not?" I asked.

He sighed and nodded. "But only because I don't want to wake up tomorrow morning and hear about how you were sneaking around some abandoned warehouse and fell off a staircase and busted up your leg and then had to lie there by yourself for hours until the night-shift security guard found you."

"We're not going to an abandoned warehouse."

"You get my point."

"It's a stupid point."

He laughed.

I pulled the folded-up newspaper from my skirt pocket and went around to the passenger side of the truck. With a ballpoint pen I found in the glove box, and using the dashboard as a flat surface, I wrote a note for Zeb in the empty margins, then tucked the paper under the windshield wipers where it was impossible to miss.

"Ready?"

Travis glanced down at my skirt. "Is that what you're wearing?"

"Unless you brought me a change of clothes, then yes, this is what I'm wearing." I flounced past him, walking in the direction of the Attic.

Travis caught up with me quickly. "So," he said. "Where are we going?"

ollie

Papa Zeb returns to the house alone. He tosses a crumpled newspaper into the trash and goes upstairs. When I am sure he's not coming back down, I take the paper out of the trash and spread it flat on the counter.

> *Went to the movies with Travis. Don't wait. I'll get*
> *a ride from him. Be back before dinner.*

Lies written out in my sister's slanted hand.

She hates going to the movies, says the speakers are always too loud, the picture too close, the smell of stale popcorn too disgusting. The last movie she went to was three years ago, when Mom made her come—"It's your sister's birthday. Do it for her." She brought earplugs and sat in the back row and complained the whole ride home. She might be with Travis, but I know for a fact she's not at the movies.

I ball up the note and throw it back in the trash.

Nana Fran comes into the kitchen and sees me scowling at the table and mistakes my anger for boredom. She says, "There's a deck of cards in the closet under the stairs. Go grab it and I'll teach you how to play rummy."

There are more than just cards in the closet under the stairs. There are blocks and dominos and plastic tubs filled with broken crayons. There are stacks of board games teetering together on narrow shelves. Chess and checkers and Monopoly and Life.

To get the cards, I have to stand on tiptoe, and when I pull them down, other things come too. Boxes and dice and boards and cards and plastic army men collapse around me.

"Everything okay in there?" Nana Fran shouts.

I bend and start picking up the pieces.

She pokes her head through the kitchen door and, when she sees the mess, comes over to help.

"I keep meaning to clean this old closet out," she says, picking up a box that has been torn in many places and taped back together.

I recognize the letters on the side and take the game from her.

She laughs a little. "A girl stayed with us once who claimed she could channel the spirits of all the dead presidents. Papa Zeb brought this home for her one day, and I don't think a minute went by that she wasn't doing some kind of hocus-pocus."

I open the box and take out the board, lay it on the floor. The letters are worn and scuffed, but they are clear enough. The wooden planchette slides smoothly, my fingers pushing it from one corner of the board to the other.

The one who follows me laughs, and I know she thinks it's just a stupid kids' game, but maybe there's something more to it.

I think, *Are you mad at me for what I did?*

The planchette doesn't move.

I think again, *Are you mad?,* and this time look straight at her.

She stops laughing, crouches down beside me, and puts her hand over mine. The planchette shivers. She moves the planchette under our hands to the word *NO* at the top of the board.

I think, *Do you still love me?*

Her hand moves my hand again, over the *YES*. She whispers, *For always.*

Franny says, "It's yours if you want it."

I do.

sam

Travis stopped the bike in front of Deputy Santos's driveway, but he kept the engine running. He looked over his shoulder and shouted, "What are we doing here?"

Her driveway was empty, and the curtains in the front window were drawn. The garage door opened at the house across the street, and a black Suburban backed out. A few houses down, a woman in a blue bathrobe watered her roses. She lifted her hand, shielding her eyes, and looked in our direction.

I leaned close to Travis, slipped my arms around his waist again, and shouted, "Park down the street. Behind those bushes."

At the very end of the cul-de-sac, a yellow post marked the start of a narrow dirt path that cut behind the houses. There was a culvert back there, too, the perfect cover. Travis parked his bike up next to a row of overgrown laurels.

I climbed off the seat and straightened my wrinkled skirt, then removed the helmet he'd let me borrow and, handing it back to him, said, "Thanks."

He hung the helmet from the handlebar, then got off the bike and pulled on the collar of his T-shirt, shaking out the places where it had gone damp and flat, where I'd pressed up against him, clinging tight the whole way here. It was my first time on a dirt bike, on any kind of motorcycle actually, and at every turn and bend in the road, I'd clung to him, certain we were mere milliseconds from a very fast and spiraling, painful death.

"So," he said. "You going to fill me in now or what?"

I stretched my arms above my head, clenching and unclenching my fingers, trying to work out the numbing, tingling sensations, the feeling that my soul, if there even was such a thing, was peeling away from my body, already half gone.

"We're breaking into Deputy Santos's house," I said, and stepped around the yellow post toward the culvert.

"Wait, what?" Travis hurried after me.

The path went about a hundred yards before dead-ending against a waist-high chain-link fence. On the other side was a narrow dirt ledge that dropped off into the culvert, an open half-pipe, about fifteen feet wide and eight feet deep. Beyond the culvert was another chain-link fence and beyond that, a vast stretch of undeveloped land. Scrub mostly, dirt and loose gravel, a few scraggly trees that were barely hanging on.

I cut left and, sticking to the path that ran between the chain link on one side and cedar plank fencing on the other, followed the culvert toward Deputy Santos's house. The weeds were all trampled down, and there were cigarette butts scattered everywhere. Behind me, Travis kicked an empty beer can and it clanked against the chain link.

I glared at him over my shoulder.

He shrugged and mouthed, *Sorry.*

I counted the houses as we passed behind them and when I reached eight, I stopped and stood on tiptoe to peek over the fence.

"This is it," I whispered. "Give me a boost."

"No." Travis crossed his arms over his chest and shook his head. "No way."

"You said you'd help."

"Not this. I'm not going to help you break into a police officer's house!"

"Fine," I said. "You can wait with the bike."

I inched onto the support beam, a two-by-four that ran parallel to the ground along the back of the fence boards, reached up, and grabbed the top of the fence. It would have been easier if I'd been wearing jeans, but even with the skirt knotting around my legs and catching on splinters, I somehow managed to heave myself up and over the top into the yard below.

Travis cursed. Then he grabbed the top of the planks and swung himself over into the dead grass beside me. Wiping his hands on his pants, he said, "Do you have any idea how much trouble we could get in for this?"

I ignored him and jogged to the patio. Flowerpots lined the brick edge, but all the plants were brown and wilted. I tried the sliding glass door. Locked, but the curtains were open, and I could see into her empty living room. The television was off. A dirty plate and fork had been left on one of the couch cushions, three coffee cups sat on the end table, and there was a pile of laundry heaped in the middle of the floor, like she'd been about to fold it, but something had distracted her.

Footsteps crunched in the dry grass behind me and Travis whispered, "It's locked? Let's take it as a sign and just go."

Along the back wall of the house there were three windows. One was too high and narrow to even consider, the other two were closer to ground level and big enough for me to slip through if I went in sideways.

To reach the bigger windows, I had to squeeze behind a row of tall hedges and through a sticky cobweb mess. A broken branch raked across my calf. The first window was shut and wouldn't budge. The second was cracked open, just barely. I popped out the screen, pressed my fingertips against the plastic edge of the window, and wiggled the crack wider, enough to slip my fingers around the frame and push the window all the way open.

Travis shoved through the bushes after me. He said, "Sam! This is a really shitty idea." He swatted at a branch blocking his way. "They can put you in jail for this, you know? Breaking and entering. It's a felony."

I lifted my skirt up around my knees and swung my legs over the ledge.

"What if she has an alarm?"

I froze half crouched on the beige carpet in Deputy Santos's bedroom, listening, ready to spring back outside and run like hell if any alarm went off. In the kitchen, the refrigerator clicked and thrummed. Somewhere outside a car horn honked once. No other sounds. No alarm. No panicked beeping. No one was coming, and we were alone.

I stuck my head out the open window and waved at Travis to come inside. He shook his head.

"You've already come this far," I said.

He glared at me, glared up at the sky.

"Come on, I need you to keep a lookout."

"Sam?"

"What?"

"What the hell are we doing here?"

"I need to know what they have on Bear," I said. "I need to know why they think he's guilty."

I ducked inside again.

Travis climbed into the room after me but hesitated at the door.

"Hurry," I said.

We crept through the living room and into the kitchen. The table was still strewn with papers and files, even more than I remembered from a few days ago. There was too much to go through all of it right now. I'd need several hours, maybe even a whole day. I ran my fingers over the top layer of papers, my eyes blurring the letters and numbers, overwhelmed by the staggering amount of information here, the impossibility of finding the answers I needed.

Travis whistled softly through his teeth. "You think there's something important in all that mess?"

I nodded and picked up one of the reports. A quick glance told me it was a statement from the manager of the Meadowlark confirming Taylor Bellweather had rented a room for four nights and paid with a credit card. He said he might have seen a man coming out of her room late Sunday night, but he couldn't be sure, he hadn't really been paying attention. I tossed the statement aside.

Travis reached for a slip of paper. He held it close to his face and then put it down again where he'd found it. "What exactly are we looking for?"

"*I* am looking for whatever they haven't told the public yet," I said. "What has them so convinced it was Bear. *You* are looking out the front window. So you can tell me if anyone's coming."

Travis looked over at the entryway and the long, slim window set in the wall parallel to the front door. Then he looked back at the piles of paper on the table. "You sure? This is a lot to go through by yourself."

I nodded.

He went to stand in the shadows, where he could see out onto the street, but someone looking in would only see reflections. "I don't get it, Sam. Why now? Why like this?"

"Because I need to know what happened."

"But why not just ask Deputy Santos?"

"She won't tell me."

"So why not just wait for the trial?"

"By then it'll be too late. A judge will award custody to my grandparents, Ollie and I'll be living in a Boston retirement community or someplace even worse, and no one will ever know the truth. They think Bear did this," I said. "And they've stopped looking for any other suspects. If I don't do something, they'll just build a case around Bear being guilty whether it's true or not. They'll twist the facts to make them fit."

I sifted quickly through a stack of phone records and credit card receipts.

"What makes you so sure?" Travis asked.

I looked up from the statement I'd been reading, a small paragraph from a gas station attendant confirming that two days before Taylor Bellweather's body was found she had filled up her Toyota Corolla, a white four-door like the one they pulled from Blue Heron Pond.

"That Bear's innocent?" I said.

He nodded.

I shrugged. "I just know."

Travis was quiet for a second and then said, "Sometimes the people we love most are the people we know least."

"You're supposed to be watching the street."

He turned his face to the window. "Hurry up," he said and settled into mumbling about how stupid this was and how much trouble we'd be in if anyone found us here, how his mom was probably calling the sheriff right now to file a missing person's report and if they didn't catch us here first, when he finally did get back to the store he'd be grounded for the rest of the goddamn summer and what was I thinking dragging him into this shit, if we got busted for this, there went his clean record and any chance for a college scholarship and then what would he do, run the cash register at his parents' store for the rest of his life, never making more than minimum wage? This was a bad idea, a really bad idea.

I sifted through the paperwork faster, skimming over insignificant notes and shorthand, chicken scratches only Deputy Santos understood. Whenever I saw my father's name, I slowed down and read a little more carefully, but though everything seemed important, none of it was exactly what I was looking for, nothing clearly pointed to Bear as the suspect.

I found the autopsy report and scanned to the bottom where the medical examiner had written in the cause and manner of death. Blunt force trauma to the head, homicide. Deputy Santos had also highlighted other sections of the report noting Taylor Bellweather had multiple contusions around the throat and chest as well as defensive wounds on her hands and arms. Fingernail samples had been taken, but here in the margin, Deputy Santos had scratched a note that any physical evidence had probably been destroyed, washed clean in the river. I set the report down and kept looking.

There were notes scrawled on loose sheets of paper, things like *Victim's purse is still unaccounted for, as well as several pieces of jewelry,* and *Suspect's alibi unconfirmed,* and *Victim's clothes torn, but no sign of sexual assault.* There were statements from both of Taylor's parents, saying they had spoken to her two days prior to her death and had no reason to fear for her safety. There was my statement, too, the things I'd told Deputy Santos the day Bear was arrested, typed and printed out in damning black ink. Reading over it now, my own words shouting back at me, I realized how bad this was for Bear, how it seemed like even his own daughter believed him guilty. Maybe I did for a brief moment in time, barely a blink, but not anymore. I pushed the papers aside.

There had to be something else more substantial than pages and pages of meaningless words, a connection between Bear and Taylor Bellweather, a chain, a rope, a thread, even a wisp, something linking them together that would be impossible to ignore.

I came across Joe Mancetti's statement, the one he'd given to Detective Talbert over the phone. Here, in black and white and plain text, Mancetti told Detective Talbert that Taylor Bellweather had been in Terrebonne to interview Billy Roth about his upcoming show. It was supposed to be shocking, raw, unlike anything he'd ever done before. It was supposed to put him back on top.

"Billy and I go way back," Joe Mancetti had told Detective Talbert. "We were college roommates. I still help him out when I can. Thought a feature article might generate the buzz he needed to get him moving in the right direction again. After the accident, losing Delilah the way they did . . . well, he's just been down for so long, it's good to finally see him fighting his way back."

He'd sent Taylor because Mrs. Roth had requested a new reporter, someone who didn't know much about Billy's past and didn't have a connection with the sculptures he used to make. Someone who might bring a fresh perspective. Joe Mancetti thought it was a good story for his newest reporter to cut her teeth on. The interview was scheduled for Monday evening, and Joe had expected Taylor to call after it was over, so they could talk about what she'd managed to get and if it would be enough for the front page, or if she needed to keep digging, take a few more pictures, ask a few more questions. He was at the office until midnight, but she never called. And when he tried her motel room, no one answered. He said Mrs. Roth had called the next morning to complain about Taylor standing them up for the interview. They waited and waited for hours, but she never came. There was a sticky note attached to the last page of Joe Mancetti's statement with Billy Roth's name written and then crossed out with black ink.

I glanced over my shoulder at Travis. He twirled an unlit cigarette in his fingers, his gaze fixed out the window. The glass danced reflections, shifting, churning eddies of light, across his face. He looked up, caught me watching him, then smiled and said, "What?"

I shook my head and went back to digging through the paperwork.

"Find anything good yet?"

"Maybe," I said. "How's the street looking?"

"Clear," he said. "So far. But I got a bad feeling—"

"Another few minutes. Okay?"

Several seconds passed and then Travis said, "You've got ten, tops. Then we're going."

I flipped quickly through a stack of photographs. Scene photos mostly, of the shoreline where they found Taylor Bellweather's body, of the park and picnic tables nearby. There was a close-up of her body in the water, her face turned up toward the sun, her eyes all dark pupil and no light. I slipped that photograph behind the rest and set the whole pile to one side.

Inside an unlabeled folder I found what looked to be an interview between Detective Talbert and Pastor Mike. Many of the pages were out of order and some were even missing, but after I'd sorted and shuffled, enough of the interview remained to understand this was it, this was why they were so keen on Bear. Here, typed and printed on thick, white paper, was the cornerstone to the case they were building. Set this up next to the rest of it—the jacket, the scratches, the key, the timing—and, if I hadn't seen those boot prints, I might have been convinced too.

DETECTIVE RANDY TALBERT: Now what time would you say all this happened?

MIKE FRESHOUR: Around a quarter to five. I didn't check the time exactly, but Rosalee called me at four thirty and it takes me about fifteen minutes to get to the Jack Knife from my house.

RT: And when did you first see Mr. McAlister?

MF: Well, I had to let my eyes adjust to how dim they keep that place, but I saw him a few seconds after I came through the door. He was at the bar, which surprised me considering his past trouble with drinking.

RT: He was alone?

MF: There was a woman beside him, but I didn't think they were together at first. I'm so used to seeing Bear by himself all the time, it just didn't occur to me that he might be meeting someone.

RT: And when did you first realize he and the woman were together?

MF: I wouldn't say "together" exactly.

RT: What do you mean?

MF: He didn't seem to be enjoying her company very much.

RT: He was upset?

MF: I'd say annoyed. Put out. She kept leaning in really close to him and he kept leaning away. And he wasn't looking at her. That's why it took me a few minutes to realize there was something going on between the two of them. Because he didn't look at her for a really long time. He kept his eyes pointed straight forward, staring at the mirror behind the bar.

RT: Was Mr. McAlister drinking?

MF: He had a full glass of something by his elbow. Scotch, I think. Or whiskey. I'm not much of a drinker myself, so it's hard to say.

RT: What about the woman?

MF: Was she drinking?

RT: Yes.

MF: I think so. There was an empty martini glass in front of her.

RT: Did you know the woman?

MF: No. Well, yes. Sort of. I wouldn't say I knew her. Exactly.

RT: Had you met her before?

MF: Yes. Sunday night. At Patti's.

RT: Go on, Mr. Freshour. Please describe your first encounter with Ms. Bellweather.

MF: It's just, there she was, this pretty young lady sitting all by herself, eating alone. I went over and introduced myself. Welcomed her to town. She said she wasn't staying long. I asked if I could buy her a drink. She turned me down. And that was that.

RT: Did you have any other interactions with her prior to seeing her again at the Jack Knife?

MF: . . . No, sir.

RT: Mr. Freshour?

MF: Well, I guess I should tell you . . .

RT: You're starting to worry me here a little bit, Mr. Freshour. I need you to be completely honest about what you know. Okay?

MF: Yes. Yes, sir. Of course. I want to help however I can. This whole thing. It's just so awful. She was so young. Full of life. I just can't figure out what our Good Lord was thinking, letting a thing like this happen.

RT: Mr. Freshour, did you see her again?

MF: Uh . . . no.

RT: Mr. Freshour—

MF: I didn't! God's honest truth. But I did go to her hotel room. On Sunday night after she turned me down at Patti's.

RT: And?

MF: And she wasn't there. Or at least, she didn't open the door when I knocked.

RT: And then?

MF: And then I went home, warmed up a can of tomato soup, and watched *Murder, She Wrote*. Now, Jessica Fletcher, she knows how to solve a mystery.

I skipped over the next few questions where it seemed Pastor Mike had taken over the conversation, rambling on about little details, nothing that really mattered. My eyes snagged on my father's name and I went back a few lines, started reading more closely again.

RT: Let's . . . why don't we go back to Monday night? Why don't you tell me about when the fight started?

MF: Right, so . . . I went and found Rosalee and I was helping her to her feet when all of a sudden Bear just up and started shouting.

RT: Do you remember what he was saying?

MF: He wanted to know how she'd found him. She said something about it not being too difficult, considering, and then Bear started in about how none of this was any of her goddamn business and she should just go back to where she came from and leave him the hell alone.

RT: When you heard the yelling, what did you do?

MF: I settled Rosalee back down in the booth and told her I'd only be a second, then I went to see if I could help. By that time, of course, Vic was there, leaning his hands on the bar and telling Bear he needed to calm down or take his business elsewhere.

RT: And Ms. Bellweather? What was she doing during all of this?

MF: She had out a small notepad and a pen and was jotting something down. Bear kept trying to grab the notepad from her. She was asking him questions, but Bear and Vic were shouting so loud, I couldn't hear a word she was saying.

RT: And then what happened?

MF: Bear grabbed hold of her and started to shake her. I tried to pull him off, but he swung back with his elbow and hit me in the jaw. I gave him some space after that. She fought him hard, though. Scratched up his face, I think. He let her go after Vic started to dial 911.

RT: And then?

MF: He left.

RT: Mr. McAlister did?

MF: Yep. Got up and walked right out.

RT: And Ms. Bellweather?

MF: She went after him.

RT: What did you do?

MF: Well, Vic got me a bag of ice. For my jaw. It was hurting pretty bad about then.

RT: Did you do anything else, Mr. Freshour?

MF: Sure. I went out to the parking lot. I didn't like the feeling I was getting about the whole thing.

RT: And what kind of feeling was that?

MF: Have you ever woken up short of breath? You know you've had a nightmare, a really bad one this time, but you can't quite remember what it was about? All you remember are glimpses, dark flashes, tremors? All you remember is being terrified? It was like that. A bad feeling.

RT: What happened in the parking lot?

MF: Nothing.

RT: Could you be more specific?

MF: Nothing happened. By the time I got out there, they were both gone.

RT: Did you see where they went?

MF: No.

RT: Anything else you remember?

MF: Before he left the bar, Bear said something like, forgive my language, "If you threaten me or my family again, I'll break every single one of your goddamn fingers. I'll make sure you never write another damn word."

The interview ended here. Abruptly. I shuffled through the stack of papers looking for the rest of the pages but couldn't find them. I pulled one of the chairs out from the table. The feet scraped against the linoleum, squealing sharply.

"You okay?" Travis asked.

I sat down. If Pastor Mike was telling the truth, then Bear had lied. To me. To Ollie. To everyone. I covered my face with my hands.

"Sam?" Travis left his post by the window and came and stood over me.

I said the only thing that made any sense. "This can't be right."

Travis took Pastor Mike's statement from me and flipped through each page. He said, "Jesus Christ," and then returned the papers to the folder.

He grabbed my arm, tried to pull me to my feet. "Let's get out of here."

"No." I jerked away from him, even though he was right. We'd been here too long already. But in that moment, I didn't care about getting caught.

"There has to be something else here," I said. "Something I'm not seeing."

"What else could there be? This interview makes things pretty clear, don't you think?"

"Or Pastor Mike's full of shit." I stood and started looking through the folders and loose papers again.

"Sam."

I kept shuffling through the papers.

Travis rested his hand on top of mine. "He threatened her."

I pulled away from him, shaking my head.

Travis continued, "The newspaper said she died sometime Monday night. Pastor Mike said they left together."

"No, he didn't. He said he saw them fighting. Then Bear left."

"And so did she. Right after."

"According to Pastor Mike." I returned to shuffling papers, brushing Travis aside. "One man's word against another's. It doesn't mean a damn thing."

"Sam, listen to yourself. The bartender was there. Other witnesses. It would be pretty easy for Detective Talbert to find out if Pastor Mike was lying."

I slammed my hand down on the table. "Bear didn't kill her."

"I know you want to believe that . . . I get that you want him to be innocent. But look at the facts. Look at all these things stacked up against him." And he started lifting papers and scanning through the reports, saying out loud everything I already knew. Finally, he held up the folder containing Pastor Mike's statement and shook his head. "Sam, I'm sorry."

I leaned over the table again, shoved papers out of the way, looking for something else, I didn't know what. Something that contradicted Pastor Mike's statement.

I said, "Fine. Let's say it happened the way Pastor Mike said. Let's say it's all true. There has to be a good reason why Bear was upset, why he said those things. Why they were fighting. She must have provoked him. So he gets angry. He shouts. He makes a scene. But he didn't . . . he would never . . ."

"Then who?"

"I don't know. Maybe Pastor Mike did it."

"What? That's ridiculous."

"No, think about it." I picked up a thick, rubber-banded folder with my father's name printed on the tab. "Taylor Bellweather turned him down. Maybe he got angry about that. Maybe he felt humiliated that she'd embarrassed him that way. Then he sees her and Bear fighting at the Jack Knife and he tries to ride in like some hero to save the day, but she ignores him again. Maybe he follows her out of the bar and tries to kiss her or something and she pushes him away and he gets even angrier and maybe things get out of control."

"Sam . . . stop. You're upset. You're not thinking straight."

I slipped the rubber band off the folder and kept talking, thinking out loud, trying to make the pieces fit the way I needed them to. The longer I talked, the more I started to believe that maybe what I was saying made sense. Maybe I was onto something.

"So he hits her or pushes her down or something. She cracks her head open. Maybe he didn't mean to kill her, but maybe he did. And now he needs to cover it up. He needs someone to frame. Who better than Bear, right? Everybody in this stupid town hates him."

"Sam. He didn't do it."

"He went to her hotel room. Don't you think that's weird?"

"Listen to me," Travis said. "Pastor Mike didn't kill her."

"You don't know that."

"Yes, I do."

I stopped flipping through papers and looked at Travis, waiting for him to continue.

"He was at my house that night."

"What?" My stomach sank.

"He was at my house Monday night. He came over for dinner sometime after seven, maybe seven thirty, and stayed until well after midnight. He and my dad were out on the porch drinking beers and talking so loud I couldn't sleep. He would have had to come straight from the bar."

I clutched the folder to my chest and asked, "What about the interview Taylor was supposed to have with your father?"

"What about it?" Travis shook his head, frowning. "It wasn't supposed to take very long. A couple questions. A couple pictures. But none of that even matters. She never showed up."

I stared at him.

"Taylor was never there. The interview never happened," he insisted. "Pastor Mike was the only person who came over that night."

"God's honest truth?"

He said, "Of course it is," and I believed him.

"What time did he leave?" I asked.

"Pastor Mike?"

I nodded. "Because maybe he killed her later. After he left your house. Maybe he stuffed her in the trunk of his car and then—"

"I'm not doing this."

"—after dinner he drove out to some secluded spot in the woods and dumped her body in the river and that was that and now he has this perfect alibi. There was time, you know. He had plenty of time before and after, and maybe—"

He grabbed my arm. "Sam. Stop it. You have to stop. Bear did this."

I glared at him, then shook his hand off and opened the folder again.

Inside were old employment records from years ago when Bear

had a real job, bank statements showing balances hovering danger-
ously close to zero, my mother's obituary cut from the newspaper and
pasted to a single sheet of white paper, the photocopy version blurred
and hard to read. Every minuscule and boring detail of my father's
tragic life. Nothing and nothing and nothing. And then a paper-
clipped stack of papers, public records, court documents, criminal history. And I had a sudden recollection of the arraignment hearing and
how the prosecuting attorney had mentioned a prior arrest and how
it hadn't really made an impression on me at the time because there
was so much else going on and I thought it was just something all
lawyers said at those kinds of hearings because my father had never
been arrested before.

Outside, a car door slammed.

Travis swung his head toward the front door. "Shit. Sam! We have
to go. Now!"

He grabbed my arm. I pushed him off, scanning the papers,
trying to make sense of the numbers and abbreviations, the code and
garbled text that regular people weren't meant to understand. Finally,
I read something that I could grab hold of: Criminally Negligent Homicide, Vehicular Homicide, DUI. There were dates, too, coinciding
with the day Bear disappeared and the day he called home, two years
later. Arrested. Convicted. Sentenced. Time served. Released on pro-
bation. And somewhere out there was a family grieving, left in pieces
because Bear had done the one thing I never thought him capable of
doing. I thought about all the times I'd asked my mother where he
was, all the times she refused to tell me. My knees bent. I sank into
the chair again.

Someone was coming up the porch steps. Keys rattled.

"Sam!" Travis pulled me to my feet. He took the papers, threw
them on the table, and dragged me out of the kitchen, down the hallway, into the bedroom.

My legs were made of stone. I couldn't get them to work right.
Travis pushed me out the window. The front door opened.

"Go!" Travis pulled me across the yard to the fence.

I jumped and grabbed for the top of the planks, but slipped and fell backward into the grass. A splinter jabbed into my palm. Travis jerked me to my feet again, wrapped his arms around my legs, and hoisted me over the fence. My skirt caught on a nail near the top. I ripped the fabric free and tumbled into the weeds on the other side. Travis jumped down beside me a few seconds later, grabbed my elbow, and dragged me toward the chain-link fence. We clambered over and slid to the bottom of the culvert, pressed our backs up against the concrete side, and didn't move.

"Shit," Travis whispered. "Shit. Shit. Shit. What the hell was that? What the hell were you thinking?"

I gathered my knees up close to my chest and buried my face against my legs, shut my eyes, counted off the seconds.

A sliding glass door opened, and I knew we were caught. A few seconds more, then Deputy Santos would come over that fence and down into the culvert, she'd say my name and I'd look up and see her standing above me, maybe with her gun drawn, with that same disappointed look she'd had when I brought her Taylor Bellweather's necklace. I would look up and see her blotting out the sun.

The sliding glass door slammed shut.

I lifted my head and looked sideways at Travis.

"Is she gone?" I whispered.

He shook his head and shrugged.

We listened for a while longer, waiting for footsteps in the grass, the clink of handcuffs, Deputy Santos calling for us to come on out now. We waited. We listened. A blue jay shrieked. Somewhere far off a bass thump pounded, and it echoed the thump in my chest. I stretched out my legs and inspected the tear in my skirt. A two-inch-long, jagged hole just below my left knee. I leaned my head back on the cement. Franny wasn't going to be happy when she saw that.

Travis's shoulder brushed mine. He took a deep breath. I did, too.

Whenever I closed my eyes, I saw my mother gray and dead. I saw

Taylor Bellweather beaten, torn apart. And dead. Every true thing in this world, everything I thought was real: dead, dead, and dying.

Except.

I turned my head, and Travis was looking back at me. I leaned in before he could say anything and pressed my lips to his. He tasted like salt and dust and stale smoke. He tensed at first, then relaxed and brought his hand around, burying his fingers in my hair.

I kissed him because I wanted to be close to someone warm, someone who was breathing, to see what it was like, taking in life, giving my own. I wanted to feel something, anything. I wanted to feel alive. But instead I felt only rough skin and a slight pressure against my bottom lip. No tingling fingers or singing angels. No rush of heat to my cheeks. No spark or snap or blinding light. Nothing that meant anything at all. A kiss was supposed to bring people together. A kiss changed everything, that's what Laura had told me. A kiss was a beginning, an awakening, an exchanging of souls. I didn't believe in souls. This kiss was just a kiss, and the dead were all still dead.

I pulled away from him. "We should go."

"Yeah," he said, but then leaned forward again, reaching for me, wanting more.

"Your mom's probably worried." I pushed him off and rose to my feet, brushed dirt and bits of dried grass off my skirt.

He scrambled after me and tried to take my hand, but I moved ahead of him before he could.

When we reached his bike, he said, "Hey. Are you . . . are we okay?"

I grabbed his helmet and shoved it down over my head.

ollie

Wednesday night and the pews are full. So are the rafters.

The people bow their heads.

The Shimmering float quietly above, calmed tonight by so much remembering. The ones who are unattached, who follow no one, come to places like this. Churches, mosques, temples, cemeteries. To pray and sigh and wait.

They whisper, but there are no words. It is, instead, a sound like breathing, like a single, final, fading gasp. Candles flicker on the altar and in holders along every wall. It is dark enough and light enough that the Shimmering look like the people they used to be, and that makes me nervous. There are so many here, so many I do not know.

When they are all energy and light, it is easy to pretend they're not real.

But with shape and form and face, they are impossible to ignore.

The one who follows me drifts up and down the center aisle. When she passes our pew, she smiles and looks so much like my mother that

I start to cry. I let the tears fall. They are not out of place here where everyone but my sister has damp eyes and trembling lips.

"It's not a funeral," Franny said on the drive over after my sister asked why we had to go. "It's a memorial service."

"But why even have one at all? She wasn't from around here. And no one knew her before . . ."

"People want to express their sympathies and show support. To find closure and then move on. Pastor Mike's offering a safe space for our community to gather. To heal."

"It's weird," my sister said.

Pastor Mike leans over the pulpit. He is drenched in sweat and keeps dabbing his eyes with a balled-up handkerchief. He says, "When someone so young and still so full of life is taken from this world in such a violent manner, the easiest thing to do is blame God. Or question his love, his mercy, his sense of justice. But we must not blame God. God is love. God is good. He did not create evil in this world. He does not cause it. It is our sin and shortcomings. Our own poor choices. We may never fully understand, never know why. The best we can do is pray and trust our Lord and Savior, find our peace in him."

My sister rolls her eyes and squeezes her hands together in her lap. She doesn't believe in God.

After our mother's funeral, when everyone came over to the house for lemon cake and raspberry punch, my sister pulled me into a room alone and said, "What these people are saying, it's bullshit. You know that, right? You're never going to see Mom again. There's no heaven. No bright tunnel of light. She's not looking down on us. She's not our guardian angel. She's not going to be there to help us cross over. Don't believe any of it, Ollie, okay? It's better if you just say good-bye now and get on with things."

It's hard to say good-bye to somebody who's still here.

Pastor Mike is talking now about a bigger plan, a reason for our losses.

The one who follows me stops beside our pew. She spreads herself thin above me and my sister and Nana Fran and Papa Zeb. She spreads thin and rains blue fire down on our heads.

I want to tell her I'm sorry for what I said all those weeks ago and how I made her cry, but I think if I do, she'll leave. Only this time she won't come back. She'll go wherever it is they go when their business is finished here. To heaven or some distant cluster of stars.

She'll go. And I'm not ready yet.

My sister leans across me and whispers to Nana Fran, "I'm going to the bathroom."

Nana Fran pinches her lips together, but doesn't say no.

My sister slips out of our pew and down the aisle through the double doors. The one from the river goes with her, slowing a little as she passes the very last pew where Mrs. Roth and Travis sit together. Billy Roth is not with them; neither is the pale girl. Mrs. Roth watches my sister leave, then touches Travis's leg and whispers something in his ear.

Pastor Mike says, "Though we cannot say our good-byes in person, I believe she is able to hear us from heaven." He smiles, though he's not happy. He lifts his eyes to the ceiling and folds his hands. He says, "You are remembered. You are missed. You are loved." And then he moves his eyes over the rows and rows of tragic faces but does not settle on any one. "Let us all bow our heads for a moment of silence and remember Taylor Bellweather. Pray for her family in this difficult time. Pray they will find comfort. Finally, pray they will always remember their daughter for how she lived rather than how she died."

He bows his head.

From the silence comes weeping and sighing and sniffling and rustling tissue. Someone coughs.

The Shimmering stir the air and make the candles sputter.

And in the very last pew, Mrs. Roth stands and moves into the aisle, hurries through the double doors after my sister. Travis goes with her.

I am the only one who sees them leave. I start to get up, but Nana Fran puts her hand on my knee and shakes her head.

s a m

Pastor Mike's office door was wide open. I glanced over my shoulder. The foyer was empty. I was alone and would probably never have another chance as good as this one. I didn't know what I was looking for exactly, or if there was even anything to find. But I'd need something more than cobbled-together hunches to prove Pastor Mike was lying about what had happened the night of Taylor Bellweather's death. I ducked inside and shut the door behind me.

The streetlights outside were close enough and shining through the picture window bright enough, I didn't bother looking for a light switch. In the middle of the room, taking up most of the space, was a large wooden desk. If Pastor Mike had been sitting in his leather chair, he would have been the centerpiece. Bookshelves lined one wall. On the other hung an assortment of framed photographs and certificates. Set atop a filing cabinet in the corner was one of Billy Roth's sculptures. It was similar to a piece I'd seen in a newspaper clipping a few years ago, surreal and, at first glance, repulsive, but take a second look and you might see something beautiful.

The one in the clipping took up half a room, but the piece on Pastor Mike's cabinet was much smaller. The base was butter-brown wood carved to look like tiny, rolling mountains covered in pine forests. Four stumps grew up from the base and spread roots into the body of a fox. A real fox. Dead, now, of course. Taken apart, stuffed, and sewn back together. His legs had been cut off, his torso mounted on these intricate wooden replacements. His mouth was open, his head tipped back like he was howling, and long twists of wire shot past his sharp yellow teeth and into the air. Tiny metal birds in midflight had been welded onto the end of each wire. The fox's tail was curved into an unnatural-looking S-shape, and a section of skin on its right hind leg had been peeled away, revealing bright white bone underneath. I could have stared at it for hours, but I knew if I stayed away too long Franny would send Zeb to come get me.

I turned my attention to Pastor Mike's desk. The top was uncluttered. No papers strewn about, no haphazard piles, no pencils teetering on the edge, no jotted notes. Just a phone, a blank notepad, one pencil, a simple wooden cross, and a day planner. I flipped the day planner open to August. Most of his days were filled with things like board meetings and hospital visits, a counseling session with Mr. and Mrs. Dunsworth, the usual comings and goings of a small-town pastor. I closed the day planner and put it back exactly where I'd found it, lining the edges up with the corner of the desk. I bent and tried opening the drawers, but they were locked. I straightened a paper clip and jammed it into the keyhole, wiggled it around a little, but the lock stayed fast.

I scanned the bookshelves, running my finger across the spines, looking for something interesting, something that seemed out of place. Mostly there were the usual books about God and religion and how to counsel people who had post-traumatic stress disorder and depression, people who were alcoholics or drug abusers, people who had lost their way. There were books about financial planning, too, and how to run a business, books about strategic leadership and woodworking and how to cook Italian food. And Bibles. So many Bibles. All different versions and bindings and one written entirely in Hebrew.

I moved on to the wall of photographs and certificates. Here were diplomas and other various achievements alongside pictures of Pastor Mike with his parishioners. Smiling, happy, arm-around-shoulder pictures. Potlucks and fishing trips and volunteering at a soup kitchen. There was one of him and another man I recognized immediately as Billy Roth. They were standing waist-deep in a river, holding up the two fish they'd caught, still on hooks, swinging dead in the air. Both men were grinning like it hurt. Beside it was another picture of Pastor Mike, this time with the entire Roth family posing in front of one of Billy's sculptures. Baby Travis was perched on his mother's hip. A blond-haired girl who must have been Travis's sister had her arms wrapped around Billy Roth's legs. The sculpture they stood in front of was like the one I remembered from the news clipping, huge and grotesque.

It was hard to tell from the photograph exactly what the sculpture was. The main bodies looked like reindeer, but I couldn't tell if they were real or carved from wood—though based on the fox sculpture, I imagined it was some combination of both. I counted four heads and sixteen hooves, or maybe there were seventeen. Antlers rose together, higher and higher, making a tangled column so tall it almost touched the ceiling. There were places too, where it looked like the insides of the reindeer had exploded out through their skin, where colored blobs hung frozen in midair. Maybe it was supposed to be some kind of metaphor, but I didn't get it.

Out in the foyer, a door opened and closed. Two people started arguing in hushed voices. I was trapped in Pastor Mike's office until they left.

I moved closer to a watercolor painting hanging beside the door that I hadn't noticed earlier. Fine brushstrokes and saturated colors came together in the form of a beautiful church that seemed to be made almost entirely of glass. The architecture was simple. Straight lines and steel beams, a one-room sanctuary, a steeple reflecting the sun. Inside were pews all in rows, the pulpit, the altar, a cross behind. But even more beautiful than the church's simplicity and beveled edges was what surrounded it on the outside. A quilt of wildflowers, a lush green tapestry, statuesque trees, and off in the distance, a sparkle of blue, hinting at water, at a river flowing into forever. At first I thought it was just something nice, something lovely for Pastor Mike to look at and dream about when he grew tired of his own white, clapboard, shake-shingle-roofed building surrounded by asphalt, but then my eyes focused on what was hanging on the wall beneath it. Blueprints. I took the frame carefully off the wall and brought it close to my face so I could see the fine lines better.

Not blueprints exactly, more like a rough sketch. Here was the glass church, and here was a river running behind it. I squinted to read the writing that curved alongside the water. *Crooked River*. A hard knot formed in my throat. My eyes moved over the drawing quickly now, jumping from label to label, allowing just enough time to take in the name and move on. *Service Road 19. Blue Heron Pond. Lambert Road. Johnson Farm*. All familiar places. Places I'd spent the past eight summers exploring. The glass church was sketched inside a wide open space encircled with trees a quarter mile east of Zeb's barn if you followed the dirt road to the hemlock stump. Underneath the building were the words *Terrebonne Baptist*. A church that hadn't been built. Yet. A church that would never be built as long as Bear had any say in the matter. But Bear was in jail now, thanks to Pastor Mike's statement. Bear was in jail and no longer had a say in anything. I hung the plans back on the wall.

Outside the voices had gotten louder, right up close to the door. Someone said, "She's not here. Let's just go back inside."

A second person, a woman, said, "She couldn't have gone far."

"She's probably in the bathroom." I recognized Travis's voice now and felt pretty sure he was talking to his mother. "I'm sure she'll be back in a few minutes. Come on."

"Just let me . . ." The handle turned.

I took a step back, searching the room for someplace to hide. Too late, the door opened.

Mrs. Roth didn't seem at all surprised to see me. Instead, she smiled. "What are you doing in here, dear?"

"I . . . uh . . ." I took another step back and bumped against the desk. "I was . . . Pastor Mike told me I could borrow one of his books."

Mrs. Roth glanced at the bookshelves and then at my empty hands. She said, "Travis told me about your mother. Poor thing. I'm so sorry."

I gave her a halfhearted smile.

"I was worried about you when I saw you leave the service." She gestured to Travis who was still standing in the foyer. "*We* were worried."

Travis moved into the doorway behind her. When he dropped me off yesterday at the house, Ollie was waiting for me on the front porch swing. So I'd just thanked him for the ride, and he left. There'd been no time in between for us to talk about what we'd found at Deputy Santos's house, or about the kiss and how quickly I'd pushed him away.

He stood in front of me now, blushing and staring at his feet.

"I'm fine," I said.

Mrs. Roth came into the office. She crossed to the wall of photographs and tapped her finger on the picture of her family taken so many years ago. "Did you see this? I've always loved this picture."

"Mom," Travis said.

"This was the sculpture that made my Billy famous." She leaned in closer, squinting, and wiped the glass with her sleeve, then turned and gave me a hard stare. "Travis told you about the show?"

I nodded.

"Only a few more weeks now."

The congregation had started singing, and I wanted to return to the sanctuary, but Travis was blocking the doorway.

Mrs. Roth took a small step toward me. "It's been ten years, you know. Since he's been in his studio. Ten long years. Hard years." She had a run in one of her stockings, from her ankle to her knee. "This piece he's working on now? It could change everything."

"Mom," Travis said again.

She glared at him and then back at me. "Our family is depending on this show. All of Terrebonne is."

The fox stared down at us from the top of the filing cabinet. His eyes glinted like Mrs. Roth's. I licked my suddenly dry lips and backed toward the office door. Travis moved out of my way. I turned my back on them and hurried through the foyer toward the sanctuary doors.

I slipped inside as quickly and as quietly as I could, but Pastor Mike still noticed. He looked up from the hymnal spread open on the pulpit and lost his place in the song. He stumbled over the words, found them again, then sang louder, stronger, giving his whole attention once again to the sheet music in front of him.

Ollie and I sat between Zeb and Franny in the front seat of the truck, all of us squeezed together. They stopped to pick up a pizza and when they asked us what we wanted, I shrugged and said nothing because my stomach hurt. And Ollie shrugged and said nothing because she was still pretending to see ghosts. Zeb turned on the radio and asked what kind of music we liked listening to. I shrugged and said nothing. Ollie did the same. Franny turned off the radio and asked us if we wanted to talk about anything.

"The service," she said. "Your father's arrest. Your mom?"

I shook my head. Ollie slumped down in the seat and crossed her arms over her chest.

We used to play this game on long car rides where we would both turn our faces away, pretending to look out our respective windows, and slowly, very slowly we'd start to turn inward again, toward each other. If we both turned at the same time, we'd both whip our faces back around to our windows. If one person was looking and the other person wasn't, the looker would stare and stare until the person being looked at started to turn, then the looker would have to whip her head around fast, pretending she hadn't been staring at all. We called it Look, Don't Look, and the point was to not get caught, or maybe the point was just to make each other laugh.

Ollie was always the first one to start laughing. Her shoulders would bounce up and down, and then she'd snort and giggle, gasping, "Stop it, Sammy. Stop!" And when I didn't, when I made her laugh even harder, so hard tears rolled down her face, she'd clutch her stomach and say, "My seams! They're splitting!" And then, if I still didn't stop, she'd say, "Sammy! I'm going to pee my pants!" And after that we'd collapse into each other, arms and hands tangled, laughing and laughing until we'd forgotten what had been so funny in the first place.

I stared at Ollie's profile, her stretched-thin lips and tired eyes, so much weight, so much sadness. In this dim light, her hair looked gray, her skin see-through, like she was a tiny, old woman. I tried to take her hand, but she pulled it away from me, curled it in her lap instead. The last two miles back to Zeb and Franny's house, no one said a single word.

At the kitchen table, I picked the pieces of pepperoni off my slice of pizza and stacked them on the edge of my plate. Ollie kicked her feet against the chair rungs and started in on her third piece. She kept her eyes down, staring at the tablecloth.

Franny was talking about how Pastor Mike should have decorated with lilies instead of roses tonight because roses were too festive and fit better at weddings and birthdays than memorial services.

I picked up my slice of pizza, then set it down again without taking a bite.

"Got something on your mind, Sam?" Zeb asked, cutting Franny off midsentence.

She sniffed loudly, her only protest, and dug into her pizza with a knife and fork.

I wiped my fingers on a napkin. "Are you going to sell the meadow?"

Zeb snorted. "Where'd you hear a fool thing like that?"

"Travis told me." It seemed a good enough answer as any.

Ollie stopped kicking her feet against the chair.

Zeb said, "Boy doesn't know what he's talking about."

Franny nodded in agreement.

"You're not going to sell it to Pastor Mike so he can build a new church?" I asked.

Zeb wiped his mouth with a napkin, then cleared his throat and said, "Well now, a while back Pastor Mike came asking after that bit of property. Said he thought it would be a real nice place for a sanctuary, what with it so close to the river and looking out over all that green space. Offered me a fair bit of money for it, too. 'Course, I turned him down."

"Zeb," Franny warned.

He waved his napkin at her and continued, "Bear was here first, and he's never once been late with his rent. Can't turn a good man out for no reason. Plus, he and your mama—"

"Zeb!" Franny said, giving him a hard look across the table and shaking her head.

He bent over his plate and started eating again.

"But now that Bear's gone?" I pressed.

Zeb shrugged. "He's paid up through the end of September. Don't see anything changing until then. And maybe not after, either."

Nobody spoke for a while after that.

I ate a few bites, but my slice was cold and my stomach still hurt. I pushed my chair back from the table and left without asking to be excused.

Franny called after me, but Zeb said, "Let her go, Mother."

A half hour later, he came and found me.

I was out on the front porch swing, rocking slowly, my bare feet brushing across the worn-smooth boards.

He leaned on the railing, crossed his arms over his chest, and said, "Something else bothering you?"

I stared past his shoulder.

The edges of the barn blurred in the deepening twilight. The gray ribbon road, threading between the fields and disappearing into the trees, was smudged charcoal. Taylor Bellweather had been dead for nine days. My mother for thirty-seven. Almost five days had passed since Bear's arrest, four since I'd last gone to the meadow. I knew it was time to check on the new hive, make sure the bees were building their comb the right way and the queen was laying eggs. If there were problems and I didn't catch them early enough, we could lose the whole colony. A thousand bees dead because I was too scared to do what needed to be done.

I shifted my gaze to Zeb and said, "Did you know about Bear being in prison?"

"He's in jail," Zeb said. "Not the same thing, kiddo."

"No, not now. Ten years ago. He was driving drunk, killed somebody. They sent him away for two years. Did you know about that?"

Zeb cleared his throat and looked down at his feet.

"Do you know what happened? In the accident?"

He looked at me, and the weight of eighty years pressed down on his shoulders, making him collapse and sag, making him old. When he spoke, his words were sighs. "Yes. Yes, I do."

I waited for him to continue, and when he didn't, I asked, "Aren't you going to tell me?"

He pushed away from the railing, rubbed his bad hip, and went back inside the house. I stopped rocking but didn't go after him.

I stayed on the porch until the last drops of day bled into night, and the stars came out. I stayed until the square patch of yellow shining from Zeb and Franny's bedroom window onto the grass disappeared. I stayed until dew began to form on my eyelashes and darkness squeezed so tight around me it got too hard to breathe.

When I went inside, Zeb was sitting on the couch in the living room. Just sitting there in the dark. Silent and still. His hands were on his knees, and he stared straight ahead at nothing, even when the screen door squealed open and banged shut.

I stood at the bottom of the staircase, watching him, and thought maybe he'd fallen asleep like that and maybe I should wake him and help him upstairs to bed. Then he turned his head. I couldn't see his face or his eyes or mouth or anything, just the silhouette of an old man sitting alone.

He said, "I'm taking you to see your daddy tomorrow. Seems to me you got a lot of questions and seems to me he's the one who should be answering. Now get on upstairs and get some rest. Got a long day in front of us."

ollie

My sister's voice drifts into the bedroom through the open window. Papa Zeb's voice, too. But they are talking too low for me to hear all the words. Something about Bear. Something about an accident.

And then they are quiet. The screen door opens and closes.

I take the Ouija board from the top of the dresser and sit with it on the bed, stare at the door and wait.

The one who follows me moves back and forth between the bed and the door. A swirling river of fire and light. She brushes my hand. I flinch, but I don't pull away.

We will spell out the truth for my sister. We will point her in the right direction. And finally she will see. She will understand.

She will help us fix this.

When the truth is told, the one from the river will leave and Bear will come home and we will be a family again. And the one who follows me will be happy seeing us together and safe.

She will forgive me and go. Ready or not.

The day before she died, Mom was making plans. She wanted us to move to the meadow to live with Bear. Me and her and Sam. All of us together.

I heard her talking about it on the phone.

I was supposed to be playing at Margo's house, but Margo ate something that made her throw up and so I came home early and found Mom at the kitchen table with an architecture magazine spread open in front of her.

She didn't see me come in.

"I think vaulted ceilings will make all the difference." She listened to the other person for a minute and then said, "Yes, as much light as possible." Another pause. "We're thinking about leaving the floors unfinished. Just having all that bare wood under our feet," she said and then smiled. "It's going to be so beautiful. Bear is going to love it. And I think the girls really will too."

"Love what?" I said.

Mom turned and frowned and said, "Heather? I have to go. Yes . . . Ollie . . . I'll call you back in a few minutes."

She hung up the phone and patted the chair next to her. "Sit down."

She told me she was sorry she'd kept it a secret. There were so many details to work out, and she wanted to make sure it was really going to happen before she told us. She didn't want to get our hopes up or make any promises she couldn't keep.

"But isn't it exciting, sweetheart? All of us together again under one roof?"

She waited, wanting so badly for me to want this too. But I didn't.

I ran to my bedroom and slammed the door shut.

When she came to apologize and explain, when she reached out her arms to hug me, I pushed her away. I told her I hated the meadow and I hated Bear and I hated her.

She said, "Sweetheart—"

"Just leave me alone!"

She reached for me one last time. "Please, Ollie. Try to understand—"

I threw myself onto my bed and buried my face in the pillows.

When she left my room, I thought about what it would be like if she were dead, how much easier my life would be.

Five weeks, three days, exactly.

And I wish I could take it all back.

I wait a while, but no one comes up the stairs. I'm about to put away the Ouija board and try again later when the screen door opens and closes a second time.

Voices murmur in the living room. The staircase creaks and sighs.

My sister enters our room, looks at the box in my lap, looks at me, says, "Ollie, it's time for bed," and changes into her pajamas.

I open the lid and spread the board out on top of the quilt. The one from the river spirals above me. Gray and white and blue and green and black, forming a ceiling hurricane.

I tap the planchette on the board.

My sister sits on the edge of her bed and says, "It's late."

I tap the board a second time.

"Put the game away, Ollie."

I point at the board and wiggle my eyebrows.

She doesn't laugh. She doesn't smile. There are purple-gray shadows under her eyes.

I put the board away. The one from the river sighs and sinks to the floor, curls into a cold, black ball at my sister's feet.

"You have to start talking to me," my sister says.

I sit across from her and stare at my hands.

"You're the only one I've got left, Oll."

I look up at the hitch in her voice. She's crying.

"You're all I've got and I need you to talk to me again, okay?"

I go and sit next to her.

"Please?"

The one who follows me drapes my sister in streamers of gold and silver, curls red ribbons around her hands and ankles, whispers love against her cheek.

"Just try and say something, Oll. One word."

I reach for her hand, but she pulls it back and rolls onto her side away from me. She turns off the lamp beside her bed and we sit in the dark not moving, not speaking.

I get up from her bed and go to my own.

"You're not the only one who misses her, you know," my sister says. "But this whole not-talking, pretending-to-see-ghosts thing won't bring her back. She's gone, Ollie. We can't have her back."

I lie under the covers and stare up at the ceiling where the one who follows me is dancing. A small flame, barely visible in the moonlight. She sings us a lullaby.

sam

Zeb gave the man at the front desk our paperwork in exchange for badges to hang around our necks.

"Don't take these off until you leave," he said. "Or we might mistake you for a prisoner and throw you in an empty cell." He laughed at the joke. Zeb and I didn't.

We went through a metal detector and a man with a gun led us down a gray corridor through a gray door into a gray room crowded with people, waiting on chairs and benches, leaning up against the walls. No one paid us any attention.

"Station three," the guard said, pointing to the middle booth in a row of six that lined the far wall. "Wait your turn. When we bring him in, you just lift up the phone and you'll be able to talk to each other. Twenty-five minutes is what you're allowed, but if things get too rambunctious or we just don't like the way you two are looking at each other, visit's over. Okay?"

I nodded.

Zeb said, "Thank you."

The guard went out the same door we'd come in.

There was someone at station three already, a young woman with purple hair. She was talking to a man on the other side of the glass who had a shaved head and lots of tattoos on his arms and neck. He saw me standing behind her waiting and grinned. His teeth flashed gold. I looked at the floor.

Zeb put his hand on my shoulder and said, "How are you doing?"

I shrugged.

The purple-haired woman and her tattooed boyfriend talked for another few minutes. Then she hung up the phone and left, dabbing at the corners of her eyes with a tissue. The man on the other side of the glass went back to his cell.

I took my place on the stool facing the partition. Zeb patted my shoulder twice, then sat down on a bench somewhere behind me. I stared at the empty stool on the other side of the glass, stared and went over silently what I was planning to say to Bear. *I know about the DUI. I know you went to prison. I know you killed someone, and I want to know who. I want to know why. I want to know about the drinking and everything that happened the night of the accident and after. I want to know where you were and what you were doing during those two missing years. I want to know why you and Mom kept it from me, why you never told. I want to know why you lied.*

A buzzer sounded, and the door of the inmate area opened. Bear entered and crossed to station three.

His chin was dark with stubble. The bruise under his right eye was starting to heal, turning green and pale yellow around the edges, but still plum black in the center. The two scratches on his cheek were gone. He sat down on the stool and picked up the phone.

I stared at him through the glass. My hands lay frozen in my lap.

He pointed to the receiver. Then tapped the partition lightly. He mouthed, *Pick up,* and pointed to the receiver again.

I lifted the phone from its cradle and pressed it hard against my ear. I could hear him breathing.

"How are you?" He sounded tired and undone.

"Fine."

"And your sister?"

"She's fine, too."

"They told me you're staying with Zeb and Franny? Until Grandma and Grandpa can come get you?"

I nodded.

"Good. That's good." He switched the phone to his other ear. "They're good people."

I picked at the narrow shelf in front of me where the linoleum was starting to peel along the edge.

Bear sighed.

At another station, a woman laughed loudly. A man shouted, "To Denver. I told you this last time!"

I pressed my hand to my ear and leaned closer to the glass.

"You know, it won't be so bad. Living with Grandma and Grandpa," Bear said. He rested one arm on the shelf on his side of the partition. "Your mom said their condo's big, plenty of room. There's a park close by. And good schools. They love you and Ollie very much. You know, they might even let you have a dog."

"I don't want a dog."

"A cat?"

"I hate cats."

Bear sighed again, louder, longer, the smothering sound of a man who's reached his end.

And the words I had practiced, all the things I was going to say, jumbled and rattled to pieces. If I tried to say them now, out loud, if I tried to put them together again, they'd come out mangled and wrong, they'd make no sense.

I squeezed my eyes shut and opened them again. I said, "It's only temporary, right?"

"What?"

"This." I waved my hand in the air at nothing, at everything. "You being in jail. Me and Ollie living with Grandma and Grandpa."

Bear rubbed his eyes. He said, "Sam . . ."

"Because you're going to get out of here. You didn't do anything wrong."

"I wish it were that easy."

"It is."

He shook his head.

"Just tell them the truth."

"I did. They don't believe me."

"Tell me, then."

"Tell you what?"

I leaned close to the glass. "What happened with Taylor Bell-weather?"

"Nothing happened. Nothing. That's the whole story."

"You saw her the night she died."

"How do you know that?"

I shrugged. "That's what they're saying."

He slumped forward and hung his head so I couldn't see his eyes.

"You saw her, didn't you? You had a fight? At the Jack Knife?"

He nodded.

"Why? What was it about?"

He kept his eyes lowered and didn't answer.

"Tell me. Please."

He lifted his head, looked straight at me.

"Please," I said again. "I want to believe you. But you have to tell me the truth. All of it from the beginning."

He hesitated, drew in a long breath, let it out again. Finally, he said, "She wanted to know about something that happened a long time ago, something that was none of her damn business. I told her to leave it alone, to leave *me* alone, but she kept asking questions. So I shouted at her, I said things I shouldn't have. I made a scene. And then I left. By myself. I lost my temper and I made a mistake behaving how I did, but she was alive when I left the bar. I never saw her again after that. And that's it. That's what happened. That's the whole story."

"And?"

"And what?" He scowled at the ceiling.

"What about the jacket?"

"I told you already, I found it in the bushes."

"You didn't know it was hers?"

He paused a few seconds before answering. "She wasn't wearing a jacket at the bar. I didn't think anything about it until you told me you found her body in the river." He leaned close to the glass, holding my gaze. "Sam, listen. If I'd known that jacket was hers, I would have left it right where I found it and called the police. I would have never brought it back to our meadow."

I dropped my gaze. He'd wanted to take the jacket to the police from the start. He'd wanted to tell the truth about everything. But I'd been so afraid. I hadn't trusted him at all.

"Sam."

I looked up again. He laid one hand against the glass.

"This isn't your fault."

I chewed on the inside of my cheek.

"It was my responsibility. I'm the parent." He pulled his hand away from the glass and looked down at the counter. "Sometimes I forget how young you still are."

"What about the key?" I asked.

He shook his head. "I don't know how it got there."

"You lied to me about the scratches."

He rubbed his eyes again, nodding.

"Why?"

"I didn't want you to think . . ." He took a deep breath and looked at the ceiling. "It doesn't matter why. I'm sorry. I should have told you. I should have told you everything."

"Like how you went to prison for driving drunk and killing somebody?"

He jerked back like I'd slapped him, and tightened his grip on the phone.

I said, "That's what you and Taylor Bellweather were fighting about, wasn't it?"

Bear's mouth twitched, and his jaw tensed, and I saw just how much of himself he'd been hiding behind his beard.

I continued, "That's why you got so upset? Because she kept pushing? When all you wanted to do was forget?"

Bear took a deep breath.

"Why didn't you tell me?"

He scraped his lips over his teeth and was quiet for so long I was afraid he wasn't going to answer me, that I would have to leave this place still not knowing. Then he sighed and propped his head in his hand. "Have you opened the new hive yet?"

"What does that have to do with anything?"

"Don't wait too long," he said. "That burr comb can get bad faster than you'd expect. And if the queen's not laying—"

"Bear, stop. I know how to take care of the bees."

We stared at each other.

I switched the phone to my other hand and asked again, "Why didn't you tell me about the accident?"

He shrugged. "You were just a kid when it happened. And then a couple years went by and I was starting to feel like I was getting my life back again. Like maybe I could even put it behind me and move on."

"You should have told me. I deserved to know. Ollie, too. We both deserved the truth."

"It just never seemed like a good time." He leaned his forehead against the palm of his hand. "I'm not the same person I was back then, and I couldn't stand the thought of disappointing you."

"You were gone for two years! You left us and we had no idea where you went. You didn't call. You didn't write. You just vanished. I was worried sick about you. And Ollie, she was just a baby and I was worried about her too. And Mom wouldn't tell us anything." My hands were shaking. "Those two years were the worst years of my life."

"Sam, I'm sorry. I called. I wrote. I did all those things, but your mother . . ." He shifted his weight on the stool and sat up a little straighter. "We both thought it would be best if you didn't know about the accident and my time in prison. We were trying to protect you. We thought it would be better for you in the long run."

I clamped my teeth down hard, biting back all the words I wanted to scream at him, all the ways he'd failed us. I thought about the unfinished letters I'd found in the teepee, how it seemed he'd started to tell me, but the words had slipped his grasp. All the explanations and apologies in the world couldn't change what had happened. We carry our pasts with us, no matter how hard we fight to break free. He knew it, Mom knew it. I knew it now, too. I took a deep breath, and then another. I came here for the truth, and that's what Bear was giving me—take it or leave it.

I started to hang up the phone.

"Wait," Bear said.

I brought the phone to my ear again, but I didn't look at him. I stared at the scabs on my knees.

He said, "It's nearly impossible for a bee to join a colony she wasn't born into. Did you know that?" He paused, but when I didn't respond, he continued, "She can bring gifts. Pollen, nectar. And maybe the hive will accept her as one of their own. Maybe. Usually, though, it doesn't end well. It's the pheromones. She doesn't smell right. They can tell she doesn't belong."

I lifted my head.

Bear laid his palm flat against the glass again. "I tried, Sam. I wanted to come back. I wanted to start over. And I wanted us to be a family again, but . . ." His mouth stayed open, stuck on some excuse that wouldn't fix anything. He shook his head. "I'm sorry. If I could go back in time, I would. If I could do everything over . . ."

I watched him a few seconds, taking in the way his shoulders sagged and how his hand moved across his chin, pulling at a beard he no longer had. I said, "The night Taylor Bellweather died? That night you left me and Ollie alone all night in the meadow?"

He blinked at me.

"Where were you?"

"It doesn't matter."

"To me it does."

"I was alone, Sam," he said. "The whole night. No one saw me. No one can give me an alibi. So, no, it doesn't matter."

"I want to know where you were." I leaned close to the glass. "I want to know what was so important you left us alone."

He closed his eyes. After a while, he opened them again and said, "I was visiting your mother."

I pulled back a little. "At the cemetery?"

He nodded.

"Why?"

"I needed to . . ." He swallowed hard and fast and wiped his hand down his face. "I needed to say good-bye."

He had skipped Mom's funeral. I'd pleaded and Grandma had argued for over an hour, but he still refused to leave the house with us. He said he wanted to remember his wife alive and smiling, not laid out in some ridiculous coffin, lowered into the ground, and covered in dirt. I told him he was selfish. He'd shrugged his shoulders and told me maybe when I fell in love I'd understand.

Bear tapped his finger on the shelf. "I let her down so many times. I let you all down."

I leaned close to the glass again, waiting for him to continue.

"I shouldn't have gone to the Jack Knife that night. I shouldn't have been there. But I wanted to do something symbolic, some-thing to show that I was ready to start over. Really start over this time. With you and with Ollie." His eyes pleaded with me to un-derstand. "I ordered a scotch straight up, but I wasn't going to drink it. Honest to God. I was going to leave it there on the bar. I was going to get up and walk out and leave it all behind." He shook his head. "And then that reporter. She just showed up out of nowhere and sat down next to me like we were old friends. She sat down and started asking questions and digging up ghosts, and all the worst parts of me came rushing back. After I left, I just . . . I couldn't come back to the meadow after what happened at the bar. Not right away. I needed to be alone for a while, get my head straight."

He rubbed his chin.

I gripped the phone tighter.

He said, "I went to your mother. I wanted to tell her how sorry I was for everything. For ruining our family and for not being a better father to you and Ollie. For failing her as a husband. I wanted to tell her I was sorry and I missed her and that things were going to be different starting now. I was going to change. I was going to look after you and Ollie the way I should have been doing all these years. I was finally going to be the father you both deserve."

He closed his eyes, and I wanted to tell him he hadn't let anyone down, that he was a good father, the best, but the words jammed in my throat. When he opened his eyes again and looked at me, something had changed, something I didn't understand right away.

He stiffened his shoulders and took a deep breath. He said, "You and Ollie are going to be fine now. Grandma and Grandpa will take good care of you. Better than anything I could ever do."

I pulled back, startled, realizing what was happening, not wanting it to be true. "What do you mean? You're not thinking of . . . you can't stay here. You can't let them . . . you didn't do anything wrong!"

"I will never be the father you need me to be, Sam. I've tried. And I just can't. I already had my chance. And I blew it. I belong in here." He sighed and lowered his head, hiding his face from me. "It's better for you and Ollie this way. It's better for everyone."

"No," I said. If there hadn't been glass between us, I would have reached out and grabbed his chin, forced him to look me in the eyes and say those words again.

"I know you're upset now, but you'll get used to the idea," he said. "You'll see I was right. Just give it some time."

"You can't give up now." My voice rose louder. "You have to keep fighting. For us. For me. And Ollie. And Mom. What about Mom? She wouldn't want this."

He glanced over his shoulder at the guard by the door and nodded, then turned back to me and said, "I'm sorry, Sam."

"Bear, don't do this!"

He hung up the phone, stood, and walked away from me.

"Dad!" I pounded on the glass and shouted for him to come back, but it was an underwater sound, too weak to carry very far.

The buzzer sounded. The door on his side opened. And then he was gone.

Zeb and I sat in his truck in the parking lot outside the jail. The keys were in the ignition, but the engine was off. I cranked down my window and turned my face to catch the breeze. Zeb buckled his seat belt. Then he unbuckled it again, rubbed his hands across his knees, and said, "You know, when I found your daddy in the meadow, I didn't know what to think at first."

A group of people came out of the jail, walked down the front steps, went to their separate parked cars, drove away.

"He was half starved and not dressed right for the winter we were having," Zeb said. "I brought him up to the house, gave him some supper and a clean set of overalls, a nice heavy coat. Even offered him a bed for the night, but he said it'd been too long since he slept out under the stars. Said if it wasn't too much trouble, could he just stay awhile in that old pasture I wasn't using anymore? I told him he could stay there as long as he needed, but he'd have to give me fifty dollars a month when he had it so I could tell anyone who asked he was renting the place, not just squatting. He wanted to give me three hundred that night. Said it was all he had. I took a hundred and told him to use the rest for food and a nice warm sleeping bag."

I propped my chin on my hand, stared out the window, and tried to imagine Bear's first, cold night. The hard ground, the chill creeping into his bones. The shame he must have felt for what he'd done, how heavy it all must have been to keep him from coming home to his wife and daughters. I imagined him looking up, seeing nothing but black space and glinting stars after all those months in prison and beginning to feel the first sparks of freedom and stirring of possibility, a longing to start over. I'd been to the meadow enough times now to understand why he'd stayed.

Zeb said, "We all knew who he was, a'course."

I looked at him. He was staring out the windshield, gripping the steering wheel with both hands.

"What do you mean?" I asked.

Zeb turned and met my gaze. The hard lines around his mouth softened into a weak smile. "Well, now. The accident happened west of here, out near Suttle Lake. Your father was driving back to Eugene. The other car, coming on home to Terrebonne."

"Did you know the other driver? The person who died?"

Zeb bit his lower lip, hesitating a moment, then saying, "It wasn't the driver who died."

"But you knew them?"

Zeb nodded. He twisted his hands on the wheel, his knuckles protruding sharply beneath his thin skin. "It was Billy Roth driving the other car. His daughter, Delilah, was riding along with him."

"Travis's sister?" I pinched the skin between my finger and my thumb, but it didn't make the pain in my stomach hurt any less.

"Yep," Zeb said. "She wasn't too much younger than Ollie is now when it happened."

I leaned back against the seat and closed my eyes. "Was it quick?"

Zeb coughed once. "Don't know. I expect so. Those roads can get real slick in the winter, real icy. Hard enough to drive that pass sober. Papers said your daddy crossed the center line, scraped along the side of Billy's car, and pushed them through the guardrail over the edge of a short cliff."

I snapped my eyes open, not wanting to picture it, not wanting those dark images to form.

"They hit a tree."

"Oh God."

"I'm sorry, Sam. Really, I am. I know this is hard to hear."

I nodded. "Yeah. No, it is. But it's . . ." And I couldn't think of how to describe what I was feeling, a sort of sinking heaviness in the pit of my stomach, and yet light and tingling at the same time, like my body was getting too big to fit in my skin.

"It's better to know," he said. "I would have said something a long time ago, but your mama asked me to keep it a secret."

I leaned my head back against the seat and sighed.

"She thought she was doing what's best," Zeb said, reaching and taking my hand, squeezing it once, then letting go. "I never once thought your daddy was a bad man. Some people did, even I suspect your daddy himself, but not me. Not Franny. During the trial, and even after. We always just said he was a man who made a bad mistake. That's all. And he deserved a second go at life just like the rest of us if we ever found ourselves in a similar situation. When he came around again, I wasn't surprised. Figured he still had his own demons to fight. And maybe, too, he wasn't done doing penance. Whatever his reasons for returning, I thought the least we could do was give him a safe place to stay until he put himself back together again, until he was ready to go home. What I didn't figure was that he'd stay so long. Or that he'd start to feel so much like family. And I sure as hell didn't figure on you and your little sister."

He laughed quietly to himself, then said, "For what it's worth, though Lord knows it ain't worth much, I know your daddy didn't kill that reporter."

It was me reaching for his hand this time around and when I had it, I didn't let go.

Franny was waiting for us at the kitchen table with Deputy Santos. They were deep in conversation but stopped talking when Zeb and I came through the door. Deputy Santos was in plain clothes, jeans and a button-up green shirt. No hat, no badge, no gun. We made eye contact, but I didn't smile at her, and she didn't smile at me.

Franny started to get up.

"Sit down, Mother," Zeb said, resting his hand gently on her shoulder. "It's just us."

Franny lifted a plate of oatmeal cookies from the table and offered them to me. "How's your father?"

I shrugged and took a cookie even though I didn't want one.

Zeb said, "Seems to be gettin' on all right." He opened the cupboard above the coffeemaker. "Fresh pot?"

Franny nodded. "Left some for you."

Zeb took down a gray mug, then glanced over his shoulder at me. "Hot cocoa?"

"Sure. I'll get it," and I stepped up behind him to grab my mom's mug. I moved aside a white and yellow one, and one that said I'D RATHER BE FISHING, but I couldn't find her ruby red one with white polka dots. And it suddenly seemed the most important thing. As if wrapping my hands around it would be the same as a hug. As if touching my lips to where hers had been would be the same as a kiss. As if somehow, I could be close to her again, find comfort, feel protected.

I turned away from the cupboard to look in the dish rack by the sink. Zeb finished pouring his coffee and sat down at the table beside Deputy Santos who lifted her cup to take a drink. Rounded red sides, white polka dots. My mother's cup. The cookie I'd been holding was now a crumbled, sticky mess. I threw it in the trash before anyone noticed.

"Sam, honey, come sit down." Franny patted the empty chair next to her. "Deputy Santos was just telling me she was able to talk to your grandparents this morning. They're on their way to the airport as we speak."

I sat down and leaned my elbows on the table, and even though I tried to look at something else—the knickknacks on the wall, the salt and pepper shakers in front of me—I couldn't keep my eyes from wandering back to Mom's coffee cup, awkward and out of place in Deputy Santos's rough hands. Her nail polish was chipped so badly it was almost gone, her cuticles shredded. There was a burn scar on the back of her left hand—from what I had no idea—but that didn't matter so much as the plain fact that her hands didn't belong to my mother. My chest hurt. I wanted to grab the mug and smash it on the floor.

"Sam? Are you listening?"

I looked at Deputy Santos.

She said, "They're going to call with flight information as soon as they have it, but they should be here sometime tomorrow night. Saturday morning at the latest."

One day. That was all I had left. To check on the bees. To pack. To say good-bye. To uncover the truth and prove Bear's innocence and salvage the pieces of our family. All of it so impossible.

"And then what?" I asked.

"And then they'll take you home." Franny reached over to pat my hand.

I pulled away from her, tucking my hands in my lap underneath the table. "We don't have a home. Not anymore."

"Oh, sweetheart," Franny said. "Of course you do."

"It's their home. Not ours."

"It'll be a good change," Deputy Santos said.

"How do you know?"

"Sam," Franny scolded.

Deputy Santos tapped her thumbs against the side of my mother's coffee cup. "You just need to give yourself a little time is all, to get used to everything."

"What about Bear?"

Zeb coughed into his fist. Franny shifted in her chair, and the wood creaked beneath her.

Deputy Santos tightened her grip around the mug. "What about him?"

"Did you follow up on those boot prints? The tire tracks?"

"I'm sorry, Sam. I can't talk about the case with you."

"You did before."

"I know. And I shouldn't have."

"I want to stay here." I leaned back.

"You know that's not possible," Deputy Santos said.

"As long as Bear's in jail, I'm not leaving."

"You're still a minor, Sam."

"So?"

"So it's not for you to decide."

"Then whose decision is it?"

Franny smoothed her fingers along the edges of the place mat in front of her. When she spoke, her voice was faint and stretched thin with emotion. "Your grandparents think it'd be best if you and Ollie were with them right now. With family."

"But you and Zeb, you're our family, too. We were going to stay here with you anyway, if Bear hadn't found a place by the end of September. Can't we just stick with that plan?"

Franny gave me a half smile. "It might not seem fair to you now, but your grandparents just want to make sure you and Ollie are in the best possible place. They're trying to protect you the only way they know how."

"Mom would want us to stay."

"Your mama's not here, child," Franny was whispering now, and her eyes dropped away from me, down to her hands laid flat on the table. "Nothing else to do but put on your best face and carry on."

"Besides," Deputy Santos said, "school's going to be starting up again in a few weeks. Better to be back with kids your own age, don't you think? Make some new friends."

"Bear registered us at the schools here."

"It won't be hard to get all your paperwork to the school district in your grandparents' neighborhood," Deputy Santos said. "It's not your responsibility to worry about any of that anyway."

"But I don't want to go."

"Sam." Deputy Santos leaned closer to me.

I leaned away.

She said, "It'll be better for you to be away from all of this. Better for Ollie, too. Trust me."

I pushed away from the table and hurried out the sliding glass door before they had a chance to say anything else. I went straight to the barn where Zeb had cleared a place for our bikes, grabbed the handlebars of the black-and-red Schwinn, swung my leg over the seat, and then just sat there, feet on the ground, not going anywhere, suspended and trying to decide.

Deputy Santos came out to the barn and stood in front of me. She folded her arms across her chest. "Joe Mancetti called me last night."

I picked at a small hole forming in the handlebar grip. "Who?"

"Don't play stupid. I know you called him pretending to be me."

I bit down on my lower lip and shrugged.

"Why?" she asked.

I shook my head. "I don't know what you're talking about."

"Did you break into my house, too?"

I stared at the rafters, where the sun was shining in through the open loft door, spreading yellow light into dark corners.

Deputy Santos sighed. "It's an election year. Did you know that?"

I shrugged again.

"People around here haven't exactly been thrilled with the way Sheriff Harper's been handling the department. They haven't been so thrilled about having a woman on the force, either. This case is high profile, Sam. We have to tread carefully, do everything by the book. If something happens that jeopardizes our investigation, if I take even one step in the wrong direction, I could lose my job."

I started to push the bike around her.

She grabbed the handlebars, slamming me to a stop. "If you're planning something else, Sam, just forget about it. Leave it be. I know you want to protect him, but you're going to make things worse."

"Do you think he did this?" I pushed a strand of hair behind my ear. "Do you think Bear's guilty?"

She hesitated, then said, "Yes. I do."

"And you want me to believe that, too, don't you?"

"I just think it will be easier if you start working through it now."

"Easier?"

"To move on. To get over this and get back to being a kid and having fun." When I didn't say anything, she continued, "I know how hard this summer's been for you, Sam. First you lose your mom. Then this whole awful thing with Bear. But you're strong. You're young. You'll bounce back." She smiled.

I gave her a cold stare, and she sighed, shook her head and said, "Ollie needs you right now. She needs someone who can look out for her and set a good example."

"What about me?" I wrenched my bike out of her hand. "Who's going to look out for me?"

I jammed my feet onto the bike pedals and rode hard away from her, around the barn, to the dirt road that would take me to the meadow and the bees and the river and all the very best things I loved about August and my father. I rode with my head lifted high and my eyes wide open, taking it all in, every yellow grass blade and white butterfly, every flitting cloud and grasshopper. If this was going to be the last time I saw this place, I wanted to memorize every last inch, shadow, and crinkled leaf. If this was going to be the last time, I wanted to be able to remember every good thing.

Just before the hemlock stump, I slammed on my brakes.

Wide tire tracks cut deep ruts around the stump, carving holes in the brush and shredding the grass, leaving flowers trampled and wilting, trees scarred and bent, pushed aside by whatever silver, shiny, barreling beast had come through here. Our path into the meadow was narrow, meant for people walking, not a truck ramming, shoving its way into a place it had no business going. I dropped my bike in the dirt and ran the rest of the way through the trees.

The air changed as I entered the meadow. The shadows grew darker, turning into something thick and shifting. Bees swarmed, spinning in mad clumps, humming so loud I had to cover my ears. The tire tracks cut straight through the center of the meadow and into the apiary before circling back around, back to the path and the hemlock stump, the dirt road leading to the highway. Whoever'd been in the truck had also turned over the picnic table and spray-painted black and violent words on the outside of our teepee: FREAK and MURDERER and BURN IN HELL. But it was the apiary they'd focused on most, the destruction here ruthless and assured.

Two hives had been knocked onto their sides, and the tops were broken open, bees visible on the inside, working to save what they could. A third had been tipped and then run over, smashed beyond recognition. Shattered frames and spoiled comb littered the now damp and sticky, amber-tinted ground. And everywhere: bees. Lost bees, wandering bees, angry bees, dead bees. The ones who'd survived flew in mad circles around me, which meant this damage was recent, maybe even as early as a few hours ago. There hadn't been enough time for the colonies to regroup and fly off to new homes. They were still reeling from the violence and counting their dead.

I stood apart from the hives, watching the bees tumble and riot, unable to catch my breath, trying to think, trying to reason the who and why, but I couldn't. There was no sense to this destruction.

If Bear were here, he'd tell me we could salvage the pieces. He'd tell me to start at the beginning. Rebuild the boxes, replace the frames. Leave a jar of sugar water and let the bees do the rest. "They'll carry on," he would have said. "They'll work harder. They'll fight. They'll survive." But Bear wasn't here, and I didn't have the equipment to do any of that. Nor the skill.

A bee flew right up close to my face. I waved her away, but she came right back, darting and weaving in erratic patterns.

"What do you want?" I felt a little stupid talking to her, but she was the only one here to listen. "What? What the hell am I supposed to do?"

The bee landed on my arm. I froze. Her delicate feet whisper-danced over my skin, her wings fanned slowly up and down. She crawled in tiny circles.

I whispered, "Go away."

She walked the length of my arm from my wrist to my elbow, moving toward my sleeve.

I whispered, "I can't help you."

She turned and walked back down to my hand. I tried to shake her off, but she kept returning, landing on my arm again and again.

I drew her close to my face. "I don't know what you want from me."

My breath moved her wings, and she stopped walking. She turned her huge black eyes on me, waiting. There was something alarming about the stare of that bee—like she was looking inside me, seeing everything, even the parts I stuffed way down and hid deep. Like she knew me better than I knew myself and knew what I was going to do even before I had decided.

I glanced at the broken hives, the comb scattered across the grass, the abandoned, vandalized teepee, and the overgrown garden. I looked again at the bee and whispered, "You're on your own now. He's gone and he's not coming back."

The bee plunged down her abdomen too quick for me to fling her away, and the sting came hot and furious, a small patch of skin swelling red almost instantaneously. I yelped and tossed the bee off my hand. She stumbled away, flying off somewhere to die. With my fingernail, I picked out the stinger she'd left behind.

I couldn't sleep. I closed my eyes and saw cars flying off cliffs and felt bees crawling over my skin and heard someone moaning and thrashing. I opened my eyes and returned to the quiet, dark bedroom at the top of the stairs and there was only the rustle of blankets when Ollie rolled over and my throbbing hand keeping me awake.

Franny had made me soak the sting in an ice bath and then applied a warm oatmeal paste. It had helped for a few minutes right after, but now it hurt again. And itched something awful. When she'd asked me what happened, I'd told her I was checking the new hive.

"Without any gear?"

"Bear does it."

"He lives every day with those bees," she'd said. "They've reached an understanding."

I didn't tell her about the damaged hives or the threats scrawled black on white, because I didn't want her to worry. I was afraid, too, that somehow Bear would find out and I didn't want him to know how badly I'd failed the bees, failed him. Tomorrow I'd go back to the meadow with Zeb's old suit, the one he kept in a plastic box in the barn just in case, and fix what I could. Try, at least. I'd do what Bear would do if he were here. I'd start at the beginning.

I got out of bed and put on jeans and a sweatshirt, my socks and shoes. Bear had said he'd driven to Eugene the night Taylor Bellweather was murdered. To the cemetery. And maybe Deputy Santos and Detective Talbert didn't believe him, but I did. And maybe they'd stopped looking for the real killer, but that didn't mean I had to. Bear had returned the truck to Zeb and Franny with a nearly full tank, which meant he had to have bought gas somewhere between here and there. Which meant someone must have seen him, talked to him.

Someone who could give him an alibi, even though he said there was no one. There had to be someone. There had to be.

I grabbed a flashlight and the folded-up newspaper I'd been keeping in my duffel bag since Bear's arrest. As quietly as I could, I tiptoed downstairs and out the back door.

The truck was unlocked. I got into the driver's seat and felt under the visor for the spare key Zeb kept there for Bear, so he could use the truck anytime he wanted. I had my learner's permit, and Mom had been letting me drive with her to the grocery store and back every week. I'd even driven this truck once last summer when Bear and I were checking fences for Zeb. Bear had given me the keys and said, "Go easy on the gas pedal." As long as I didn't speed, or break any laws, as long as I didn't attract any attention, maybe I could get away with it.

I turned the key in the ignition. The engine roared awake. I glanced at the house. The windows were still dark, but I doubted they'd stay that way for very much longer. I turned on the headlights and jumped so high out of the seat, I hit my knee on the bottom of the dashboard.

Ollie stood in the driveway directly in front of the truck, holding a small, flat box with one hand, keeping the other on her hip. A crooked apparition in the dim yellow lights, she'd shown up out of nowhere.

I rolled down the window and leaned my head out. "Go back to bed."

She came around to the passenger side, opened the door, climbed into the front seat, and buckled her seat belt.

I didn't have time to argue with her, or push her out, or ask her what the hell she was doing out here wearing nothing but pajamas and slippers, because lights turned on inside the house. First, the light in Zeb and Franny's bedroom. Then the one in the kitchen. Then the floodlights on the front porch snapped on, burning white hot across the grass.

Ollie locked her door.

"Goddamn it." I put the truck in drive and stepped hard on the gas.

I didn't need a map. I'd been there twice already, but even just once would have been more than enough. When I buried my mother, it was like I'd buried some small part of me, too. For the rest of my life, I will always know how to find my way back to her. I could drive there with my eyes closed. Highway 126 two hours due west until you see a flagpole. Driveway is on your left.

ollie

My sister stops the truck in the empty parking lot in front of the mausoleum and turns off the engine. "Maybe you should just stay in the car."

I open my door first and get out, holding the Ouija board safe under my arm.

My sister scrambles after me. "Ollie! Stop! Where are you going?"

The one from the river runs ahead of us. In the flashlight beam, she is a bright green snake, weaving through the grass, a glow-in-the-dark jump rope dragged along by an invisible hand. The trees bow at her passing.

The moon is a thin sliver, casting pale light over the cemetery. The headstones that rise from the ground look like hunched old men. The grass is gray. The trees are black. The shadows in between are constantly changing shape.

And the one from the river goes faster.

"Ollie, this isn't the right way," my sister says, but follows me still.

We veer off a gravel path and tiptoe between rows of grave markers that are buried flush to the ground. The one from the river stops in front of a plot where the earth is still mounded and the grass laid over the top is lined with seams.

My sister puts her hand on my shoulder and says, "Come on, Oll. This isn't where we want to be. Mom's over there."

I shrug off her hand and point to the temporary plastic grave marker.

My sister moves closer and shines the flashlight so she can read the name. She squints and then jerks her head around to me again, her eyes wide and confused and more angry than afraid.

"How did you know she was here?" she says, backing away. "Did Franny tell you?"

The one from the river sits on her grave and traces the letters of her name.

T-A-Y-L-O-R-B-E-L-L-W-E-A-T-H-E-R.

She does it again and again and hums a little to herself.

I sit on the grass beside her and take the Ouija board out of the box.

My sister grabs my arm and tries to drag me to my feet. "No. No, absolutely not. There are no such things as ghosts, Ollie. No such things as unsettled spirits or happy spirits or any kind of spirits at all. And I'm not going to play any of your stupid games."

The one from the river purses her lips and blows at my sister's face. A rush of cold air moves across both of us and my sister's hair flutters. She lets me go and takes a step back. She shivers and hugs her arms. She looks left and right and up and down, but the trees are still and the night is warm.

I pat the empty grass beside me.

My sister shakes her head.

The one who follows me laughs, and it sounds like a fireworks explosion. The stars twinkle brighter.

Our noise has attracted others. They inch out of the darkness, hobbling and sliding and skipping closer. Their whispers swell inside my head and I cannot think. Their energies fill my chest and I cannot breathe. I ask them to leave us alone. I say, *Go away. It's not your time.*

The one from the river hisses. The others retreat into the darkness. The one who follows me sighs and settles into the open arms of a nearby concrete angel. My head stops throbbing, the pressure in my chest releases. I rest my fingertips on the wooden planchette and nod to the one from the river. She puts her damp hands over mine.

I look up at my sister who can see only my hands. I raise my eyebrows and shrug one shoulder.

"Fine." She rolls her eyes. "Fine. I'll play. But it doesn't mean anything."

She waits until I nod, and then she says, "Who killed Taylor Bellweather?"

I turn my attention back to the board and think, *Who did this? Who murdered you?* Her hands move my hands, and the planchette skips across the board to the first letter.

sam

I was supposed to be the practical sister, the no-nonsense one, the older, wiser, ghosts-are-for-little-kids-and-crazy-people sister. I was supposed to be watching out for Ollie, keeping her safe, not dragging her to a cemetery in the dead middle of night, breaking who knew how many laws. So when she set up that stupid board game, the only thing I was thinking about was how to get her moving again so we could go to Mom's grave and then get the hell out of here.

"Fine," I said. "I'll play. But it doesn't mean anything."

Her pale hands, ghost hands, barely touched the fat wooden pointer she moved across the lettered board.

Who killed Taylor Bellweather?

R

Who dumped her in Crooked River?

O

Who in Terrebonne has something to hide?

T

Ollie moved the pointer to the last letter.

H

She looked up at me.

"That's not funny, Ollie."

But she wasn't laughing.

A rustling noise started up somewhere behind me. Like foot-steps swishing through dry grass, strange voices muttering in the dark. I spun around, sweeping the flashlight beam in a wide arc, but the shadows that surrounded us were too thick to see much of anything besides hulking gravestones, scratching tree limbs, and crouching bushes. No shapes moving closer, no animals scuffling through the grass. The air was heavy and stale and still. No wind tonight. Not one gust. I was letting my imagination get the best of me.

I shined the flashlight back on Ollie and her stupid game. "Put it away."

Ollie lifted her hand to block the light. Her eyes were black smudges, her lips straight, gray lines.

"Put the game away," I said again. "And let's go."

When she still didn't move, I kicked the edge of the board. The pointer skittered and hopped away from the *H,* landing on the word *NO* scrawled in the top corner. I took a step back. Ollie grabbed the pointer and clutched it to her chest. She scowled at me.

"It doesn't mean anything," I said. "I told you. It's just a stupid game. Anyway, how do I know you didn't just move that pointer your-self, by your own strength? It doesn't prove anything."

Her scowl deepened.

"I shouldn't have let you." I crouched and laid the flashlight on the ground. The beam pierced a bright tunnel through the grass. I folded the board along its well-worn seams, in half and then in half again, and returned it to its box. "It's disrespectful."

I held out my hand for the pointer. "Give it to me."

Ollie shook her head.

"We're done playing."

She looked over her shoulder where faded moonlight was falling down silver, brushing soft light on a concrete angel. When she turned back to me, her mouth was open like she was about to speak.

I dropped my hand to my side. "Well, say it."

Ollie took a breath.

"Go on. Say something." I stood up and put my hands on my hips. "Call me names. Shout at me. Tell me what an awful, horrible sister I am. Go on. Cuss, spit, scream. What's the matter? Ghost got your tongue?" And I said it in a way that wasn't nice.

Ollie snapped her mouth closed, tossed the pointer into the box, and replaced the lid. Gathering the board game under one arm, she rose to her feet and started to walk back to the truck. Her toe caught the end of the flashlight, spinning it in a circle so the beam was illuminating Taylor Bellweather's name. I snatched the flashlight up from the grass and swung it after Ollie, but she had already melted into the dark.

A few seconds later, the truck door popped open. The cab light blinked on and then off again as Ollie slammed the door shut. Maybe Franny and my grandparents and, yes, maybe even Deputy Santos, were right. Maybe Terrebonne wasn't the best place for me and Ollie right now. I'd had this idea that Ollie might pick up talking again once we got to the meadow, that she could shake off whatever sadness was keeping her silent, but now I was beginning to understand it wasn't going to be as simple as that and staying here was only making things worse.

I waited for Ollie another few seconds beside Taylor Bellweather's grave, but she stayed in the truck. I thought about going after her, opening the door, taking her hand, and making her come with me to Mom's grave the way Grandma had tried last week when we came by here on our way to the meadow. Ollie had refused to get out of the car that day. The only time she'd been to Mom's grave was for the funeral, but I couldn't think of any good reason to force her now.

I kept the flashlight pointed down at the narrow, gravel path and walked deeper into the cemetery. I'd only ever been here during the day when the landscape was bright and airy and layered with color. At night, with just this blue-white beam illuminating no bigger than a three-by-three patch of the world at any given time, I started to feel pressed in, like any second I'd run into a wall or fall into an open grave. I tried telling myself that this place was no different than any other place, but then the flashlight beam would sweep over a crooked stone and I would remember all the buried bodies. Hundreds of men and women, husbands, wives, sons, daughters. Decomposing and falling to pieces right here under my feet.

I kept the beam pointed as straight as possible and followed the path to the left and up a small rise, then into the grass, six headstones in and three rows below a large stone cross. It's hard enough trying to find a certain gravestone in the day. At night, it's nearly impossible.

The flashlight danced over graves and flowers and names, stones worn almost flat by time and rain. Here lies Mr. John C. Gordon, may he rest in peace. His wife was buried beside him. Their two daughters and their husbands took up space nearby. I spun in a slow circle. She was here. Somewhere. Six headstones in, three rows below the large stone cross. Or was it above? I walked up the hill, past the cross to the third row.

Because it had only been a few weeks and the headstone wasn't ready yet, her grave was marked with a small placard, a piece of paper shoved into a plastic sleeve. Printed black on white was her name, Sara Bethany McAlister, the day she was born, March 2, 1949, and the day she died, July 4, 1988. These would be carved on granite, along with the epitaph Grandma had picked out because Bear hadn't wanted anything to do with it. *Beloved Daughter and Mother.* As if that was all that counted. As if an entire person was made up of only two parts.

She was other things, too. Stargazer, storyteller, bibliophile, chocoholic and something of a weekend wino, gardener, collector of roosters and spoons and oddly shaped rocks, a good hugger, a better back-scratcher, a terrible cook, loyal, passionate, ever the eternal optimist, wife. A loving wife. Despite how it may have looked to people on the outside, or how many times Grandma had begged her to file for divorce, or all the days, weeks, months they spent apart, Mom had never stopped loving Bear. And he had never stopped loving her. And maybe someday, no matter what Grandma or anyone else thought, maybe someday Bear would have come home to her, to us. We could have been a family again.

I moved the flashlight from left to right across the placard. Grandma had left roses when we'd stopped here on our way to the meadow, but they were dead now, brown and drooping over, their dried petals falling to the dirt. I crouched to take them out of the vase, planning to throw them out in the garbage can in the parking lot, and that's when I saw the honey settled down in the grass, a pint jar with a yellow label and red ribbon.

I picked it up, turning it in my hand, and shined the flashlight on it. The honey glowed, like something on the inside was trying to burn its way out. In ancient Egypt, people used to bury their loved ones with sealed honey pots so they would have something to eat in the afterlife. A waste of good honey, if you asked me.

There was writing on the lid, black marker scrawl, and I recognized Bear's handwriting from the receipts he'd written out for people who bought honey and from those letters he'd started but never finished.

On the lid, he'd written, *My love for always. Forgive me.*

I put the jar back in the grass beside the vase. So here it was. Proof that Bear had been here, that he was telling the truth. Grandma and I could both be witnesses for the defense. "I swear to tell the truth, the whole truth and nothing but the truth. So help me God. No, the honey was not in the cemetery Saturday morning when we stopped to leave flowers at my mother's grave. Yes, that is my father's handwriting. No, I did not actually see him in the cemetery on Monday night, but . . ." It wasn't enough. It meant something to me, but that was all. No one else would be convinced.

If I could set up the timeline better . . .

If I could find someone who'd testify that they saw Bear in the area between the time he left the bar and the time he showed up for breakfast . . .

If he would fight harder for us . . .

Ifs and ifs and ifs. Our entire future dependent on conditional clauses.

I'd been carrying Mom and Bear's honeymoon picture around with me since I'd taken it from the teepee. I slipped it from my pocket now and tucked it in beside the jar of honey. It seemed the right place to leave it.

Something rustled in the grass, like someone was walking over to me. I swept the flashlight beam to one side and then the other, and then over my shoulder, then around to the front.

"Ollie? Is that you?"

Another sweep of the beam. I didn't see anyone or anything and the sound had stopped, but I couldn't shake the feeling that I was being watched. Probably just a raccoon. I switched off the flashlight and walked through the shifting camouflage of darkness and pale moonlight back to the truck where Ollie was waiting, her seat belt buckled and ready to go.

Along the highway between the cemetery and Zeb and Franny's farm, I counted six gas stations. Four were shuttered and dark, and when I pulled the truck through, the signs in the windows all said CLOSED, and though the hours varied a little from station to station, all four had been closed since at least 10:00 P.M. and would stay closed until at least 5:00 A.M. Only two of the six stations still had their lights on, welcoming late-night drivers.

The first one I tried was a Chevron. The attendant was a rough-looking man with gray scruff and slicked-back hair. His lower lip bulged, and just before he reached the truck he turned his head and spat.

He leaned into the open window. "Awfully late for two young birds like you to be flitting about, isn't it?"

One of his eyes wandered, taking its own initiative and looking off in some more interesting direction.

I held the newspaper folded to the front page and Bear's mug shot out to him. "Do you recognize this man?"

"You buying gas?"

I shook my head.

He said, "Nope, never seen him," without even looking at the picture.

I dug a wadded-up five-dollar bill from my pocket and shoved it out the window alongside the newspaper. "What about now?"

The man took the five dollars, then leaned in close and squinted at the grainy picture. He shook his head real slow. "Nope. Still never seen him."

He pocketed the money and sauntered back to his post inside a small, glass-enclosed office where he settled down onto a tall stool and lit a cigarette. The smoke crowded up against the glass, obscuring the man for a few seconds before breaking apart and disappearing through the cracked-open door. He kept his face pointed away from me.

We drove on.

The second open station was an Arco and the lights glowed bright on the horizon for several miles before we actually came up to the driveway. A blue sedan was parked at one of the pumps, the driver a hunched silhouette tapping his thumbs on the steering wheel.

I didn't pull up to any pump this time. I parked in front of the convenience store and left the engine running.

"Stay here," I told Ollie and got out of the truck.

A bell above the double glass doors rang.

The kid behind the counter looked up and said, "Can I help you?"

His skin was dark, his eyes golden brown. He smiled and his teeth were shining white. He was only a few years older than me, and cute, too. Any other summer, I probably would have been too embarrassed to even say hi. I slid the newspaper in front of him, and he leaned his elbows on the counter, bending close for a better look.

"You know him?"

The kid looked up at me, nodding. "Sure, I do."

And my heart lifted. And my feet wanted to dance across the ceiling.

"He's that crazy hobo who lives out in the woods. In a teepee or something, right? He beat that girl to death a couple weeks back."

Ten days. It had only been ten days since Taylor died. And no, my father hadn't beaten anyone. Those were just rumors and terrible lies. I pulled the paper away from him and held it down beside my leg.

"You ever see him around here?" I asked.

The kid leaned back on his stool. "No, but if I ever did . . ." And then he punched his fists in the air, one-two-three, quick jabs meant to break a man's nose.

"Yeah. Right. Thanks," I mumbled and returned to the truck.

I tossed the newspaper on the floor at Ollie's feet. She bent, picked it up, and stared at Bear's picture for a few seconds. Then she spread it out flat and laid it on the seat between us, keeping her fingers on the newsprint close to Bear's face.

I drove back onto the highway and headed toward Terrebonne, keeping the speedometer steady at fifty-five. Ollie, still holding the Ouija board in her lap, leaned her head against the door. Now was as good a time as any to tell her what I had learned about Bear, about his accident and Delilah Roth, about how he'd fought with Taylor Bellweather the night before she died and maybe he wouldn't ever be coming home.

I glanced over at her. Her eyes were closed. A car passed in the op- posite direction and the headlights swept through the glass, brushing gold over her face.

"Ollie?" I whispered.

Her eyes stayed shut. Her mouth was open a little, something that always happened when she fell asleep in a car. Turning my attention back to the highway and the double yellow lines rolling on for miles, I let Ollie sleep.

When we finally got back to Zeb and Franny's, it was closing in on three in the morning. The lights were still on, and before I even had a chance to shut off the engine, the front door of the house opened. Franny hobbled across the porch, stopping at the top of the steps and leaning one hand on the railing. Zeb followed her, taking his time. They were both dressed, though Franny had on house slippers and her hair was pinned in curlers. I turned off the truck and took the keys out of the ignition.

Zeb went down the steps slowly, pausing at the bottom to rub his hip and tug at his belt before going on.

I nudged Ollie's shoulder. "We're back."

She shifted and raised her head, saw Zeb coming toward us, and turned to look at me. There was still sleep in her eyes. She rubbed at it with knuckled fists.

"I'll tell them it was all my idea," I said, because it was. "I'll tell them I made you come with me."

She started to shake her head. I reached for her hand and squeezed it gently. "It'll be okay."

Zeb tapped on my window. I opened the door, and he took a step back.

He crossed his arms over his chest. "Where in hell's blazes have you two been?"

I climbed out of the truck. Ollie climbed out after me, holding the Ouija board under her arm. We left the newspaper crumpled on the seat.

I said, "We went to see Mom."

From the porch, Franny shouted, "Are they all right, Zeb? Is everything okay?"

"They're fine, Mother." He never moved his eyes from me.

"Do you know what time it is?" he asked.

I stared at the ground and scuffed my shoe in the gravel.

He said, "I would have taken you, if you'd just said something."

"We wanted to go alone."

He shifted his attention to Ollie, taking in the board game tucked under her arm. "Is that right?"

"We didn't want to bother you." I reached for my wallet in my back pocket. "I have my learner's permit. And I know how—"

He waved the card away. "We were this close to calling the police," he said. "You could have been hurt. Or killed. You could have killed someone else." He pinched the skin between his eyes and exhaled sharply. "Both of you. Get inside."

When Ollie got to the front porch, Franny gathered her under one arm and took her into the house. I started to say something about paying for the gas I used, but Zeb just shook his head and held out his hand.

"Keys," he said.

I handed them over.

Just before he pulled open the front door, Zeb stopped and turned and said, "What were you thinking?"

The floorboards overhead groaned as Franny and Ollie shuffled down the hallway. Franny's muffled voice drifted downstairs, but I couldn't make out the words.

If Mom were here she'd know what to do, how to fix this mess we'd gotten ourselves into. She'd be the one to decide. But it was just me and Ollie left now, so I had to do what I thought best. I had to make the decision for both of us.

"I'm sorry," I said. "Really, I am. And I won't do anything like this ever again. I promise."

Ollie and I slept in the next morning and missed breakfast.

When we finally came downstairs for lunch, Zeb didn't say one word to us. The three of us ate our ham and cheese sandwiches in silence, while Franny rattled on about one thing or another. When Zeb finished, he laid his napkin over the crumbs on his plate, pushed back in his chair, got up, and, leaving his dirty dishes on the table, went out the back door. He didn't look at me the entire time, not even a passing glance.

I picked at my sandwich, eating a few bites before pushing the plate away from me.

Ollie ate half her sandwich and poked holes into the other half with her finger. We were both slouched in our chairs, frowning at nothing in particular.

"Well, aren't you two a lively bunch," Franny said, getting up and clearing our plates from the table.

"Did my grandma call yet?" I asked.

"About an hour ago." Franny left the dishes in the sink and came back to the table. "Their flight arrives in Portland tonight, around eight thirty. They wanted to rent a car and drive straight here, but I convinced them to get a hotel, get a good night's rest, that you and Ollie were safe with us. They'll be here to get you sometime before lunch tomorrow."

"Guess we should pack," I said.

Ollie got up from the table and left the kitchen. Franny and I listened to her footsteps on the stairs and then overhead. The bedroom door slammed shut.

Franny leaned her chin on her hand and stared at me. "What happened last night, Sam?"

I shrugged and crossed my arms over my chest.

"It's just, you're usually so responsible. Especially when it comes to Ollie."

I stared at the ceiling.

Franny sighed and leaned back in her chair again. "I suppose we shouldn't be surprised. Not really. Not after all that's happened."

"Did you tell my grandparents?"

Franny shook her head. "No one was hurt, praise the blessed Lord, so there isn't any reason to go and make a fuss about it."

I relaxed a little and settled more comfortably into the chair. "Thanks, Franny."

She clicked her tongue on the roof of her mouth. "Now don't you go thanking me, young lady. I was all ready to tell your grandma exactly what kind of trouble you two girls had been up to until Zeb told me to hold my tongue. He said since you were in our care and it was our truck and our house, then that made it our business and no one else's."

"I'm sorry, Franny. I really am. I'll pay you for gas or rent or whatever."

She snorted and flapped her hand in the air. "It's all right. I know you're not going to go and do something like that again. Won't really have much of a chance to, I suppose."

We sat quietly together.

Franny cleared her throat. "'Course, we can't just close our eyes and pretend it never happened. That wouldn't be the right thing either."

I rearranged the salt and pepper shakers so they sat side by side in the middle of the table.

"We decided that the best thing would be to ground both of you girls for the rest of your time here." She paused, as if waiting for me to put up a fight.

I stayed quiet.

She continued, "Until your grandparents arrive, you and Ollie are not allowed to leave the house. I want to know where you are and what you're doing every single second, okay?"

I nodded.

She seemed surprised that I was agreeing to her punishment so easily, but the truth was, I was done. I quit. I was giving up. Bear had, so why couldn't I? Last night, seeing Ollie standing in the dark in her pajamas and slippers, seeing how worked up she got over that stupid Ouija board, then seeing her sleeping so peacefully with the headlights moving over her face, all of that reminded me that the other stuff I'd been so focused on—finding out what really happened to Taylor Bellweather, trying to save a man who didn't want saving—

none of it mattered as much as making sure Ollie was happy again. Happy and safe.

Franny sighed, then stood, went to the sink, and started filling it with hot water.

I reached for a folded-up newspaper that was sitting in the middle of the table and opened it to read the headlines:

OVERTURNED LOG TRUCK CAUSES FOUR-HOUR

TRAFFIC JAM

ONE-HUNDRED-DEGREE HEAT WAVE

PREDICTED FOR NEXT WEEK

Nothing about Taylor Bellweather or Bear or the pending trial. And so life goes on.

I laid the paper down again and started to get up from the table.

Zeb poked his head through the back door. "Seems like you're gonna want to get your shoes on, Sam, and come on out here with me."

Franny turned toward him, wiping her hands on her apron. "What's going on?"

"It's the hives," he said. "Somebody took it upon themselves to come in and smash things up a bit."

"Oh no," Franny said, touching her fingers to her cheek. "Oh, that's just awful. How bad is it?"

With all that had happened last night, I'd forgotten about the bees. But Zeb seemed to understand by my reaction—or lack of one—that none of this was news to me. He gave me a pointed look, like I'd let him down, and then just shook his head.

"There are a few worth saving," he said. "But I could use Sam's help."

Franny said, "We agreed they aren't to leave the house."

"I'll be with her the whole time," he said, and then he waved me to follow him out the door. "Come on, then. I haven't got all day. Plus, if you're planning on leaving these bees here for me to take care of until your daddy gets out of jail, I'm gonna need some instructions on how to keep the little buggers happy."

I said, "I don't have my gear."

"I've got my old suit in the barn," he said. "You can use that."

"What about you?"

"This'll do just fine." He gestured to his long-sleeved flannel shirt and overalls. "Your daddy once said bees won't sting if you move slow. Figure that should be easy enough for me."

Franny sighed and shook her head and reached under the kitchen sink for a bottle of dish soap.

I pulled on my boots and hurried outside.

ollie

I'm supposed to be in the guest room packing. That's where I was an hour ago when Nana Fran came in to check on me and said I couldn't leave the house. I'm supposed to be grounded. I hand the librarian a slip of paper.

He squints at the name I scribbled down and then looks at me with eyebrows raised, lips curled in amusement. "Roth, huh?"

I nod.

"Getting an early start on next year's homework?"

I nod again.

He laughs and says, "Well, let's see what we can find, shall we?"

This library is smaller than the one I normally go to, but I like how close I am to all the books here. How, as I walk between the shelves, I can reach my hand and brush my fingers along their spines, and we are connected. I feel safe with all these stories around me.

I feel invincible.

The librarian shows me to a round table near the reference desk.

"There aren't any books written solely about Billy. His career was just getting started when the accident happened. Though, now that I think about it, even back then he was never much for the spotlight. He's only included in one or two art books, a few paragraphs, nothing substantial. But there are certainly a lot of articles and newspaper clippings that discuss his life at length, his art, the accident. His head injury and ongoing recovery, his rise and slow fade into obscurity. More than enough to keep you busy for a few hours, I should think."

He pulls an oversize book from the shelf and lays it on the table. The cover is brown leather, and inside are pages and pages of newsprint bound together with string. The librarian opens to the first article, dated January 1, ten years ago. Something about Bend's annual New Year's Eve Party ending in fireworks and a barn burning to the ground.

"If you can't find what you need here, let me know and I'll see what I can find in the basement."

I pull the book closer and scan the first page, but there is nothing here about Billy Roth. I pinch the bottom corner and turn to the next page.

The librarian bends over my shoulder and whispers, "The good stuff starts in February."

I flip forward and snag on the front-page headline from February 19:

LOCAL ARTIST INVOLVED IN DEADLY
COLLISION NEAR SUTTLE LAKE

Here I see Billy Roth's name and his daughter's, Delilah. Here I see my father's name, too. His real name, Frank McAlister. I run my fingertip across the letters, wonder what he was doing so far from home that night. Wonder how much of this my sister knows. If anything.

"I'll leave you to it, then," the librarian says. He claps his hands together, straightens his shoulders, and in a voice too loud for the library says, "In addition to the *Bulletin,* we also maintain collections of the *Register-Guard* as well as several other major newspapers. The *New York Times,* the *Washington Post,* the *Oregonian . . .*" He ticks them off on his fingers.

I smile at him, then bend my head over the newsprint.

"Good luck, then," he says and goes.

In the next dozen articles, I learn everything there is to know about Billy Roth and Frank McAlister, the man who became Bear.

Husbands.

Fathers.

College graduates with such promise, each moving along his own path to greatness, their families still young, their futures stretched out in front of them, the wide world waiting.

And then Bear went to a bar and got drunk.

A moment of bad judgment. A split second. Blink. That's how long it takes for whole lives to fracture and souls to collapse into shadow and screaming.

On the wall nearby, light weeps, dripping down the beige paint like tears, pooling gold on the red carpet beneath. The one who follows me is crying, and so am I. I ask her to stop. *Please,* I think. Her tears, her sorrow, it feels too much like drowning.

I close the book. I don't remember when Bear left us. I was too young. And I don't remember him coming back, either. But I've read enough to know now why he stayed in the meadow away from us and what needs to happen next. When I leave, the librarian is nowhere to be seen. On the street, no one tries to stop me.

If I go to my sister with only the news clippings, she will say, "So what? So Bear and Billy knew each other? What does that have to do with Taylor Bellweather? What does that have to do with anything?"

Everything, I would say if I had the words. *It has everything to do with everything.* And I would tell her, too, that I know how to fix it. How to bring Bear home. And then I would say, *Don't give up on us.*

If I had the words.

Without them, I need something more. Proof my sister and Nana Fran and Papa Zeb and Deputy Santos and everyone else can see with their very own eyes.

The basement door of Delilah's Attic is propped open with a piece of broken concrete. I peer through the crack.

The light is on, but no one's down there. There's no movement, no sound, no shuffling or rattling or thumping. I open the door a little wider.

The one who follows me waits at the bottom of the stairs. I feel her impatience like a stone in my throat, and I know that whatever it is she wants me to find is still here and whatever I find, I will show my sister and she will understand and say the right things and Bear will be released. The proof is down those steps, in that basement.

Somewhere.

I go straight to the desk and search through the papers on top. Receipts, inventory lists, business cards of other shops and antique dealers, brochures from New York art galleries, news clippings reviewing recent and upcoming shows in all the major art cities around the world. Words and names have been circled and highlighted. Notes written in the margins.

I don't know what I'm looking for.

A connection where one plus one equals one. She was there and he was there and they were there together. Then she washed up dead.

The papers shift under my fingertips. I dig. And dig. The layers shift and underneath I find a calendar. I push everything else aside. August 27 is circled and starred and exclamation-pointed. Inside the box, the words *Opening Night! Resurrection!!* Other dates are marked with reminders like *Bonny Moliere's Estate Sale, Pick up Dry Cleaning, Dentist Appointment, Register Travis for Fall Classes.* Things so everyday and unimportant and written in black ink.

I stare at Monday, August 1.

Red ink and capital letters:

7:00 P.M., BILLY'S INTERVIEW

The night before my sister and I found a woman dead and drifting.

Or another way: the night before she found us.

Attached to the edge of the calendar beside this date is a business card. Taylor Bellweather's name curls across the top and beneath it, *Journalist*.

Here, a single thread.

It's not enough, but maybe it's all there is. I tear off part of August and stuff it into my pocket between *Alice*'s pages.

The one who follows me sparks around the handle of the bottom drawer. I pull it open. The wood squeals like last time, but there are no rushing footsteps overhead, no voices calling down, asking who's there. The door leading into the store stays closed.

But something is different. Something has changed.

The gun.

The gun is gone.

And for a second, I want to run as far from this place as I can. For a second, shadows press too close, and the air fills with whispers. The birdcage swings side to side. The dolls sit up and turn their heads. Green eyes blink down at me from a dark top shelf. The one who follows me tells me it's all right, I don't have to be afraid.

Look, she says, in a voice I recognize.

And I do. I look.

And the shadows retreat. The birdcage is caught in a breeze coming in through the open door. The dolls stare up at the ceiling. That gray tabby cat that's always hanging around here jumps down from the top shelf, meows, and comes over to wind around my legs.

I take a sketchbook out of the drawer and flip through pages filled with someone I recognize. Billy Roth's pale girl. Delilah. A few of the drawings are complete, her head and shoulders and face sketched with loving detail, but more of the pages are filled with bits and pieces, as if he was having trouble seeing her, as if he was trying to remember.

Halfway through the book, the drawings change from profiles and portraits to sharp angles and bolted parts, carved wood and twisted wires. Art imitating life, and piece by piece by terrible piece, he tries to put his daughter back together again.

I slam the sketchbook closed and shove it back into the drawer.

Keep looking.

I open another drawer, push aside more papers, a calculator, a box of broken crayons. Way in the back, wrapped in baby pink tissue paper, I find a purse. It's small and soft and tan with a metal clasp and a long, thin strap to go over your shoulder. Blood drops stain the front. And there's another smudge, a thumbprint maybe, where the strap connects with the bag. I know it's blood because there was blood on her jean jacket, too, and the color, the texture, look the same. And I know this purse is hers because inside I find her wallet and inside that, her driver's license.

This is it. This is what I came here to find. I start to wrap the tissue paper around the purse again.

The one who follows me is exploding, bursting red and yellow and orange, but I do not listen to her.

I do not listen.

And when someone grabs my arm and says, "What the hell are you doing here?" I drop the purse and take a breath to scream.

Travis clamps his other hand hard over my mouth, and I choke. The gray tabby at my feet screeches and leaps away, disappearing into the shadows under the desk.

"Be quiet," Travis says into my ear and drags me backward. "You have to leave. Now. If she knew you were down here snooping around . . ."

But it's too late.

She's at the top of the stairs looking down at us and smiling.

She says, "Oh. Hello again," and takes a step down. "You really should come through the front door next time, dear. The basement isn't a safe place for kids. Too many jagged corners and rusted bits of metal."

"She was just leaving." Travis pushes me toward the back door.

"Please," she says, cocking her head to one side. "Stay."

And somehow she has come all the way down the stairs and crossed the room to where Travis and I are standing, though I didn't see her move. She was there at the top of the stairs. Blink. Now she's here in front of me.

Smiling with only her mouth.

Her eyes are mist and vapor, shape-shifters and phantoms. They are grief and they are fear. They are dark and light, half empty, half full. Confused and, at the same time, determined.

"Are you down here all by yourself?" She looks around the basement and sees the desk drawer open and the purse on the floor close by.

Her eyes narrow on me again. All crackle and heat and panic. She knows I know what I shouldn't, what she has tried so hard to hide. She knows I know the truth. And she knows, if given the chance, I will tell everyone.

"Well, now." She bends, picks up the purse, and sets it on the desktop. "You and your sister are quite the little detectives, aren't you?"

"Mom," Travis says. He's taken his hand away from my mouth, but he's still holding on to my arm, pushing me behind him, blocking me with his body. "Mom. Just let her go. Let's just . . . She isn't part of the plan."

Mrs. Roth smiles at her son like she's disappointed she even has to say it. "Plans change."

And then she takes the cowboy gun from behind her back.

Travis says, "Mom, no."

Mrs. Roth reaches around him and grabs my arm, pulls me to her. Though she keeps the gun pointed at the floor, her grip is firm and steady, her impatient finger hovers over the trigger.

The one who follows me licks like fire across the ceiling, but I am the only one sweating, the only one choking on smoke. There's nothing she can do to help me now.

Mrs. Roth holds me against her body with one arm and speaks to Travis over my head, "Go find Sam and bring her to the house."

Travis shifts his feet. "Why?"

"You know why." When Travis doesn't move, Mrs. Roth says, "Travis. Go."

"Are you going to hurt her?"

"Of course not," she says. "It's just time we had ourselves a heart-to-heart. So she knows what's at stake here. With all of this." She waves the gun, bringing it too close to my head.

"And Ollie?"

"I'm not going to hurt either one of them." But when she says this, she squeezes tighter, bruising my ribs and keeping me still. "She's just a bit of insurance. In case Sam decides she doesn't want to cooperate."

"And after? When Sam agrees to keep quiet about everything? To stop snooping around? You'll let her go? You'll let both of them go?"

Mrs. Roth gives me another squeeze, like we're buddies this time, and says, "Of course I will."

But I don't believe her.

sam

The sleeves of Zeb's jumpsuit fell down over my hands, and the helmet kept slipping to one side even after I tightened the strap. I rolled the pant cuffs to keep from tripping over them and wrapped duct tape around my wrists and ankles so there weren't any gaping holes or loose cloth for the bees to crawl into. Finally, I lowered the long veil over my face, slipped on a pair of thick gloves, and entered the apiary.

"Any idea who did this?" Zeb righted one of the tipped-over hives.

The bees that had made their home inside it were long gone now. They'd left behind their broken comb and smashed brood, their spilled-out honey stores, their dead. Those who'd survived the violence had flown away, the only sensible thing to do. To get through the long winter months and protect what remained of their colony, they needed to go and find some better place, a new hive where they could start over. They had to move on.

I answered, "Teenagers? Some drunk bastard who hates Bear maybe?"

Zeb snorted a laugh, then said, "Seems unfair to take all that out on the bees."

I nodded but didn't say anything else. A lot about this summer was unfair, and I was ready for it to be over.

I pushed a bundle of smoking pine boughs close to the entrance of a hive that hadn't suffered as much damage. Since the sheriff's department was still holding all Bear's tools as evidence, the slow-burning branches were the next best thing to a real smoker.

Bees flew drowsily in and out and crawled up and down the sides of the box. I thought they'd be more frenzied, hurrying here and there, rushing and angry, but perhaps they were in mourning. Even though their colony had fared better than the rest, perhaps they still sensed the nearby losses and were grieving the destruction of their neighbors and fellow bees.

"Pick through those frames carefully," I said. "If there are any with the comb mostly intact and it's being used for honey stores, not brood, we can put them in an extra box for the hives that are still working."

Zeb grunted his acknowledgment.

We worked quietly side by side, moving between the boxes, saving what we could and throwing out the rest. In the end, we were left with four working hives, two that were abandoned and empty but in good enough shape to be filled with a new colony at some distant point in the future, and two that were too busted up to be of any use. Zeb hauled the broken hives out of the meadow to his truck waiting by the hemlock stump and tossed them in the back.

When he returned, we stood together at the edge of the apiary, taking sips of lemonade from a thermos.

"What now?" he asked.

"Just let them be," I said. "They'll repair their broken combs and refill them with honey as best they can before the cold sets in. Since we didn't harvest this year, they should have plenty to hold them through spring. And hopefully by then, Bear'll be . . ." But the words felt impossible, so I didn't finish.

"Of course he'll be back by then," Zeb said. "Of course he will."

I was willing to let him have faith enough for both of us.

"Just in case," I said. "You should pile hay around their hives in November or December, before the snows hit. It'll help them stay warm."

Zeb bent and yanked a long piece of grass from the ground. He pinched off the roots and stuck the smooth end between his teeth.

"You should leave them a jar of sugar water every week, too," I said. "Especially in February and March when they're most likely to be running low on stores."

Zeb said, "You know I always told your daddy that if he ever left this place, he'd have to take his goddamn bees with him."

"If he had a choice, I don't think he'd ever leave. He loves it here."

Zeb chewed his long piece of grass, then nodded and said, "Ain't that the truth." And then, "You know, a few months before your mama passed, Bear came up to the house wanting to talk to me about buying this land."

"He did?"

"He wanted to build a house."

I readjusted my grip on the helmet.

"Nothing fancy. Just a two-bedroom cabin. Something big enough for all four of you."

It hurt to swallow. It hurt to breathe. It hurt to do anything but stare at the tiny, dark shadows flitting in and out of their cozy, white boxes.

"I remember him saying your mama refused to sleep on the ground, even though he told her the meadow grass was softer than any mattress you could buy. He said he wanted to build her a proper bed and a proper roof, one with a skylight so he could still see the stars. He said he wanted to give you girls a real home with all of you together, and he thought this was a better place than most because at least here you had fresh air and vegetable-growing soil and a river to sit by and me and Franny within hollering distance." Zeb laughed a little and swept his hand over his thinning hair. "Don't see really what we have to do with any of it, but sweet Franny, now she was pleased as punch when I told her what he'd said."

A bee flew right up close to my face, then dodged away.

"Maybe after all this craziness settles down a bit, he and I can pick up that conversation again. Maybe it won't be too long before you and Ollie are back here seeing to these bees properly. Lord knows what'll happen if I'm in charge of them for too long."

Everything Zeb was saying would only make it that much harder to leave.

When Mom dropped me off last August, we'd done something we didn't normally do. We all walked out to the meadow together. Ollie and me and Mom and Bear, like a real family. Halfway there, Bear and Ollie slowed to watch a fuzzy caterpillar inch across the dirt road and into the leaves on the other side. Mom and I kept walking, kicking at stones.

She asked me if I liked staying here. I told her it was my favorite place in the whole world. She said, "The world's a pretty big place, Sammy," and I told her even if life took me on a grand journey to all sorts of different countries and cities and wild lands, even if I saw the northern lights and stone castles and a field full of perfect red tulips, even then, my heart would always bring me back to the meadow and Crooked River.

"Why do you like it so much?"

"Because it's ours."

I picked a daisy for her to wear in her hair.

When we came out from the trees, she stood in a patch of bright sun, tipped her head back, and closed her eyes. I held my breath, watching her. I had talked about this place for years, trying to convince her. Now she was here. She was seeing, breathing, listening, becoming a part of it. I remembered thinking, *Finally.* She opened her eyes just as Bear and Ollie appeared at the edge of the meadow, and I waited for her to tell them she'd had a change of heart, she was staying, we all were. But a few minutes later she was kissing me good-bye and telling me to be good; she was waving and walking with Ollie back into the trees. And then, three weeks later, we were driving back to our house in Eugene and leaving Bear behind and nothing had changed.

Now I thought she'd probably known about the house all along, that they'd been working on it together, but had kept it a secret from Ollie and me, wanting to surprise us. It helped, a little, believing that when she died her thoughts were of a bright and smiling future, in which her daughters lived with their father in the most beautiful place in the entire world and, there, found a way to be happy again.

Zeb held the thermos out to me for another sip of lemonade, but I shook my head, afraid my stomach wouldn't be able to handle something so sweet. We stood side by side saying nothing for another few minutes. The bees hummed in the apiary, but softer than I remembered and less enthusiastic, as if they were only half going about their work now that Bear was gone.

There's a tradition among beekeepers, an enduring superstition that if something important happened in the household, if the beekeeper, or someone in his family, got married or had a baby or had to go away for a while or died, then someone had to go and tell the bees. Otherwise, the colony would swarm and leave their hive, or worse, in midflight fall right down dead. I guessed Bear had told his bees about Mom already, and he would want me to tell them now about his arrest and how he might not be coming back, but I just couldn't bring myself to do it, not in front of Zeb.

A twig snapped in the trees somewhere behind us.

Zeb and I both turned toward the path that led back to the hemlock stump. At first there was nothing but trees and dull shadows. Then the shadows trembled and shuddered, and Travis stepped into the meadow, striding toward us, crushing clover and dandelions under heavy boots. His eyes were hidden behind a pair of reflective sunglasses. When he reached us, I started to take a step back, remembering last night, how swiftly Ollie's fingers had moved the pointer, but then I stopped myself, shifting my feet a little in the dirt, hoping he hadn't noticed.

He nodded to Zeb and said, "Mrs. Johnson said I might find you two out here."

"Just cleaning up a bit." Zeb gestured toward the apiary. "And getting a quick lesson in beekeeping."

Travis glanced at the hives, then tipped his chin toward the teepee. "That paint's not going to come out easy, you know. Probably best to just get a whole new canvas."

Zeb nodded and snapped the lid back on the thermos. "They wrecked things pretty good around here."

Travis shook his head. "It's a shame."

Zeb looked at me, then at Travis, who was fidgeting his hands in his pockets and scuffing his boots across the ground like a nervous horse, then back at me, then at Travis again. He cleared his throat and said, "Well, if we're done here, we should head on back to the house. Franny'll be wondering."

"Can I say good-bye?" I asked.

Zeb thought about it a second, then nodded and took the helmet and veil from me. "Fifteen minutes. That's it. If you aren't back by then, I'll be telling your grandparents all about last night's joyride. Okay?"

I nodded, then stripped off the gloves and the rest of his bee suit and handed it over to him. "Fifteen minutes."

"Fifteen." He winked and then left me alone with Travis beside the apiary.

Travis said, "Joyride?"

"It's nothing." I walked to the overturned picnic table.

Travis followed. I grabbed one end, he grabbed the other, and we turned the table upright again. The wood was covered in a thick layer of dust. I leaned against the edge and crossed my arms over my chest. Travis stood in front of me, fumbling with his pockets.

"So you're leaving soon?" he asked.

I nodded. "My grandparents are driving in tomorrow morning."

"But you'll be back."

I tapped my thumb against my elbow. "Doubt it."

"But the trial? You have to come back for that, right?"

I shrugged. "I don't know."

Travis nodded and nodded, like he didn't really know he was doing it, like once he got started, he wasn't able to stop. He reached into his back pocket and pulled out a cigarette and that gold lighter he was always carrying around. He tapped the cigarette against his palm, tapped and tapped. Finally, he lifted it to his lips, cupped the lighter, struck a flame, and inhaled sharply. Smoke billowed from his mouth and nose.

"You still think Bear's innocent?"

I waved away the burning cloud. "Of course I do."

"Have you found your proof yet?"

I thought of Ollie's hands floating above the wooden pointer, barely touching it. She'd closed her eyes, squeezed them tight.

"If I did, Bear wouldn't still be in jail," I said.

"You said you found something by the river, didn't you?" He blew smoke above our heads. "What about that?"

I shrugged again. "Dead end."

Travis flipped the lighter off and on, striking a tiny flame, then extinguishing it again. I thought back to the day he'd brought us cobbler in the meadow, how Ollie had acted and, too, how she'd behaved a few days later at Patti's Diner.

"Bear's innocent," I said.

"But how do you know?"

Ollie blowing spitballs, tracing her finger over the storefront window, writing the name Delilah over and over in the air, sitting in the grass beside Taylor Bellweather's grave—all the ways she'd tried to make me see.

"My gut, I guess."

"And what's your gut say?" he asked.

"That things are never as simple as we'd like them to be."

Travis's thumb worked the lighter. Click, flame, smoke. Click, flame, smoke.

"Why are you here, Travis? Really."

"I came to see you." He tapped ash from the burning end of his cigarette.

"What for?"

He brought the cigarette up to his mouth again, inhaled. His hands were shaking.

"She came to your house, didn't she?" I asked.

"Who?" He fumbled with the lighter, trying to shove it in his pocket.

It slipped from his fingers and landed in the dirt at our feet. We both bent to pick it up at the same time and our hands brushed. Travis jerked back like he'd been burned.

"You know who." I picked up the lighter and turned it over for a better look. A coiled rattlesnake had been carved into one side, its tail up, its eyes narrow and angry. "She was there, wasn't she? She showed up for the interview."

"No, I told you already. No." He threw his cigarette butt on the ground and stomped the ember out with his boot. "She was never there."

He reached for the lighter.

I curled my fingers around it. "I don't believe you."

He scowled at my fist, then shoved his hands in his pockets again, took them back out, rubbed his neck.

I said, "I think you know what happened to her. Maybe you even had something to do with it."

He shook his head. "It's not what you think."

"You put that key in my bag, didn't you?"

He couldn't look me in the eyes.

"And this lighter? It's hers, isn't it?" I rubbed my thumb over the etching.

"Listen to me, Sam. I can explain everything. Just stop talking for a second. Just stop . . ." He reached for me.

I tried to get out of the way, but I was stuck up against the table. He grabbed my wrist, held me still.

"You're hurting me." I twisted my arm, but he squeezed harder, forcing my fingers open.

The lighter fell to the ground.

"There's something you need to know. Something important. Your . . . there's . . ." He clamped down on the words, then took a deep breath and said, "Come with me."

"What? Why? No. No way."

"Please. Don't make this any harder for me than it already is."

I stared at him and in his mirrored lenses saw my mouth stretched thin, my teeth clenched, my freckles darkening against my pale skin—I saw myself scared and all alone.

I said, "I'm not going anywhere with you."

He looked down for a second. The muscles in his neck tightened, released. When he lifted his head again, something in his face had changed, the lines hardening, bearing down. "Yes, you are."

I leaned as far away from him as I could, but he was still holding on to my wrist, and the table pushed sharp into my back. There was nowhere to go.

"I'll scream," I said.

"They won't hear you."

"Why are you doing this?"

He said nothing.

"Travis. Please. Let go."

Before either of us could say or do anything else, a loud horn blasted through the meadow, and Zeb's truck roared to a stop somewhere on the other side of the trees. Travis and I both turned toward the path. A door opened but didn't close, and the engine kept running.

"Sam!" Zeb shouted through the trees.

Travis relaxed his grip.

I jerked my arm away from him, pulled it close to my chest, and rubbed at the red sore spots forming on my wrist.

"Sam!" Crashing, crashing through the brush.

He broke into the sunlight and kept coming, hobbling across the meadow toward us with one hand on his bad hip, the other grabbing the air and throwing it behind him, saying my name over and over.

I pushed away from the table and ran to Zeb. He grabbed hold of me, leaned. I put my arm around his shoulder and held him up. He was out of breath and panting. Sweat beaded his forehead. His cheeks were flushed red and his eyes glittered moist.

I hushed him and told him to calm down. "What's happened?"

"It's Ollie," he said. "She's gone."

Those were the exact words Grandma had used the morning after Mom died when she sat me and Ollie down on the couch and said, "Sometimes life's not fair. Sometimes we pray and pray and God says no." *She's gone.*

An invisible hand grabbed my throat and squeezed. It was hard to tell at this point if Zeb was leaning on me, or if I was the one leaning on him.

Zeb said, "She took her bike."

The invisible hand released me, and I could breathe again.

"She didn't tell Franny where she was going?" I asked.

Zeb shook his head. "Franny said she didn't even hear her come downstairs."

"Okay," I said. "Okay. Let's not panic." More for my sake than his. "I'm sure she's fine. I'm sure she just got bored and went for a ride. She probably went into town. I bet she's on her way back now."

Zeb nodded. "I hope so."

"But maybe we should still look for her, just in case?"

"You know where she likes to go?" he asked.

I squeezed his hand. "We'll find her."

I glanced over my shoulder to where I'd left Travis by the picnic table, but he had disappeared. I took a few steps in that direction, scanning the meadow, the apiary, the trees all around, but he was no-where. Just like that—vanished into the bright sun.

Zeb said, "Sam, let's go."

Beneath the table, the rattlesnake lighter winked and glinted in a freckle of sunlight. I picked it up and slipped it in my front pocket.

Trying to sound more confident about finding Ollie than I actu-ally felt, I said, "We'll try the library first."

I hooked my elbow into Zeb's and hurried us along the path toward the truck.

ollie

I left something behind. When Mrs. Roth was pushing me out the back door and up the concrete steps, the gray tabby ran under her feet, and she tripped. I pretended to trip, too, and dropped *Alice* on the ground. If my sister is looking for me, she will probably go to the library first, and when I'm not there, she'll come to the store second. If my sister is looking for me, the book will be obvious, and she will know I left it behind on purpose and that there is something important for her inside the pages.

If my sister is looking.

I am in a shed, tied to a chair. Every time I move, even just a little, the ropes dig deeper into my wrists and ankles. I am in a shed, tied to a chair, and though the sun is high above the trees right now, it will set soon.

I don't want to be here after dark.

Mrs. Roth stands beside the half-open door and keeps the gun at her side where I can see it. She glances outside and then back at me. Outside and then at me.

The one who follows me won't come inside the shed. Or can't. Maybe it's too thick in here for her, the air too unsettled and broken. So she stays close to the small building's only window where I can see her out of the corner of my eye, sparking white.

Behind me, Billy Roth hammers something. The sound rings in my head and makes my teeth hurt. His pale girl is close by. I can't see her, but I hear her moaning. She is trying to let go and being ripped in half.

When Mrs. Roth first pushed me into the shed, Billy Roth turned around and smiled at me. He said, "I remember you."

Mrs. Roth shoved me into a chair and tied my hands and feet. She told me not to move a muscle.

Billy Roth leaned in close and grabbed my braid, ran it through his finger and thumb. "So much like my Delilah." He straightened and returned to his workbench, saying, "I'll be finished with her soon and then you can see for yourself."

Mrs. Roth tied double knots and stuffed a rag in my mouth. I gagged on the oil taste at first, but I'm used to it now.

Outside, there are engine sounds coming up the driveway.

"Finally," Mrs. Roth says, and then, "Billy, honey, keep an eye on her."

He strikes his hammer, down and down in a steady beat.

Mrs. Roth goes out the door but stays close enough to the shed that when the engine stops I can still hear everything she says.

"Where is she?"

Travis answers, his voice, distant at first, then getting closer and louder, "Zeb showed up before I could get her to come with me."

"Did you tell her that her sister was here?"

"I didn't have time."

They're standing together outside the door now, just out of sight.

"What do you mean you didn't have time?"

"They know Ollie's missing. They're looking for her."

"Who is?"

"Zeb, Franny, Sam. Probably the sheriff by now."

Mrs. Roth sighs, then says, "Jesus Christ," and I can't tell if she's praying or cursing.

Travis rushes his words. "I tried, Mom. But then Zeb was just . . . there. And you said no one else could know. You said she had to come alone. I didn't know what else to do. I did the right thing, didn't I? Leaving? Coming back here? Mom? Say something."

She speaks softly. "You did the only thing you could have done. You did what you thought best for our family."

"She doesn't know what really happened, Mom," he said.

"How can you be so sure?"

"We're not in handcuffs, right?"

"Don't be smart with me."

"She might have theories, but she doesn't have any real proof," he said. "So we can just forget this whole thing, right? Take Ollie home, wait for the trial, see how it plays out, keep on pretending we had nothing to do with it?"

"No," Mrs. Roth says. "No, I'm afraid not."

"But they're leaving soon. Sam told me. She said her grandparents . . . she said she wouldn't be back. So it's okay, right? We can just—"

"I wish it were that simple." And then her voice changes into something jagged and scarred with holes. "All these loose ends."

"What do you mean?"

Mrs. Roth comes back inside with Travis close behind her. He stops just inside the doorway and stares at me and the double-knotted ropes and the rag keeping me quiet.

"Fuck," he whispers.

"Language." Mrs. Roth stands a few steps away and taps her thumb against the pearl white pistol grip. Taps and taps and taps.

Travis looks behind me then, to where Billy Roth is working, and his face scrunches. He takes one step forward, then a half step back, like he can't decide what to do. He says, "What the *hell* is that?"

Mrs. Roth says, "Keep your voice down."

"This is what he's been working on?" He shuffles closer, but not too close, squints and tilts his head. "Is that . . . ? What's that at the base? Are those . . . are those *bones*?" He stumbles backward, staring at his mother and shaking his head. "It's made out of wax, right? Or wood? It's not real. I mean, it's not—"

"Travis!" Mrs. Roth slices her hand sharp through the air, silencing him.

There is a moment where we all hold our breath, waiting for something to happen. Then Travis wipes his hand down his face and turns away from his father's sculpture, focuses on me instead.

"We have to let Ollie go." He moves toward the chair. "We have to just untie her and set her loose in the woods. That'll buy us enough time—"

Mrs. Roth grabs his arm, stopping him from coming any closer to me. "Leave her."

He looks at her, fear darkening his eyes. "You can't be serious."

"We can still fix this."

"What? How? Mom. Listen to me." He's talking fast now, his words tripping and mashing together. "We're in way over our heads, we can't just, this isn't the way it was supposed to go. You promised everything would be okay but it's not, it's a goddamn fucking mess and there's no fucking way we're ever going to fix it, not like this, not now, no fucking way."

"Language," she says calmly, and then, "Call her."

Travis shakes his head, his mouth opening and closing like a fish.

Mrs. Roth continues, "Call Sam and tell her that if she ever wants to see her sister alive again, she won't tell anybody what she knows, not the sheriff, not Zeb, not a single person. She'll come straight here so we can work things out. And she'll come alone. Do you understand?"

Travis nods.

Mrs. Roth turns and smiles at me.

A silver-white moth bangs against the window.

sam

The librarian nodded and said, "Sure, she was here. Real cute kid, right? With pigtails and purple glasses?"

"Yes, that's her. That's Ollie." I gripped the edge of the counter so hard my knuckles turned white.

The librarian scratched his cheek and glanced at the ceiling. "Yeah. Yeah, I remember her. She came in about three hours ago, around two thirty, maybe. Looking to do some research on Billy Roth. Not a very talkative one, now is she?"

"When did she leave?"

"Now, let's see . . ." He stared over my shoulder and drummed his fingers on the countertop.

I shifted my weight from one foot to the other, one foot, the other. Zeb was waiting in the parking lot, engine still running. I glanced at the front door. The bottoms of my feet itched. My palms itched. I leaned closer to the librarian.

He stopped drumming his fingers and said, "Actually, I'm not really sure."

"What do you mean you're not sure?" I had to unclench my teeth to get the words out.

"Well now, well, let me think." His fingers scratching and scratching at his five o'clock shadow. "She was still here when I ducked into the back to load up a cart with returns. That was around three, I think, maybe a little before . . . and that took about twenty minutes . . . and when I came back up to the front, your sister was gone. Cleaned up her work area and everything. Nice girl. Why? Has something happened?"

I glanced at the clock hanging on the wall above the librarian's head. A lot could happen in three hours. So much could go wrong.

"Is she okay?" The librarian started to come around the desk. "Did she—"

I ducked away from his questions and hurried outside. I climbed back into Zeb's truck, slammed the door closed, and said, "She's not here."

Zeb reversed, spinning the truck's front end toward the driveway exit. "Where to next?"

The sign in the Attic's window was turned to SORRY WE'RE CLOSED, PLEASE COME AGAIN, but I tried the front door anyway, rattling it inside the frame.

I knocked on the glass. "Hello? Mrs. Roth? Are you in there? It's me. It's Sam."

Zeb leaned out the passenger-side window and waved me to come back to the truck idling at the curb. "If they ain't home, they ain't home."

"I think there's a back entrance," I said, and when he started to protest, "It'll only take a few seconds."

He nodded and settled back into his seat.

I went around the corner of the building into the alley. A shock of bright green stood out against the dull gray asphalt. I bent and picked up the hardcover book, rubbed my fingers over the embossed white rabbit. I looked up and down the empty alleyway.

"Ollie?"

No answer.

I went down some concrete steps to a closed door that I assumed led into the Attic's basement. I pounded and pounded and shouted her name, but the only response was my own muffled echo. I tucked her *Alice* book under my arm and returned to the truck where Zeb was waiting, one hand hanging out the driver's window.

"Anything?" he asked.

I showed him the book, then slipped it into my back pocket. "She was here, but I don't know how long ago."

He nodded and leaned across the bench seat to open the passenger door.

I said, "We should try Patti's."

"You think she's there?"

"No," I said. "But maybe somebody saw something."

He rolled up his window and turned off the truck.

We went inside Patti's together. Most of the booths and tables were empty. An old man sat at the bar. He turned when we came in and nodded at Zeb.

Zeb nodded back and said, "Albert."

The old man Albert hunched over his coffee cup again.

Belinda pushed through the swinging doors from the kitchen carrying a plate piled with a roast beef sandwich and fries. She glanced at Zeb and me waiting by the front counter and said, "Be right with you folks."

She took the sandwich to a booth near the back of the diner. When she returned, she straightened her blouse, reached for two menus, smiled at us, and said, "Just the two of you today?"

"We're not here to eat," I said.

She frowned and dropped the menus back into their rack.

"We're looking for a little girl," said Zeb.

Belinda's penciled-in eyebrows shot up.

"You remember my sister?" I asked. "Ollie? Remember we came in on Monday? For lunch? She ordered tomato soup and grilled cheese. She's about this tall. Wears purple glasses and pigtails that go all down her back . . ."

"Of course I remember," Belinda said.

Albert was watching us now, leaning close.

"Did she come in here today?" I asked.

The lines on Belinda's forehead creased, and a dimple formed in her chin. "No, sweetheart," she said. "No, I haven't seen her since the two of you came in here together."

"Sam?" Deputy Santos was standing a few feet from us in the middle of the diner, dabbing her mouth with a napkin.

She was in plain clothes, and her dark hair was pinned back from her face with hot pink barrettes. She must have been tucked away inside some booth when we came in, just out of sight, but she came closer now, saying my name again and then, "Is something wrong?"

Everything. Absolutely everything.

She lifted her eyes to Zeb.

"Ollie's took up missing," he said.

Deputy Santos was close enough now to put her hand on my shoulder. "Tell me where you've looked already."

Zeb left out the part about me and Ollie being grounded for taking his truck, but he told her all the rest.

When he finished, Deputy Santos pulled out her wallet and handed Belinda some money. "Change is yours," she said, and then to Zeb, "You and Sam go on back to the house now in case she shows up. Double-check the meadow again, and down by the river. I'll call in a report, then swing by the hospital."

Belinda said, "Oh dear, oh dear," and then put her hand over her mouth.

Deputy Santos continued, "I'll take a couple passes through town, too, drive out Smith Rock Way and then down to Lambert. If she hasn't turned up in the next hour, we'll get some search-and-rescue dogs out to your place."

Albert tossed a five-dollar bill on the counter and said to Zeb, "I'll round up Clinton and Mack and some of the others who ain't got nothing better to do on a Friday."

Zeb nodded. He put his arm around my shoulder.

Belinda untied her apron and laid it over the cash register. "I'm coming, too."

Deputy Santos checked her wristwatch. "It's almost six. Let's plan on everyone meeting at the Johnsons' in an hour." She rubbed her thumb over the watch face and then looked at me. "I'm sure she'll be back by then and we'll all just end up sitting around eating some of Franny's famous hot-from-the-pan crullers." But she rushed out of the diner like she believed something else entirely.

Zeb ushered me toward the door. Over my shoulder, I asked Belinda, "Is Travis working today?"

"He was scheduled for the lunch shift, but he never showed. Kids." She shrugged in a way that made me think he'd skipped out on work a few times before this, and then she disappeared into the kitchen to tell the rest of the staff she was leaving.

On the ride back to Zeb and Franny's, the knot that had been forming in my stomach since we left the diner grew and pulled tighter with each mile. I stared out the window, rubbed my thumb along the spine of Ollie's *Alice* book, and played Travis's words over in my head. *There's something you need to know. Something important. Come with me.* I spun my wrist in a quick circle, feeling the bruises where he'd grabbed on so tight I thought my bones were going to snap in two. *What does your gut say?*

"Please," I said, my voice barely above a whisper. "Please, Zeb. Go faster."

He pushed down on the gas pedal, and I did something I hadn't done in years. I closed my eyes and prayed.

When Zeb pulled into the driveway, I jumped out of the truck before he could even turn off the engine and ran into the kitchen, where Franny was waiting at the table, staring at the phone on the wall like she thought, if she only stared hard enough, she could will it to ring and Ollie would be on the other end, telling her everything was all right.

I stopped in the doorway. Franny spun her head around to look at me. Our eyes met and what small glimmer of hope she had blinked out in the time it took me to say, "Anything?"

Franny shook her head real slow and twisted a napkin in her hands. She turned her attention back to the phone and said, "I think it's about time we called the sheriff."

"We saw Deputy Santos at Patti's," I told her. "She's getting a search party together. They're all meeting here in an hour."

Zeb came into the kitchen behind me. "No use sitting around worrying yourself half to death, Mother. Might as well keep your hands busy."

Franny rose from the table. She went to the sink, filled a pitcher with water, poured in a packet of powdered lemonade, and stirred in ice with a wooden spoon. Then she put a saucepan on the stove, measured in water, butter, sugar, and salt and settled in to stirring, waiting for the ingredients to boil. She worked methodically, slowly, putting all her worry into the familiar routine of making crullers. I left them in the kitchen and went upstairs to the guest room.

Ollie's duffel bag was still on the floor beside the dresser. Her pajamas were folded neatly on the end of the bed. I searched for a note. On the desk, the dresser, her bed, mine, on the window, behind the door. Nothing. A corner of the Ouija board peeked from underneath her bed. I pulled it out and opened the lid. The wooden pointer had slid into one corner.

I placed my fingertips on the edge of the pointer and whispered, "Is Ollie safe?"

The pointer didn't move. I jammed the lid back on the box and placed the game on top of the dresser.

I sat down on the end of Ollie's bed, then stood right up again and took her *Alice* book from my back pocket. She carried this book with her everywhere, and if she'd left it behind, it was for a good reason. I thumbed quickly through the pages. Tucked near the beginning was a small piece of paper torn from a larger calendar page. August 1 and some of August 2 and 3, too, but it was that first day, the day of Billy's interview, that Ollie wanted me to see. Under this was another piece of paper, folded in fourths. I unfolded it and only had to read the headline to recognize it as a photocopied article about Bear's accident and the awful, horrible night ten years ago that changed the entire course of our lives. On the opposite page, she'd underlined a passage in her book in thick, red ink:

> *"It was much pleasanter at home," thought poor Alice, "when one wasn't always growing larger and smaller, and being ordered about by mice and rabbits. I almost wish I hadn't gone down that rabbit-hole—and yet—it's rather curious, you know, this sort of life! I do wonder what can have happened to me! When I used to read fairy tales, I fancied that kind of thing never happened, and now here I am in the middle of one!"*

I looked at the news clipping again. Billy Roth's name was circled so many times the paper was starting to rip, and in the blank space at the bottom of the paper it looked as though Ollie had tried to write something, but the letters were all jagged and streaked and crossed through with lines, and I couldn't make out a single word. But it didn't matter. I knew what she was telling me, what she'd been trying to tell me all along, and I knew, too, where to find her now: in the exact place I'd prayed she wouldn't be.

I left the book on the bed and ran downstairs. A map showing the farm and the meadow and a long stretch of Crooked River was spread out over the coffee table, but the living room was empty.

In the kitchen, Franny was at the stove turning a cruller in crackling-hot oil. She'd already fried up two plates' worth, but the mixing bowl was still half full of raw dough.

"Where's Zeb?" I asked her.

She waved her free hand toward the sliding glass door. "He took Albert and a couple other men to search along the river."

"Is Deputy Santos here?" I asked her.

"Not yet." Franny wiped her forehead with a dish towel and narrowed her gaze on me. "Sam? What is it? Did you find something?"

I ignored her questions and took the stairs two at a time back up to the second floor and Zeb and Franny's bedroom, where I could have some privacy. I shut the door behind me and left the light off. There was a phone on the nightstand beside the bed. I picked it up and listened to the dial tone for a few seconds. Then I punched in Deputy Santos's phone number. It rang and rang and rang. I slammed the phone back in its cradle, feeling stupid. Of course she wasn't going to answer. She was out searching for Ollie. I'd have to call 911, have them get her on the radio and tell her to come straight here. I reached for the phone again, but before my fingers wrapped around the receiver, it rang.

I jerked my hand back. The phone rang a second time.

I grabbed it off the cradle and pressed the speaker to my ear. "Hello?"

For a few seconds, there wasn't anything on the other end but silence.

Then, raspy breathing and a low voice. "Sam?"

I didn't say anything.

"Sam? It's me. It's Travis."

I closed my eyes, opened them again, stared at the ceiling, tried not to imagine the worst.

From downstairs Franny called, "Sam, honey? Who is it?"

I blinked, took a breath. "What do you want?" I asked, even though I was pretty sure I knew what his answer was going to be.

"We have Ollie."

Franny shouted my name again, louder this time, like she'd moved from the kitchen into the living room. I pressed my hand down hard against the mattress.

"We have Ollie," Travis said again. "At the house."

"Please. Don't hurt her. Just tell me where to go. I'll come. Please . . ." My voice was a scratch below a whisper.

"Take Smith Rock Way north. About a mile outside Terrebonne you'll see a gravel driveway on the left. Our name's on the mailbox. You can't miss it. Oh, and Sam?" His voice hostile, my name dagger-sharp. "Come alone."

I hung up the phone.

The bedroom door opened. Franny stood half in shadow, half in light, with streaks of flour on her forehead and grease spots on her apron.

"Who was that?" she asked.

"Wrong number." I got up from the bed and pushed past her into the hallway.

"Sam?" She called after me.

"It wasn't her." I called over my shoulder.

"Sam!"

But I was down the stairs already, moving toward the front door. I shouted, "I'm going to go help Zeb," and slammed through the screen door onto the porch.

The truck wasn't in the driveway. Zeb must have taken it. I ran to the barn, grabbed the black-and-red Schwinn, and rode as hard as I could toward the road.

On the uphills, I stood and leaned over the handlebars and set my body on fire. On the downhills, I switched to the hardest gear and spun my legs into taffy. The wind screamed in my ears and drew salt tears from my eyes. And when it started to become too much, when my muscles and ligaments and cells begged me to stop, I imagined I was made of gears and cogs and greased-up bearings. I imagined myself a machine, incapable of pain.

I sped down Lambert Road, then Smith Rock Way, and all the way through Terrebonne, the fields and houses passing in a blur. Another mile to go now, give or take, and my legs were going numb. I dug way down deep, found a shallow reservoir of strength, and pedaled even faster.

ollie

I pluck at the rope with my fingernails. Twist my wrists one way, another, rubbing my skin raw. I squirm and lean side to side, feeling for a sticking-out nail or splinter, something sharp. There's nothing.

Mrs. Roth watches me struggle but doesn't try to stop me. She says, "Things didn't have to happen like this, you know."

I slump down in the chair. The one who follows me beats her silent wings against the window. She wants me to be brave and keep fighting. I turn my face away from her.

"If you and Sam had just had the sense to leave well enough alone." She looks at the pistol in her hand. "Maybe this will be better, though. For everyone."

Someone's running up the path. Mrs. Roth spins to face the door and raises the gun, pointing it at chest level, ready to shoot.

But it's only Travis.

"Jesus Christ!" He stops short.

Mrs. Roth lowers the gun quickly. "Did you do it?"

Travis nods and enters the shed. He says, "Now what?"

"We wait."

Travis begins to pace. After a while, he stops and stares at the sculpture behind me and says, "Tell me that's not really her under there. Please tell me that's not my sister."

Mrs. Roth hesitates a beat too long.

"Mom," Travis says, and then when she still doesn't answer, "Oh my God. How could you let him do this?"

"Keep your voice down." Mrs. Roth glances at her husband hunched over his workbench. She speaks to Travis in an almost whisper. "I had no idea this is what he was doing out here. Not until that night. When I realized what he'd done, that he'd gone into the woods and . . . I tried to talk him into doing something else, leaving her out of it, but he refused."

"You aren't really going to send this to New York, are you? I mean, now that you know, you aren't really—"

Billy Roth slams his hammer down. "Quiet!"

Travis glares at his father. Mrs. Roth glares at her son. And for a while, except for our breathing, the shed is silent. Then the clinking, clanking, tinkering starts up again.

Mrs. Roth whispers, "Your father's worked hard on this project, Travis. It's the first time since the accident he's wanted to be in his studio. The first time he's made something important. Something that has the potential to shake up the art world, change its very essence."

"This isn't art," Travis says. "It's . . . it's wrong and awful and—"

"Remarkable," says Mrs. Roth, raising her voice to drown out her son's. "Groundbreaking, really. The work of a true genius."

"Of a lunatic."

A loud crash behind me and Billy Roth shouts, "Enough!"

Travis ducks. A wrench flies overhead and dents the wall.

"Billy!" Mrs. Roth shouts.

Travis takes a step back. "Shit!"

"Language!"

Billy Roth says, "Coming in here, criticizing, cutting me down.

Flapping and squawking. Telling me what is and isn't. Acting like you know better. Like you're all high and mighty and above. You have no idea. None."

"Billy, honey, calm down. Travis didn't mean—"

A jar of nails crashes to the floor. Mrs. Roth screams. So does the pale girl, a sound like screeching tires and breaking glass. A sound of shattering bones.

"I don't want you in here!" Billy screams. "Go! All of you! Get the hell out!"

"Billy, honey, listen to me. Listen." Mrs. Roth goes to him. "He doesn't understand what you're trying to do. You need to finish her so he can see. So he can understand."

I rock back and forth, trying to get the chair to move, but it's too heavy, and I'm too small. Travis stares at me but does nothing.

Mrs. Roth continues, "You're so close now. Look. Look at what you've done. She's beautiful. You're going to make history with this one, Billy. You're going to be bigger than Dalí."

Billy Roth murmurs something so soft I can't understand, and then there is a single pop, a paint can being opened.

Mrs. Roth returns to Travis and says, "You need to calm down too. You're not helping, getting him all riled up like that."

"But—"

"Enough." Mrs. Roth gets right up close and puts her hand on his chest, looks straight at him and doesn't look away. "I know I'm asking a lot from you right now. I know that, but I need you on my side. I need you to trust me."

Travis bites his lip and rubs his neck. He lowers his head, hiding his eyes.

"Travis." She reaches and lifts his chin, stares at him with a trembling smile. "We're too far in to turn back now."

He jerks from her grasp and steps back. "I told you, didn't I? When you asked me to help clean up his mess, I told you it would only make things worse. From the very beginning I've said this was a shitty plan!"

"Language," Mrs. Roth says through gritted teeth.

"We should have called the sheriff right away."

"Your father would have gone to jail. He doesn't deserve that."

"He killed that woman, Mom. He just . . . he killed her."

"No, it wasn't like that." She reaches for him, but her hand can't cross the distance. She says, "She showed up early for the interview. If she had come to the front door instead of going straight to the shed . . . but she just barged in on him, came into his space, and started asking him all these questions about Bear and you know how your father gets, and then she saw the sculpture and, understandably, she was upset. But she could have just walked out. She didn't have to start tearing him down, calling the whole thing a desecration. She didn't have to threaten to call the police, either. She pushed him first. Your father . . . he felt trapped. What was he supposed to do? But it was an accident, Travis. I swear to you. He didn't mean to push her that hard. If she had fallen any other way, we wouldn't even be here right now, talking about this. It was an accident."

"Then what are we protecting him from?"

"You know how hard it's been for him since the crash. With his headaches. His episodes. And remember how they raked him over the coals when he tried to go back to work? How they said he'd lost his edge? They won't understand. They'll think he did it on purpose." Mrs. Roth shakes her head. "Prison is the last place he needs to be right now. He'd die in there."

Travis stares at the sculpture, says nothing.

"He needs this, Travis. He needs *us*."

"He needs to be in a mental hospital," Travis mumbles.

"So we'll find him a doctor. After the show, we'll get him help."

"And what about that woman's family?" His voice loud again. "Who's going to help them?"

Mrs. Roth doesn't answer.

And I imagine her, the one from the river. Taylor Bellweather. I imagine her lying there in a pool of her spilled-out blood. Her body broken, but her soul still awake. Waiting for someone to come.

sam

I rode down the Roths' long and narrow, winding driveway. The first fifty yards or so were gravel, but then it changed to rutted dirt with patches of soft sand. My tires kept slipping. Fir trees crowded me on both sides, their limbs intertwining overhead and blocking the sun. The farther I went, the darker it got. The light changed, and the colors shifted from a dust-and-orange summer to a shadow-and-blue midnight. The sun couldn't be setting. Not yet. It wasn't that late, but sweat was drying on my skin, cooling me, and I couldn't see more than a few feet into the trees. And the birds—there were none. That scared me more than anything else.

Dirt became gravel again as I finally came around the last bend, and the narrow road widened, ending in a turnaround driveway big enough to park two cars and Travis's dirt bike. Black handlebars stuck out of the open back of a Jeep Wrangler. I skidded to a stop beside the car and looked inside to find Ollie's blue-and-white Schwinn crammed between the backseat and the tailgate. Keys dangled from the Wrangler's ignition.

Travis hadn't told me what to do once I got here. I thought he'd be waiting, but he wasn't. I got off my bike and leaned it up against a tree that was set back a few feet from the road. My legs shook and my elbows were numb. My palms were red from gripping the handlebars so tight. I wiped my hands on my jeans and walked toward the house.

I'd never seen anything quite like it before. All hard edges and sharp corners, it looked like three giant shipping containers stacked one on top of another, each end turned a slightly different angle. The roof was flat, and wrought-iron balconies jutted from two dormers facing the driveway. One lower-level wall was made entirely of glass, but no lights were on and I couldn't see inside. The sepia-colored siding was going a bit green with moss on the north side, and there were mobiles hanging from every railing and empty space—delicate bird skeletons wired together, wings stretched in midflight, so perfect it was impossible to tell what they were made of, if they were real bones or something else entirely. Sculptures littered the front garden, lunging from behind azaleas and rosebushes and clumps of ferns. Many were like the fox in Pastor Mike's office, some unholy combination of carved wood and real animal, but a few were made of glass and metal, bits of things welded and twisted together to make abstract shapes and whorls of color and light. I went up a winding staircase that curved twice around a pole inlaid with colored glass and tiny mirrors before reaching the upper level and what I hoped was the front door. Instead of a regular brass doorknob, there was a clenched metal fist the color of blood. I grabbed it and turned.

The door swung open, and when I walked in, it was like stepping into a tomb. Dank, suffocating, crowded. The air reeked of wet dirt and mold and something else, something long dead. The room was dark except for an old film projector set up in the middle of the floor with a spent reel that hissed and clattered, flickering bright white light against the opposite wall. Hanging from the ceiling above my head, a rainbow-colored and shimmering banner shouted HAPPY 9TH BIRTH-DAY!! Limp gray streamers sagged from the center of the banner to the corners of the room. I took a step toward the couch and a cardboard party hat crunched under my foot. I kicked it aside and lifted a framed photograph from the coffee table.

A barefoot, blond-haired girl with buckteeth grinned up at me. She wore a light blue swimsuit and goggles around her neck. Behind her, brightly colored slides spiraled into a large, indoor swimming pool. She had wrapped a beach towel around her shoulders like a cape and was clutching the corners together just under her chin. She stood beside a birthday cake ablaze with candles. Her cheeks were flushed, her eyes glittering. Hanging from the table's edge was a rainbow-colored and shimmering banner. The exact same banner that hung over my head now. All these years later. I returned the picture to the coffee table and then turned off the rattling projector. The house settled into silence and twilight.

"Ollie?" I whispered, though I wasn't sure what good that would do. Louder, I called out, "Travis? I'm here. Hello?"

I stepped over a stuffed bear that was missing one eye and coming apart at the seams and moved past a bookcase filled with taxidermy raccoons and squirrels, blue jays and crows and something that looked like a bobcat. Their glass eyes twinkled and seemed to move with me, watching, disapproving. A few steps more, past a desk strewn with sketches and pictures of the same blond-haired girl, and I reached the sliding glass door that opened onto a balcony overlooking the woods behind the house. About fifty yards down a bark mulch path was another building, a shed, similar in color and style to the house, but smaller, a single cube instead of several stacked together. The lights were on inside.

I turned to go back out the front door, but I stopped halfway there and stared at my empty hands. I curled my fingers into fists. So small and fragile, so completely useless. I searched the living room, but nothing seemed right. In the kitchen, I grabbed a frying pan from the hook hanging over the stove and swung it once, twice, like a baseball bat, but it didn't feel heavy enough to me. I needed something menacing, something I might not even have to use once they got a good look at it. I put the pan back on its hook and started opening drawers instead. I found the butcher's knife in the third drawer alongside a lemon zester and a bottle opener. The knife was almost as long as my arm, heavy and sharp and glinting silver. This.

Keeping the blade pointed away from me, I ran back through the living room and outside. A light wind had started to blow, setting the trees grumbling like angry old men. A thin orange ribbon twisted through their thick black trunks. The sun was flickering out, collapsing into night.

The shed door was ajar. Hushed voices drifted toward me.

"If you have a better idea, I'd love to hear it," Mrs. Roth said.

"I just think . . . maybe we should go to the sheriff first." This was Travis. "Right now. Before we make it worse. If that's even possible. Just tell them everything. Tell them the truth."

"The truth."

"Yes."

"Tell them everything?"

They were quiet for a few seconds, enough time for me to get right up close to the shed and hunker down behind a stack of firewood. I clutched the knife in both hands now, holding it close to my chest.

Mrs. Roth said, "We're as guilty as your father now, Travis. Our hands are covered in just as much blood."

"But maybe if we tell them—"

"What? Tell them what, exactly? There's nothing we could say to fix this."

"So . . . what? What do we do?"

Mrs. Roth didn't answer.

I needed to see what was going on inside, what I was up against. I needed to see Ollie. Staying low to the ground, I inched around to the other side of the woodpile, closer to the door.

"We could run," Travis said.

"Where?"

"I don't know. Mexico? Canada? Wherever. Somewhere far away from here."

"And what about Sam?"

Something tickled the back of my arm, making circles near my elbow, then walking toward my sleeve, but I didn't dare move. I was close enough now to see inside.

Ollie was tied to a chair. A sock or a handkerchief, some kind of cloth, had been shoved into her mouth, and her hands were tied behind her back, her legs tied together at the ankles. My grip tightened on the knife. I couldn't see Travis, but from the sound of his voice, he was close to the door. Billy Roth was at the back of the shed, busy with something at his workbench. Mrs. Roth stood in the center of them all. I stared at the gun in her hand, stared and tried not to panic.

Travis said, "When she gets here, we tie them both up and that will buy us a few hours. Enough time to pack up a few things and get the hell out. If we drive fast enough, we might even make it to the Canadian border. We could disappear."

"And then what?" Mrs. Roth said. "Keep running? Keep hiding? For the rest of our lives? Always looking over our shoulders? No. Absolutely not. Not when we're this close. Not when it's almost over."

Whatever creature had been crawling around my elbow was almost to my armpit now. I twitched my arm, but I could still feel it creeping around, tickling its tiny legs over my skin. I brushed at my sleeve and a honeybee fell into the dirt. Dazed, she hobbled in circles for a few seconds, then gathered herself up again and flew away, circling around me and landing somewhere in the woodpile.

Mrs. Roth was still talking. "No, we stick with the original plan."

"And if Sam doesn't agree to it?"

Another bee landed on my jeans. I brushed her off.

"She won't have a choice."

"What do you mean?"

I leaned closer to the crack in the door, sticking my head out far enough that if either of them looked over, they would see me plain as day. But Mrs. Roth had her back to me now, reaching for something I couldn't see, and Travis, a few steps from the doorway, was too busy watching her to notice me. Ollie saw me, though, and started squirming and grunting. I pulled back into the shadows.

Mrs. Roth said, "Hush, dear. No use working yourself into a fit. This will all be over soon."

Ollie fell silent.

Mrs. Roth asked, "Do you still have the lighter?"

Travis said, "I lost it."

I shoved my hand in my front pocket, took the lighter out, cupped it in my palm.

Mrs. Roth sighed loudly, then said, "Oh, it doesn't matter. The purse will be enough."

"Tell me again how this is going to work?"

"We'll give it to Sam, have her take it to the sheriff. She'll tell them she saw Bear with it the day after the murder, that she saw him throw it in the woods, but she was too scared to come forward with it until now. We've planted enough evidence already, everyone thinks he's guilty. But just in case. If they have any doubts, they won't after this."

"She won't do it."

"She'll have to," Mrs. Roth said. "This won't come back to us. I won't let it."

"You're not going to . . ." There was a long stretch of silence, and then Travis said, "You promised you wouldn't hurt them!"

"You understand what would happen if anyone else were to find out what we've done, right?"

Silence and then Mrs. Roth continued, "We're the victims here, Travis. You, me, your father. We wouldn't have to be dealing with any of this if your sister was still alive, if that accident had never happened. This is Frank McAlister's fault. You know that as well as I do. He's the bad guy, Travis, not your father. He's the monster who started all of this. Try and remember that."

The door opened a little wider, and Travis's shadow stretched long across the orange swatch of light bleeding onto the grass. I leaned back against the woodpile, as far away from the opening as I could get. Two bees twirled and buzzed in the air around my head. I stayed still, hoping the shadows were thick enough to make me invisible.

Travis moved away from the door again. "Where is she?"

I couldn't wait any longer. If I was going to do something, I had to do it now.

I crawled to the other side of the woodpile and scooped up dry pine needles and small twigs, making a messy pile of kindling that butted right up against the side of the shed. My timing would have to be perfect. I held the lighter to the bottom of the pile and struck a flame. A twig caught fire, then sputtered and died. Smoke curled away from me.

"It shouldn't be taking her this long," Travis said.

I tried again. Snick, pop, flare. I cupped my hand around the flame this time and blew softly on the fragile embers. Some leaves caught fire, then a bundle of dry moss. More smoke lifted, carried away by the wind. The twigs were burning on their own now.

"She's told the sheriff. I know she has. We're fucked. Completely fucked."

"Language," Mrs. Roth said. And then, "If she'd told the sheriff, they would have been here a long time ago. She'll be here. Have a little faith."

I reached for a small log teetering near the top of the woodpile. When I brought it down to the fire, the dim light caught the movement of fluttering wings and marching legs and yellow-and-black wiggling bodies. Half a dozen bees roamed up and down the stick. I rose to a half crouch to get a closer look at the woodpile.

The bees were coming from a large, hollow stump that was up against the side of the shed, teetering on the edge of a rotting pallet. From what I could see, the comb inside was new and thin and still growing, so they had only been here a few days, if that. They were starting to gather inside now, clustering together for warmth, whispering their bee secrets as night settled around them. I desperately wanted to believe they were Bear's bees, the ones whose hives in the meadow were so recently destroyed, and I wanted to believe they recognized me. But even if they didn't, even if they came from someplace else entirely, their low and steady hum still gave me courage.

My pile of kindling was starting to die, the embers smothering, turning gray and puffing bits of ash into the air. I left the bees and dropped another handful of dry tinder onto the fire. The flames shot up again, angry and red and hotter this time. I added a small log and the flames grew bigger still, taller and meaner. They thrashed against the side of the shed, snapping like devil tongues. The smoke bulged and shifted with the wind, burning my throat and making me cough. Sparks sprang from the center and then settled in the dry grass, and it was only a matter of time before something else caught fire, and the whole world went up in flames. If that happened, the bees with their wings would be all right, but I couldn't say the same for Ollie and me. Too late, now.

I buried my mouth and nose in the crook of my elbow and ducked around the corner of the shed. I followed the walls around the back and then around another corner, and then I was at the front of the shed again, but opposite the fire, which was burning hot now, filling the night with noise and smoke and shifting red shadows. I held the butcher's knife steady with both hands and waited.

"Do you smell that?" Mrs. Roth asked.

"What is that?" Billy Roth's voice grew louder, coming toward the door. "Is that smoke?"

He thrust his head through the doorway, saw the rapidly growing fire, then disappeared back inside. Something scraped loudly across the floorboards.

"Get a bucket of water!" he shouted. "Hurry!"

Mrs. Roth rushed outside. Her eyes were red burning embers, reflecting the firelight. She kicked dirt at the flames, but the fire kept burning, devouring the siding now, grasping at the eaves.

Travis came, carrying a bucket. Water sloshed over the sides. He hurried to his mother and the flames and shouted, "Move! Get back!"

Their full attention on the fire, I slipped into the shed.

Ollie's eyes widened, and she bucked in the chair, straining against her ties. I pressed a finger to my lips and held out the knife. She nodded and settled down.

Billy had his back turned to me. He was coughing into his elbow and trying to cover something with a canvas sheet, trying to drag it as far away from the door as he could.

I crouched behind Ollie and cut the ropes around her wrists first. They were made of soft nylon, the weave loose, and the knife went through them as if passing through butter. Ollie rubbed at the bruises and raw spots, and then pulled the gag from her mouth. She bent, reaching for the ropes around her ankles, but I pushed her hands away and hacked with the blade. The last thread snapped, and Ollie leaped to her feet. She threw her arms around my waist and buried her face into my chest. I pushed her away.

Hurry, I mouthed.

The scraping sounds and coughing stopped.

I turned to find Billy Roth scowling at me, one hand still holding on to the thing he'd been dragging.

"How did you get in here?" he asked.

I pointed the knife at him.

"Maggie knows I don't like people seeing my work until it's finished." He dropped his hand and came toward me. "She shouldn't have let you in."

I pushed Ollie behind me and started to shuffle backward toward the door.

"Stay back." I slashed the knife through the air.

He tried to grab my arm.

I jerked out of reach and then shoved Ollie. "Go!"

But she didn't move. She pressed back against me.

I glanced at the door. Travis was there, framed in smoke and flickering light, holding the empty bucket, staring at me and Ollie and working his lips between his teeth.

I pushed Ollie toward the other side of the room. "The window!"

Travis shouted, "Dad! Don't!"

Billy clamped his hand around my wrist. I dropped the knife. It clattered to the floor. I reached for it. He got there first and snatched it out from under my fingers. He twisted around and laid the knife on the closest corner of the workbench, well out of my reach.

He grinned, his hand still clasped around my arm, squeezing tighter. "Little girls shouldn't play with such sharp toys."

I kicked his shin, dragging my heel hard down the length of his bone. He yelped and let go of my wrist. I spun away from him and ran to Ollie. She'd managed to push the window up a few inches, enough to bring in a gust of fresh air, but not enough for her to escape. The wooden frame was swollen and stuck.

Travis dropped the bucket and came toward us. "Sam! Wait!"

I pounded my hands against the window, then jimmied my arm into the gap and pushed up as hard as I could. The wood squealed and gave another inch. I pushed up on the window frame even harder.

Billy pressed his hands to his temples, saying, "I can't work like this. It's impossible. All this noise. So much noise."

Mrs. Roth stepped into the shed. "What is going on in here?"

She gaped at me and, for a stretched-out second, stood frozen in the doorway, the gun hanging useless at her side. Then she raised her arm, pointed the barrel straight at my head. "Come away from the window, dear. Before someone gets hurt."

"Mom, the fire!" Travis reached for Ollie's arm. She slapped at him and kicked his shin and spat in his face. He backed away, wiping his eyes.

Mrs. Roth said, "It's out. I got it out." And then, "Stupid girls."

She came toward us, gun still raised.

I'd managed to push the window open wide enough so I could crouch and get my shoulder up under the frame. I heaved and shoved and pushed and slammed. The window squealed, sliding open only another half a foot, but this time it was enough.

Ollie grabbed the ledge and pulled herself up and over. She squeezed through the gap and tumbled into the dirt below, then sprang to her feet and motioned me to hurry. I took a single step toward the window, and then I was jerked backward.

Mrs. Roth twisted my arm behind my back, pulled it up so far between my shoulder blades, I heard a pop and pain burned down into my fingers. I cried out.

"Tell your sister to come back inside," Mrs. Roth spoke softly into my ear, her breath warm across my skin. She smelled like smoke and wet ashes.

Through the glass, Ollie was a blurred and pale figure hovering in the dark, floating farther and farther away from me.

I screamed, "Run, Ollie! Run!"

Mrs. Roth yanked me from the window and threw me into the now empty chair. She kept the gun pointed at my head.

"Go after her," she said to Travis.

He stumbled toward the door. At the threshold, he stopped and looked over his shoulder. "Should I bring her back here?"

"No," Mrs. Roth said. "Take her to the meadow. We'll meet you there."

Travis hesitated, glancing at me, his expression impossible to understand. He seemed about to say something, but then Mrs. Roth shouted, "Go on! What are you waiting for?"

He turned away from me and ran into the night.

"No!" I tried to go after him.

Mrs. Roth shoved me back down in the chair and pointed the barrel at my chest, right above my heart. "Careful, now, Sam."

I stopped struggling and stared out the window into hollow darkness. Somewhere close by, Travis's dirt bike roared awake, a sputtering, choking awful sound that turned into a shrill banshee scream as he sped into the forest after my sister.

ollie

I run into the woods behind the shed.

I run into the dark.

I run.

Serpents and ogres reach and grab and try to drag me down. Fangs and claws tear my skin. An owl screams.

I run and run and do not stop.

I can't breathe. I do not stop.

I can't see. I do not stop.

I stumble over a rock and twist my ankle. *Keep running. If you stop, they will find you.*

My tears taste like oil and smoke and blood.

When I looked back through the window, the pale girl Delilah was screaming and weeping, clinging to her old dead bones. But there was nothing I could do to help her, and then my sister yelled, "Run, Ollie! Run!"

She did not tell me how far or which direction. But I know to go fast.

Fast and faster.

There is no moon tonight, and clouds blur the stars. I have no way of knowing if I'm running in a straight line, but every step that does not take me back to the shed is a good step. I try to keep my body pointed forward, in one direction—away—but I am running blind and going nowhere.

The one who follows me is somewhere close by, but there is not enough light for her to show me the way. Like a firefly she darts in and out of sight, and even though it's all she can do, I feel stronger just having her with me, braver knowing I'm not alone.

She runs beside me, whispering encouragement, urging me on.

We run faster.

I hear the engine sounds first, like a snarling wolf, crashing through the brush behind me, chewing up the miles in between. A few seconds later a single beam of light shoots through the darkness, bouncing off tree trunks and cutting through shadows. The light chases me, coming closer and closer, growing brighter, and I know I only have a few more seconds before I am eaten alive.

Hide.

A word so quiet I almost miss it, thinking it's only the night crying, only a moth brushing against my cheek, only a whisper in my head.

Behind me, the engine revs louder, close enough now that when I glance over my shoulder I see the dark shape of Travis's dirt bike breaking through the trees. A nightmare.

I duck left and out of the yellow spotlight.

The motorcycle turns, catching me in the beam again.

Dodge right, into the dark between two pine trees, but the headlight finds me here, too.

I run in a zigzag line, crossing in and out of the light too quickly, making it hard for him to follow me, and as I run, I look for someplace to hide. A hollow space, an oversize rock, a log big enough to tuck myself under, somewhere, anywhere to disappear.

He shouts something, but I do not look back.

I do not stop running.

In front of me, the earth drops off. The world ends and, above the roaring engine, I hear water gurgling. I twist away from the headlight of the motorcycle one last time and when I am in the dark again, I run straight off the cliff.

I hit the dirt hard, and my knees buckle. I tuck and roll and then I'm on my back, looking up at the stars. The clouds have gone, and the stars are many and bright. A rushing river is all I hear now, water crashing against stones.

The drop wasn't far. A few feet, maybe. More a long step down than an actual cliff, but I am below the headlight now, out of sight for at least a few seconds. Time enough.

I roll onto my stomach and inch on elbows and knees across the damp sand toward a log that's half buried in the dirt, half drowned in the river. I crawl over the log to the other side and scrape my knee on the rough bark. The pain is worse than when I twisted my ankle earlier, but I bite my lip and don't scream. Thistles scratch my legs and arms and face. Blackberries tear my clothes. I burrow down into a low spot behind the log. I am hidden between weeds and rotting wood. Hidden inside darkness.

The one who follows me spreads herself thin across the water. She is white and silver and blue and gray. She is starlight reflections and waiting. She is beautiful and bright with love.

A yellow beam sweeps over the cliff, stretches halfway across the river. It stays steady, not moving back and forth, not searching the trees. Just stopped there at the edge of the world.

"Ollie!"

It's Travis, but he sounds funny. His voice raspy, like he's been crying.

"Ollie! Please come out. I won't hurt you."

The one who follows me dances like fire on the water.

"It's not what you think, Ollie," he says. "We never meant for any of this. Please. I can explain everything. Just come on out now."

He waits for me, silently, but I know he's still here because the headlight pierces the dark. Then he screams. He screams and howls and kicks rocks that clatter down the cliff and splash into the water.

He screams, and I am torn apart. The energy he lets go makes the stars tremble, the trees shudder, makes me curl over my knees and weep without a sound. For all the things we had, and all the things we've lost, and all the things we'll never be.

He is not evil. I am not good.

We are the same: broken and put back together again.

If this night was different—if we were friends and not enemies, if my sister wasn't in danger, if I had my own words—I would go and take his hand and tell him that he still has all his pieces, that just because you can't see something doesn't mean it isn't there. I would tell him that the people who love us love us for always, even when we say mean things or make bad choices, even when we hurt them in the worst possible ways. Even then, they love us and keep loving us and will go on loving us forever. Love is a wide-eyed believer in second chances and impossibles, I would say, and then I would tell him to open his eyes.

His screams have fallen silent now. The dirt bike revs, and he backs away from the edge of the cliff. The headlight grows dimmer and disappears.

Travis is gone, and I am lost in the dark woods.

But I am not afraid anymore.

My mother is here with me.

sam

Mrs. Roth shoved a broken pencil and a piece of notebook paper at me. "I want you to tell them you're sorry."

I sat on my hands and turned my face away. She laid the pencil and paper in my lap.

"I want you to tell them that life just got too hard," she said. "That your grief for your mother overwhelmed you, your shame over what your father did was too much to bear. I want you to tell them you killed your baby sister to protect her from the evil, awful things in this world, and then you killed yourself."

"No."

"Tell them you didn't want to be a burden, that you wanted to go and be with your mother."

"Go to hell." I spat in her face.

She drew back, wiping off the spit with her sleeve.

Billy Roth spun away from his workbench and came at me. He struck me across the face, a single, violent blow. My head jerked. My jaw popped. Searing pain rolled through my skull, and blood rushed into my mouth.

"Billy, don't!" Mrs. Roth's voice rang and rang like a distant buzz-ing hive. "We can't leave any suspicious marks. We have to do it right. No mistakes this time, okay? No mistakes."

I tipped forward in the chair and let my head hang down, stared and stared at my so faraway feet. A drop of blood fell from my lips and splashed into my lap, onto the clean, white paper. A bright red splat of blood. My blood.

I sat hunched over like that, like a broken doll, for another minute or so, until the jabbing pain in my jaw subsided to a dull ache and the ringing in my ears faded. Until Billy Roth grabbed a fistful of my hair and jerked me straight again. "Do what she says."

Mrs. Roth smiled the way a waitress might smile if she'd gotten your order wrong, with an apologetic look she doesn't really mean. "Write it."

I picked up the paper and pencil. Billy let go of my hair and turned back to his work. Looking Mrs. Roth straight in the eyes and not blinking, I broke the pencil in half, crumpled the paper into a ball, and dropped everything onto the floor at her feet.

Billy started to turn toward me again, his hand raised. Mrs. Roth pushed him back.

"It doesn't matter. I can do it." She snatched up the paper and spread it flat again, then went to the workbench, took another pencil from the jar, hunched over and started to write.

Billy stood with one hand on my shoulder, pressing me into the chair.

I closed my eyes and imagined myself stretched out on my back in the meadow. The grass soft underneath me. The sun warm on my face. I imagined Bear whispering to the bees, and the bees whispering back. I imagined Ollie stretched out beside me.

"Billy, honey," Mrs. Roth said, shattering my thoughts. "Go and bring the Jeep around."

His hand lifted off my shoulder, and I returned to the shed and the smell of wet paint and lingering smoke and the realization that I might never see my sister again, might never be able to tell her how sorry I was for not listening, not believing. And Bear. He'd already lost so much. It wasn't fair for him to lose us, too. None of this—for anyone—none of it was fucking fair.

Mrs. Roth grabbed my arm and jerked me to my feet. She pressed the gun into my side and said, "The sooner we get there, the sooner this will all be over."

She started to push me forward. I dragged my feet, pressed back against her, struggled, did everything I could to keep from going out that door.

"Why are you doing this?" I asked.

"If you hadn't been so nosy," she said. "If you hadn't insisted."

"I couldn't let Bear go to prison for something he didn't do."

"After what he did to my Delilah? And to Billy? To my *entire family*? He deserved a life sentence."

"All of that was an accident. A terrible, awful mistake."

"No, my dear. Your father made a choice. And that choice, his choice, cost us everything. He should have never been released." Mrs. Roth squeezed my arm harder, pinching her fingers down to the bone.

I squirmed, but that only made it worse. "She wouldn't want you to do this."

She stopped trying to force me out the door. We were a few steps from the threshold now. I could feel cool air, smell pine trees and twilight dew.

"Do you know what it's like?" Mrs. Roth's voice was barely a whisper. "To lose something so precious? To wake up every morning wishing you were dead, too?"

"Please. Please don't."

"I don't really have a choice, *now,* do I?" She sighed and for a brief second, the gun lifted away from my ribs, but only a second, then it was right there again, cold through my shirt and unyielding.

"You know," she said. "I keep going back over it in my mind, trying to think of a way things could have turned out differently.

Maybe if I hadn't called Billy, insisting they come home. He told me the roads were icy, that he didn't feel comfortable driving the pass, but I pressed him. I made him feel guilty for leaving me all alone to take care of Travis. His fever was so high, I was scared. Or maybe if we hadn't spoiled Delilah so much. Maybe if we hadn't agreed to have her party at that fancy water park. But you see, try as I might, I just keep coming back to your father. A selfish, stupid man who thought he could still drive after drinking a half bottle of scotch. He's the reason my Delilah's dead. The reason my Billy lost his way. He took everything from me. *Everything.* And all they gave him was a slap on the wrist. A couple of years in prison and then free to go. Just like that. Free as a bird. While my family continues to suffer."

She started to push me toward the door again, and I fought her as best I could, but her grip was firm on the gun. The gun. My tears made it blurry, made it disappear, but I could still feel it pressed solid against my side.

"But now, look where we are. It's like the universe is finding balance again," she said. "Finally, making things right."

From somewhere far off came the high-pitched whine of a dirt bike, and then it was here, stopping right outside. The engine shut off.

A few seconds later, Travis burst into the shed. He stopped just inside the doorway, looked at his mom, then at me, then at the gun. He twisted his fingers and said, "She got away."

And my first reaction was to smile. A twitch at the corners of my mouth, a rising, bubbling feeling inside my chest that might have turned into a laugh if I hadn't swallowed it quickly down.

"What?" Mrs. Roth jabbed the gun harder into my ribs.

"She got away," Travis repeated. "I looked and couldn't find her. She's gone."

My second reaction was to hold very still and, with only my eyes, scan the room for something I could use to protect myself. Something that would draw blood. There were screwdrivers and pliers and wrenches hanging on a Peg-Board wall. Hammers of all sizes and crowbars and long shards of metal and even a blowtorch sitting on top of the workbench. The butcher knife was there too, in the exact place Billy had left it. But all those things, even the knife, were beyond my reach.

Mrs. Roth's hand started to shake. "Impossible."

"It was dark," Travis said. "I couldn't see a damn thing."

Mrs. Roth lowered the gun so it wasn't pressing against me anymore, but she kept her grip tight around my arm.

"I tried," Travis went on. "I looked all over, but there were just so many different ways she could have gone. Back toward Terrebonne. Out to the river. She could be anywhere by now."

Mrs. Roth shook her head. "Hush a moment. Let me think."

Travis stuffed his hands in his pockets and shifted back and forth on his feet, sneaking glances at me that I refused to return.

Outside, the Jeep pulled up to the shed door. Billy honked the horn.

Mrs. Roth sighed and shoved me back into the chair. "Don't move." Then she turned to Travis and said, "I'll go find her myself. You wait here and make sure Sam stays put. We'll figure this all out when I get back."

She started to move toward the door, but Travis stepped into her path. She tried to step around him, but he moved with her.

"Travis?"

"She's gone, Mom. She's gone."

I couldn't see Mrs. Roth's face from where I sat, but I saw her shoulders sag a little and her hand tightened around the gun. "You had her, didn't you?"

He placed his hands on Mrs. Roth's shoulders and leaned down so their foreheads were almost touching.

"Oh, Travis. Do you realize what you've done?"

"I'll tell the detective it was me," he said quietly. "I'll tell them I killed Taylor. I'll tell them I covered it up, too. You and Dad, you didn't know anything about it. That's what I'll say."

"No," Mrs. Roth's voice cracked.

"It's going to be okay. Everything will be fine. You just tell them I've been losing my temper a lot lately, acting strange. Tell them I've been smoking and skipping work, and that you've been worried about me for some time now." He let go of her shoulders, took two steps to the bookcase, and picked up the tan purse. He wiped it off with his sleeve, then gripped it tight with both hands. "My fingerprints are all over her bag. See? And my boots. They match the prints down by the river. The Jeep tracks. I'll sign a confession. It'll work. They'll believe it. You just stick with our original story about how she never showed up for the interview, and everything will be fine. Tell them I must have snuck out after you went to bed. Tell them you had no idea."

"Travis, stop," Mrs. Roth said. "I won't let you do this."

Billy honked the horn a second time, a loud, long, persistent blast. Mrs. Roth glanced at the open door.

"It's going to be all right, Mom. Just let Sam go. I'll take the blame. Please. Let her go." He looked at me when he said this, looked at me and said, "I'm sorry. This should have never happened. We panicked. And the whole thing got so out of control. But I'm going to make it right, okay? You'll help me?"

I nodded, not sure what he was asking, but willing to say whatever he wanted if it meant getting out of here alive and seeing Ollie again.

"You'll tell them I killed her?"

I nodded faster.

Mrs. Roth grabbed Travis's arm and pulled him close. "They'll put you in jail. You'll grow old and die in there."

"It's okay. Listen, it'll be okay. You and Dad, you'll be fine. And Sam and Ollie, they'll be safe, too. And I'm still a minor. Maybe they won't be so hard on me. Or maybe I can cut a deal. Maybe they'll—"

"No," Mrs. Roth said. "No! I won't let you do this."

"I can't think of any other way to fix it."

"I have a new plan. It's foolproof. It's—"

Travis shook his head. "I'm sorry."

He slipped from her grasp and came toward me, stretched out his hand, and said, "Come on, Sam. I'll drive you back to Zeb and Franny's on my way to the station."

I stood.

Mrs. Roth grabbed Travis's elbow and pulled him back. "Don't do this."

Travis smiled sadly at her. "It's over, Mom. I'm done."

A car door opened. Boots crunched through the gravel, and then Billy came back into the shed. "Are we going or not?"

He didn't wait for an answer. Instead, he brushed past us and went straight to the sheet-draped object on the other side of the shed. He pulled on one end, sweeping off the cloth, revealing the sculpture underneath. It was beautiful and terrifying at once. Shaped delicately from a tree trunk, a girl rose like a Phoenix from a pile of tin cans and ash-colored dirt. Both of her arms were stretched to the ceiling, her head tipped back, her hair streaming gold behind her. She had two faces that looked in opposite directions. One was serene and gentle and smiling, the other grotesque, the mouth twisted open in a silent scream, tears carving lines in her cheeks. I recognized her. She was the girl in the picture standing beside the birthday cake with candles that would never go out. She was Delilah. I looked closer at the base, could see now the shape of something curled there, a sleeping child with fingers stretching bone-white through the gray, reaching and reaching for something that would always be just beyond her grasp. I turned away, dizzy and sick to my stomach.

"I was thinking of adding a bow," Billy said. "A blue ribbon with white polka dots. Right here." He touched a spot at the very top of the sculpture.

Travis pinched his lips between his teeth, grimacing.

"Sounds lovely, dear," Mrs. Roth said. "A nice touch."

"Mom, please," Travis whispered. "Don't let him do this."

Mrs. Roth gave him a sharp look and shook her head.

"Delilah wouldn't want this," he said.

Billy's mouth twitched.

"Travis." Mrs. Roth's voice was low, a warning.

Travis clenched his fists at his side and moved toward the sculpture. "I won't let him do this. It's not right."

"Travis. Please. Just leave it be."

"No." He was almost there. "This was your daughter, Mom. And look, look what he's done to her."

Billy said, "I think you should leave."

"She deserves better than this," Travis said, crouching down and laying his hand over her reaching fingers. "Delilah's gone, Dad. You can't bring her back this way."

Billy rolled his head in a tight circle. "Get out."

"Travis," Mrs. Roth said, moving away from me, taking a step toward the sculpture. "Do as your father says."

"No." Travis closed his eyes and shook his head. He opened them again and rose to his feet. "No. We'll just have to cancel the show. Postpone it. We'll just have to think of something else. I won't let her be remembered this way. I won't . . ." He started to pat the wooden part of the sculpture, like he was trying to find a latch to pull or a button to push, something that would make it disappear.

I tried creeping sideways toward the window.

Mrs. Roth saw me from the corner of her eye and whipped her head around. "Where do you think you're going?"

I stopped shuffling and spread my arms open. "Nowhere. I'm just—"

Silently and with such speed I didn't even have time to scream, Billy Roth rushed Travis. He'd grabbed the butcher knife from the corner of his workbench, raised it now above his head and brought it down, fast and hard, plunging it into the soft slope of Travis's neck right above his collarbone. Travis gasped and stumbled backward.

The scream rising in my throat got stuck and came out instead a strangled sputtering.

Mrs. Roth turned. "Billy?"

Travis pressed his hand to where the knife had gone in and come out again. Blood everywhere. So much blood. Squirting through his fingers. Dripping down his arm, spreading a crimson stain on his white T-shirt.

"Billy?" Mrs. Roth said again and took a staggering step toward Travis. "What did you do?"

Billy laid the knife on the workbench and calmly wiped his hands on a rag like nothing had happened, not a single damn thing. He returned to the sculpture with a clean rag and tin of beeswax and started buffing the places Travis had touched. He hummed a little as he worked.

Travis leaned back against the workbench. His mouth opened and closed around silent words. He looked at me, then at Mrs. Roth who was reaching out her arms, grabbing him, embracing him. He shook his head and his knees bent underneath him, but Mrs. Roth wasn't strong enough to hold him up. They collapsed together on the floor.

Mrs. Roth pulled Travis into her arms and rocked him and rocked him and pressed her hand to the gaping wound and brushed bloody fingers over his pale cheeks and whispered words I couldn't hear but hoped were filled with love.

I backed slowly toward the door, feeling the way with my hands because even though I tried, even though I told myself—*Go! Run!*—I couldn't. My heart wasn't working right. It was pounding too hard, sending out too much blood—so much blood—and all my limbs felt heavy, every joint swollen and stiff. And I couldn't get my legs to go. I couldn't make myself turn and run and leave him here.

I bumped into something solid, a shelf or a table, maybe, and knocked a jar of bolts on the floor. They crashed and spilled across the concrete, echoing crassly in the quiet room.

Mrs. Roth lifted her head, turned, and stared at me.

I was at the door, my hands groping empty air.

Mrs. Roth whispered something in Travis's ear, then laid him carefully on the floor, grabbed a rag from the workbench, and covered his wound, made him hold it there with his pale, trembling hand. She kissed his cheek and said, "I'll be right back. Hang on for me, okay? Hang on."

She stood and came toward me.

The gun looked so much smaller from this angle, a glinting sliver and nothing to be afraid of at all. I walked backward. Mrs. Roth matched me step for step. My shoes scuffed gravel.

I was outside. She, in the doorway, a looming silhouette.

The night hummed. I took another step back.

"I wish you had left all of this alone." She brushed her face against her sleeve. Her hands were shaking. "You should have just stayed out of it."

I wanted to turn and run, put all this behind me, but her finger was on the trigger and I didn't stand a chance. I kept thinking, *Someone will come for me. Someone will come.*

No one was coming.

"You understand why I have to do this, don't you? I can't have you . . . I can't." She closed her eyes and drew in a deep breath, gathering herself, steadying her hold.

The gun pitched down. It was only a few seconds, but it was enough time for me to scoop up a handful of rocks, some small, some bigger, the size of golf balls. When she opened her eyes again and readjusted her grip on the pistol, I was standing with my arms at my side, standing like I hadn't moved at all.

She said, "I'm sorry, Sam. I'm so, so sorry."

I drew back my arm and hurled one of the bigger rocks at the woodpile. The trick is to aim a little higher than your target. The stone hit the hollow log with a decisive thump.

Mrs. Roth flinched, but the pistol stayed fixed on my chest.

The second rock hit the exact same spot on the exact same hollow log. The log teetered from the impact, then fell off the pallet and onto its side in the dirt. There was a moment where neither of us moved or spoke, where time slowed to a near stop. Then the log exploded. Bees poured into the night, swelling into a blacker-than-black cloud and vibrating the air with angry wings.

"What—" And that was all she had time to say.

She took a step back and waved her hand in front of her face. She yipped and slapped and then started to thrash.

I turned and ran. Hard, fast, shoes pounding, knees shuddering, arms pumping, faster, faster. Her screams grew louder and more frantic, turning into something wild. I didn't look back.

I was halfway down the path, almost to the house when a single shot ricocheted through the trees. Something with sharp teeth and a poison dart tongue dug into my calf. I stumbled and cried out and pitched forward, skidding my hands and knees across the bark mulch. I lay there a moment, my cheek against the hard ground, my throat swelling, my eyes filling with tears.

This is it, I thought. *Only a matter of time before I'm dead, good-bye, Bear, good-bye, Ollie, give Zeb and Franny and Grandma and Grandpa my love . . .* and then my hands were underneath me, pushing up and I was struggling to my feet, struggling to stand. I swayed on my good leg, biting back a scream, and tried to put weight on the other one, the one that was burning and throbbing like a thousand stinging bees wreaking havoc under my skin. My stomach heaved into my throat. I swallowed and blinked away bloodred sparks. I took a trembling step forward because I couldn't stay here. Pain rammed deeper, digging straight through me, clawing its way to my very center. I took another step because Bear was innocent and someone had to tell them. I took another step and another, grinding my teeth and telling myself the bullet hadn't gone in, hoping, praying this was true, that she'd missed and it was only a nick, needing maybe a few stitches, that was all, nothing permanent. I took step after step, even though it hurt like hell, because Ollie was out there, somewhere, alive.

Somewhere between the backyard and the front driveway, I managed to find a rhythm, a half jog, half drag, and the farther and faster I went, the less my leg hurt. My body seemed to take over for me, moving without my permission, pushing on because that was the only thing it knew how to do. I could see my bike now, where I'd left it, leaning up against a tree. A few more steps and I was there.

I grabbed the handlebars and swung my good leg over the seat. The stretching motion was worse than running, and I cried out and slumped down over the handlebars. I took long, deep breaths. The hard part was over. Pedaling was easy. Just get to the road. Get to the road. I lifted my head, put my feet down on the pedals, and pushed off slowly. Every time I thought the pain was getting to be too much, every time I wanted to quit, I thought of Ollie and kept going. The trees swayed their overhanging branches and whispered her name, urging me on, faster and faster.

This driveway was so long . . . I'd forgotten how long . . .

A car engine revved in the darkness behind me, coming closer, tires sliding in gravel. I glanced over my shoulder. Headlights swept around a bend and for a second I was blind. There was only a brilliant, crushing stream growing brighter. I squinted and blinked and faced forward again, leaned my head down and pedaled hard.

The headlights illuminated the edges of the road, dancing and darting between the trees, making it seem like the forest was running alongside me. I took another quick glance back. The boxy grille of a Jeep bore down. A hundred yards away, then ninety, eighty . . . the engine sounds thrummed in my chest, diesel burned my throat, the driver, a shadow monster hunched over the wheel, blasted the horn . . . seventy, sixty, fifty yards now. Only seconds to decide.

I jerked the bike hard to the right and steered it off the driveway and into the trees. I thought it would be narrow enough, I didn't think she would try it, but if she did, she wouldn't get very far. Tires and brakes squealed. I looked over my shoulder. The Jeep swerved left, right, left again.

I should have been watching where I was going. I should have never looked back.

My front tire crashed into a rock sticking up from the dirt just as the Jeep skidded too far to one side and started to tip. I flew over the handlebars and slammed, shoulder-first, into a tree. My head hit second, but just as hard. I slumped to the ground beside my smashed-up bike. Stars poked holes in the dark canopy above me. I couldn't move. I tried, I did, I tried so hard, but my body refused to cooperate.

There was a loud crash somewhere to my right, near the road. Crumpling metal and splintering wood. Then a hissing sound, like steam escaping, and a click-click-shudder of a dying engine. The Jeep's headlights were flickering. Dark, light. Dark, light.

Dark.

Before the night pulled black around me, this is what I saw: white smoke, curling through the branches, and a woman with hazel eyes and dark hair crouching over me, whispering, "Thank you."

ollie

We stay close to the river, following its curves. Mom walks in the shallows. I walk on the shore. I reach for her hand and it's like holding steam. I want to go slow and look for animals in the stars. I want just a little more time.

To say all the things I need to say, all the things she already knows.

She urges me to go faster. *Your sister needs you right now.*

Funny, I always thought I was the one who needed her.

I guess it comes down to this: Sam and me, we need each other.

I start to jog. I don't know exactly where I am, but I know this is Crooked River and I know I'm a little north of Terrebonne because Mrs. Roth turned right, not left when she drove us out of town earlier today, and I haven't passed Smith Rock yet. If I keep going, I'll run into town eventually. I just hope when I get there, I'm not too late.

After I run through tall grass and tangled weeds for a few minutes, the shoreline widens and flattens. Up ahead I see streetlights.

Almost there.

Mom streaks like a firecracker to the first building we've seen since we left Billy Roth's shed. It's the hardware store and across the street is a pay phone. My legs burst forward with sudden energy. I am flying. My braids snap in the wind behind me. I pump my arms. I've never moved so fast in my entire life. And when I reach her, she softens her edges and smiles. I stare a little too long, trying to memorize the shape of it so when she's gone I won't ever forget.

Hurry, she says.

I pick up the phone and dial zero and a recording says, "Please deposit twenty-five cents or press 1 to call collect."

I press 1.

"Say your name after the tone."

There is a long beep and then silence.

I say nothing.

A click and then, "Please dial the number you wish to call."

I punch in the numbers my sister made me memorize on the drive up here, just in case.

Only a few seconds go by before I hear Nana Fran's voice on the other end, wide awake and shouting, even though I'm certain it's well past her bedtime.

"Hello? Hello? Who's there? Who is this? We must have a bad connection."

Mom is standing right beside me, right up close, waiting, flickering slowly pink to purple to green to yellow.

"Speak up, please. My hearing's not what it used to be. Speak up."

I open my mouth, close it again. I am still afraid the words won't come out right. I'm afraid they won't be my own.

Mom is a tornado of gold and silver, red, white, and blue.

"Hello? I can hear you breathing."

And I have to try. For Sam. For Bear. For me.

For all of us.

I open my mouth and say, "Nana Fran?"

"Olivia? Is that you?"

"Yes," like a croaking frog.

"Child! Where are you?"

I say, "She's going to kill Sam."

"Who is? What are you talking about? Where are you?" And then, "Zeb! Get in here!"

I say, "You have to get Deputy Santos."

I say, "You have to tell her to go to Mrs. Roth's house."

I say, "Tell her it's an emergency."

I say and say and say.

I say everything.

sam

Is this what dead feels like? An in-between place of dreaming and waking where you keep thinking, *Wake up, wake up, open your eyes,* but you don't. You can't. So you lie motionless, your mind and body apart, and you wonder if anything you're seeing, hearing, feeling is real. I thought dying would feel more like soaring. No, that's not true. I thought I would feel nothing. Because when you're dead, you're dead and that's it. That's all there is.

I am dead.

Say it again. I am dead.

Say it again, until you believe it. I am dead and dead and dead. But then why can I still hear myself think? Why can I feel my rushing blood slow, my fevered skin grow cold? Why can I see the trees swaying above me, dancing for no one?

Ollie would say it's my soul, my ghost, my Shimmering, trying to separate from the part of me that is bound by rules like gravity and aging. I strain against my bones, begging to be set free, at the same time begging to stay.

My mother is here with me. Here. Where am I? Nowhere. Everywhere. Here and dead. A dim light flickers white, red, white. A baby cries. Or is that me? It can't be me. I am dead. I am silent. Someone—not me—cries. And my mother is here.

The edges of her are jagged and spinning rainbows, like a pinwheel. But her face is clear and her smile warm, and I am calm.

Mom.

Nasty little bump you got there.

She reaches over and brushes light and heat across my forehead. A flash of remembering all the things I'd rather forget.

Ollie?

She's here.

And now I hear her. She's the one crying. She's saying my name. She's saying, "Sam, look at me. Sammy. You have to hold on."

And I want to laugh because there are ghosts around. Mom is one and I am one, and Ollie is still talking. "I know you can hear me. Please. Try. Don't give up. Not yet."

My sister, talking, and her voice tells the most beautiful story.

I can't see her.

She's still here.

I want to see her.

Open your eyes.

I try. I can't.

"I'm here, Sam," she says. "I'm right here."

There are other voices floating around me, too, words like buzzing bees, and I do not know to whom they belong. Ollie's is the only clear voice. Her words, the only ones that matter.

"I need you to stay."

The stars are so much brighter when you're dead. The dark, so much darker. The trees are whispering, but I do not feel any wind. I want to feel the wind.

There is pressure against my chest and it hurts. Oh God. It hurts. Mom starts to fade. She is a faraway lighthouse beam sweeping the night. I imagine myself shattering this body, these bones. I imagine streaking after her, and then the pain goes and Mom is bright again, blinding and up close.

I want to stay here with you.

If that's really what you want, just think of the place you love best, the place where you feel most safe. Imagine yourself there and then let go.

I'm in the meadow. And Bear is somewhere close by and Ollie is right beside me, and I'm telling her about the bees. See that? How she's slowly fanning her wings? She's sending out a special scent, calling the lost ones home.

From a far-off place, I hear Ollie saying my name over and over, telling me to stay. I hear my sister, and I come back to myself. I come back.

I'm not ready.

You have to decide soon.

But what if I can't?

You can.

I want to go with you. And I want to stay. I want you and her and him and us all together again.

That's not possible.

It's not fair.

No, it never is.

Did you know? About the house he was going to build?

It was my idea.

It was?

He couldn't come home to us, so I decided to bring us home to him.

I wish none of this had ever happened. I wish . . . I wish. I wish so badly I could go back and change everything.

None of us can.

I start to think about the meadow again.

"Sammy," my sister says. "Sam! Please! I'll talk to you, I promise! I'll say anything you want. I'll . . ." She's still talking, even though it's hard for me to hear her now. She's talking and talking. So many things left to say.

I'm being pushed down, squeezed back into my bones. This time, I don't fight it. The pain doesn't come all at once. It starts as a memory, a low tide lapping at my bare feet. Mom flickers. Her sky blues turn gray, her cherry reds dim beige.

Is it lonely?

Never.

Do you miss us?

Always.

I feel pine needles now, under my hands, poking the skin at the back of my arm, and there's something jamming into my side, the hard root of a tree. I smell burning oil and forest rot. The wind tugs my hair. Gray shapes move around me, whispering and brushing against me. My mother spins between the stars.

Forgive your father.

I already have.

Tell your sister I love her.

She knows.

Tell her anyway.

I don't think I can do this.

You're stronger than you give yourself credit for, Sam. Braver, too.

She sings me a familiar lullaby, though I can't remember where I've heard it before.

There is a moment of bright pain and fireworks exploding, and I see the past and present and future ripping apart and then collapsing together again. There is a moment where I am nowhere and everywhere, nothing and everything. I am crushed and torn in half. I am pummeled by stones and lashed with barbed wire. It hurts, all of it; God, it hurts so much I want to die. And then someone squeezes my hand.

Her fingers are smaller than mine, but they are strong and warm and insistent. I squeeze back so she knows I am still here. I try to speak, but the words come out in a groan.

"We've got her!" a woman says, and there is a rush of movement and noise.

Faces I don't recognize bend over me, tugging and pulling, sticking needles into my arm, strapping a mask over my face, pumping me with air, making it impossible to talk. My eyes dart, panicked, and then I see her, close to my left shoulder.

Her cheeks are red, her eyes puffy behind her purple glasses. One hand wipes snot from her nose, the other refuses to let go. The paramedics keep trying to push her away from me, but she won't budge. They work around her, rolling me onto a backboard and lifting me off the ground onto a gurney. Ollie stays close, keeping her hand in mine.

"Did you see how beautiful Mom was? How happy?" She looks off into the trees and then back down at me, her eyes a little sadder than before but still smiling. My sister is smiling.

"She's gone now," Ollie says to me.

But I'm here. We're here.

"She told me to tell you she loves you," Ollie says. "For always."

I know.

She leans in closer, whispers, "Thank you for saving me."

If it didn't hurt so much, I'd laugh. I didn't save her, she saved me.

We move out of the trees toward the road where an ambulance waits with red and white lights flashing. The gurney wheel bumps against something, jostling me, screaming pain through my bones. Every single fragile one. I close my eyes. Just for a second.

"Sam? Sam!" Ollie shakes my arm.

For all her courage, there is still fear.

I open my eyes, stare into hers. I want to tell her it's okay to be scared, that I'm scared too. I'm scared of so many things. I want to tell her we can be scared together. Let someone else be brave today. I squeeze her hand as tight as I can.

She squeezes back and says, "Does it hurt bad?"

I nod. I think I nod.

She says, "Remember when you were eleven and you were doing circles on your bike and you fell and broke your arm? Does it hurt bad like that?"

I haven't thought about that day in a long time. How the circles got tighter and tighter, faster and faster, and the world became a blur of color and light and wind and for a second it felt like flying, and then the bike slipped out from under me and I was falling, falling. I remember hearing my bones crack before feeling any pain, remember staring at a strange lump forming, watching it turn red and purple, watching it swell, then become searing hot and all-consuming. I remember screaming and screaming and screaming and Mom and Ollie running out, helping me to my feet, taking me to the hospital. My cast was blue. Ollie was the only person to sign it. After six weeks the cast came off. My arm was fine. The bones healed exactly the way they were supposed to, and the pain that had once been so sharp and terrible faded into memory.

The pain I'm feeling now will fade, too. One day and soon. It has to. For us to keep on living, loving, being who we are, we have to forget how badly the worst parts hurt us. We have to heal.

We reach the ambulance. A paramedic says, "You need to step back now. You need to give us room."

Ollie says, "I want to go with her."

From somewhere close by, I hear Deputy Santos telling Ollie it'll be all right, the paramedics will take good care of me. She says, "You can ride with me. I promise we'll stay right behind them until we get to the hospital. Lights and sirens, the whole way."

I hear Zeb now, too, asking the paramedics if I'm conscious, if I'm awake, if I'm going to live. And I think . . . I think I hear Franny off to one side praying. But I can't see them, and I can't see Deputy Santos either. My head is strapped down, my neck in a brace. Ollie's face is the only familiar one leaning over me.

"They won't let me go with you," she says. "But you'll be okay?"

I squeeze her hand twice.

She bends to give me a hug and then steps away from the gurney. The paramedics lift me into the back of the ambulance, buckle me in, and shut the doors. I close my eyes when the sirens start and think about my mother, wonder why I never noticed it before. Her smile. Ollie's is exactly the same.

Bear says that in September the light in the meadow softens and the air turns crisp and tart. The days get shorter. The flowers die. Life is loss and nothing lasts. The leaves change green to red to yellow and dance off the trees like tiny ballerinas, and sometimes you wake to silver frost on the ground and your breath forming white clouds. "It's a different kind of beautiful," he tells us. "You'll see." But summer isn't over. Not yet. There's plenty of time left for us to walk barefoot in the grass, splash in the river, and talk to the bees, to fall asleep counting stars.

ACKNOWLEDGMENTS

Profound thanks to the many wonderful people who had a hand in the creation of this book. Enthusiastic high-fives and fist bumps to Laurie McGee, Laura Cherkas, Ashley Marudas, and the rest of the team at William Morrow for your attention to detail as well as your care and dedication in making this book a book and bringing it to readers. Special thanks to my editor, Emily Krump, who saw into the heart of this story and drew out the best parts. And to my agent, Julia Kenny, whose determination, confidence, and unfailing support found this book its best home and whose business savvy makes it possible for me to write and keep writing: thank you and thank you and thank you.

Warm hugs and chocolate chip cookies to my family and friends who have been cheering me on since the beginning. To my parents, who indulged my book obsession and never once told me to get a real job, thank you for your boundless love. To my big sister, my cheerleader, my best friend, thank you for listening and sticking with me through the best and worst days. To Mike, Suzanne, Joyce, and Ralph, thank you for welcoming me into your family and for your enduring optimism. To Alisa, thank you for asking the right questions at the right time and helping me bring these characters to life. To Caroline and Kate, thank you for your invaluable feedback, continued encouragement, and gracious friendship—you two keep me sane.

Finally, my deepest gratitude to Ryan, my partner and biggest supporter, for reminding me all those years ago that "real writers write." Thank you for giving me enough time and space and love, and for helping to make the impossible possible. Let's keep this adventure going!

ABOUT THE AUTHOR

Valerie Geary is a full-time writer and a fair-weather gardener. Her stories have been published in The Rumpus and *Day One*. She lives in Portland, Oregon, with her family. *Crooked River* is her first book.

valeriegeary.com